She

And Fire . . .

Dominique's hand moved and the gown slipped away, baring first the smooth perfection of her shoulders, then the full lushness of her breasts and the tiny indentation of her waist.

For a moment, it rested on the curve of her hips before she pushed it away and stepped out unhesitantly to stand before Paul proudly naked, unashamed, magnificent.

"Like Aphrodite," he murmured, "rising from the waves."

She smiled sweetly, surely, a smile as old as time. "No goddess, only a woman."

His hands settled lightly on her hips, their calloused touch almost reverently grazing her velvet smoothness. "Not quite," he murmured, drawing her closer. His lips brushed her belly and he felt her tremble. "But soon . . . very soon."

"Now," whispered Dominique. His arms held her upright as her head fell back, the silken hair brushing her rounded buttocks. A tremor ran through her, as though the earth itself quivered.

She cried out softly as he rose, slowly, tantalizingly, his mouth trailing fire . . .

❧❧❧❧❧

MAURA SEGER is one of America's bestselling and best reviewed romance novelists. The author of over forty books, she has received the Reviewer's Choice Award from *Romantic Times* every year since 1985.

BEFORE THE WIND

MAURA SEGER

WARNER BOOKS

A Warner Communications Company

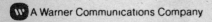

Chapter
1

Paris, Summer 1792

The girl hesitated at the entrance to the antechamber. Ignoring the fatigue that weighed her down, she straightened her shoulders and forced herself to take a deep breath. It was imperative that she remain calm. Nothing would be gained by revealing her inner turmoil. Indeed, much could be lost.

Yet despite her resolve, her slender hand trembled as she opened the door and stepped inside. The room was small, dark, and stuffy, like all those in the hulking stone mass of the Tuileries Palace. On this late-June day, it was also stultifyingly hot.

The man who awaited her, however, did not seem troubled by the heat. As always, he appeared impervious to any such human frailty. In the instant before he became aware of her presence, Dominique had a chance to study him unobserved. Paul Delamare was as tall as she remembered—several inches over six feet. Beneath the dark frock coat, his shoulders and chest were broad and heavily muscled. He stood with the easy stance of a man at once physically strong and inherently confident. In the dim light filtering through the narrow windows, his thick, slightly disheveled hair gleamed like beaten gold. When he turned abruptly, his turquoise eyes shone with a light she remembered all too well.

"Dominique," he murmured. His voice was low and deep, but it held a rough undercurrent. It made him sound hard, unflinching, exactly as she would have expected.

But there was also a hint of displeasure that sent a tremor down her back. Despite the heat, she was suddenly cold. She drew her shawl more closely around herself and met his eyes unflinchingly.

"*Monsieur.*" The single word was spoken with a measured hint of disdain that did not escape Paul. His brows drew together ominously.

"I was hoping," he said, "that there was some misunderstanding. What in the name of heaven are you still doing here?"

Dominique flushed. Unbidden, she remembered how in times past he had always looked at her with consummate gentleness and patience. Then, his rare flashes of temper, terrible though they were, had always been directed elsewhere. She had never been more than a fascinated spectator as he dealt with those whose arrogance, laziness, and simple greed condemned their fellowman to suffering. She had always felt they more than deserved to be the target of his anger. Never had she believed it would someday be turned on her.

Instinctively, she met it with the only weapon at her disposal—frigid contempt. "Is your memory faulty?" she demanded haughtily. "Six years ago, when I first went to court, Her Majesty kindly offered me a position in attendance upon her. I am glad to say that I have it still.''

"Then more fool you," Paul snapped back. From his great height, he glowered down at her, making her feel even smaller and more vulnerable.

Not that she would let him see that. She glared back obstinately, refusing to give an inch.

"Everyone with any sense has left," he went on grimly. "I took it for granted that you were gone, safe and snug in England with those relatives of yours. Instead, here you sit, right in the center of the fire storm."

Dismayed by the sudden image he invoked, Dominique took a step back. Her face was pale, her eyes dark and luminous. Shakily, she said, "It isn't that bad."

Paul made a sound of disgust and turned his back on her. Staring into the empty fireplace, he said, "If you truly believe that, you're even more deluded than I thought. France is in the midst of revolution; the old way is dying, and it remains to be seen what will come next. At any rate, this is no time for a young and unprotected girl to come and go so freely."

Dominique grimaced. His description was so at odds with her real circumstances that she couldn't help but find it macabre. Far from being free, she was living under worse confinement than she had ever imagined experiencing. Though she resided in one of the most renowned palaces in Europe, in one of the continent's greatest cities, each day she had to struggle to secure the simple necessities of life. Food, clothing, and medicine were all kept in deliberately short supply; it was a demoralizing tactic that had its effect on those stalwart few who continued to serve the royal family.

Indignities and petty cruelties were manifest. Dominique

did her utmost to ignore them, but there were times when even her normal optimism faltered. This was such a moment. She was worn out in mind and body, exhausted after a night of keeping vigil beside the queen. The added strain of confronting the man whose mere presence was enough to unleash a wave of piercing memories was almost too much to bear.

Six years ago she had been a child of twelve and he a young man of twenty-three. To her awakening senses, he had seemed the epitome of everything admirable. Her infatuation had been absolute. She had trailed after him as he went about his rounds, seeing to the medical needs of people who until that time had rarely, if ever, seen a doctor. Had it been left to Dominique's father, the duc de Montfort, they never would have, for he was firmly opposed to "coddling the peasants." Only respect for his friend and neighbor, Paul's father, the marquis de Rochford, had led the duc to tolerate the young man's activities.

Bitterness flowed through Dominique as she recalled how Paul had repaid that tolerance. He had become a traitor of the worst sort—a man who had turned his back on his social class, his heritage, and his responsibilities in order to support a cause that was nothing short of madness.

Yet he was still a doctor, and she still needed his help.

"I never thought they would send you," she said.

Paul frowned. He had not known what to expect when Dominique stepped into the room, but what he saw took him aback. In his memory, he carried the image of a young girl—happy, innocent, and dancing through life. That child appeared to have vanished irrevocably, for he now confronted a beautiful, self-possessed woman who clearly regarded him as an enemy.

Despite his resolve to remain aloof, he could not help but be struck by her loveliness. Her midnight black hair was swept up in a cascade of curls that framed the heart-shaped perfection of her face. Her features were delicate, her brow high, her nose straight and slender, her mouth ripely soft. Only the firmness of her chin hinted at the stubbornness of her nature—that, and the flash of her eyes, which at the moment were sea green, as impenetrable as the ocean, and as enticing.

She was simply dressed in a high-necked gown of rose-hued wool that hung too loosely on her. Paul felt an unexpected stab of pain as he realized that she must have lost weight recently. She was almost too thin. There were violet shadows beneath her eyes and the paleness of her face suggested that she might not be completely well.

Anger flowed through him. He was furious with the leaders of the revolution, who seemed more interested in vengeance than in reform, but he also was angry at the royal family for selfishly allowing those still loyal to them to put themselves in such danger. Above all, he was upset with Dominique for letting herself be trapped in so untenable a situation when, with a modicum of good sense, she could have avoided it.

Coldly, he said, "You gave the Assembly to understand that a physician was required. As you may recall, I am one."

"Were one," Dominique corrected. "It was my impression that of late you had found another vocation—that of . . . politician."

She uttered the last word with contempt that at the very least equaled her earlier address of him. Still, Paul refused to be provoked. However bold and disdainful she might wish to appear, he was too well aware of how vulnerable she really was. That was the only reason he had agreed to what promised to be an extremely onerous assignment.

When he had learned the identity of the lady-in-waiting who had written to the Assembly about the queen's illness, he had been first appalled, then deeply worried. Ordinarily, he would have been extremely reluctant to involve himself with the royal family—not because he feared any possible repercussions for himself, but simply because there were what he regarded as more important demands on his services. He was, at the moment, fully absorbed in trying to stem the spread of cholera among the troops of the National Guard. In his mind, that was far more important than the well-being of a handful of people who could be served by any competent physician. But learning of Dominique's presence at the Tuileries had changed everything. He would have to get involved, at least until he could remedy the situation.

"It is true," he said quietly, "that I have some dealings within the government. However, I have not given up my medical practice. When the Assembly learned that Her Majesty was ill, I was asked to be of assistance."

Dominique heard him out in silence. She was already regretting having sent the note informing the Assembly that the queen was indisposed and without medical help. Never in her wildest imaginings had she considered that the result would be Paul Delamare.

"This is all the fault of Dr. Chantain," she murmured under her breath.

Paul's slanted brows rose questioningly. "I take it that the good gentleman is no longer with you?"

Reluctantly, Dominique nodded. She hated admitting any such thing, but there was no point trying to deny what he obviously already knew. "He has not been seen in a fortnight or so."

Paul shrugged. Unlike certain of his colleagues, he had no objection to royalist sympathizers leaving France. On the contrary, the more who left, the better the chance for a relatively peaceful conclusion to the revolution that had begun three years earlier, with the storming of the Bastille.

Indeed, Paul had some regrets that King Louis XVI and his queen had not been successful in their own attempted flight the year before. Instead, they had been forcibly brought back and virtually imprisoned in the Tuileries.

The only remaining concession to their once manifest privileges was the continued presence of the household guard, the traditional protectors of the royal family. Whatever vestige of safety these men created was just an illusion, but one Paul devoutly hoped would never have to be shattered.

"I realize," he said quietly, "that Her Majesty would undoubtedly prefer someone she could regard as more sympathetic to her position. However, I do at least have the advantage of not being entirely unknown to her. Nor," he added for good measure, "is it very likely that I will suddenly take it into my head to leave France."

Dominique reluctantly had to acknowledge that he was right. Not that it would have made much difference, in any case.

The plain fact of the matter was that despite their regal surroundings, the royal family and those who served them were completely dependent on the revolutionaries to make their existences tolerable. If there had been any chance of acquiring the services of another physician, she would have taken it. As it was, she supposed she should be grateful that anyone had come at all.

"Her Majesty was sleeping when I left her," she said stiffly. "But she had a very restless night, and I am concerned that she will awaken again soon."

Paul nodded. He did not have to be told who had cared for the queen. One look at Dominique was enough to assure him that her devotion was unwavering. For the briefest instant he felt a stab of envy, and wondered what it would be like to be the recipient of such care.

"Is there no one to help you?" he demanded. "I realize the circumstances here are difficult, but surely the family could give you some assistance."

"You don't know what you're talking about," Dominique objected angrily. "Their Majesties do everything possible for each other and for their children. I have never seen more loving or considerate people."

She broke off, abruptly aware that she was close to tears. Undoubtedly, exhaustion was a good part of the cause, but there was also the fact that lately, whenever she looked at the king and queen, and at their two young children, she felt a sense of dread so black that it terrified her. It was as though a premonition of disaster hovered over them, like the dark, fluttering wing of a carrion bird.

"Never mind," she said quickly. "If you are going to be of use, you'd best come with me now."

Without waiting for him to reply, she swept out of the room. Paul followed and caught up with her in the corridor. He said nothing as they walked the distance to the royal apartments.

A member of the household guard stood immediately outside the double doors. Dressed in the traditionally ornate blue-and-white uniform, he saluted and stood aside to let them pass, but not without casting a wary glance at Paul.

Word of his identity had apparently preceded him. That was not surprising in a palace under siege, where even the simplest occurrence might have drastic effects.

"Wait here," Dominique said when the double doors had closed behind them. They were in another small antechamber, no cooler than the previous one and haphazardly furnished with a few uninviting chairs. Paul sighed and reconciled himself to the delay, but to his surprise, Dominique returned within minutes.

"Her Majesty is awake," she said. "She will see you now."

Paul followed without comment. The queen's boudoir was larger, but no more appealing than any of the other rooms in the palace. Still, an effort had been made to make it seem reasonably cheerful and comfortable.

The windows were opened to admit a much-needed and welcome breeze, despite the scent of the nearby Seine that it carried. In the center of the room stood a four-poster bed draped in burgundy curtains. They were tied back to reveal a small, pale woman sitting up against a pile of pillows.

The queen smiled and held out her hand. Her hair, casually arranged in soft curls, was more gray now than strawberry blond, and her face had lost its youthful beauty. But Marie Antoinette was still a striking woman—all the more so because her gracious, gentle looks were so at odds with the scurrilous rumors that continually circulated about her. The more rabid of the revolutionaries liked to paint her as an immoral, contemptible creature given to every sin imaginable. Paul disregarded that; he considered her to be an innocuous enough woman who had simply had the misfortune to be born in the wrong time and place.

"Madame," he said as he took her hand and bent over

it. Mindful of his responsibility to his patient's well-being, both emotional and physical, he added gallantly, "I regret the circumstances, but it is nonetheless a pleasure to see you again."

The queen smiled. For a moment, she looked almost like the young, carefree girl she had been. "How kind of you to say so, Monsieur le Marquis." Teasingly, she said, "Ah, forgive me. That is an outmoded form of address, is it not? Undoubtedly you prefer Monsieur le Docteur, or perhaps even Citoyen."

"It is true that I don't use the title inherited from my late father," Paul acknowledged. "But neither do I insist on all the latest innovations. Doctor is quite acceptable, particularly since I am here in that capacity."

At the reminder, the queen made a gentle moue of distaste. "Dominique is a dear child, but sometimes she worries too much. I am really quite fine."

Paul replied noncommittally as he slipped his fingers down the queen's wrist and discreetly took her pulse. It was rapid, but not alarmingly so.

The problem was her breathing. He could hear the congestion in her lungs. Her skin was dry and hot, and a dark flush stained her cheeks. He cast a quick glance at Dominique, who stood silent and unmoving at the foot of the bed.

"Mademoiselle de Montfort was correct to call for me, Your Majesty," he said gently. "You have an inflammation of the lungs that must be treated."

"A small indisposition only," Marie Antoinette insisted. With charming candor, she added, "Truthfully, Monsieur le Docteur, I loathe being bled, nor am I fond of the noxious potions your profession unfailingly prescribes."

"Then we will deal well together, madame," Paul said soothingly. "I don't believe in bleeding patients." At her startled look, he explained, "I realize it's the most popular treatment, but I think the theory behind it is wrong. A lack of blood is far more dangerous than too much. As to the potions . . ."

He paused and smiled at her reassuringly. "I believe whatever I prescribe can be made sufficiently palatable. To begin with, I'd like you to take a cup of milk three times a day, along with a whole egg."

The look that passed between the queen and Dominique did not escape him. He made a mental note to assure that adequate supplies were provided. There would be no further nonsense about that—not if those fools at the Assembly were serious about him doing the job.

Quietly, he gave instructions for the use of a salve and an infusion that he hoped would provide the needed relief. The queen's condition was not immediately serious, but he knew only too well that such ailments could turn suddenly deadly.

While there were men in the Assembly who might find such a royal death convenient, Paul's duty as a physician, coupled with simple human decency, demanded that he do everything possible to bring about a speedy recovery. He would need to check on his patient frequently.

"I will be back later today," Paul said as Dominique showed him out. "Try to get her to sleep more."

"Today? But I thought . . ." She broke off, staring up at him with wide, apprehensive eyes.

"What?" Paul asked quietly. "That I would simply come by, see that she wasn't precisely at death's doorstep, and disappear?" Her silence confirmed his suspicion. He grimaced and shook his head. "That isn't how I do my job."

"Which job?" Dominique demanded. She had recovered sufficiently from her surprise to challenge him. "We have enough spies here."

That accusation, coming without warning, left Paul momentarily at a loss for words. He gazed down at her in bewilderment, trying to discern what he could possibly have said or done to lead her to such a conclusion.

"You yourself requested that a doctor be sent," he reminded her. "Why should you now think that I have any other motive for being here?"

"Because," she said flatly, "your colleagues in the Assembly demand payment for everything. Even the smallest concession to our needs has carried a high price."

He was about to insist again that he came only to care for the royal family, when he hesitated. Much as he disliked admitting it, she was probably right. The chances were that the men who had sent him would expect him to report anything he saw or heard. In that case, they were going to be disappointed.

"Do you know what the Hippocratic oath is?" he asked.

Dominique looked at him blankly. "What has that to do with anything?"

Patiently, he explained. "It is the oath that doctors take, in which we swear to keep confidential any information we may glean in the course of performing our duties. The pledge that binds us is as sacred as that which seals the confessional. It cannot, for any reason, be violated."

Dominique listened skeptically. That such an oath existed she did not doubt. She was even willing to grant that Paul took it seriously, at least at the moment. But if the past few years had taught her anything, it was that the word of men could seldom, if ever, be trusted. In times of turmoil, any treachery could be justified by the simple need to survive.

"We shall see," she murmured as she opened the door leading to the corridor. With a cool nod of her head, she took her leave.

Paul was left to reflect on what had turned the joyful child he remembered into so cautious and even cynical a young woman. His thoughts did not please him. He was scowling as he walked down the wide stone steps of the palace.

As always, a crowd was gathered immediately beyond the cordon of troops that kept watch night and day. It parted reluctantly for him amid muttered imprecations and obscenities.

He ignored them as he pushed his way through, assailed by the odor of garlic, unwashed bodies, cheap wines, and stale cheese. Over all of it floated the stench of violence, barely restrained and infinitely dangerous.

The Paris mob was becoming more unruly by the day. Certain of the revolutionary leaders found that advantageous, but Paul disagreed. He believed instinctively in order and respect for the law. That seemed to be falling by the wayside these days.

A cloud passed over the sun. For a moment it blotted out the late June afternoon and brought a shadow of approaching night.

Chapter 2

"He is so handsome," the queen exclaimed. She was sitting up in bed, a smile wreathing her gentle face and a flirtatious look in her eyes. "Really, Dominique," she went on, "you might have warned me."

"My apologies, madame," Dominique murmured dryly. "I was more concerned with your health than with Monsieur le Docteur's appearance."

"So formal," Marie Antoinette teased. "But it wasn't always so between you, was it? I seemed to sense something . . . a certain understanding, perhaps. Or," she added softly, "am I mistaken?"

Dominique hesitated. The memories were so tantalizingly close and so piercingly sweet. Yet reliving them would bring her pain.

"I knew him when I was a child," she admitted finally. "But it was only a . . . casual acquaintance. When he was at court we saw nothing of each other."

This wasn't strictly true; their paths had occasionally

crossed. She still had a vivid image of coming upon Paul several years ago in a secluded corner of the great chateau of Versailles, finding him snug in the embrace of a court lady known for being generous with her charms.

Ruefully, Dominique recalled that there had actually been a time when she believed nothing more anguishing could ever happen to her.

"The family was Irish originally, weren't they?" the queen asked thoughtfully.

Dominique nodded. "They were among the Wild Geese who were driven into exile a century ago following their defeat by the English. The original name was Delaney. Delamare is a corruption; also, a reference to their being *de la mar*—of the sea."

"How fascinating," Marie Antoinette murmured, her eyes dancing as she observed the young girl. "You must have been well acquainted with Monsieur de Docteur, at least at one time, to know so much."

Realizing that she had revealed a greater knowledge of Paul than she had intended, Dominique added hastily, "Isn't it odd the things one remembers? I recall almost nothing else about him."

The queen was far too kind and considerate a mistress to point out that Dominique was being less than candid. She merely smiled gently and patted the bed beside her.

"Sit down and talk with me for a while. I get so bored just lying here in bed."

Dominique complied. She knew that the queen was not so much feeling the tedium of her confinement as she was succumbing to the ever-tightening coil of tension that gripped them so remorselessly. There was among all of them a growing sense that they were reaching some sort of watershed.

France, which had existed in a state of perpetual crisis for several years, now stood on the brink of war. Worse yet, the enemy was Austria, Marie Antoinette's birthplace and the country many still believed held her loyalty.

Dominique knew that wasn't true, but there was no way to convince the mob of it, nor the men in power who found it convenient to believe such slander.

Gently, she took the older woman's hand and smiled soothingly. "You will feel better soon. I'm sure of it."

Marie Antoinette laughed softly. "So you still have faith in the good doctor, despite your disclaimers."

Dominique sighed. The queen was an inveterate romantic, deeply attached to her husband, devoted to her children, unfailing in her friendships. Despite her recent experiences, she tended to believe the best about people. Above all, she wanted everyone to be happy—as happy as she had been in the early days of her marriage, before the world had intruded so harshly.

Choosing her words carefully, Dominique said, "I am sure that Monsieur Delamare is a skilled physician."

With some hesitation, she added, "And he does seem more reasonable than the others—not so filled with rage and the desire for vengeance."

Pain flitted across the queen's soft features. Her eyes filled with bewildered tears. "I will never understand why they hate us so. Louis has labored long and hard to improve conditions for the common people. He lowered taxes, helped trade, maintained peace—all for their sake. At first, they seemed to appreciate what he was doing, but then . . ."

She broke off as a spasm wracked her and she coughed harshly. Dominique hurried over to a nearby table and found the tincture Paul had left.

Gently, she helped the queen swallow it. A moment or two passed before her breathing grew easier and she managed a wan smile.

"So foolish of me," she murmured. "I must not dwell on unhappy thoughts; they only lead to upset."

The words sounded almost like a recital, as though the queen had repeated them many times to herself. Certainly, she'd had no lack of occasion to do so.

Dominique waited a few minutes longer, half crouched on the bed with her arm around the queen's shoulders. Gradually, the tension eased from the small, soft form. Her eyes drifted shut. In another instant, she was fast asleep.

Dominique breathed a sigh of relief. Carefully, she lowered the queen onto the pillows and covered her lightly. Still, she did not leave until she was certain that her mistress would not wake again soon. And then she went only because she knew the children would be waiting.

They were gathered as usual in a small chamber between their mother's apartments and their own. Louis, dauphin of France and heir to the throne of his forefathers, smiled shyly as Dominique entered. He was a slightly built, gentle boy of seven with shoulder-length chestnut hair and wide blue eyes.

Dominique never managed to look at him without feeling a pang of concern. Illness and frailty ran in the royal line. Louis XVI had been fortunate to escape it, but one of his brothers had not; he was so weakened by tuberculosis of the bones that he was barely able to walk upright. There were fears, though never expressed, that the dauphin might face a similar fate.

No such shadow lay over the princess, Maria Theresa, at fourteen years of age already very much the self-possessed, confident young lady who was also capable of engaging sweetness and a bright intelligence that helped considerably to ease the dreariness of their surroundings.

Just then, however, Theresa was worried. "How is Maman?" she asked. "Papa says she will be fine, but he would say that anyway to make us feel better."

"He is telling you the truth," Dominique said swiftly. She came farther into the room, shutting the door behind her, and lowered her voice.

From long-ingrained habit, anything of the slightest delicacy was discussed in whispers. It had to be when no one could know when an eavesdropper was crouched nearby, eager to report everything that was said.

"There is a new doctor," Dominique went on. "His name is Paul Delamare, and he seems . . . quite capable."

"Delamare?" repeated another young girl seated nearby on a horsehair settee. Nicole de Montfort tilted her small head to one side and regarded her sister solemnly. "Isn't that the marquis de Rochford's family name, Dominique?"

How was it, Dominique wondered, that at the tender age of nine, when most young ladies were concerned only with their lessons and their daydreams, Nicole already had an encyclopedic memory for aristocratic relationships? She could, seemingly without effort, unravel the most complicated lineage. When Nicole was barely five, and they were all still at Versailles, Dominique remembered her standing in the glittering Hall of Mirrors, blithely explaining how a particular duke and his wife were actually sixth cousins four times removed. Nicole had even managed to make it sound obvious!

"Yes," Dominique said, a shade wearily, "he is de Rochford."

"Then he is a traitor," a young boy blurted out. It was

not the dauphin, who was too polite and well-behaved to ever say such a thing. The blunt-spoken fellow was Dominique's own brother, David, at eight only a year older than the royal heir, but more than a head taller and robustly built.

"He turned his back on all of us," David continued, "when he sided with the revolutionaries."

Though Dominique agreed, she sought to minimize Paul's guilt in order to reassure the children. "There are many shades of opinion among the rebels. Not all of them are as radical as the few who seem to shout the loudest. Besides, what really counts is that he is a very good doctor."

She was convinced of that after seeing him at work. Whatever else he had done, Paul had not lost the compassion that made him such a capable physician. He was even still capable of extending it to a woman others of his ilk might prefer to see die.

Dominique's throat tightened. Though she had eaten little all day, she knew that were she to attempt to swallow anything at that moment, she would fail.

Fear, plain and simple, held her in thrall. Not simply for herself, but for all those she loved: Nicole and David, Maria Theresa and little Louis, the king and queen, who had become almost like parents to her.

They were going to die, unless something changed drastically for the better. She was certain of it, though she could not say how.

Such grim thoughts were alien to her nature, yet she recognized them nonetheless for what they were: a warning she could not afford to deny.

"I must go," she murmured with a smile for the children. At the swift look of concern that passed among them, she added, "But I'll be back soon. In the meantime, why don't you all pick out a new book for us to begin this evening? Something gay and amusing, perhaps?"

They promised that they would do so as she smiled again and hurried off.

Fortunately, for Dominique's purposes, the Tuileries was a maze of corridors and stairways that caused the uninitiated to become hopelessly lost, but which also offered ample hiding places for those who wished to be unobserved.

One such was in a corner tower reachable only by a narrow, winding flight of steps that ended in an iron-studded doorway. The leather hinges creaked as Dominique eased the door open. She stepped into a tiny room filled with stale air and lit by a single fluttering candle.

"Shut the door," a voice hissed. "Quickly."

Dominique complied, then stood silently until her eyes adjusted sufficiently to penetrate the gloom. As her gaze fell on the figure crouched in the corner, she suppressed an impatient sigh.

"It's all right, Monsieur Renault. I wasn't followed."

"So you say," the man snapped as he reluctantly straightened up and approached her. He wore the plain, somber clothes of a good bourgeois, startlingly at odds with the bold red cap draped carefully over his head. Once exclusive to the poor of Paris, it had become a popular symbol of the revolution and, as such, was adopted by everyone anxious to prove their loyalty to the new government.

"It's impossible to know who's doing what in this place," Monsieur Renault murmured. He was a young man, in his midtwenties, but appeared much older by virtue of his narrow, suspicious face and stooped shoulders.

His father owned a trading firm renowned for the quality of its silks and brocades; the queen had once been one of their most honored clients. More recently, the company of Renault et Fils had other merchandise of greater interest to those still loyal to the monarchy.

"I could lose my life," the young man whined. "In fact, I probably will. Father is mad to be involved in this."

"He is being extremely well paid," Dominique reminded him coldly. She reached a hand into the pocket of her dress and removed a pouch. "Here is the amount agreed on. The rest will be paid when the project is successfully completed."

Even here, in this hidden room, she was too cautious to speak directly of what they were about. The word *escape* never passed her lips. It never would. She was careful not even to think it.

"Madness," Renault muttered again. "The entire royal guard couldn't help them when they tried to get away last year. What makes anyone think that a simple merchant can manage it?"

"Because no one will be expecting us to try this way," Dominique said, cutting him off firmly. "Everyone thinks that if we do try to get away again, it will be an attempt like the first one, complete with royal guards and a desperate dash to the borders. Instead, it's going to be much simpler and quieter. And this time," she added tautly, "it will succeed."

Monsieur Renault continued to look doubtful, but the weight of the pouch in his hand helped to decide him. "All right," he said grudgingly, "we will continue with the plan. I'll contact you when all is in readiness."

"Do not delay," Dominique cautioned. "It must be soon."

"It will be when it will be. There is a limit to the risks we will run."

When he was gone, Dominique stood staring at the shadows cast by the flickering flame of the candle he had left behind. Long ago, in some forgotten time, the small room had been used as a chapel. On the soot-and-mildew-stained wall, the outline of a long-vanished cross could still be seen.

Staring at it, she sank to her knees and began to pray. But the solace of such simple—and quite genuine—devotion eluded her. Her heart was in too much turmoil. Unbidden, the memories she had earlier struggled to deny rose to taunt her.

Six years might have been mere hours, for all the forgetfulness they had brought. She remembered everything —the scent of fresh-cut hay on that balmy spring day; the cheerful voices of the workers in the fields, singing as they moved along the rows of golden stalks; the sudden scattering of crows as a horseman rode up.

Numbly, she shook her head. *Please, not now—later, when I am out of this place*. But the plea went unheeded. The dark, clammy stone walls seemed to dissolve around her as she heard again the shout of her father's steward.

Lefauche, get over here!

In the distant reaches of the field, a young man straightened. He was about twenty, sturdily built, with broad shoulders and a shock of rough black hair. His face was open and ingenuous until he heard the steward's summons. Then it became carefully guarded.

"Sir?" he asked tentatively as he approached the man.

From her perch in a nearby chestnut tree, Dominique observed the exchange. She disliked the steward—a loud, vulgar man she suspected of being cruel. But she was unprepared for his callousness as he said, "Your wife's whelping. The priest said to get you."

Clearly, the instruction was resented, but not even the steward dared go against the will of the Church's representative. Lefauche had no opportunity to appreciate that. He had turned pale.

"She's all right . . . my wife?"

The steward shrugged. "Think they'd call for you if she was? Go on, get out of here, but mind you, be back in the fields by first light tomorrow. I'll have no malingering."

Without waiting for an answer, he yanked his horse around and rode off. Lefauche was left on foot almost a mile from the village, with no means of getting there except to walk. Or run.

Dismayed by such thoughtlessness, Dominique slipped from her tree branch. "Come on," she said gently, "I've got my mare."

The young man stared at her dumbly. She had to repeat herself before he understood. Even then, desperate as he was to get to his wife, he hesitated.

"Mam'selle," he murmured, doffing his cap, "it wouldn't be right . . ."

"Don't be a ninny," Dominique said. Briskly, with an inborn air of command, she grasped his arm and tugged him toward the horse.

"We can ride together," she instructed as she swung agilely into the saddle. Lefauche was a good deal less graceful. For one, he had never been on a saddled horse before in his life. For another, he was extremely disconcerted to be so close to the young daughter of his lord, a creature who by all rights he should never even have looked at directly.

Dominique was not insensitive to his concerns; she merely chose to ignore them. Setting a rapid pace, she coaxed her mare on. The small, graceful horse took the additional weight well. They reached the village swiftly and pulled up in front of a small, windowless hut.

Lefauche bolted from the saddle, almost falling in the process, and raced inside. Dominique followed more slowly. Although she had visited her father's tenants from time to time, she had never grown accustomed to their circumstances. To her, the dark, dank hovels in which they dwelled were the nearest thing to hell she had ever experienced.

Yet others took them for granted. Not even the kindly priest seemed to believe that the peasants deserved any better. They lived as they always had and always would. The order of the world was immutable. The wise man accepted that.

But the man kneeling beside the tattered and filth-encrusted pallet did not. Paul Delamare's eyes flashed with fury. In a voice made all the more threatening by its softness, he said, "I should have been called hours ago. Why the hell wasn't I?"

The toothless old woman crouched beside him shook her head. " 'T'isn't done."

A pulse leaped in his clenched jaw. "Why isn't it? You know I'm a doctor and you know I'm willing to help, so why let this poor creature go so far without summoning me?"

The woman looked away stubbornly, but there was a faint look of confusion in her eyes. Meanwhile, Lefauche fell in a heap on the floor beside his wife. He seized her white and lifeless hand and began to sob helplessly.

Paul uttered a sharp curse at the same moment that he glanced toward the door. Silhouetted against the light, Dominique felt his eyes touch her.

"You . . ." he said, surprised. His tone became gentler. "Dominique, what are you doing here?"

She took a step farther into the room. Her emerald gaze darted fearfully to the woman moaning on the floor. On a breath of sound, she murmured, "I . . . I brought Lefauche."

Paul stared at her for a long moment. Slowly, the hard lines in his face relaxed. He smiled gently.

"Come here, Dominique."

That was absolutely the last thing she wanted to do. The woman on the floor, her tattered skirt yanked up around her waist to expose her grossly swollen belly, was terrifying to her. Although she could not have grown up in the country without learning the rudiments of how all things were born, she had never before seen a woman in labor, much less one in labor gone horribly wrong.

Still, the strength of Paul's voice and his compelling aura of command proved irresistible. Falteringly, she moved to his side.

His hand closed around hers. His skin was warm, his touch powerful yet almost unbearably gentle. Her knees began to shake.

"Dominique," he said softly, "can you be very brave?"

Her eyes widened, meeting his. "I can try," she whispered.

He smiled as though she was the cleverest and best girl in the world. "Good, I need your help. So does this young woman here. Don't be afraid of her. She can't hurt you. Indeed, if you and I don't manage it, she is going to die."

"Oh, no," Dominique blurted. But he was right, of course. The presence of death hovered in the room, waiting ever patient and resourceful to claim its due.

Dominique raised her head. Her small chin thrust outward. "We must save her."

If Paul found her use of the word *we* amusing, he didn't show it. Instead, he nodded gravely. "Go out to the well and fetch a bucket of clean water. Then get the fire going and boil it. Can you do that?"

Swiftly, Dominique nodded. It didn't matter that in her father's house, she had rarely so much as lifted her own clothes from the floor where she dropped them. She was certain she could carry out her entrusted task.

It proved more difficult than expected. The only bucket in sight was filthy and had to be scrubbed before it could be used. She cut several fingers on the splintering sides and had to squeeze her eyes tight to hold back the tears.

But at last she managed to lower it into the old stone well, only to discover that water was much heavier than she had thought. How on earth did the serving girls manage to carry gallon upon gallon of the stuff up to her bedroom for the daily baths she loved? Lugging a single bucketful back to the hut was almost more than she could manage.

Paul was still kneeling beside the woman. Bloody cloths lay nearby. Lefauche was swaying back and forth, moaning helplessly. His wife had ceased to make any sound at all, but lay ashen and silent, as though already dead.

"Is she . . . ?" Dominique murmured.

Paul shook his head. "Not yet. Get the fire started."

It did not seem to occur to him that she had never performed any such task in her life. Thankfully, she had seen it done enough times to know how. Nonetheless, she had to puff long and hard on the damp kindling before the flame at last caught.

A curl of gray smoke twined its way toward the hole cut in the hut's roof. With all her strength, Dominique hoisted the bucket onto a hook above the fire.

Paul glanced over his shoulder. "Add more wood; there isn't much time."

Grimly, she nodded. Half an hour later, she had a steady blaze going and was satisfied to see that the water was beginning to boil.

"It's ready," she said.

"Good, take these." He handed her a collection of strange-looking implements and directed her to plunge them into the water. As she did so, he continued to gently knead the woman's distended belly, all the while murmuring to her encouragingly, even though she appeared to be deeply unconscious.

"The baby . . . ?" Dominique asked as she came to kneel beside him. Oddly, the sight of the woman no longer frightened her. Her struggle with the water and the fire had given her a sense of competence she had not had before.

"It still lives," Paul said softly, "but it is not correctly positioned. I am trying to shift it."

Dominique paled. She had a sudden, acute insight into the battle being waged in the silent darkness of the woman's womb. Her hands shook as she struggled to her feet.

"I'll get those things . . . whatever they are."

"Be careful; don't burn yourself."

She did despite the warning, but it didn't seem to matter. She was far too fascinated by what Paul was doing. He lifted the woman enough to lay a clean sheet beneath her, then turned away to scrub his hands and forearms.

"I've never seen a doctor so concerned about a little dirt," Dominique said in a weak attempt at teasing.

Paul nodded as he returned to the pallet. "Most of my colleagues don't think cleanliness matters, but my experience indicates otherwise. More patients survive when I follow these procedures."

He picked up one of the instruments Dominique had taken from the water and turned back to the woman. Dominique watched for a few moments until her stomach suddenly rebelled. She looked away hastily until Paul ordered, "Take your hands and press down on her belly." When she hesitated an instant, he added, "Now!"

Instinctively, Dominique obeyed. She stiffened with shock as the baby kicked out at her. It felt so strong and alive, yet it was moments from death. They were all— mother, child, husband, Paul, and herself—in some nether region between the light of the world and the fathomless dark. Her resolve girded within her. No matter what, the dark must not win.

An instant later, a piercing cry broke the silence. Dominique watched in astonishment as the baby, still coated with the milky substance of the womb, slid from his mother's body. Swiftly, Paul wrapped him in a clean blanket he had brought along for that purpose.

"Take care of him," he said as he thrust the infant at Dominique.

Take care of him. She had not the slightest notion of what to do. Fortunately, the baby didn't seem to mind. He screwed his little face up furiously and bellowed with all his might. Dominique laughed with relief until she remembered his mother.

She looked quickly back toward the pallet. Paul had delivered the afterbirth and was laboring to stop the bleeding. At his direction, Lefauche managed to sit his wife up a few inches so that she could drink the liquid Paul held to her lips. Even the old crone bestirred herself.

"What's that?" she demanded.

"Tincture of ergot," Paul said quietly.

Her rheumy eyes narrowed. "Most physicians won't use that. They say it's superstition."

Paul shrugged. "Whatever it is, it stops bleeding, as I'm sure you know. If you've none of your own to give her, I'll leave a supply. She needs to have it every—"

"I know how often to dose her," the old woman broke in, "and I won't be needing any from you when I've plenty in my own medicine chest." Her tone softened as she looked at him grudgingly. "Still and all, I couldn't have done what you did, turning the babe like that. You saved them both."

Paul inclined his head, as though he was acknowledging a lady of gentle birth. "Thank you," he said simply.

A short while later, he and Dominique were both standing in the blessedly fresh air beyond the hut. A cool breeze blew. All around them was silence, save for the drone of grasshoppers and frogs. She was startled to see that it was dark.

"I had no idea we'd been so long," she murmured.

He smiled gently. "You were wonderful in there."

She flushed and looked away from him, feeling within herself the painful stirrings of newly awakened emotions —emotions that a lifetime later were still disconcertingly alive.

Chapter
3

Paul paused in front of the large, elegant building on the Avenue de Liberté. The sidewalk out in front was crowded with hurrying passersby. Men and a few women streamed in and out of the building. A few looked blankly confident, but most appeared apprehensive.

He couldn't blame them. The building was the headquarters for the National Assembly, and as such, contained the offices for the leaders of the revolution—men who were as powerful and as autocratic as the Bourbon King they had sought to supplant.

Liberté et Égalité. Liberty and Equality, the guiding lights of the revolution. They were the cornerstones of Paul's own conviction in the worthiness of tearing up a way of life and replacing it with something new and better. Except everything he saw about him filled him with disgust. France seemed in the process of devouring itself alive. It was a horrible image, but one he could not shake, no matter how hard he tried.

And now he was about to come face-to-face with the man who, more than any other, symbolized what for him had gone wrong with the struggle for freedom—the man Paul had once believed in passionately; whom he had been willing to follow into the fire. The man he was set to betray.

With a deep sigh, he shook himself from his thoughts and entered the building, merging quickly with the milling crowd.

He was quite short—only a shade over five feet tall—and slim. As usual, he was pacing up and down in the large, ornately furnished office. His nervous energy was immense. He was rarely able to sit for more than a few minutes at a time.

He was Maximilien Robespierre, leader of the Jacobin faction in the National Assembly—spellbinding orator, shining idealist, madman.

Paul watched him carefully. Robespierre was dictating to a secretary, the words spewing out of him in a flurry, his voice strident, shrill, always on the edge of cracking.

His hair was chestnut and worn in short curls. In more formal circumstances, he used a wig or had his own hair powdered. His skin was sallow and pockmarked from a childhood bout of smallpox. His eyes were large, slightly protruding, and he squinted.

"Is that you, Delamare?"

Paul glanced at the secretary—a tall, bewhiskered young man who was sweating profusely, and not entirely because of the warmth of the day. With a faint smile, he said, "You are working Hebert too hard. He looks as though he needs a rest."

In fact, it was Robespierre who appeared stretched to

the breaking point. Each time Paul saw him he was more convinced than ever that the man was seriously ill, if only in his mind.

The same instinct that made him so capable a physician enabled him to sense the poison spreading through the other man, distorting what had once been a brilliant and farseeing intellect. It was a tragedy, but it was also a danger that had to be defused.

"Sit down," Robespierre directed with a wave of his hand. He withdrew a lace-edged handkerchief from his brocade frock coat and pressed it lightly to his lips. When he removed it, the mask of congeniality was firmly in place.

"How long has it been, Paul?" he asked with a smile. "Two months . . . three . . . since I last saw you? But then," he added archly, "from all I hear, you are a very busy man."

Paul shrugged. He stretched his long legs out in front of him and made himself as comfortable as the stiff-backed chair permitted. "We all have our duties."

"Ah, yes," Robespierre agreed. "That is certainly true. But then, yours have recently expanded, have they not?"

Paul repressed a sigh of impatience. Though the revolutionary leader had not been among those who had asked him to see the ailing queen, he would certainly have known of the assignment. It was even highly likely that Robespierre had suggested Paul for the job.

If he had done so in the expectation that Paul would in turn be a ready source of information, he was about to be disappointed.

"Was there some particular reason you wanted to see me?" Paul asked smoothly. His tone betrayed exactly the right degree of restrained impatience proper to a man who has pressing demands on his time and attention—a man who could not be expected to while away an afternoon chatting amicably, no matter how much he might otherwise be inclined to do so.

Robespierre frowned. Power had made him vain. He was accustomed to deference; had come to consider it his due. No one—not even his political opponents—dared to challenge him directly. All paid him the tribute of being afraid.

Except for Paul. He had always been the exception, the one man Robespierre could not bluster or bludgeon into obedience. And as such, he was the one man whose respect the revolutionist most desired.

"Fetch us some tea, Hebert," Robespierre directed abruptly.

The secretary was so startled by the notion of the great man offering hospitality that he stumbled on his way out the door. When it had closed behind him, Paul laughed softly.

"Still keeping them on a short leash, I see."

Robespierre waved a hand dismissively. "I am surrounded by mediocrities—not like in the old days, when everything was possible."

He leaned forward, his narrow shoulders tense and straining. "More than ever, we need men like you directly involved. Only say the word and I can guarantee you a position on my staff that would make you the envy of France."

Paul hesitated. He knew his reply had to strike exactly the right balance, showing proper appreciation for the magnitude of the honor being done him while firmly rejecting it.

Not that he hadn't anticipated Robespierre's offer and

even been tempted to accept it. From the inside, he might be able to do more good—perhaps even thwart some of the more insane rumblings he heard coming from the Jacobins.

Except that he was no spy, much less a saboteur. His character was far too straightforward to hope to pull off such a role effectively. He was better off doing exactly what he was—working quietly and steadily to bring sanity back to the revolution.

He looked at Robespierre directly, holding his gaze. "Did you know that last week alone there were two hundred and twelve deaths from cholera among members of the National Guard? And those are only for the divisions in the Paris area. I don't have the figures yet for the rest of the country."

The older man shrugged. "There is always disease and death. They are a fact of life."

"But they can be conquered, or at least forestalled. We don't need to be helpless victims of our own mortality."

Robespierre smiled, somewhat indulgently. "That has always been your credo, hasn't it, Paul? Life can be better. You truly believe that."

Paul's eyebrows rose. "Don't you?" The question was far from innocuous. If Robespierre didn't believe that the human condition could be improved, he had no business leading a revolution whose goal was to do exactly that.

"What I believe . . ." Robespierre murmured. He broke off, his gaze suddenly turned inward, as though he was caught by hidden vistas that did not bear close scrutiny.

"What I believe," he began again, "is that man has been corrupted by the evils of our society. Greed and superstition are like cancers eating away at us. Until they can be cut out, there can be no hope of improvement."

Paul kept his expression rigidly controlled, but underneath he was shocked and worried by Robespierre's pronouncement.

To speak so blithely of cutting out . . . and what precisely did he mean by greed and superstition? To a distorted mind, the normal activities of business and religion might be given those classifications.

He shook his head, not wanting to dwell on the rumors that were plaguing Paris. Gossips said that the National Assembly, primarily at the behest of Robespierre, was about to make even more outrageous demands on the king than had been done previously. The demands could not possibly be met without shattering the very bonds that held French civilization together. Without the strength of their history and faith, how could the country hope to survive?

In a sudden shift of mood, Robespierre smiled again and took the chair opposite Paul. His tone became engagingly confidential as he said, "Tell me, then, how did you find Citizeness Capet?"

He was referring to the queen, using the name assigned to the royal family by the revolutionaries, who refused to accord them any other title or acknowledgment of their noble descent. Paul privately thought that it was a foolish conceit to imagine that you could belittle people simply by refusing to call them by their proper name.

"The queen," he said matter-of-factly, "is ill but not seriously so. She does, however, require the attentions of a doctor."

"I see," Robespierre murmured, his eyes on Paul. "And you will care for her?"

"I have agreed to do so," Paul acknowledged.

"Do you . . . like doing so?"

Paul frowned. The question was not clear to him. He

had a duty and he had accepted it. Nothing more was involved—unless Robespierre had somehow found out about Dominique. A stab of apprehension shot through him, which he carefully masked. Not for a moment would he let the other man sense the concern he felt for the queen's young lady-in-waiting. To do so would only place Dominique in even greater danger.

"Someone has to do it," he said carefully. "Surely it would not be politic to have the queen of France die because she had not received proper medical attention."

"Is that a possibility?" Robespierre asked. "That she might die?"

Paul shrugged. He didn't want to exaggerate this point, but neither could he totally ignore it. "There is always that chance. As you said, disease and death are ever with us."

"Yes, but is she herself in any immediate danger?"

Paul shook his head. He couldn't reconcile what he knew to be Robespierre's hatred for the royal family with his apparently genuine concern for Marie Antoinette. Far from appearing eager for the queen's death, he seemed sincerely worried that she might succumb.

"Her constitution appears to be inherently strong," Paul said, "and if she follows my instructions, she should recover in good time."

Robespierre sat back with a small sigh of relief. "I certainly hope so. It would not do for that contemptible bitch to escape so lightly."

Paul stiffened but managed to hide his disgust. Robespierre looked perfectly calm. No change of tone or expression betrayed the extreme virulence of those words, which made them all the more ominous.

"Ah, well," he went on as though he had said nothing

in particular, "a man must be patient. I've always said that, haven't I, Paul? And you're a great one for biding your time, too, aren't you?" He chuckled softly and stood up, holding out his hand in a gesture of dismissal.

"Go on with you, then. Back to your soldiers and your cholera. But don't forget to look in on Citizeness Capet from time to time. It wouldn't do to let her health be neglected."

Paul heard Robespierre's laughter as he left the office and with relief made his way from the building. His thoughts were on the Tuileries and the two women within it who had become his particular concern, each in a different way.

He did not notice the small, dark-faced man who followed a discreet distance behind him.

Chapter 4

Dominique grimaced as she glanced in the mirror. The rose dress was looking more worn than ever. She would have to turn the collar again.

Even more pressing was the need to secure a new dress for Nicole. She was growing so quickly that nothing she had fit her properly. Then there was David. He was fairly bursting out of his breeches. Something would also have to be done for him.

Automatically, she added those tasks to the already copious mental list she carried about. Her Majesty needed fresh books to read, the dauphin had requested a new deck of cards, His Majesty was almost out of ink.

So much to do, and it all tended to fall on her, simply because she had proved herself most adept at wangling from the authorities those little concessions that made life tolerable.

It was just as well; she preferred to be busy rather than to have too much time to dwell on her thoughts.

With a final tug on her dress, she hurried out. In the past week, the weather had turned mercifully cooler. The royal apartments were actually comfortable, though that probably wouldn't continue long.

Experience had taught that they would soon again be sweltering, but for the moment, at least, she was neither dazed by heat nor shivering with cold, and for that, Dominique was grateful.

Besides, the sun was shining. Outside, in the gardens adjoining the palace, birds were singing. The gravel paths were freshly raked and the hyacinths were blooming, and if she kept her mind on business, she might find time for a walk before the day was done.

The moment she entered the queen's sitting room, Dominique's optimistic mood vanished. Marie Antoinette was not alone. The king was with her, and they both looked extremely grim.

Louis looked up as Dominique entered and managed a wan smile. He was a short, somewhat plump man with a round face and a benign expression. Popular thought labeled him stupid, but Dominique knew beyond question that it wasn't true. Louis had a keen, methodical mind.

"Good morning, my dear," he said quietly. "You're looking very well."

His comment demonstrated how thoroughly distracted His Highness was, since normally he was far more perceptive.

Dominique shot a quick, worried glance at the queen. After a week of Paul's treatments, Antoinette was much improved.

Her lungs were no longer congested and she had far more energy than before. It could be said that she was back to her old self, except that she was as distracted and concerned as the king.

Dominique's hands clenched in the folds of her skirt. Softly, she asked, "Has something happened?"

The royal couple hesitated. Finally, the queen said, "His Majesty has been presented with a decree from the National Assembly, which he has decided not to sign."

"Good," Dominique said unequivocally. "It's time that bunch was set back on its heels."

The queen smiled gently. "Sometimes I forget how very young you are. When I was your age, I, too, tended to see everything in idealistic terms."

"Ideals have nothing to do with it," Dominique insisted. "I merely think things have gone too far." Quickly, she added, "I don't mean to criticize, but surely there comes a point when patience and tolerance are no longer called for?"

"And you think," the king asked quietly, "that we have reached that point?"

"Definitely. The time has come to stand up to the radicals and insist that certain basic standards of decency be respected."

Louis sighed. He sat back in his chair and stared out the window toward the garden. Several moments passed. Softly, as though he still couldn't quite believe what was happening, he said, "They want to deport the priests."

Dominique's lips parted soundlessly. She stared at him. "I don't understand . . ."

"It isn't enough that hundreds of them have been imprisoned," Louis continued, "accused of disloyalty simply because they refuse to recognize the authority of the new government above that of God. Now the radicals want me to agree to send them to some hellhole where they will most likely all die of leprosy and malaria. I simply cannot do it.''

Dominique heard him as though from a great distance. She felt as though she had been struck and was reeling from the blow. It was worse even than she had thought.

There had been rumors, certainly, but none had pinpointed exactly how virulent and audacious the revolutionaries would be.

They had placed the king in an absolutely untenable position. To comply with their demands would doom him, not only in this world but the next. There had been no choice for him except to refuse.

Which meant that they had him exactly where they wanted—in violation of the new so-called constitutional government, which Louis had pledged to uphold.

"What will they do?" she asked faintly. Instantly, she knew that she didn't want to hear the answer. Almost as swiftly, she realized that it could not be eluded.

But before Louis could reply, they were interrupted by a low, snuffling sound, like that of some great, lumbering beast. It was loud enough to penetrate the thick stone walls. It came from immediately beyond the palace gates.

At first, Dominique had no idea what it could be. Moments passed before she realized that she was hearing the sound of the mob—not the usual collection of hangers-on outside the palace, but hundreds, perhaps thousands, of enraged men.

Marie Antoinette heard it, too. She rose, hands clasped to her breasts, her face white. "Oh, my God . . .''

Louis reached out, taking hold of her quickly. "You must hide," he said, "and the children, as well. The mob must not be allowed to find you.''

"They won't get in," Marie Antoinette protested.

"Who will stop them—the citizen army? I prefer not to trust to their tender mercies. They . . ."

He did not have to finish. Both women knew what he meant. They had lived on the knife edge of disaster for so long now that they understood it completely. The mob had been known in its fury to tear people apart. There was nothing to say that such would not be their fate.

"No," Marie Antoinette exclaimed. "I will not leave you. Dominique, find the children, get help from the guard. There is still time . . ."

Before she could finish, the door to the antechamber was flung open and a man strode into the room.

"Come," Paul said brusquely. "You can't stay here."

"What are you . . . ?" the king began. He had been introduced to Paul in his capacity as the new royal physician and he also remembered him from those long-ago days at Versailles. But he had not expected him to appear so suddenly, and he was momentarily bewildered.

"It isn't the usual crowd out there," Paul cut in. "There are more than a thousand of them, and they're screaming for blood."

"The National Guard will hold them back," Marie Antoinette insisted. They had done so in the past, when angry crowds had threatened to storm the Tuileries. There was no reason to think they would not perform the same function now.

Paul swiftly banished that hope. His turquoise eyes glinted angrily as he said, "They are standing aside. I suspect they have direct orders to do so. Robespierre and the others have apparently decided to let this run its course."

Louis did not need to hear anything more. Ordinarily, he was the gentlest of men with his wife, but now he thrust her aside without further ado. "Go," he ordered sharply. "Find the children and hide."

Turning to Paul, he held out his hands. "Monsieur le Docteur, I beseech you to help them. They are innocent and helpless."

A pulse leaped in the shadowed hollow of Paul's jaw. His gaze was inscrutable as he stared at the king whose overthrow he had advocated so firmly, but who at that moment seemed the epitome of honor and decency.

"What about you, sire?" he asked.

Dominique started with surprise. She wondered if Paul was even aware of his form of address. Certainly neither he nor Louis seemed to notice it.

"I will remain here," the king said quietly. "It may yet be possible to calm the crowd and prevent bloodshed."

Marie Antoinette had begun to cry. Her slender body shook with the force of her sobs. Dominique put her arm around her shoulders and held the queen close. Murmuring to her softly, she drew her from the room.

Paul followed swiftly. The corridor was empty, but not far away they could hear the screams of the mob. Above that blood-chilling din, Paul shouted, "Where are the children?"

"Upstairs," Dominique told him, praying that she was right. He nodded and bent to lift the queen in his arms. "Go on," he said.

Obediently, Dominique raced ahead. She could hear Paul following, hear her mistress moaning softly, but her thoughts were on the children. At this time of day, they should be at their studies. But there was a chance they might have ventured outside.

A soft cry of relief escaped her when she saw that they had not. All four—Louis, Maria Theresa, Nicole, and

David—were in the drawing room. They had abandoned their studies, but only to stare out the window at the gathering mob.

"Maman," the dauphin exclaimed when he saw the queen in Paul's arms. "What has happened? Are you hurt?"

Quickly, the children clustered around, all excited and alarmed, but as yet without the hard, brutal sense of their true danger. Only Maria Theresa, at fourteen, was old enough to see what the rest were as yet still mercifully sheltered from.

"They aren't going to be stopped, are they?" she asked, still clinging to a faint ray of hope.

Paul dispelled it with a single shake of his head. "Unfortunately not. Come, we must be going."

"Where to?" the dauphin demanded. He had drawn himself upright and was looking at Paul squarely. Dominique had a sudden glimpse of the man—and ruler—he might one day be, if fate was kind enough to let him live.

"The council room," Paul said swiftly. In his earlier visits to the palace, he had become sufficiently familiar with its layout to know where the most shelter was likely to be found.

The council room faced the back of the building, farthest away from the rampaging mob. Its windows could be shuttered and it possessed stout double doors that would at least delay any assailants.

That was cold comfort to the group that huddled within, particularly when they realized that Paul did not intend to stay.

"Don't go," the queen entreated. She had recovered her composure sufficiently to reassure her children, but she was also clearly consumed by fear.

"It's all right," Paul said soothingly. "I'm going to barricade you in and there will be members of the royal guard posted immediately outside. You will be safe, provided that you don't attempt to leave, no matter what you may see or hear."

Over the queen's head, his eyes met Dominique's. She swallowed hard and nodded to show that she understood what he was saying. No matter what it took, she would keep the queen and the royal children in the council room until the danger passed.

The heavy thud of the doors signaled his departure and their own isolation. For several minutes after that, they heard the sounds of furniture being dragged into place to form a crude barricade. After that there were only the ominous shouts of the mob, coming ever closer.

"They are inside," Maria Theresa said softly. She was standing in the center of the room, arms hanging loosely at her sides, her face white and strained.

Dominique went to her. Gently, she guided the young princess over to a chair and sat her down. "We must listen to Monsieur Delamare," she said. "Everything will be all right."

Maria Theresa clearly did not believe her, but Nicole was another matter. "I'm sure Monsieur Delamare is right," she announced, her eyes shining with admiration. "He's so much nicer than I thought at first, and very brave, don't you think, Dominique?"

Her older sister managed a slight smile. "Most definitely, Nicole. David, stay away from those windows! And you, too, Your Highness, if you please."

The boys obeyed reluctantly and came to join the women. The little group fell silent. Outside they could hear the shouts and screams of men, the pounding of running feet, and an odd metallic clash, which it took them a moment to recognize.

"Pikes," Dominique murmured under her breath. "They're armed with pikes and using them to smash their way in."

Instinctively, they all glanced at the thick double doors. How long would they hold once the barricade was swept aside and the pikes let loose?

They had ample time to contemplate that possibility. The minutes dragged by. After half an hour, when they began to realize that the emergency would not end quickly, a queer, leaden exhaustion settled over them.

Dominique recognized it for what it was—the weariness of mind and body that follows hard upon terror. Such a fever pitch of fear simply could not be sustained. Eventually, it had to fade, leaving its victim like a shipwrecked survivor, stunned and bewildered.

She did her best to fight the weariness, but without great success. Numbly, she watched the hands move on the ornate, gilt-encrusted clock on the mantel. They were well into the second hour of waiting when they heard fresh shouts from the courtyard.

Dominique jumped up. She hurried to the door and pressed her ear to it, listening intently. These voices were different—not the rabid shouts of the mob, but more controlled, official sounding, yet also self-conscious, as though the men knew they were merely playing a part.

It didn't seem to matter. Within a very short time, the royal guards who had held their positions stalwartly on the other side of the door called the all-clear. Swiftly, they removed the barricade.

Barely was the door open when Marie Antoinette cried

out anxiously, "Is His Majesty safe? Has that rabble gone?"

"Yes to both questions, madame," Paul said gently. He looked tired but relieved. The harsh lines around his mouth and the shadows in his crystalline eyes were more eloquent than words. When his gaze met Dominique's, she felt herself swept by apprehension.

"Is it true?" she whispered after the queen and the children had gone on ahead. "They left peacefully?"

Paul nodded curtly. "After that fool of a mayor finally showed up. Petion is responsible for the security of the Tuileries. He should have intervened at once, but he was afraid to challenge the mob. Either that, or it was Robespierre he was frightened of displeasing."

"But he came finally?"

"Oh, yes, and eventually, even he was convinced that Louis will not sign the decree. They finally all left that poor man to his peace."

Dominique picked up her skirts as they hurried upstairs. Under her breath, she murmured, "I am surprised to hear you speak so sympathetically, Monsieur Delamare. One might almost think that you had undergone a conversion of some sort."

"Don't," he advised harshly. "My opinions are unchanged. France must become a republic. But that doesn't mean I can't admire a man who faces his enemies so courageously."

But at great cost. Louis was slumped in an armchair, his round face white and perspiring. Yet he managed a fragile smile as his wife flung herself at him, sobbing with joy.

"There, there, my dear," he said, patting her shoulder

gently. "It's quite all right. All that was needed was a bit of patience."

"They might have killed you," she exclaimed. "Truly, it is a miracle they did not."

Dominique privately agreed with her. She thought that the king had come as close to the brink as he could without expecting to be pushed over.

Again her eyes met Paul's. A silent message passed between them. Secure in the knowledge that the royal family would be too distracted to notice her absence, she slipped out the door.

Paul joined her in the corridor. Members of the royal guard were milling around, scrutinizing everyone who passed suspiciously.

"Come on," Paul said. Firmly, brooking no resistance, he drew her into a small room at the far end of the corridor. When he had shut the door behind them, he turned, hands on his hips, and glared at her.

"You understand what almost happened today?" he demanded coldly.

"Of course I do. We came very close to disaster." Thinking that what he wanted was thanks, she went on, "Naturally, we're all very grateful to you. If you hadn't arrived when you did and acted so decisively . . ."

"That isn't important," Paul broke in. "My point is that you are all hanging by tenterhooks. One wrong move and you can expect to fall."

"I realize that, but . . ."

"Do you?" Angrily, he strode across the room and took hold of her shoulders. His fingers dug into her soft flesh as he demanded, "If you are so sensible to your danger, then tell me, sweet Dominique, why are you so foolish as to trust men like the Renaults?"

Chapter 5

Dominique stared up at him numbly. She could not believe that she had heard correctly. How could he possibly know about Renault?

Her expression revealed her bewilderment. Coldly, Paul said, "Did you really imagine that I wouldn't be on guard against something like this? I know you too well, Dominique. You were always impulsive—apt to leap first and look afterward."

Dominique flinched. The words, so harshly spoken, were also accurate—as they both knew all too well. Her eyes shadowed with pain, she tried to turn away, but Paul would not allow it. His expression was suddenly gentler as he belatedly realized what she must be thinking.

"I didn't mean that," he said quietly. A smile, meant to be reassuring, lifted the corners of his mouth. "Although it's not a bad example."

"Please . . ." Dominique murmured under her breath. She knew she was being foolish, but the incident to which he was referring, which he apparently found amusing, was anything but to her.

All too acutely she remembered how in the days after the birth in the peasant hut, she thought continually of Paul. As she relived every tumultuous moment, he emerged in her mind as a heroic being vastly beyond the limits of ordinary men.

She was twelve years old, on the verge of her own awakening into womanhood. The emotions he innocently provoked were strange and frightening, and yet they were also irresistible.

"Dominique," he said quietly, recalling her to the present, "there is nothing to be ashamed of. If either of us should be embarrassed, it's me."

He wasn't being merely kind. Memories he had fought for years to repress were returning with a vengeance. All too clearly he remembered that late-summer day on the hillside behind her father's house, when she had come upon him taking a much-needed few hours from his medical rounds. Had she arrived a few minutes earlier, she would have found him stark naked after a swim in the river that adjoined their two properties. Fortunately, he'd had the sense to pull on his breeches, though his chest was bare and water still dripped from his golden hair.

She stood, uncertain as a fawn, staring at him. He felt a spurt of pleasure, his desire for solitude suddenly forgotten. He called a greeting and she came closer, but kept her eyes downcast.

Little Dominique. He had known her all her life. From his vaunted age of twenty-three, and a doctor to boot, he could not think of her as anything but a child—a curiously lovely and pleasing child, but a child nonetheless.

Somewhere in the back of his mind was the thought that

she couldn't have it very easy, what with her absentee parents leaving her to servants who seemed inclined to let her fend for herself. He wanted to be kind to her, if only because she had been so brave about helping him.

She seemed starved for affection. Her face lit up when he made some small joke. They passed a contented hour or so watching the river flow by. At her urging, he talked of Paris and his medical training. He found himself telling her things he hadn't spoken of before—about the rage he felt at those who seemed determined to use their poverty as an excuse for sinking into the greatest possible degradation, and about his shame for not being more charitable and forgiving.

She listened silently, except for an occasional murmur of surprise or dismay. Her emerald eyes were fixed unswervingly on him. Gradually, he ran out of words, as though some long-suppressed poison had been leached away. He found himself staring into those eyes, thinking that they seemed much older than her tender years—as though they had seen and understood a great deal.

Even years later he wasn't certain who moved first. He wanted to believe it wasn't him, but he couldn't be sure. The shaft of golden sunlight separating them narrowed almost imperceptibly. The hushed sounds of the forest ceased. Time itself appeared to stop.

The kiss they shared could not have lasted more than a few seconds, but that was long enough for every detail to be imprinted on their minds. He remembered lips that were warm and infinitely soft, the tantalizing fragrance of lavender mingling with summer earth, and an overwhelming sense of warm, sweet welcoming that was beyond anything he had ever known.

She recalled a mouth at once hard and tender, the mingled pounding of their hearts, the scent of pure, unfettered male, and the terrifying but exultant sensation of plunging headlong into the center of life itself.

Then it was over. Paul pulled away and jumped to his feet. He looked shaken and suddenly forbidding.

"Get up," he said. She did not even think of disobeying. Hard on the first joyful discovery of her own capacity for passion came shame more acute than she had ever known. Without a word she turned from him and ran.

But this time there would be no escape. Struggling to remain calm, she said, "You still haven't told me how you found out."

"I was suspicious that you might try something like this," Paul said bluntly. He was as glad as she to have the subject changed. That summer day still evoked feelings in him that he felt ill-prepared to deal with. Better to stay with what was immediate and comprehensible.

"I made certain inquiries," he went on. "For your information, Renault and son caved in like a couple of rotten melons. At the first sign of trouble, they were only too happy to spill everything they knew."

Dominique paled. She understood only too well what Paul was saying. If the authorities had happened to question the Renaults, she and the entire royal family might now be in far worse straits.

Still, she hated to admit that Paul had been right to do what he had done—not when she had hoped for so much.

"It might still have worked," she argued stubbornly. "And it was the best way—quiet, no fuss." She broke off, a sudden suspicion dawning. "Who else have you told?"

Instantly, she regretted the words. Paul had been looking

none too pleased with her as it was. Now he looked positively enraged.

He took a long, shaky breath, struggling to control himself. In steely tones, he said, "There are times when I think that I should have been less forbearing with you. As a child, you might have benefited from a few good whacks in the most convenient place."

Dominique turned beet red. She could feel the fire sweeping over her skin. How dare he even think of such a thing? She was a woman now, fully grown, and whatever he thought, deserving of the respect due her sex. For him to refer even indirectly to such a private portion of her anatomy, and to further suggest that he should have laid hands on it, was simply not to be borne.

"You are insufferable," she hissed from between clenched teeth. "I have never encountered a more overpowering, arrogant, pigheaded . . ."

"That's enough."

"No, I don't think it is." She drew herself up to her full height, ignoring the fact that she still came no higher than his chin.

Her own was tilted at a pugnacious angle as she said, "I don't like you, Paul Delamare—not one little bit. You are . . ." She broke off, searching for precisely the right words, and finally settled for a phrase that only dimly spoke of her feelings. "You are a bad influence."

Paul stared at her blankly for a moment. He had steeled himself for something far worse than that, and now could feel only mildly let down. Amused, he asked, "Is that the worst you can come up with?"

"That's bad enough," Dominique asserted. Seeing that he still was not taking her seriously, she added, "This is nothing to laugh at. When I was a child I thought the sun rose and set around you. But then you tore everything up, turned the world topsy-turvy, all because—''

She stopped abruptly, belatedly aware that she was crying. With a horrified murmur, she tried to turn away.

Paul almost let her. Compassion, guilt, and an assortment of other emotions almost conspired to make him end the confrontation then and there. But it had been too long delayed already.

He had a sudden, blinding insight into exactly why he had never forgotten her—why he had come running the moment he had realized she was in danger.

Love. What a damn fool emotion to encounter at the precise moment when he needed all his faculties undimmed, when he could least afford even the slightest distraction or liability. Not only did he love, but he loved a woman who regarded him as her enemy. Still he was going to do what he wanted no matter how little sense it made—no matter where it might lead him.

"A bad influence," he murmured under his breath. "Why, Dominique? Because I won't let you throw your life away on a cause that doesn't deserve it? That's what would have happened, you know. A bungled escape would have been your death. But instead, you're going to live. You might as well start right now."

As he said the last words his head came down, leonine in the shadowed sun, gleaming with the polish of hammered gold. She had an instant to grasp his intent but no time at all to try to stop him, even if she had wanted to, which was not at all clear.

His mouth claiming hers was a piercing, beguiling delight unlike any she had ever known. He tasted of brandy and tobacco—not by any means an unpleasant combination, but one that was overwhelmingly male.

By contrast, his touch was far gentler than she would have expected. He coaxed instead of demanded, drawing her down pathways new yet instinctively familiar.

A soft moan broke from her. She pressed closer to him, her breasts flattened against the rock-hard expanse of his chest and her hands tangling in his thick, golden hair. Had he been anyone other than the beloved friend and confidante of her childhood, she would never have let herself go to such an extent.

Instinctively, she understood that. But this was Paul, and whatever disagreements existed between them now, there had been a time when he mattered more to her than anyone else. Perhaps somewhere deep inside, he still did.

That was a terrifying thought—one she could not bear to pursue. Thought, reason, even sanity were rapidly slipping beyond her. She let them go gladly. For the moment, it was enough to be a creature of purest sensation, caught up in the discovery of her own passion and the need it unleashed.

She felt at once infinitely daring and totally safe. When Paul's hand—hard and callused, but so tender—slipped to her breast, she trembled with delight. Her body was flowering beneath his touch, waking with a warmth she wanted to cling to forever. For so long she had suffered the bone-deep chill of fear and growing hopelessness. There were even days when she felt old—absurd for someone who had turned nineteen a scant two months before. But perhaps that was understandable, considering that even when her parents had still been alive those feckless two had taken scant interest in her. She had always had to depend on herself.

The grinding isolation of the palace prison, the growing sense of siege, and the knowledge that in the final analysis, she alone was responsible not only for her own life but also for David and Nicole's, all combined to make her feel weighed down beyond her years.

Paul changed that. In that timeless moment wrenched out of anguish and grief, she was rediscovering what it meant to be young. Hope flowed through her, more intoxicating than any wine, tempting her to take the ultimate chance.

He made her want to trust and believe that the world was a kind place where good things really could happen. She wanted to drop the veneer of hard practicality and determination in which she had sheathed herself and be the vulnerable, innocent girl she had once been. Yet no one—not even Paul—could turn time back on its course and restore that which was lost forever.

Locked in his arms, clinging to him, her passion rising to meet his, she remembered that. And then she was awakened, unwillingly, to reality.

An angry moan of rejection rose from her throat and reached Paul even through the fog of his own shock and hunger. He was shocked because she was so much more sensual than he had expected, and he was hungry because he had no other response to her, no dampening down or restraint to save him. He might as well have been a starving man presented suddenly with a banquet.

But it was snatched away from him. Naturally, he resisted, wanting to hold on to her with all the force of his being. But her small hands pressing suddenly against his chest and the rigid stiffness of her body communicated themselves too effectively to be ignored.

One moment he was holding a passionate, pliant woman in his arms; the next she had turned into an enraged, spitting cat. Against him she was defenseless, had he chosen for it to be so. But that was a choice he could never make. Innate honor and decency put him at an insurmountable disadvantage.

With an angry curse, he put her from him. Dominique stood, breathing hard, her forest-green eyes glowing. "I was wrong," she said raggedly. "Despicable is far too polite a description for you. Is there nothing you won't stoop to?"

"If there weren't," Paul said slowly and deliberately, "you'd be on that floor right now with your legs spread, sweet Dominique. What's more, you'd be loving it."

He had the satisfaction of seeing her turn ashen at his crudity. But the pleasure was fleeting and sour at best. She was gone from him, farther than she had been even at that first encounter several weeks before.

He turned on his heel and walked toward the door. Without looking at her, he said, "You're lying to yourself, Dominique. When you're willing to admit it, let me know."

An angry denial sprang to her lips, but she never had the chance to utter it. Paul was gone.

Drinking didn't help. Paul discovered that a few hours later, sitting at a back table of the café he frequented when he felt the need for a little anonymous sociability.

It was close to the building where he rented a modest apartment—two rooms haphazardly furnished that he'd taken because they came with enough bookcases to hold his personal library. The rest was inconsequential.

His landlady cooked for him when he remembered to ask her, and her fat, cheerful daughter kept the place relatively tidy. Like many Parisian families in these difficult days, they were meticulously nonpolitical, which suited him fine.

He liked the café for much the same reason. It attracted mainly working men who came in too tired and preoccupied to much care what was going on in the world beyond. The food wasn't bad, the wine was honest, and the proprietor minded his own business. He'd chalked Paul down as safe and had left it at that.

Joseph was another matter. Barely had he strolled through the café's dark and peeling doors than eyebrows were raised. From his seat at a back table, Paul observed the proceedings with mingled irritation and amusement.

His friend had gone to great lengths to disguise his true identity. Joseph Descampes, baron de Champion, wore the garb of a Breton fisherman, or at least an eccentric version of it.

Despite the heat, he wore a bulky sweater in coarse, colorless wool, and a pair of thick navy trousers that ended an inch above his ankles. His dark hair hung in unruly fashion around his collar and a day's growth of whiskers covered his face.

As he entered the café, he looked around with studied casualness, then limped over to Paul's table. He sat down heavily and regarded his friend.

"You're sure this place is safe?"

"It was," Paul murmured dryly. "But now that misplaced Breton fisherfolk have begun patronizing it, that may not remain the case."

Joseph had the grace to look slightly self-conscious. "I suppose I did lay it on a bit thick, but then, I could hardly show up here in silk frock coat and powdered wig, could I? After all, the idea is to remain anonymous."

"No," Paul said gently, "the idea is not to attract attention. These good people know who I am. They'll be wondering about you, that's for certain. But they also have far too much sense to ask."

"I hope you're right," Joseph murmured dubiously. "God knows we're living in dangerous times. There are plenty who will as soon stick a knife in your back as look at you."

Paul suppressed a sigh. He liked Joseph and respected the young man's intelligence. But he also considered him a newly hatched cynic—someone who had only recently confronted the venality of the world and who was still reeling from that knowledge.

"How's the leg?" he asked quietly as he signaled Claude to bring them another pitcher of wine.

"Better," Joseph said. "The exercises you recommended are helping."

"Don't forget the hot soaks." Joseph had been injured in one of the many brawls that had lately rippled through Paris. He'd been coming home from the National Assembly when a group of rioters swept over him, pummeling him in the process and leaving him with a leg broken in two places.

That had been six months ago, and the leg was not healing well. Paul had set it, convinced the young man to stay put long enough for the worst of the damage to ease, and since then, he had kept after him with encouragement and advice so that he didn't lose hope of eventually regaining its full use. In the process they had become friends—and compatriots.

"You've been busy," Joseph said after he downed a long swallow of the wine. It was young, slightly sharp, but it held a pleasant fruitiness that made it palatable.

Paul raised an eyebrow. When he had received Joseph's message—suitably obscure—indicating that he wanted to meet, he had had no idea of what to expect. Nonetheless, the sudden sense that he was to be the subject of discussion was disconcerting.

Shrugging, he said, "So are most people these days."

"Ah, but not like the renowned Doctor Delamare. You go back and forth from the palace to military headquarters to the National Assembly, even to the office of the great Robespierre himself. And everywhere you go there is speculation, rumors, innuendo. No one knows quite what to make of you, Paul."

The subject of this analysis smiled wryly. Joseph was describing the story of Paul's life, though he didn't know it. No one had ever known what to make of the marquis's son who had insisted on becoming a physician, who scorned the privileges and arrogance that were his birthright.

Even Joseph, for all his advanced thinking, maintained a core of superiority that could not be challenged. He honestly believed that he and those like him were better than the vast majority of people—not by virtue of any special abilities, but simply by birth.

Paul disagreed. To him all people were equal, each as deserving of respect, protection, and opportunity as the next. Which was not to say that they were all the same. Some would always be more intelligent, stronger, or more ambitious than others.

The point was that in the eyes of the government, those distinctions shouldn't matter. All people—regardless of their origins and abilities—were equal citizens. That was what Paul believed the revolution was all about, until the madmen turned it into a personal crusade of vengeance and self-aggrandizement.

"I'm not sure I get your point," Paul said quietly. "Are you trying to tell me that your people have been keeping me under surveillance, tracking my movements? Because if that's so, it's been a bloody waste of time."

Joseph took another swallow of the wine and looked at him steadily. "I wouldn't say that, my friend. But it's interesting that you mention being followed. Did you know you were?"

Paul stiffened. He stared across the table at the other man. "By whom?"

"His name doesn't matter. What counts is that he's one of Robespierre's lapdogs. Oh, yes," he went on as Paul took this in, "it's the great man himself who wanted you leashed. Not that it seems to have gotten him very much."

"How long?" Paul asked grimly. He was berating himself for a fool. He should have been more cautious, more watchful. But instead, he'd been so caught up with his own concerns—the cholera, the revolution, Dominique . . . especially Dominique—that he'd never noticed what was happening right under his nose, or more correctly, behind his back.

But Joseph, or somebody close to him, had. And for that he should be grateful.

"I'll be frank with you," the young man said. "We were a bit curious about you. After all, you had a reputation for being an absolutely solid revolutionary, whereas we tend to be far more moderate. Suddenly, you seemed to regret your earlier stance and to turn against those who thought that way."

"It wasn't sudden," Paul protested. "I rather wish it

had been, but instead, it took me a long time to understand the mistake I'd made."

"Which was?" Joseph prompted.

Paul restrained a sigh. He'd been all through this—not just with Joseph, but with the other men who with him formed the Girondists, or moderate wing of the revolution. They were the men who opposed Robespierre and his far more fanatical Jacobins. He'd understood that they'd be slow to trust him, but he also thought that he'd proved himself by now.

When he said as much, Joseph grinned. "Truth be told, you have. But there were still some of us who felt you might be in need of a little looking after—the kind you're always so willing to give to others, but don't seem to keep much of for yourself."

Paul looked at him, taken aback. Joseph had spoken with rough affection and the sincerity of a man who knows that what he is saying is true. Paul wasn't used to that kind of perceptiveness—at least, not when it was directed at him.

"So," he said guardedly, "you've been keeping an eye on me and found out that Robespierre was doing the same."

"That's right. We also found out what his lapdog told him."

"Which was?"

"Not enough. It seems that the great man is annoyed. He wanted something solid on you—something that would have had you residing in the Conciergerie, instead of in that discreet apartment of yours."

The Conciergerie was not by any means the only prison left in Paris after the razing of the Bastille at the beginning of the revolution, but it was the most notorious. The mere mention of it was enough to strike fear into most people.

Paul brushed it off. He knew perfectly well what Robespierre would do if he ever found out that Paul was part of the group actively working to bring about his downfall. He accepted it as a necessary risk in order to be true to himself and to France. But he was vulnerable in other ways, as he was about to discover.

"The lapdog did throw his master a bone," Joseph went on. "Something about a certain Mademoiselle de Montfort, lady-in-waiting to the queen." He smiled engagingly. "It seems you've been accused of having a *tendre* for her."

Paul's face hardened perceptibly. The taut lines around his mouth grew even firmer. His eyes narrowed to shards of ice-blue steel.

"Does Robespierre believe it?"

"Who knows? What really matters is whether or not he thinks he can use it." With studied ease, Joseph asked, "Are you by any chance involved with the delectable Dominique?"

Instead of answering directly, Paul asked, "You know her?"

Joseph shook his head. "Only by reputation, alas. She is alternately described as a creature of impeccable beauty and an ice princess whose mere glance is enough to strike men down. But perhaps," he added shrewdly, "you know her better."

Did he? He wasn't actually sure. For a brief moment earlier that day he had thought that he knew her completely. But then she had backed away, turning on him, and his certainty had ebbed.

Not that it mattered. After what Joseph had told him, he was sure of two things: he had to stay away from Dominique in order to divert Robespierre's attention, and, even more important, he had to get her out of the Tuileries and out of France.

The only problem was how he was going to manage to do both at the same time.

Chapter
6

Dominique saw very little of Paul in the weeks that followed. He still paid his calls at the palace to check on the health of the royal family, but he contrived to do so at times when she was busy. Their paths crossed on only a handful of occasions, and then he was always cool and distant.

That troubled her. She was caught between desperate need for him and the terrible feeling that were she to give in to that need, she would end up sacrificing everything she believed in.

He had already cost her the Renault escape route; she had not seen or heard of Monsieur Renault in weeks. Paul's warning had apparently been taken to heart. Dominique had still not admitted to herself that he had been right to do what he did.

She clung to the hope—more correctly, the dream— that they could all have slipped away quietly and safely. Instead, they were trapped, and though no one spoke of it, they all had a sense of the noose drawing ever tighter around their necks.

Even David and Nicole were aware of it. As she sat with her younger brother and sister late one afternoon in early August, enjoying the peace and relative coolness of the garden, Dominique tried hard not to listen to their conversation. She was supposedly reading—Thomas Malory's tales of King Arthur in the English edition—but her attention kept wandering to Nicole and David. They were slouched on the ground near her bench, playing idly with a set of jacks and talking between themselves.

"Old Girard says they're going to kill us all," Nicole said matter-of-factly. "He says they won't rest until the last aristocrat is dead."

David nodded thoughtfully. "Madame Santerre says that the streets will run red with blood. She thinks it's going to be the end of the world. I wonder if she's right."

Dominique listened with growing horror. They spoke casually, but that didn't fool her. Children often pretended that something really wasn't important when it was at the center of their nightmares. It was a way of protecting themselves.

How long had they been talking about death like this? And why hadn't she noticed sooner?

Maybe she had and just hadn't been able to come to terms with it. She'd known that they were feeling the strain, like everyone else, and she'd kept promising herself that she would do something about it.

She put her book down with a thump. "Come over here, please."

They looked at her blankly, as though only just remembering that she was there.

"What's the matter?" David asked, not alarmed yet but

suspicious, wary that she was going to tell them something bad.

"Nothing," she said quickly and held out her arms. "I only want to talk with you both."

They came, reluctantly, and perched on the bench on either side of her. She put her arms around their shoulders and drew them close. For a few moments it was enough simply to hold them like that, to feel their young, trusting bodies instinctively softening against hers.

It had always been like that, right from the beginning. She been ten years old when Nicole arrived; eleven when David was born. Each time, after a single glance, she had fallen in love with her sibling.

Her parents had found that amusing. Neither had cared much for children, preferring the gay life at court with no entanglements. Dominique had been their one attempt early in their marriage to get an heir for de Montfort. When she turned out to be a girl, they had given up the effort until all those years later, when a combination of too much wine and being briefly without other partners led seren-dipitously to Nicole.

Dominique had never known for sure, but she suspected the encounter had been startlingly satisfying to them both, despite its outcome. After more than a decade of an ar-ranged and politely distant marriage, it had caused the marquis and marquise to become lovers. And that had led to David.

Two years later their mother was dead, thrown from her horse during a too-frantic gallop, and Dominique was taken into the household of the queen, who had counted her mother as a friend. Six months after that, the Marquis de Montfort left his mistress's house on the rue de Plessis, walked down a narrow street, and disappeared.

His body was found four days later, floating in the Seine. There were no signs of violence. He had either fallen into the river by accident and drowned, or he had taken his own life.

The Church was suitably discreet; in the absence of definite evidence of suicide, Charles de Montfort was buried in the family crypt beside his wife. To this day, Dominique had no idea what had actually happened.

She had reached the point where she thought about it rarely. So much else had intervened since. But as she held her brother and sister, she allowed herself to admit how very alone the three of them were in the world.

"It's all right," she said softly. "I know things seem very bad now, but they will get better. I promise."

With all her heart, she prayed that it was a promise she would be able to keep. In the garden, all was beauty and peace, but beyond there was neither. And soon they would have to confront that.

Not far away, Paul was thinking much the same thing as he sat listening to Joseph. They were meeting again at the café. It was stifling hot, but neither man noticed. They were too caught up in their thoughts. "This is madness," Paul said. "It will tear the country apart. Unless, of course," he went on, "your information is incorrect."

Joseph glanced at him in a chiding gesture. "I'm sorry to say it is all too accurate."

He leaned forward across the scarred and pitted table. "These men—Robespierre and the rest—want to bring down a great wave of destruction on us. They believe the new France—their France—will rise phoenixlike from the ruins. Louis is a symbol of the old. He must perish, preferably in as public and dramatic a fashion as possible."

Paul heard him out in silence. Despite his instinctive rejection, he didn't really disbelieve Joseph. The scenario he evoked was all too chillingly real.

"How long do we have?" he asked quietly.

The younger man spread his hands. "That, unfortunately, I don't know—at least, not for sure. I'm not certain there is a precise timetable, or if they simply plan to wait until there is another incident such as occurred a few weeks ago and then seize the moment. Either way, it doesn't much matter—the results will be the same."

Paul couldn't help but agree with him. But at the moment, he had even more urgent matters to consider. What Joseph had revealed only added to the driving need he felt to get Dominique out of the Tuileries.

A tight wave of frustration mingled with fear rippled through him. Not for himself—he understood the risks and accepted them. But he feared for her, the beautiful, proud, infuriatingly stubborn girl he was in love with.

"What's the matter?" Joseph asked. "You look like you're about to tear somebody limb from limb."

"Not quite that bad," Paul said. He even managed a smile, which he was far from feeling. "All right, there's going to be an incident, and then all hell will break loose. But before that, I've got a favor to ask of you."

Joseph leaned back in his chair and folded his hands over his flat abdomen. "Go ahead."

"I need to get somebody out, but there are problems involved in it, and so far, I haven't been able to come up with a way that will work."

Listening to him, Joseph's eyes had widened. He gave him a look that suggested he couldn't decide whether Paul was crazy or joking. "I should think not. You know how tightly guarded the borders are right now. Nobody with the brains of a gnat is going to try to get through them.''

"Still," Paul reminded him, "people are getting out."

"A few," Joseph acknowledged. "A whole lot more are getting shipped right back—to the Conciergerie, the Temple, and some of the other less pleasant prisons in our fair city. And then there's the crowd that's turning up just plain dead. I hope you're not thinking of joining them?''

Actually, Paul had given no thought at all to his own safety. His only interest was Dominique. He was more than willing to put his own life in jeopardy in order to protect her. But he couldn't find a way that would give even a decent chance of her making it out safely, much less with her younger brother and sister.

Seeing his concern, Joseph sighed deeply. "This person you're so worried about, I don't suppose she's by any chance a member of the bourgeoisie—someone nice and middle class who might not be missed?''

"I'm afraid not," Paul said.

Joseph muttered something under his breath. He took a long swallow of his wine and swiftly refilled the cup. Glancing at the empty basket beside it, he said absently, "Doesn't anyone work anymore? There's hardly a loaf of bread to eat in Paris, or anything else, for that matter. It's as though some giant, insane holiday has been declared.''

Paul didn't reply; there was no point. They both knew that the fabric of their civilization was being destroyed. But both were determined to salvage as much as they could from the ruins.

"You know," Joseph said absently, "I'm fond of women—sometimes *extremely* fond." He looked at Paul intently. "However, I've never been tempted to take hopeless risks for one of them.''

Paul was about to reply, but Joseph forestalled him. Quietly, he said, "If she's who I think she is, my friend, she's trapped. There's simply no getting around that and no polite way to put it. She should have gotten out a year ago, even six months ago. Now it's too late."

A nerve twitched in Paul's lean jaw. He rose, hands clenched at his sides, his voice rigidly controlled. "I can't accept that."

It was Joseph's turn to remain silent, but he stared at his friend with great concern, as though gazing at a man who was teetering on the edge of a cliff, and who seemed determined to fall off.

Paul left the café a short time later. He returned to the military hospital to visit patients and review the latest reports of new cholera cases. Ordinarily, it would have required no special effort to turn his mind in that direction, but his disquieting conversation with Joseph prevented it. He could not easily dismiss the younger man's conviction that no safe way would be found to get Dominique out.

He worked late and did not emerge from the hospital until it was almost midnight. Despite all he had seen and done in the intervening hours, Dominique was still very much on his mind.

A full moon in a cloudless sky showed him the way home. He was following it automatically, his mind on the problem of her escape, when his thoughts were interrupted by a sudden, hard drumming sound that seemed to be welling up out of the street. It felt like a great engine, perhaps one of those used to control the giant mechanical toys built for festive displays, but instinctively he sensed that it was not.

A moment later, the mysterious force was explained. A

shouting, waving mob rounded the corner, bearing down directly on him. In the ghostly moonlight, their faces were devoid of color. They looked like gray specters risen from the grave and destined to return to it with the coming of dawn.

Even more ominously, above their heads danced waving pikes, their razor-sharp tips gleaming in the silver light.

Automatically, Paul stepped into a doorway while the mob streamed past. He watched them go as though in slow motion, every face and gesture imprinted on his mind. Oddly, he was not afraid.

That would have been a perfectly normal reaction under the circumstances. Any man, no matter how innately strong or courageous, could be expected to know fear before such an onslaught. But all he felt was cold, calculating knowledge.

He knew, without knowing how, that this was *the* mob—the one all Paris had been expecting these many months, for whom all the others had been mere rehearsal. This was the mob that would finally rise unchecked to break the last, slim bonds of control and ring down a dark curtain over what had once been one of the most beautiful and gracious cities in the world.

The mob—fueled by inchoate rage and blood-maddened lust, shorn of any pretense of humanity—was like a ravening beast. It was the kind that existed not in nature itself, which was far too benign, but in the depths of the human soul. With proper care, it could be brought to the surface by men clever enough, and ruthless enough, to turn ordinary people into a weapon of death. It was aimed directly at the Tuileries. There was no question of the route they were following, or of their intent. Watching them, Paul knew beyond the shadow of a doubt that this time, no amount of courage or patience would turn them aside.

He began to run.

Dominique was asleep when she heard the sound. She woke suddenly, at first thinking that they were in the midst of a summer storm. She ran to the window and glanced out, surprised to see that the sky remained completely clear. Odd, that, since she could have sworn that she heard thunder.

But the noise was something else. It was pounding, rolling, coming ever closer.

With a gasp, she ran back to the bed. Nicole shared it with her. Quickly, she awakened her sister and told her to dress.

Nicole was dazed and bewildered, but she obeyed. As she did so, Dominique hurried over to the door that separated her room from the small chamber where David slept. She yanked it open to find that he was already awake and fumbling into his clothes.

Quickly, Dominique did the same. All three had barely finished when there was a pounding at the other door, the one leading to the corridor. Dominique opened it to find the queen's chamberlain, distraught and pale, but doing his utmost to control himself.

"You must come at once, mademoiselle. Her Majesty needs you."

Dominique did not hesitate; she knew her duty and fulfilled it readily. But she also made sure that David and Nicole came along with her. Instinctively, she understood that this was no time for them to be separated.

The hallways of the Tuileries were in pandemonium.

Members of the household guard raced back and forth, responding to conflicting orders shouted out by officers who had seen the mob coming, had guessed its intent, but weren't quite certain what to do to stop it.

Dominique saw one young boy—he looked barely old enough to wear the blue and white of a guardsman—his face pale and strained, clutching his musket so tightly that she wondered his fingers didn't snap.

For a moment their eyes met. So great was the terror and despair in his that she felt a chill, icy as the grave, run down her spine. Hastily, she looked away.

Outside the council chamber, Louis was personally giving instructions to rally his forces. The King looked tired and worried, but otherwise calm. He smiled gently at Dominique as she dropped him a curtsy on her way past.

The night passed slowly. By morning, a vast crowd filled the open area in front of the Tuileries and extended deep into the surrounding streets. Dominique heard the size of the mob was estimated at twenty thousand, and had no reason to disbelieve it.

There were also other, even more ominous signs. While the royal household troops had rallied to the king and taken up defensive posts, the National Guard, which was supposed to be protecting him, had gone over to the mob. Guardsmen could be seen joking and laughing with them. To leave no doubt of their position, they had gone so far as to unload their cannon.

Standing at a shuttered window through which he could look out without being seen, the king shook his head bleakly.

"The fools," he said, not with contempt but with sadness so profound that it struck Dominique to the quick.

"They are playing into the hands of the very men who will rob them of everything they hold dear."

Nearby, Marie Antoinette looked up from her tightly clenched hands and regarded her husband. "I don't understand how you can speak of them so pityingly. They are animals—savages who are bent on destroying us. Fortunately," she added with a hard glint in her eyes, "we can hold out against them."

Her husband turned to her. He walked over to the chair where she sat and gently, insistently, took her hands in his. Looking directly into her eyes, he said softly, "No, *mignon*, I don't believe that we can."

The queen paled even further. Her delicate features looked stricken. In a hoarse whisper, she murmured, "What are you saying?"

"That I must think of the safety and welfare of my family and those who serve us. The mob is bent on violence this time, that is clear. It is not like before, when they were content merely to speak with me. The troops will not intervene; that also is evident. Our own men will fight— and die—bravely, but they will not be enough to protect us."

He straightened up and glanced around the room, where his wife and children, as well as a dozen or so retainers, were gathered. Quietly, he said, "There is nothing more to be done here."

Dominique went to her mistress's side. She said nothing, only laid a hand on Marie Antoinette's shoulder. The queen made a soft, sighing sound, as though all the air had gone out of her, along with the light and hope. A single tear trickled down her pale cheek.

They left on foot, walking swiftly, heads held high.

Dominique was directly behind the king and queen and their children. She held Nicole and David by the hand. Around them the grenadiers of the household guard formed a phalanx.

There was only one place to go where they had any chance of safety—to the old riding school near the palace, which had since been taken over by the revolutionaries and transformed into the National Assembly.

They were almost there when Dominique became aware of a skirmish off to the side. Fearful that the mob was breaking through, she stiffened. But there was only a lone man striding through the guards, waving away their ineffectual efforts to stop him.

Paul came toward her—dark and powerful, his turquoise eyes gleaming with all the wildness of the sun-seared sky. Even the king stopped at the sight of him.

"Your Majesty," he said, inclining his head. His gaze locked on Dominique. It was to her that he spoke, as much as to the king. "I gather from your presence here that you understand the full seriousness of the situation."

Louis nodded curtly. "We understand that the crisis is at last fully upon us, Doctor. Now I trust you will understand that we cannot linger."

The king made as though to move on, only to stop again as Paul stepped directly in front of him. His expression was sympathetic, even contrite, but it was also clear that he was not prepared to give an inch.

"Wait," he said. "There are others at risk here besides yourself. Once you step inside the Assembly, it is impossible to say what will happen. Let those who can leave now do so."

A murmur ran through the tiny group of retainers. No

one precisely wanted to admit to the desire for escape, but to have the possibility suddenly raised was tantalizing. Even Dominique, unswerving though she was in her loyalty, had to acknowledge that the thought filled her with desperate yearning.

Quietly, with great dignity, Louis nodded. "Monsieur le Docteur is correct. In light of the dire seriousness of the situation, we will fully understand any desire to leave our service without further delay. However," he added, cautioning, "remember that it will not be enough simply to escape the confines of the palace and elude the mob. One must then somehow survive in Paris or contrive to get out of it very swiftly."

The murmur turned to a whisper of fear and disappointment. They all recognized what the king was saying. Each of them was sufficiently well-known to be an immediate target of the revolutionaries. The thought of what that blood-crazed mob would do was enough to strike terror into even the most stalwart heart.

Once more Louis turned to go, but Paul again stopped him, this time laying a hand on his arm in entreaty. "Your Majesty," he murmured as the king looked at him in surprise, "I realize the impropriety of this, but the circumstances are desperate. I believe that I can protect Mademoiselle de Montfort, her brother and sister. Let them come with me. I swear to you that I will do my utmost to keep them safe."

Dominique inhaled sharply. She could not for a moment doubt the sincerity of his plea, but she was nonetheless shocked by it.

If she went with Paul, she would be trusting him not only with her life, but with the lives of her brother and sister. Moreover, she knew that she could never overcome the sense that she had abandoned the royal family at the time when they needed her most.

Still, she was tempted. Standing there in the golden sunlight, his body hard and strong, his manner utterly determined and remorseless, he offered her a haven of strength that was all but irresistible.

It was on the tip of her tongue to say that she would go with him, when she hesitated. Unbidden, the thought rose of the emotions he so effortlessly provoked in her. First the poignant yearning of childhood, then the hatred of betrayal, followed by dark, primal passion, frightening in its intensity and even more terrifying by the whispers of something she feared very much might be love.

Paul drove her to extremes she simply did not experience with any other man. Yet he was an enigma to her—someone whose life was guided by principles she neither understood nor shared.

How could she possibly trust him?

And how could she betray some of those she loved in order to go with him?

Her throat was tightly clenched as she gazed at David and Nicole, both of whom were watching her anxiously. They looked to her to save them. Could she turn their lives over to a man who might ultimately betray them all?

Could she not?

The screams of the mob were becoming more insistent. The king was waiting. Ahead she could see the riding school, where the Assembly was meeting. As far as she knew they were sane men who, though misguided in their beliefs, would not want to be party to the great and terrible crime of regicide. They would be flattered by the king's faith in them and they would respond by doing their duty to France and to the royal family. They would be safe.

Or so she struggled to believe as she looked at Paul and slowly but firmly shook her head.

Chapter
7

Paris, Winter 1792–3

Dominique rose in darkness. It was bitterly cold. Beyond the dank stone walls, the wind howled. Her hands shook as she fumbled for the candle beside her bed. With an effort, she managed to light it.

A soft sigh escaped her as the flame caught. It was the first victory of the day, small but significant. She glanced over her shoulder to where Nicole was still sleeping, wrapped in blankets as in a cocoon, only the top of her tousled head visible.

Let her sleep, Dominique thought, *at least a few more hours. Let her escape into sweet oblivion for as long as she can.*

For her there was no such escape—not physically or mentally. That had been the case since the August day when the National Assembly had failed them. Despite Louis's best efforts, the politicians had lacked the courage to uphold the constitution they themselves had voted into place.

In complete violation of it, they had allowed the royal family and their retainers to be taken off to prison, where they had since languished four long months without charges being brought against any of them.

Whereas the Tuileries had been merely uncomfortable and tiresome, the Temple prison—named for the Knights Templar who had once owned it—was far worse. Built in the twelfth century, the gloomy stone fortress lacked even the most basic amenities. The stone walls were encrusted with ice, the chimneys smoked, and the air was fetid.

Dominique had developed a dull, persistent cough, which she did her best to control whenever she was with Louis or Marie Antoinette. They had both let her know of their regret in not ordering her to leave them when she had the chance. But then, neither had suspected what the Assembly would do.

Determined not to think of what might have been, she pulled on her threadbare dress and left the chamber. The guard, posted all night outside her room, grinned lewdly as she passed. Dominique ignored him, as she did all such slights and improprieties.

Their guards were all drawn from the rougher classes, men made callous by the hardness of their own lives and eager for the chance to lord it over those who had been their betters. She understood that, though doing so made it no easier to bear.

Outside the queen's chamber another guard stood. He scowled and murmured a curse under his breath, but did not attempt to bar her entry. She stepped into the room quietly, on the chance that Marie Antoinette still slept, but as usual, she was already awake.

She smiled gently when she saw Dominique. "Come

in, my dear. We have a treat this morning—fresh brioches and butter to go with them.''

That was a rarity, one Dominique could not help but appreciate. While they were not denied food, it tended to be of poor quality and rarely fresh. By comparison, the golden puffs of sweet dough still succulent with the aroma of the baking oven seemed fit for gods.

Dominique did not hesitate. She sat down across from the queen and accepted the plate held out to her. A moment later her eyes closed in pure pleasure as the first flaky morsel slid over her tongue.

"Oh, that is good," she said with a small laugh. "Far, far better than I'd remembered."

Marie Antoinette nodded gently. "Isn't it odd how all our senses seem heightened here? The least little thing is suddenly exquisite. Only yesterday I heard a tiny finch sing and thought that all the orchestras and chorales that used to entertain at Versailles could not compare to it."

"It is true," Dominique replied, "that whatever else this experience has done to us, at least we no longer take anything for granted."

"Not even," the queen said with a wry laugh, "the most mundane things." She gestured with her hand toward a pile of linen heaped on a nearby chair. "I suppose we'd better get back to that."

Dominique grimaced. The much-needed linen had arrived the day before, to the great relief of both Dominique and the queen, who had both begun to wonder how long they could continue to repair underclothing that was all but in shreds.

Barely had the new supplies made their appearance when

the prison commissioner noticed that they were embroidered with the royal initials surmounted, as was usual, by crowns. In a screaming tirade, he had threatened to confiscate the lot.

Desperate, the women had promised to pick out the offending needlework. Satisfied that they were once again subdued and humiliated, he had relented, but not without displaying the vicious satisfaction that characterized all his dealings with them.

Neither woman spoke of that as they finished their breakfast and resumed work on the linen. They had worked for perhaps half an hour in companionable silence when Dominique suffered a renewed spasm of coughing. The queen looked up worriedly.

"My dear, something really must be done about that."

"It is nothing," Dominique said when she was able to speak again. "Merely the dampness."

"On the contrary, that can be very grave. I remember how ill I was while we were still at the Tuileries, and that was still in summer. This is much more serious. If only Doctor Delamare would come . . ."

She broke off, abruptly aware of the effect her words had on the young girl. Dominique had gone suddenly pale. Her gray-green eyes fell, but not before the queen glimpsed the bleakness in them.

"I am so sorry," Marie Antoinette murmured. "I spoke without thinking. Naturally, you are upset by his absence."

"Only because it would be better for Your Majesties if you still had a physician in attendance," Dominique said.

The queen cast her a gently skeptical look, but did not persist. For that Dominique was grateful. The wound caused by Paul's defection was still too fresh and raw to bear any probing, even by one as well-intentioned as the queen.

Not that she blamed him totally. She had rejected his help if not precisely with scorn, then certainly with no visible display of gratitude. From the beginning she had made it clear that she neither liked nor trusted him. Not that the lack of either emotion had prevented the maelstrom of desire that seized her when their bodies touched. But she absolutely would not think of that.

Paul was gone, back to his revolution, his ideals, and his dream of a new France. Though how he managed to live with himself, given the results of what he had helped to bring about, she could not imagine.

A shiver ran through her as she remembered the day a few short weeks after their incarceration in the Temple when the mobs of Paris had once again run riot. This time their targets were the hapless aristocrats, priests, and others held in various prisons.

Having been denied royal victims, they set upon these substitutes with unparalleled savagery. The terrible, tragic remnants of that fury had been paraded on pikes past the windows of the royal prison, causing the queen to faint and the king to cry out to God for surcease from such agony.

How did Paul—a man who had dedicated his life to saving others—rationalize such brutality in his own mind? How did he manage to rise each morning, look at himself in the mirror as he shaved, and refrain from slitting his own throat?

Dominique could not begin to guess. She only knew that she felt betrayed all over again by him. Within the privacy of her heart, she had vowed that never again would she nurture the slightest flicker of tenderness or desire for Paul Delamare.

He was anathema to her—the very personification of everything she loathed and despised. Should she ever meet him again, she would tell him so to his face, no matter what the consequences. A tear then fell on the linen she clutched, followed by another. Silently, the queen reached out and placed her hand over Dominique's. Together, the two women waited for whatever the day would bring.

Paul paced restlessly across the confines of Joseph's drawing room. Stretched out in a comfortable chair, the young man watched him warily.

He had the sense that he was watching not a man, but a tiger or perhaps a leopard—one of those exotic beasts brought to the royal zoo from far-off India.

They, too, were proud, untamed, and possessed of a killer instinct so profound as to be all but palpable. Cautiously, he said, "You seem well, my friend."

Paul eyed him coldly, not because he was angry with him, but simply because that was how he looked at the world these days, and everyone in it.

"You mean," he said, "for a man newly released from the great Robespierre's clutches?"

Joseph shrugged. Still treading warily, he said, "Your stay in prison doesn't appear to have afflicted you much." On the contrary, it seemed to have left him honed to a fine edge, razor-sharp and deadly.

"Why not? I had the place virtually to myself. If any ghosts lingered from those poor devils who were slaughtered, they didn't trouble me."

Joseph blanched. Young though he was, with all the resiliency of youth, not a day had passed since the September massacres that he didn't give thanks to God for not having been included among its victims. It would be bad enough to die at the hands of a mob, but to be trapped and helpless, stripped of even the slightest hope—that was unendurable.

"Perhaps," he said softly, "they left you in peace because you tried to help them."

"Tried and failed," Paul said grimly. He could not think of the massacres without feeling the rage boil up inside him.

Instinctively, he understood that anger was his best defense against the images forever imprinted on his mind. They were the stuff of nightmares . . . and insanity.

"But that is in the past now," he went on swiftly, "and cannot be changed. We must concentrate all our attention on what can be done to stop Robespierre and his kind."

Joseph sighed. He stood up and walked over to the sideboard. As he poured brandy from a decanter into two crystal goblets, he said, "My friend, there are times when a man must assess the odds against him and know that the only chance for victory lies in patience. We are in such a period now."

A dull flush spread across Paul's high-boned cheeks. He took the brandy, but set it aside without tasting it. "You and the others with you counsel delay, even knowing what the Jacobins intend to do?"

Joseph had the grace to look embarrassed, but he made no attempt to apologize for his position. To his mind, it met the chief criterion of the revolutionary world—survival.

So cleverly and ruthlessly had Robespierre worked his will that most of his opponents had been driven underground, or out of France entirely. Those few—Paul among them—who had dared to speak out against him in the aftermath of the September massacres had been imprisoned.

In recent days, however, many of them had been released. Much as their freedom was appreciated, few doubted that it signaled a new, even more ominous period.

"Robespierre and the others with him are anxious to solidify their power," Joseph said. "They believe that they have adequately demonstrated their ability to crush any opposition, so they can afford to let people like yourself out of prison now. Such apparent magnanimity is the carrot to their stick."

"And the prelude to even greater troubles."

"Alas, I agree with you, but you must realize that the pendulum has not yet swung against them. The army still supports Robespierre and the others, as does the mob. With those two forces on their side, they are invulnerable." Gently, Joseph said, "We must wait, my friend, painful and distasteful though that is."

Softly, as though to himself, Paul murmured, "What price such patience?"

Joseph swallowed his brandy, heedless of the excellent vintage. He poured himself another. Without looking at Paul, he said, "You are thinking of the mademoiselle."

A wry smile played over Paul's hard mouth. He was beyond evasion. "Of course."

"You are a fool."

"I do not deny it."

"She had her chance and refused to go with you," Joseph reminded him curtly.

Paul shrugged. "That changes nothing."

The younger man murmured an obscenity, sharp and to the point. "The saints preserve me from any such love that turns a man into a lunatic."

Paul couldn't help but echo that sentiment, even as he knew that he was powerless to alter the emotions Dominique provoked in him. Through the long weeks of his imprisonment, as he lay confined within a narrow, dank cell, never knowing if he would see the next dawn, only the thought of her had kept him whole. He would, no matter what the cost, set her free.

But time was growing short. He had chafed in prison, grudging each day for the lost chance it brought. If he was to act, it had to be now.

"Do as you will, Joseph," he said as he picked up his cloak and walked toward the door. "Perhaps you can afford to wait. I cannot."

"You will get her killed," Joseph protested, "and yourself with her."

Paul ignored the words. He strode on, his face grimly set and the cold light of determination burning in his eyes.

"Mademoiselle," a soft voice whispered, "you must come."

Dominique turned away from the gown she had been laboriously pressing. A startled look passed over her face as she found the dauphine of France at her elbow.

"It is maman," Maria Theresa murmured. "You must come."

Thinking that the queen was ill, Dominique hastened to do as she was bid. But when she entered the royal chamber, with the princess close behind her, she found Marie Antoinette sitting upright in a chair beside her worktable, apparently undisturbed.

Only the blankness of her features and the unfocused glaze of her eyes betrayed that something terrible had happened.

"Madame," Dominique said as she went down on her knees in front of the queen and took her hands in hers. "What is it?"

The older woman did not appear to hear her. Dominique had to repeat the question twice before there was any response.

With a visible effort, Marie Antoinette roused herself. She gazed into Dominique's deeply concerned eyes and said softly, "The National Assembly has decided to put His Majesty on trial."

At first, Dominique did not think she had heard her correctly. Put the king on trial? The very notion was absurd. What could they possibly charge him with? Then she realized how easy it would be for them to distort the truth to serve their own purposes, and dread rippled through her.

"Surely not, madame," she murmured. "Not even they would dare to go so far."

The look the queen gave her was almost pitying, as though Marie Antoinette truly regretted the innocence and loyalty that prompted such an assertion.

"I am afraid," she whispered, "that the world is a much more terrible place than I had ever dared to think."

With that, she bent her head into her hands and began to sob. Instinctively, Dominique put her arms around her. Over the royal head, she saw the dauphine, pale and strained, gazing at her mother.

Forcing herself to speak calmly, she asked, "Where are Nicole and David?"

"In the antechamber, I think," the young girl replied, her voice trembling.

"Go and stay with them. I will take care of Her Majesty."

Maria Theresa hesitated, but after a moment she did as Dominique said. The two women were left alone as outside, the great bell of Notre Dame began solemnly to toll the midday hour.

Louis Auguste Bourbon, fifth in line of his dynasty, sixteenth of his name to rule France, went on trial for his life on the eleventh of December, year of the Lord 1792. But the documents assiduously scribbled by the law clerks attending the trial were dated month of Nivose, first year of the Republic. The pretense of having the past cast off and the world begun anew, marked the general tone of the proceedings. All that was old—law, tradition, even simple human reason—was thrown by the board. In its place reigned madness cloaked within a mask of rigid formality.

Accusations were stated, evidence was presented. "Never mind," said Joseph grimly at one point as he and Paul crossed paths in a corridor outside the hearing room, "that the charges are baseless and the evidence fabricated. Still they will have their little drama, playing at justice like other men play at dice."

Paul was surprised by the young man's vehemence. Generally, Joseph was far too cautious to reveal himself in such a fashion, but it seemed that rage had finally overcome his self-control.

"Easy," he murmured softly, laying his hand on his friend's arm. "This isn't the place."

The reversal of their recent roles was enough to jolt Joseph back to reality. He took a deep, steadying breath and glanced around. Ordinarily, his expression was hooded, faintly bored. Now he looked afraid.

"They are going to kill him."

"Yes," Paul said quietly, "I know."

Joseph shot him a startled look. "You accept it?"

"Of course not. I accept nothing that is happening to any of us. But by the same token, there is nothing I can do to help Louis. He has become the symbol of everything they loathe and they will rip out his heart rather than let him continue."

Even as he spoke, Paul hoped that he wasn't being prescient. People had died in horrible ways during the turmoil that had engulfed France. The best Louis could hope for was to be granted a swift and merciful end.

"Do you think he realizes?" Joseph asked, curious despite himself.

Paul shrugged. "I have no idea. After all, it's been months since I was anywhere near the royal family."

Joseph grimaced. "A condition I understand you have been attempting to remedy."

That was true enough. Determined as he was to see Dominique, Paul had decided to approach the situation directly. He had gone to the Temple prison and demanded entry, identifying himself as the physician for the royal inmates. He had been turned away, as he had expected. But the attempt would certainly reach Robespierre's ears. He was hoping that the Jacobin leader would respond true to form.

As it turned out, he had little time to wait for Robespierre's reaction. Barely had Joseph taken his leave than Paul saw the short, bespectacled revolutionary coming down the corridor toward him. As usual, Robespierre was accompanied by a clutch of hangers-on and sycophants— men desperate to be near the source of such terrifying power.

He stopped when he saw Paul. A faint smile played around his lips. "Delamare," he said, "what a pleasant surprise. I had despaired of seeing you here again."

The hypocrisy of that—coming as it did from the man who had ordered his imprisonment—was almost enough to wring an angry reply from Paul. But he, too, smiled.

"Where else would I be, my dear Maximilien? After all, isn't this the very heart of France these days?"

Robespierre frowned slightly. The deliberate casualness of Paul's address did not escape him. Very few dared to speak to him so familiarly. Still, it suited his purposes to appear magnanimous, a true man of the people, unlike the mealy-mouthed aristocrats whose extermination he was looking forward to with such eagerness.

"Well said, my friend," he declared jovially as he clapped a hand on Paul's back. "The very heart, indeed. Still," he added archly, "I understand there was at least one other place you desired to be recently." With a chiding wiggle of his finger, he added, "The Temple is not the place to be paying social calls."

"That wasn't my purpose," Paul declared smoothly. "Months ago I was appointed physician to the royal family. Lately, I have been unable to discharge my duties, but now there is no reason not to resume them."

"No reason?" Robespierre echoed softly. "There are very few men who would make such a statement in these times."

Paul shrugged that off. "I realize all the world seems obsessed with politics, but life does go on. People still get sick and need the care of a doctor."

"I have heard of no illness among the Capets and their litter."

Carefully, knowing how much could be riding on it, Paul said, "Wouldn't it be better to be sure of that?"

Robespierre shot him a quizzical look. In a city riddled by plots and counterplots, it was never possible to tell who might have information and how it might be communicated. Paul had deliberately raised the possibility that the royal family could be concealing an illness, perhaps to rob Robespierre of his long-awaited bloodletting.

"A good point," he said thoughtfully as he stroked his chin and glanced at the men around him. "Why didn't any of you think of that?"

None dared to answer. They merely stared, wide-eyed, like mice in thrall to a serpent.

"So," Robespierre continued, "you would be willing to resume your duties?"

Since Paul had already said that, there didn't seem much point in confirming it. He did, however, nod.

"Good, good," Robespierre said. "Why not drop by there this afternoon?"

Paul allowed as to how that would be convenient. Robespierre lingered a few moments longer, then moved on, trailing his entourage. Paul watched him go, a wry smile playing around his hard mouth.

Pray God Robespierre would continue to think him a fool for at least a little while longer.

Chapter
8

By the time Paul returned to the Temple, the king was also there. A postponement had been granted in the trial —ten days during which Louis was supposed to prepare his defense. It appeared that the formalities of justice would be observed to the bitter end.

He did not see the king, who was closeted with advisers, but he was admitted to the queen's presence. Marie Antoinette was seated at a small table set near a window. That was the only source of light in the narrow, low-ceilinged room.

Some effort had been made to make the surroundings more appealing—there was a rug on the floor and curtains had been hung around the bed. But overall, the effect was oppressive even to a man who had spent the last few months in more austere and threatening circumstances.

Her Majesty glanced up as he was admitted. For a moment, a look of surprise flitted across her face. It was followed swiftly by a frown.

"What an unexpected honor, Doctor Delamare," she said coldly. "But I'm not at all sure that it is one we welcome."

Paul came farther into the room and shut the door behind him. He did not resent the queen's annoyance. Since she had no way of knowing that he had been imprisoned, he could hardly blame her for resenting his apparent defection.

Inclining his head graciously, he said, "I regret, madame, that circumstances prevented me from coming to you sooner. Unfortunately, the gentlemen in charge of the Conciergerie are no more accommodating than I suspect the wardens are here."

Antoinette's eyes widened. She looked at him in dawning comprehension and dismay. "Monsieur le Docteur, do I understand you? You were arrested?"

He nodded. "In September." Briefly, he sketched the circumstances for her. It was hardly necessary to go into any great detail. Indeed, the mere mention of the month was enough to make the queen flinch.

"*Mon Dieu*," she murmured. Impulsively, she held out her hand to him. "I am so sorry, Doctor. I had no idea that you were in distress, but now I realize that I should have at least considered the possibility."

"Actually, madame," he said with a smile, "I would never have expected you to give me the slightest thought. Further, I am far more interested in your situation than my own. I hope you have been well?"

The queen gestured him into a chair beside her. As he sat down, she said, "Through the grace of God, but that reminds me. You have been very much on my mind—not in the least because I have wished you were here to see to Mademoiselle de Montfort."

Paul stiffened. He had been hoping to lead the queen gently to talk of Dominique. Instead, she had anticipated him.

"What is wrong with Dom—the mademoiselle?"

Antoinette hid a smile. She had believed all along that there was more between this pair than either wanted to admit, and now she was sure of that.

Romantic entanglements were like a ray of sunshine penetrating the dark, dank prison. They suggested that there was a world beyond the madhouse in which they all dwelt—a world in which a man and woman might still come together as one.

"What is wrong?" she repeated softly. "Nothing, I suppose, that escape from this horrible place would not cure. But if she remains here . . ."

She sighed deeply, her own guilt and remorse uppermost in her mind. "I made a mistake, monsieur. I should have sent Dominique away long before. Alas, she is so loving and generous in her nature that I have clung to her out of my own fear."

"You can hardly be blamed for that, madame," Paul said gently. It was true he had nurtured angry thoughts against the queen for keeping Dominique with her, but seeing Marie Antoinette's genuine distress, he could not help but feel sympathy for her.

She was, after all, a woman who had been protected and coddled all her life. Naturally, she sought to maintain that even when it was no longer possible.

"I, too, have been thinking about Dominique," he said quietly, "and of the need to remove her from this place."

The queen sighed deeply. Her mouth trembled. "You know what happened today?"

He nodded. "The trial began."

"Naturally, His Majesty will prepare a sterling defense. After it has been presented, it will be impossible for anyone to believe him guilty of the preposterous charges."

Paul did not reply. To agree with her would be to lie. To tell her the truth would be an unnecessary cruelty.

"Still," the queen continued, her voice high and taut, "it is merely sensible to prepare for the worst, if only to prevent it from occurring. If Dominique leaves now, then perhaps she can return at some later date, after everything has settled down again. We might even go back to Versailles, where we were all so happy . . ."

She broke off, tears slipping down her pale cheeks. Instinctively, Paul leaned forward. He took the queen in his arms and held her gently as the storm of her weeping exhausted itself.

Thus it was that Dominique saw him when she entered the royal chamber.

She stopped stock-still, her mind unable to comprehend what her eyes insisted they were seeing. Paul, here? Embracing the queen?

No, not embracing. Comforting, as she was quick to realize once her initial astonishment faded. Moreover, Marie Antoinette looked not at all abashed, merely exhausted and oddly relieved.

"Come in, dear," she said as she wiped the last of the tears from her eyes. With a visible effort, she took a firm grip on herself. "Sit down. We have much to discuss."

Dominique barely heard her. All her attention was focused on Paul. He appeared as hard and strong as she remembered; there was precious little evidence that the turmoil of the last few months had had any effect on him, until she looked into his eyes and found in their crystalline depths shadows she could not comprehend.

Hardly aware that she did so, she slid into the chair the queen indicated. Her pulse was racing and the tightness in her throat made it difficult to breathe. Dominique was perilously close to tears herself, yet was determined not to shed them. Not for anything would she give him the satisfaction of knowing that his mere appearance affected her so.

For his part, Paul was conscious of little else other than Dominique. He was struck first and foremost by her beauty. In the hard winter light, her ebony hair gleamed like polished silk.

Her face was pale, making the vivid emerald flash of her eyes all the more striking. The gown she wore was simple—plain to the point almost of ugliness—but it could do nothing to detract from the gentle swell of her breasts and the fluid curve of her narrow waist.

Too narrow, he thought after the first jolt of seeing her gave way to a more measured assessment. During the summer he had thought her too thin, but now she was even more so. There was a fragility about her that belied the proud tilt of her head and the stubborn inward insistence on strength.

"Dominique," he said quietly as he rose in acknowledgment of her presence. "It is good to see you again."

Before she could reply, the queen interjected. "Paul has just told me the most horrible thing. He was imprisoned in the Conciergerie all these months. That's why he couldn't come to see us."

"Indeed?" Dominique murmured. Her gaze locked on him. She did not precisely look doubtful, only extremely cautious.

"That must have been very distressing for you," she said expressionlessly.

Paul suppressed a wry grimace. If he'd nurtured any thoughts about her returning his feelings, they had just been firmly quashed.

The notion of him languishing in jail did not seem to disturb her much at all. Granted, she looked a bit paler than a moment before, but that could be a trick of the lighting.

"I survived," he murmured. "More to the point, Her Majesty and I have been discussing the immediate future." He glanced at the queen, waiting to see if she wished to speak, but Marie Antoinette merely gave a slight nod of her head.

"We both feel," Paul went on firmly, "that it would be best for you to leave here."

Dominique's eyes widened. She was having difficulty enough with his sudden reappearance, without adding to that the apparent fact that he had been discussing her with the queen. Furthermore, he had also seemingly convinced Marie Antoinette of something Dominique believed she would never have come to on her own.

"Your Majesty," she began, struggling for words, "this is really most outlandish. Monsieur Delamare can hardly be considered an ally under the best of circumstances. For him to suddenly reappear after all this time and try to persuade you that I should not remain, is—not to put too fine a point on it—suspicious."

From the corner of her eye, she saw Paul frown and knew that she had managed yet again to anger him. But that could not be helped. The queen had to know how foolish she was being.

Marie Antoinette, however, did not see it that way. Quietly, with uncharacteristic firmness, she said, "Paul has done nothing of the sort. I had already come to that conclusion before he arrived.''

More gently, she added, ''You must go, my dear. I am sorry, but there is no longer any alternative. For your own sake, as well as Nicole and David's, you must accept Paul's help.''

It did not escape Dominique's notice that the queen had, three times in short succession, called Paul by his Christian name. Such familiarity was a rare sign of royal favor—and trust.

That he should inspire such emotions should have been incomprehensible. Yet, Dominique had no difficulty understanding it. He provoked the same feelings in her, despite her best efforts to deny them.

Seeing the queen's wan face and the nervous flutter of her hands, Dominique rose and went to her. ''Please, Your Majesty,'' she murmured, ''I fear you have overstrained yourself. I'm sure Monsieur le Docteur will understand if you rest now.''

This last was said with a glare in Paul's direction, strongly suggesting that if he attempted to impose himself on the queen any further, Dominique would personally take his head off.

Since his own preference was to get Dominique alone as speedily as possible, he was only too happy to agree. He waited in the hallway while the queen retired, ignoring as he did the bullying stare of the guard.

When Dominique at last emerged, he took her arm and guided her swiftly away, all the while saying loudly, ''Come along then, Citoyenesse. I have other patients to see and no time to waste.''

Dominique muttered under her breath but made no effort to get away from him—at least, not while they were still in sight of the guard. The moment they turned the corner, she jerked her arm free.

"How dare you?" she demanded. "How low and contemptible can you be to come back here after all these months and try to worm your way into Her Majesty's trust? And especially now, when she is worried about the king and fearful of the future?"

"She is right to be afraid," Paul broke in coldly. He would not waste time or effort defending himself yet again. If she wanted to believe him a scurrilous rogue, so be it. At least she wouldn't be able to deny the truth of her own danger.

"The noose is tightening," he said. "If you think otherwise, you are a fool."

Dominique inhaled sharply. It was one thing to confront her fears in the privacy of her own heart. It was quite another to have them spoken aloud.

"Listen to me," Paul said as he took hold of her again. He was out of patience, exasperated by her lack of trust, and desperate to convince her. Forgetting for a moment his great strength, he shook her angrily. "If you won't do what's right for yourself, at least consider Nicole and David. Do you want them to die, too?"

Instantly, he regretted his harshness. Dominique had been pale before, but now she turned gray. A moan broke from her and she swayed helplessly.

He cursed under his breath even as he caught her up in his arms. Her weight was ominously slight. Moreover, there was a heated dryness to her skin that set off alarms within him.

Farther down the corridor he found a small room furnished with two cots, a rude wooden table, and a couple of equally rough chairs. It might have been the home of a peasant—one who happened to be very neat. The room had been meticulously swept and the covers on the cots were crisply taut.

Carefully, he lowered her onto the blanket. She was conscious but her pulse was weak. Barely had her head touched the pillow than she was struggling upright again.

"Let me go," she protested, her voice faint and breathless. In her agitation, she pushed against him, with no more effect than a bird battering against a stone wall. She was about to say something else, undoubtedly less than complimentary to him. But before she could do so, she was seized by a sudden paroxysm of coughing.

Paul observed it grimly. He was not surprised; everything added up to her being ill—the weight loss, her uncharacteristic weakness, the fever. The queen had even hinted at it.

But none of that made any difference in his reaction. He was starkly, stunningly afraid. The mere thought that Dominique could be taken from him, before he even had the chance to save her, struck him so forcibly that he all but cried out against it. He managed to restrain himself, if barely. On the nearby table was a chipped pitcher of water and a wooden cup. He filled the latter and brought it to her, waiting until the coughing subsided sufficiently for her to drink.

"Slowly," he murmured, his arm around her shoulders and the cup at her lips.

She drank, coughed, drank again. At length, she shoved the cup away and sat upright.

"Please leave." Her voice had recovered some of its strength, but by no means all. Additionally, the cough gave it a rough, husky edge. Several pins had fallen loose from her hair, allowing ebony strands to tumble in disarray around her shoulders. She looked and sounded like a woman exhausted by passion.

He ignored her stilted request for his departure and instead sat down in a nearby chair.

"How long has this been going on?" When she did not respond, he made a gesture of exasperation. "I am a doctor, Dominique—the only one you are likely to see anytime soon. So why not take advantage of my presence and tell me what's been happening?"

Put that way, it was difficult to resist. She had been concerned about her deteriorating health, although she had done her best not to think about it. Softly, she said, "About a month."

"Since the cold weather set in?"

She nodded. "It comes and goes. I take hot water with a little of the medications left over from when you treated Her Majesty."

"That won't be enough—not while you're trapped in this godforsaken place."

"Nonsense," she said crisply. Without looking at him, she swung her legs over the side of the cot and stood up. Smoothing her skirt to hide the trembling of her legs, she continued, "I refuse to make this into something it isn't. I feel perfectly fine, and you aren't going to convince me otherwise." Pointedly, she added, "I suppose that's standard practice for you medical men, but I'm having none of it."

With an effort, Paul suppressed a surge of anger. His gaze swept over her with slow deliberation. At length, he said, "All right, let's forget it, then. We have more important things to discuss. I will arrange for you to depart a day or two from now."

Dominique stared at him. His face was impassive—

nothing there to indicate what he was thinking or feeling. Only the single, blunt-tipped finger tapping away on the chair arm betrayed his irritation.

She took a deep breath and was relieved that she didn't begin coughing again. Now was not the time.

Quietly, she said, "I cannot go."

For an instant she wondered if, purely coincident with her making that statement, something terrible had happened to Paul. All the color drained from his face. His mouth pulled hard and taut. He looked for all the world like a man who had suffered a sudden burst of agonizing pain and was doing his utmost not to yield to it.

Slowly, he rose and stood over her. His eyes, blue as shards torn from the sky, glinted ominously. Meticulously pronouncing each word, he said, "You are the stubbornest, the most foolish, and the most infuriating woman I have ever encountered.

"However," he continued before she could interrupt, "it had not occurred to me that you were also selfish, callous, and unconcerned about the safety of your brother and sister."

"That isn't true," Dominique shot back, aghast. "I'm desperately worried about both of them."

"But you won't leave."

"*I* can't," she murmured, misery stamped on her face. Hardly aware that she did so, she spread her hands in entreaty. "Please, try to understand. The queen has been far more to me than merely sovereign and employer. It is no exaggeration to say that she is more a mother to me than my own mother ever was."

Paul frowned. He could hardly dispute that. The marquise de Montfort had been a shallow, self-absorbed woman with no time or patience for her children.

"How can you expect me to turn my back on her now, when she needs me most?" Dominique asked. "What sort of person would I be if I were capable of doing that?"

Paul was tempted to tell her that she would be alive, free, whole, and with a chance to rebuild her life. But he stopped himself. Her conscience simply would not allow her to do as he wished, no matter what her refusal might cost her.

That did not, however, mean that his cause was lost.

Without inflection, he said, "What about Nicole and David?"

Dominique took a deep, steadying breath and looked at him beseechingly. "I know it's a great deal to ask. You're annoyed with me, and . . ."

"I'm not."

"Oh . . . well, I thought you were. No matter. If you could get the three of us out, then surely you could manage just Nicole and David? They're only children, it's true, but very intelligent and obedient. They wouldn't give you any trouble."

Her shoulders trembled. She turned away from him for a moment, struggling to regain her composure.

Before she could resume trying to convince him, Paul said, "All right, I'll get them out. They're to be ready tomorrow night. Naturally, I don't have to caution you to say nothing to anyone, and that includes the children. They aren't to know until the last possible moment."

Mutely, Dominique nodded. She was astounded by his abrupt agreement. She had expected him to argue, to try to use her concern for her brother and sister as a bargaining chip to get her to come along herself. If he had done that, she would have been in an untenable position. But instead, he had simply agreed to do as she so desperately asked.

She wondered if she had wanted him to try harder to convince her otherwise.

What was happening to her that she should be suspicious of a man who almost anyone would believe was motivated by no more than simple human decency? Moreover, he was prepared to act on those feelings at a time when most other people were looking solely to their own survival. It was because he had agreed so quickly.

Long after Paul had left, Dominique sat contemplating that question. She had told him the truth when she said that she loved the queen as a mother and could not bring herself to leave. But she was also human . . . and afraid. She did not want to die.

With a little shake, she got control of herself. There were limits to what people would allow, even during times of madness. The king's trial would proceed, he would defend himself ably, and everyone would realize how utterly outlandish and absurd the Jacobins were. She was certain that this would be the turning point. The king would be exonerated, Robespierre would be disgraced, honorable men would take over the government, and life would slowly return to normal.

Then, in six months or so, it would be safe for Nicole and David to return. They would all resume the life they had once known, and the events of the past few years would become nothing more than a vaguely remembered nightmare.

She was nineteen years old, with all her life before her. She could not possibly die. With the instinctive faith in one's own immortality that is the blessing and the bane of the young, she cast her fears aside and began the business of deciding which of their meager belongings Nicole should take along.

Chapter
9

Paul was busy for the remainder of the day and into the next. He stopped by the hospital and made sure that all his records were up-to-date.

That done, he had a light supper at the café near his apartment and lingered a short time over the wine. Not until it was fully dark did he leave. But instead of returning home, he set off on foot.

At the best of times, the streets of Paris were as unsafe as those of any large city. Few ventured out, preferring to remain behind locked doors. Those who had no alternative took pains to go by carriage.

Only someone who had most urgent business, and who wanted to be discreet about it, would venture alone into the narrow lanes and alleys of Les Halles after dark. The riverfront section—site of an ancient market that had grown over the years into a warren of warehouses and shops—was deserted at that hour. In a few more hours, just before the first gray rim of light shone at the horizon, the area would be teeming with a multitude of hawkers and buyers. Now it slumbered under a miasma of rotting garbage and skittering rats.

Paul walked swiftly, a tall, hard figure clad in a cloak, riding boots, and breeches. He was bareheaded, despite the snow that had begun to swirl down from the moonless sky. At a corner, he paused and glanced around, as though deliberating which way to go before he moved on.

He found the narrow doorway about midway down a wall of ramshackle buildings pressed one upon another and careering sharply out over the street, as though a good wind would blow them over. The door creaked as he opened it and stepped into darkness. Softly, he cursed. A tinder flared and the wick of a candle caught.

"Come on, then," a man's voice said. "Don't stand around all night." His voice was hard, uneducated, and faintly slurred, as though he had not been able to get through the hours of darkness without the help of a drink or two.

Paul suspected it was not the lack of natural light that troubled the man. He was locked in a darkness of the soul from which there could be no release.

"Monsieur Crenay?" he asked.

The man jerked his head in acknowledgment. He was fat with long, greasy hair of an indeterminate color and narrow, squinting eyes. The rest of his features were all but buried between pendulous jowls. He was dressed in a shirt and pantaloons that, though costly, were stained and wrinkled, as though he hadn't bothered to change them in many days.

"Sit down," he wheezed at Paul as he pointed to a stool not far from him. "Been waiting long enough for you. Let's get this over with."

Paul agreed. He reached into the inside pocket of his cloak and removed a pouch, which he tossed on the table between them. Crenay seized it avidly, emptied the coins into his lap, and counted them one by one.

"It's all there," Paul said, allowing an edge of annoyance to creep into his tone.

"No harm in checking. I'm a cautious man." He licked his lips and eyed Paul with cordial geniality. "Now then, I understand there's something you'd like shipped out of the country."

"Four somethings," Paul said. "To be ready tomorrow night."

"Destination?"

"Dover."

The man whistled softly. "It's a lot you're asking for."

"Which is why you are being so well paid," Paul pointed out coldly. "However, if the commission doesn't interest you, I will go elsewhere." He made to rise.

"Hold on," the man said. "I didn't say I wouldn't do it; just that it's not going to be easy."

Paul gestured to the heavy pouch in the man's hand. "I'm sure that will help you smooth the way."

Crenay frowned. "Yeah, I suppose." He made a show of reluctance, but the outcome was already certain. He was far too greedy to let such a prize escape him.

"Where's the pickup to be?" he inquired.

Paul hesitated, as though suddenly assailed by second thoughts.

"Come on, come on," Crenay grumbled. "You have to tell me; otherwise, how am I to help you?"

"All right . . . it's the Temple."

The man whistled. He looked at Paul as though he feared that he might be mad. "You're not thinking of . . ."

"Of course not," Paul broke in. "I've no interest in them. It's servants who will be coming out—ordinary people who should never have been stuck there in the first place."

Crenay looked unconvinced. He hefted the pouch again. "There'll have to be more."

"I told you, it's servants."

"Doesn't matter who they are. If they're coming from the Temple, I'll need more."

Again, Paul hesitated, as though considering whether or not to argue. At length, he shrugged. "All right, you'll have that again when we're out of the city."

"I'll have it now or there's no deal."

"That's absurd—" With sudden impatience, he relented. "Oh, all right, take it. But," he added menacingly, "you had damn well better be there, Crenay, or it'll be your head that rolls."

Crenay stood, all smiles now as they swiftly worked out the details of the plan. Their parting was hurried. The smuggler was clearly eager to see him on his way.

Half an hour later Paul was at his apartment. He spent most of the rest of the night going through his books, selecting those that were most important to him. These he put together in a bundle that he set beside his door.

From a closet, he took a long, flat belt that unrolled to reveal a series of silk-lined pouches. These he filled with the contents of a small chest kept under the loose floorboards beneath his bed.

That done, he lay down on the bed, still fully dressed, and stared up at the ceiling until darkness gave way to day.

* * *

Paul was not alone in his long vigil. Dominique also lay awake, listening to the quiet breathing of her sister and thinking about her brother, who lay close at hand on the other side of the wall.

Tomorrow they would be gone. For all her optimistic thoughts, she had to face the possibility that she would never see them again, and not because they wouldn't make good their escape. That she couldn't even contemplate, but because events might unfold in such a way as to make it impossible for them ever to be reunited as a family.

Still, whatever happened to her, she had the comfort of knowing that Nicole and David would be well cared for. Although Dominique had not seen her English grandmother in almost ten years, she had fond memories of that indomitable lady.

Unlike her daughter, the late marquise de Montfort, Lady Amelia Haverston, duchess of Clarendon, was far from being either frivolous or self-centered. Though she was now well into her seventies, she remained very much the leader of the family, the matriarch none dared to defy.

Except Dominique. She flinched inwardly as she recalled how she had rejected her grandmother's pleas to come to England three years before. Lady Amelia had foreseen the course of events in France and had tried to get her grandchildren out, only to be stymied by Dominique's insistence that they had nothing to fear. She would welcome Nicole and David with open arms. Undoubtedly, she would also have a few choice things to say about Dominique's decision to remain behind.

Would Paul take them to England himself? She realized that she should have insisted on more details of the escape plan, but at the time, she had simply been too overcome to think clearly.

Surely he must be intending to flee himself. Having helped them, he could not possibly remain in Paris, for he would be the most obvious suspect in their escape, and as such, would be hunted down and punished.

So they would all be in England—Nicole, David, and Paul—far from the vengeful hand of Robespierre, while she would still be in Paris, in Temple Prison, trapped like a bird in a cage and conveniently accessible whenever the madman chose to deal with her. She squeezed her eyes shut, battling against her fear. Silently, she reminded herself that she came from a long, unbroken line of stalwart men and women who had seen their duty and done it unflinchingly. On both the French and British sides, her lineage was impeccable. Granted, the Haverstons and de Montforts had their share of wastrels, rogues, and general incompetents, but they harbored no cowards. She would not be the first.

At length she slept, only to dream of hair the color of beaten gold and eyes born of the sky and sun—eyes that, oddly enough, smiled at her and promised all would be well.

Shortly after dawn, Paul left his residence. On his way out, he knocked on his landlord's door. Gaston Foulard was a big, beefy man who still retained the rude good looks of his native Lombardy, despite living twenty years in Paris. He was by trade a silversmith, though of late, there had been little call for such skills. He had been getting by doing odd jobs at a nearby forge run by a friend.

Fortunately, he and his wife had long since put aside the money to buy the building where they lived. That provided them with a roof over their heads and the income

from lodgers who appreciated the Foulards' instinctive cir-
cumspection.

Paul handed him the books. "I would appreciate it if I
could store these with you for a bit."

Foulard looked at him closely. He saw a young man of
twenty-eight years, handsome in a hard, relentlessly masculine way, a man of undoubted intelligence and decency
who had never given him any cause for alarm. On the
contrary, he had bestowed a certain prestige on his estab-
lishment merely by his presence there. He was a man who
Foulard had thought had the sense to stay out of trouble.

It saddened him that this was apparently no longer the
case, but he was not about to involve himself any more
than he had to. Because he despised the imbeciles who
were savaging his beloved France, and because he was by
nature a close-mouthed man, he would say nothing to
Paul—or to anyone else.

"I see," he murmured as he accepted the books. They
could be hidden away easily enough above the rafters in
the kitchen. There was a false ceiling there that provided
useful storage space for all manner of goods a wise man
did not leave out in the open these days.

"They will be well cared for," he added out of respect
and, perhaps, compassion.

Paul nodded, satisfied. He inclined his head graciously
and took his leave. The snow of the previous night had
gathered in small eddies and heaps along the cobblestone
pavement. Already it was turning to slush.

Paul frowned. He had hoped the day would be colder,
less inviting—the kind of weather that would inspire a
bored and overworked guard to be less than attentive.

Never mind; he would simply make the best of what he
had. To do otherwise was unthinkable.

He patted his inside pocket as he walked swiftly toward the corner, where it would be easier to hail a carriage. Satisfied that he had everything he needed, he gave the driver directions to the Temple. The man grumbled, but did not object. There were few enough paying customers in Paris these days without turning one away.

At the Temple, he was admitted readily by a guard who looked as though he had spent the night quaffing raw wine and the morning regretting it.

The queen was waiting for him in her chamber. Dominique was with her. Both women were pale and grim. Paul spoke with them for some time, quietly and gently explaining what would occur. Afterward, he left them alone. That seemed the kindest thing to do.

He left the Temple around noon and did not return until early evening. By then, everything was in place.

Nicole and David had been told. They were flushed with excitement—and fear. As he entered the small chamber where they were all gathered, they looked at him as though he were an apparition. He smiled at them gently, but had no illusion that it helped.

"Is everything ready?" he asked.

Dominique nodded. She had already made her farewells to her brother and sister, and they to her. Now, as the final seconds slipped away, she struggled to retain some semblance of self-control. Desperately, she concentrated on what Paul was saying, focusing all her attention on his words so that she might think of nothing else.

"Crenay will be waiting at the south gate with a cart. Naturally, Robespierre's men will be somewhere in the immediate vicinity."

"You're certain of that?" David asked. Though he was still a child, he understood perfectly well the risk they were running. If Paul had miscalculated, they were all doomed.

"There is no doubt," Paul said quietly. "Crenay has been working for Robespierre for some time. He's part of the reason why so many have tried to escape and failed."

Nicole's eyes widened. "You mean, they went to him for help and he betrayed them?"

"Exactly, although up until recently, no one knew that it was Crenay who was responsible."

"Who found him out?" David asked.

Paul shook his head. He was not about betray Joseph's reluctant confidence. The younger man still thought him mad for what he was doing. Paul wasn't convinced he was wrong.

"You don't need to know that," he said quietly. "Be certain, however, that after tonight, Crenay will be taken care of."

He walked toward the door and eased it open. After a quick glance outside, he said, "We will go through the north portal. Each evening at this time, empty wine barrels are removed through that route. The only difference tonight is that they will have something in them."

Nicole and David looked fascinated by the prospect, their imaginations caught despite all the fear and risk. Even Dominique was reassured.

Clearly, Paul had planned this with great care. While Robespierre and his men were looking in one direction, they would be leaving in another.

Vastly relieved, she took a step forward and held out her hand to Paul. "There is no way I can ever adequately thank you," she began. Her voice was soft and husky, whether the residue of the cough or some emotion he could not say. At any rate, it was her eyes that held him. They were wide and luminous, catching the harsh winter light and transforming it into something that might otherwise have been found in a sylvan glade in the midst of summer when all was fresh and alive, filled with promise and hope.

Her lips were slightly parted. He stared at their moist fullness and felt the hardening in his body, the driving need to possess her that went beyond mere sexual desire, into a realm where he had never before ventured.

But there was no time to be thinking of that. Through the narrow, barred window, he could see that it was almost dark. The day was ending. Soon, the last of the routine chores would be done and the prison would once more be sealed up for the night.

"Come," he said quietly, "walk a little of the way with us."

Dominique hesitated. She had thought to part from her brother and sister right there, but the chance for even a few more moments with them proved too tempting. With a quick nod, she agreed.

The sight of the queen's young lady-in-waiting walking through the prison corridors was so commonplace that few took any heed of her going. Similarly, her brother and sister were such fixtures that their seemingly ordinary behavior raised no curiosity. Paul might have been a different matter, but his presence had been explained the day before. The guards presumed that he must be Robespierre's man and accordingly gave him a wide berth.

"I think you could have gotten us out of here on your order alone," Nicole said with a soft giggle as they hurried along.

Paul smiled gently at the child's faith, even as he wished her sister might trust him half so much.

They rounded a corner not far from the kitchens and came upon the wine barrels stacked neatly against a wall. There were half a dozen of them, all about four feet in height and broad enough around to make it impossible for a man to lift one unaided.

Silently, Paul gave thanks to the combination of circumstances that had placed the barrels in precisely the time and place where they were most needed. Harsh though conditions were in the Temple prison, it would never have occured to the wardens to deny the inmates their usual beverage.

If they'd been allowed water, instead, only a fraction of them would have survived to stand trial, it was so polluted. Rather than be cheated of their prey, the authorities followed tradition and supplied the cheap but relatively safe wine.

And the wine barrels.

"How long will we have to be in them?" David asked in a whisper. There was no sign of any of the guards, who had long ago given up watching the utterly routine operation of the barrel removal and would not notice that the workers had been paid off and replaced by men loyal to Paul.

"Not long," Paul said soothingly. Quietly, he added, "I realize how hard this is on both of you." He looked at the children as he said, "You don't want to leave your sister, do you?"

Beside him, Dominique flinched She could not believe that he would be so insensitive, so cruel as to bring that up now. What could he possibly be thinking of to mention it to David and Nicole?

She'd already had such difficulty convincing them that

this was what she had to do. If they started to cry again or to beseech her to come with them, as they had done before, she didn't know how she would manage.

Abruptly, her thoughts broke off. Paul was looking at her grimly. Nicole and David had suddenly glanced away, abashed. What was that in Paul's hand? A handkerchief? Why was he bringing it toward her? That smell. . . .

She grasped his intention an instant too late and tried to fight, but his strength was far too great. She was helpless to tear the camphor- and laudanum-soaked cloth from her face.

The sweet, cloying scent filled her lungs. She gasped and cried out, only to find the world whirling away from her as she fell down a long, dark tunnel leading to infinity.

Chapter
10

Dominique was dreaming. She was a child again, astride her pony, Chantal, riding through the forests that dotted the vast de Montfort estate. The day was warm and sunny. Beneath her she could feel the rhythmic roll of the little horse, carrying her ever onward toward some enchanted adventure.

She sighed softly and turned over, only to abruptly become aware that all was not as it should be. Still half asleep, she frowned. There was something she needed to remember.

Her eyes shot open. Directly ahead she saw an expanse of rough wood that was swaying up and down.

Shock gripped her—the terrifying confusion that comes with the sense of being cut off from the known, predictable world.

Hard on it came memory. She sat up abruptly, only to cry out with pain as her head slammed against the ceiling of the bunk in which she lay.

She was rubbing the injured spot and muttering under her breath when the cabin door was flung open. Paul strode into the room.

His golden hair was in disarray and clinging damply to his head. He wore a rough cotton shirt and breeches. There was nothing about him to suggest the gentleman, much less a physician and scholar.

"Dominique," he said with evident relief as he saw her sitting up, apparently whole and unharmed despite the scream. "You're awake."

"Obviously." The look she shot him was scathing. "No thanks to you. Is drugging women some sort of new medical procedure, or is it simply something you enjoy doing?"

His eyes narrowed to ice-blue chips. With an angry jerk of his hand, he slammed the cabin door behind him and advanced into the room.

"Fully recovered, too, by the look of it. Certainly your sharp tongue is back in working order."

"How could you?" Dominique exclaimed. Heedless of the thin blanket that had drifted to her waist, she went on. "Just when I was beginning to trust you, to think that you might actually understand what was important to me— how could you betray me in such a fashion?"

Paul's mouth thinned to a hard, taut line. A jagged pulse beat in his lean cheek. Seeing it, Dominique swallowed hard. She knew that sign and what it meant. He was furiously, almost uncontrollably angry at her. But she didn't care, or so she told herself. He had been wrong to do what he had done. She had trusted him and he had betrayed her.

"Betray you?" he repeated, his voice dangerously soft. "Because I refused to let you offer yourself up as a sacrifice to some damnably twisted notion of love? Because I wouldn't stand by and see you fall into Robespierre's hands? Because I had the utter effrontery to believe that your life was worth saving—enough so to risk my own? Is that how I betrayed you, Dominique?''

She made no attempt to answer, but instead stared up at him, her eyes huge and filled with apprehension. She could hardly argue with such a statement. He had placed his own life on the line, there was no evading that. And he might—just might—have saved her own. But she still felt so at odds about what he had done, as though being in debt to him to such an extent left her unable to cope with anything else.

''I'm sorry,'' she murmured, dropping her eyes. So preoccupied was she that it took her a moment to realize that from the waist up she was clad only in a thin night rail that left very little to the imagination. A heated flush stained her cheeks as she grasped the blanket and pulled it back up.

Paul barely noticed. Under other circumstances, he would have been achingly aware of her dishabille. But just then there were far more important issues on his mind.

''What are you apologizing for?'' he demanded, glaring down at her. He couldn't remember her ever apologizing before. On the contrary, she was always lashing out, challenging him, being Dominique.

He crossed the narrow cabin and stood directly beside the bunk in a pose that should have been intimidating, but which was oddly comforting instead.

''For being so ungrateful,'' Dominique said quietly. She raised her head and looked at him directly. ''You took a terrible risk.''

''Others have taken worse.''

''Perhaps. The point is that you didn't have to do it.''

The fine edge of his anger softened, but he remained wary. "I'm not sure whether I did or not, but at least you're out now."

"Where exactly is out?" she asked with a faint smile.

Glad of something neutral to discuss, he said readily, "On board a small merchant ship, the *Saint Honore*. Ordinarily, she plows the route from Le Havre to Amsterdam carrying produce from Normandy. But this time she'll be making an extra stop, near Dover. We'll put ashore there."

He didn't add that the *Saint Honore* had done the same more than once before. Her captain had come highly recommended by the reluctant Joseph.

Dominique didn't ask how he had managed to arrange for their transportation. She was certain that he wouldn't tell her, if only to protect the others who must be involved. But that didn't mean there weren't plenty of other questions to which she expected answers.

"How long have I been unconscious?"

"We left Paris two days ago."

That shocked her. How could she have lain unaware for so long? Yet she must have for them to have already reached the coast and taken ship. As she shook off the last of her drugged stupor, vague memories surfaced.

There had been another boat—no, that was wrong, a barge. A river barge. She remembered lying on a narrow bed, recalled something sweet pressed to her lips—more of the laudanum.

"You kept me drugged all that time," she said accusingly.

He made no attempt to deny it. "I couldn't take the risk that you would awaken and try to turn back." He didn't add that he had watched her every moment, carefully monitoring her heartbeat and breathing to make sure that she was in no danger. Not until he was sure that the drug was wearing off had he left her alone, and then only for a few minutes. He perfectly timed each new dose so that she would remain in a gentle sleep for the better part of forty-eight hours.

"There's no chance of that now, is there?" Dominique said quietly.

"Not unless you feel inclined to swim." Ordinarily, her dejection would have disturbed him greatly. But now he was grimly glad that she was accepting the reality of the situation.

By this time, Dominique's escape—along with that of David and Nicole—would certainly have been noted. Robespierre would know that he had been duped and would be enraged. If she were to fall into his hands again, she would suffer terribly. But that, Paul reminded himself through the haze of his own fatigue, wasn't going to happen. With each moment that passed, they were closer to safety.

Softly, Dominique asked, "Did Her Majesty know what was going to happen?"

"I didn't tell her the actual details any more than I did you," Paul admitted, "but I am certain she knew. She was determined on her own part that you leave, and I believe she broached the subject to me because she sensed that I would carry it through for her."

Dominique nodded slowly. While the violent political storms swirling around her might leave the queen baffled, she had always understood men and how to get them to do as she wished. Dominique could envy her that, even as her eyes filled with tears at the thought of the queen even more alone than she had been before.

Futilely, Paul searched for words that might comfort her

but could find none. She would have to come to terms with the situation in her own mind.

"I will leave you now," he said quietly. "Nicole and David are anxious for some time with you."

At the mention of her sister and brother, Dominique started. She could hardly believe that she hadn't immediately asked after their welfare. The only possible explanation was that she so completely trusted Paul to look after them that it had never crossed her mind that anything could have gone amiss.

Nonetheless, she was grateful when he said, "They are both fine. I must say I've never met more intelligent and courageous children." A light flared in his eyes. He gazed down at her with a sudden tenderness that made her breath catch in her throat.

"Unless," he continued huskily, "you count a certain little chit I used to know."

He said nothing more, only turned and walked out of the cabin, shutting the door quietly behind him. For a few moments she was alone, but that was not long enough to sort out the whirling, contradictory emotions he had set off in her. Before she could even begin to do so, the door banged open again and Nicole and David rushed in.

Immediately, she was engulfed in a flurry of arms and legs as they threw themselves at her. Forgotten for the moment was the fact that they were a young lady of nine and a young gentleman of eight. They were only children, excited and afraid, reunited with the person they loved most in all the world and whom they looked to as the source of all security.

"Are you feeling terrible?" Nicole demanded, her forehead creased with worry. "Monsieur Delamare said that you might, but that it would pass quickly."

"Was it awful?" David asked with a small boy's avidness. "Did the drug smell dreadful?"

"No, no, and yes," Dominique said as she held them both close and gave silent thanks that they were all together. Much as she deeply regretted leaving the queen, she realized with hindsight that her brother and sister needed her more. It wasn't enough that they had family waiting for them in England. They needed the comfort of her presence in what promised to be a strange and frightening new world.

Only her refusal to admit the true direness of the situation had prevented her from seeing that before. Now she had to acknowledge that the hopes she had nurtured were nothing more than fantasy, for had she remained, she would have become simply one more weapon to use against the royal family. Perhaps the queen had been thinking of that, at least in part, when she decided that Dominique should go.

If she thought any longer just then about those still trapped within the grim confines of Temple Prison, she was going to cry. Better to concentrate on anything else and not upset Nicole and David further.

"Well," she said as calmly as she could manage, "this has turned into quite an adventure, hasn't it? I understand that we're on a merchant ship."

Immediately they both nodded and together launched into a description of the *Saint Honore*, her crew, and everything they had seen and done since climbing into the wine barrels.

"It was Monsieur Delamare's men who picked us up," David explained, "instead of the regular workers. That's why no one said anything about some of the barrels being too heavy to be empty."

"His men," Dominique repeated. "Yes . . . they would have had to be." So the escape plan was even more elaborate than she'd realized. Paul must have contacts she knew nothing about, not to mention people who were willing to trust him with information which, should he reveal it in the wrong places, would lead to their deaths.

Still trying to come to terms with that, she said, "I think I've lain abed quite long enough. Nicole, if you would be so good as to find my dress . . ."

"I'll wait outside," David said with solemn courtesy. More eagerly, he added, "Madame Renée said to bring you to the galley as soon as you were ready."

"Who," Dominique asked after David had left, "is Madame Renée?"

"Francois's wife," Nicole said, as though that explained everything. "Oh, I forgot, you haven't met Francois. He's the captain; this is his boat. Madame Renée is his wife. She comes along on all his trips. I heard one of the men say she's really the boss."

"She's very nice," Nicole rattled on as she helped do up Dominique's dress in the back. "It was she who undressed you after we came on board."

She giggled behind her hand. "She gave Monsieur Delamare a very bad time for what he had done. She said that you looked like a sick chicken and he ought to be ashamed."

Dominique frowned. She could only hope that she hadn't looked quite that bad. Even under the circumstances, certain allowances had to be made for vanity.

Once more suitably, if plainly, attired, she followed Nicole out of the cabin and down a narrow corridor toward a short flight of stairs. Immediately before it, within sight of the hatchway leading to the deck, was an open area that served as the galley. It was outfitted with a small stove, several basins, a table and benches.

It was also almost completely filled by the woman who stood there stirring a pot of stew and muttering to herself.

Dominique had never seen anyone as large as Madame Renée—at least, not a woman. She stood six feet tall and weighed well over three hundred pounds, all of it swathed in an immense red and blue cotton print, undoubtedly some of the newly popular material imported from India. She had a gigantic white apron tied around herself. On her head perched an absurdly small lace cap such as a kitchen maid in an affluent household might wear.

At the end of one large, work-worn hand, she grasped a wooden spoon that she was using to stir the contents of the pot.

"There you are," she said as they appeared at the entrance to the galley. "Don't stand around gawking. Come in and sit down."

As they did so, she looked Dominique over critically. "Well, you're looking better, I must say. Seems as though Monsieur le Docteur knew what he was about after all. Still, with him hovering over you the way he did, I suppose you couldn't have really come to any harm."

As Dominique silently digested this bit of information, Madame Renée said, "Sit down." She began ladling stew into wooden bowls, setting one in front of each of the three de Montforts. Tin spoons followed after being carefully wiped on the immense apron.

"Eat. You all look as though the first good breeze will blow you away."

Nicole and David glanced at Dominique, instinctively looking to her for permission. The aroma of the stew was delectable; it made her mouth water. But more than that was the kindness of this woman who might more easily have been resentful of them for endangering her and her own.

"Thank you," Dominique murmured as she picked up her spoon. Her brother and sister needed no further encouragement; they fell to with a will. For several minutes the galley was silent except for the ladling of stew into hungry mouths and the soft crackle of the fire in the iron stove.

When her stomach could hold no more, Dominique set her spoon down and smiled at the older woman. "That is the best meal I've had in a very long time," she said sincerely.

Madame Renée nodded matter-of-factly. "Everything tastes better with freedom," she said as she selected an onion from a basket and began briskly to peel it.

Without glancing up again, she said, "Monsieur le Docteur is on deck. He asked that you join him after you'd eaten."

The children needed no further invitation. They bolted from the table and were almost to the door when Dominique called them back to thank Madame Renée properly. Son and daughter of nobility they might be, but she had never felt that excused them from having good manners.

Dominique insisted on staying to help clear the table. She felt it was the least she could do under the circumstances, but she was also reluctant to see Paul again. As the last lingering effects of the drug wore off, she realized how shrewish and ungrateful she must have sounded. Slowly, she began admitting to herself that helpless fear and rage had distorted her perceptions. Certainly she owed the royal family a full measure of loyalty and respect. But she also owed it to herself to live. By insisting that she do so, Paul challenged her to turn away from death and confront the world head-on. It was a frightening but exhilarating prospect.

As she dried the last of the bowls and placed it carefully away in the cupboard, she felt Madame Renée watching her. Hesitantly, she smiled.

"Thank you again for the meal and for your kindness."

The large woman shrugged. "The food was here, you might as well eat it. As for kindness, that costs nothing."

Dominique thought of all the people she had met at court and elsewhere who behaved as though the smallest kindness would cost them years of their lives. Either Madame Renée was an innocent—an unlikely prospect given her milieu—or she chose to deal with the world on her own terms.

"You and your husband," Dominique said, "take a great risk in helping people like myself."

Madame Renée shot her a quick, piercing look. "Are you telling me something I don't already know?"

Flustered, Dominique shook her head. "I only meant that you are very brave as well as kind. I cannot tell you how much I appreciate it. My brother and sister . . ."

Abruptly, the older woman's face softened. She held out a work-roughened hand and patted Dominique's cheek gently. "The little ones will be safe, mam'selle, as will you be. If we could, we would save them all, but at least we get a few out."

Looking into the deep, black eyes that appeared almost impenetrable, Dominique murmured, "Why? What prompts you to do this?"

Madame Renée was silent for a moment. She moved away from Dominique and stood with her back to the room. Finally, she said, "It isn't only the high and mighty who are dying, milady. Ordinary people are being picked up off the streets and hustled to the guillotine without even the pretense of justice. My brother was one of them."

She turned and looked at Dominique directly. "Before the rebellion, things were bad. Everywhere we went along the river, we saw people struggling to find enough food to keep their children alive. They were living in hovels and dying of disease because the fine lords and ladies couldn't be bothered to help them."

Dominique's lips parted. She wanted to deny what the woman was saying, but she knew from her own experience that it was true. Her father had been such a *seigneur*, uncaring of the welfare of his people, and he was hardly unique. Despite their own genuine goodness, the king and queen had never managed to have much effect on the system itself. It went grinding on, brutalizing people without thought.

"I was all for the uprising," Madame Renée continued. "The night they burned the Bastille, I cheered myself hoarse. I thought, now everything will change, life will be good." She laughed harshly. "What a fool I was. The evil continues; it runs rampant over this poor land. We have to fight it even if that means someone like me, who had always hated the aristocracy, ends up helping someone like you to escape."

The idea of being hated wasn't new to Dominique. She had experienced it aplenty while imprisoned. But she had been able to shut herself off from the coarse, ignorant guards who always seemed to be merely parroting what they had been told.

Madame Renée was different. She was real, immediate, and direct. She could not be dismissed. Slowly, Dominique said, "I'm sorry."

A look of doubt, the first she had shown, crossed the older woman's face. "For what?"

"I don't know . . . exactly. Perhaps simply for being who I am."

Silence drew out between them until Madame Renée said, "Who you are is a young girl on her way to a new life. Take advantage of it, and when you have the chance to give back kindness, do it."

One more long, penetrating look and she was gone, bustling out of the galley on a wave of onion, sage, and plain good sense.

Slowly, Dominique made her way up to the deck. The brisk coastal breeze blew the heat from her cheeks and helped to lighten her spirits. Curiosity stirred in her as she glanced around.

The merchant ship looked as all such vessels did—a long, low deck, broad at the midpoint, narrowing slightly toward the prow and stern. Behind the hatchway was a single mast from which a broad, tattered sail flew.

Various bundles and barrels were strewn around, seemingly haphazardly. Only upon closer inspection was it clear that they were all neatly lashed down.

Two men—boys really—were twining rope. They shot her quick, surreptitious looks, but did not speak. David and Nicole were already up by the prow. Both were laughing, their faces were flushed, and their hair blew in the wind. With a pang, she realized that it had been a very long time since they had appeared so relaxed and happy.

The indisputable source of their pleasure was smiling down at them. Paul stood silhouetted against the sun. In the rough white shirt and breeches, with a cloak thrown carelessly over his shoulders, he looked unabashedly male.

He was bareheaded, his hair gleaming like gold lit by

fire. His skin was burnished and his eyes aglow with amusement. As she watched, he threw back his head and laughed—a deep, rich sound that rippled through her.

"There she is," David said. He ran over and grasped her by the hand, pulling her toward the edge of the deck. "Look," he said pointing, "isn't it beautiful?"

Dominique slowly turned her head, seeing all around them the gray winter sea, foam-flecked and sullen despite the fair weather. Only those whose vision had been so long circumscribed could wax enthusiastic over such a scene.

Softly, she said, "It is very lovely, but so is England. You will see when we get there how nice it is."

That seemed to satisfy them. Side by side, they leaned against the railing and talked quietly among themselves of what they were seeing.

Dominique watched them for a moment before she was satisfied that her brother and sister were truly all right. Thank the Lord they were, as Paul had said, intelligent and courageous. They would need both qualities in abundance before all was done.

She wrapped her cloak more securely around herself as she gazed out over the water. "What happens once we get to England?"

"I will escort you to London," Paul said.

And then? She wanted to ask further what his plans were, but she could not bring herself to do so. Certainly any obligation he felt extended no further than seeing her safely to her family. Then he would have his own life to remake in a new land.

The thought that she would soon be separated from him caused Dominique a sharp pang. She struggled valiantly to suppress it but could not.

Daring greatly, she glanced at him, seeing his profile etched against the sky. He looked utterly unbending, relentless, untouched by any aspect of human frailty. Clearly, the prospect of starting over caused him no concern.

But then, why should it? His skill as a doctor would assure that he was welcome wherever he chose to go. Even his republican tendencies would be forgiven in light of his imprisonment and exile. Moreover, he spoke English fluently, as she herself did. No, Paul would have no difficulty settling in.

While she—? Dominique closed her eyes for a moment, struggling against the emotions that threatened to overwhelm her. She had to be strong and sensible, if only for the sake of the children.

It would not do to let herself think too much about this man with whom she had battled and argued. She had leveled the most terrible accusations against him, had called him traitor and spy. Always her instinct was to attack him, to drive a wedge between them.

Why?

Once she had loved him—it had been a child's dream, nothing more. She would be a fool to think anything else.

Once she had found passion in his arms—tremulous, uncompleted, but still tantalizing. It was a memory to lock away and try to forget.

Cool salt spray struck the wooden railing. Dominique barely noticed it. She held herself tightly coiled within, struggling against thought, hope, desire. Any of those could shatter her. She had to hold on—be strong, be sensible. Life allowed for no other alternative.

A gull cried overhead. She looked up and her gaze was

caught by a wall of white cliffs rising on the distant horizon. The sun shimmered over it, a fairy haze beckoning, inviting.

Behind the wall—strong, impregnable, proud—lay England, the fortress that stood firm against the howling wind of madness. The sanctuary of safety and freedom. The place she must learn to call home.

Her glance fell again on Paul. He appeared unmoved by the sight, as closed off within himself as she was. They stood only inches apart, yet the distance between them might have been miles.

And that, more than anything else, turned the golden, glittering day to ashes.

Chapter
11

The Wayfarers' Inn was on a small back street not far from Dover's docks, yet well removed from the chaos that reigned there.

No, Dominique thought wearily, it was not chaos. There was order to the rapid comings and goings of people over the broad wooden docks. It was just that she had been so long removed from ordinary human activity that it struck her as bewildering.

At least the inn was quiet and clean. Paul had told her that he remembered it from his student days in London. Part of his medical education had been gleaned at the Surgeons College there. He had traveled back and forth frequently, staying at the inn along the way, and was well known by its proprietors—sufficiently so for them not to appear overly surprised when he arrived with a bedraggled young woman and two children in tow.

"There now, Doctor," a round, apple-cheeked woman

said, "yer a sight fer sore eyes, aren't yer now? 'Ow long 'as it been? Three or four years?"

"Longer than that, Mrs. Mullworth," he said with a smile. "I trust you've all kept well?"

"Aye, sir, though it's glad I am if the same can be said for you." She cocked her head in the general direction of the Channel over which they had just crossed. "Bad doings they are. Why, a body's not about listening to a bit of dockside gossip fer fear of hearing what's happened next."

Her assertion to the contrary, Mrs. Mullworth's avid gaze suggested that she was in fact eager for more information. She scanned Dominique closely, taking in the well-made but worn gown, the pale but perfectly formed face, and the soft, slender hands.

"French, is she?" she murmured as though Dominique could neither hear nor speak for herself.

Paul did not answer directly. He merely took Dominique by the arm and gestured to the children to follow. "We will require three rooms, Mrs. Mullworth. I trust that won't be a problem. Also, we could all benefit from some of your excellent cooking. In particular, I remember the cottage pie. Would there be any chance of some this evening?"

Caught between her avid desire to know more and her pride at being so complimented, Mrs. Mullworth dithered, but only briefly.

Vanity and the instinctive practicality of the innkeeper won out. Without further ado, she showed them upstairs and promised that dinner would be ready shortly.

Nicole and David were eager to explore their new surroundings. In their case, there was the added fact that they had been confined for so long. They were dissuaded only when Paul pointed out that it was almost dark.

"Dover is like almost every other port," he said, "not the place to be roaming around after sundown. Besides, by tomorrow we will be en route to London, where there will be more than enough for you to see."

Placated by that, they agreed to remain where they were and get ready for dinner. Paul had the first room near the top of the stairs. Since it was too small to accommodate more than a single bed and a chest, David had a room of his own immediately next door. Dominique and Nicole were at the end of the corridor in the largest room.

Barely had they set foot inside than a servant girl arrived with a pail of hot water for their washing. She glanced at them with the same eagerness Mrs. Mullworth had shown, but did not presume to question them.

"So, this is England," Nicole murmured as she glanced around the sparsely furnished room. She gave a Gallic shrug of her slim shoulders. "I suppose we shall get used to it."

"Don't resign yourself so quickly," Dominique said with a soft laugh. She removed her cloak and hung it on a peg beside the door. The servant girl had also lit the fire for them and already it was giving off welcome heat.

Outside, night was falling and a chill wind blew off the sea, but inside was comfort and coziness.

"Even this is an improvement over what we have known recently," Dominique said as she poured water from a ewer into a basin and began to wash her face and hands. "But once we get to London, I think you will be surprised by the comforts."

In fact, she had no real idea of what to expect once they reached the capital. She spoke to reassure her sister, who, despite her brave attempts, could not help looking tired and afraid.

She rattled on, conjuring up everything good she had ever heard about London, describing the great houses and parks, the balls and fetes, the promenades and theaters— all the things a young girl would find fascinating.

And she was not disappointed. Nicole's small face lost its pinched look and became far more relaxed. She even laughed with eagerness when Dominique told of the pleasure garden at Vaux Hall, with its nightly display of fireworks.

"Shall we go there?" she asked as she took her turn at the basin. "And to the shops in Mayfair and St. James, to Hyde Park and Covent Garden? I want to see all of it, every bit. It's like being reborn, Dominique—like getting a wonderful second chance, when all this time I thought that we would never—"

She broke off, abruptly aware of what she was saying. Grief and guilt shone on her face, where a moment before there had been happiness.

"Oh, Dominique," she murmured, "how can I be like this when Their Majesties are still trapped? All through the journey I kept thinking how much the dauphin and Maria Theresa would have enjoyed the adventure. And now, here I am, thinking of nothing but myself."

Dominique put her arms around the child. She stroked her hair softly. "It's all right, sweetheart. We've all got our feelings mixed up. One moment I'm so enormously relieved that I can hardly stand it, and the next I'm feeling so guilty that I think I'm about to cry."

"You, too, then," Nicole said softly. "David's the same, as well. We can't seem to know whether to be glad or sorry."

"I expect we'll be both for a good long time, darling. But what you must remember is that there was nothing else we could do. There comes a point when we simply have to accept our own limitations and learn to live with them.''

"Will they forgive us then?" Nicole whispered. ''The king and queen, little Louis and Maria Theresa—will they understand why we went?''

"Oh, yes, darling. They understand, I'm sure.'' Dominique drew a long breath, her eyes shut tight against the tears that threatened to fall at last. ''You see, they love us, all of them, even as we love them. And when you love someone, you want what is best for that person. Sometimes it means letting go when you most want to cling. But we still keep our memories and there's comfort in them.''

She took a step back, gazing down at Nicole tenderly. "Remember all the good times, sweetheart. Concentrate on them and accept that it was fate that drew you here.''

Slowly, the little girl nodded. She looked up at her sister with complete trust and love. Softly, she said, ''I'm so glad you're here, Dominique. You make everything so much better.''

They hugged again quickly before each remembered the passing time and hurriedly returned to the task of making themselves presentable for dinner.

And what a dinner it was. Rising to the occasion, Mrs. Mullworth had outdone herself. Without needing the situation clarified for her, she had decided that her humble roof sheltered French nobility who were about to spend their first night on British soil. As she was their hostess, so she was her country's ambassador of sorts, and it was up to her to welcome them properly. She proceeded to do so with such gusto that Dominique was left frankly stunned.

''Madame Renée's stew was marvelous,'' she said as

she gazed at the array of dishes set out on the table before them, "but I never quite imagined anything like this."

"Merely simple English fare," Paul said with a laugh that made mock of his words. He, too, was impressed by Mrs. Mullworth's endeavors and silently thanked the woman for her kindness.

The children simply stared as though they were waifs with their noses pressed up against a shop window until Paul laid a hand on each of their shoulders and pressed them gently forward.

What followed was pleasure, pure and simple—a celebration of life in its most innocent and eternal form. They ate and drank and talked and laughed within a circle of light from which all darkness was forbidden.

All the good things of the earth were theirs—sweet, fragrant oranges from the Mediterranean, where summer lingered; hearty kidney stew swimming with butter; crisp, freshly baked rolls; succulent lamb chops; all followed by a flummery pudding that left the children rolling their eyes.

For Nicole and David, there was also sweet milk, while Dominique and Paul shared a bottle of more than passable Bordeaux, clearly the fruit of smugglers who ran the blockade with shameless regularity.

When the last of the crumbs was gone, they sat back in their chairs replete. Mrs. Mullworth, for all her curiosity, was roundly praised. Only on the crest of a second thought did Nicole voice any doubts.

"Are all the meals in England like this?" she asked. "If so, we shall very soon not fit into our clothes."

Paul laughed and assured her that while they would undoubtedly find themselves surrounded by a host of temptations, they could also presumably exercise sufficient self-control to withstand them.

Both children were clearly pleased by his trust. When a short time later Dominique tried to shoo them up to bed, they resisted, even though they were drooping in their seats.

"Can't we stay just a little longer?" David asked, his large hazel eyes round with fatigue but his spirit unflagging.

"Don't worry," Paul said gently, "I'll be with you all the way to London. But now, it's time for you to get some rest."

Whereas the boy had been predisposed to argue with his sister, he obeyed Paul unquestioningly. Dominique was about to follow them when he delayed her with a light touch. "They're perfectly safe here. If you don't mind, I'd like to talk with you for a few minutes alone."

Far from minding, the prospect delighted her, even as it filled her with trepidation. As she took her seat at the table, after cautioning Nicole and David to go straight to their rooms and to bed, she warned herself not to read too much into Paul's sudden desire for her company. It seemed almost at once that she was right.

"There are a few practical matters," he said quietly after he had refilled their wineglasses.

"Yes, of course," she murmured, keeping her eyes carefully averted. The events of the last few days had left her sadly without her usual defenses.

She felt achingly fragile and vulnerable. Pride as well as simple self-preservation demanded that she do everything possible to keep him from discovering that.

"We have no way of knowing," Paul went on quietly, "exactly what your reception in London will be. Not," he added quickly when she began to interrupt, "that I doubt what you have told me about your grandmother. But her ladyship may not be immediately available, or there might be other factors that could interfere with your reunion.''

"Such as?" Dominique asked.

"Some other member of your family who does not look upon new dependents with too great cheer.''

Her response was a smile so filled with tenderness that it fairly took his breath away. "Ah, but you do not know our *grandmere*. She is an extraordinary person. I cannot imagine anyone in the family daring to deny her whatever she might wish.''

"A tyrant?" Paul asked, returning her smile.

"Oh, no, on the contrary. Say rather a loving despot. At any rate, I really think that once we find *grandmere*, everything will be all right.''

Paul should have been relieved to hear that, but instead, he felt an odd twinge of regret. He did not altogether despise the notion of Dominique being dependent on him. On the contrary, he was shocked to discover how much he welcomed it.

"What I am trying to say," he went on, "is that I have ample funds for all of us. There is no reason for you to experience any lack. For instance, I thought that before we started for London, we would see to new clothing for you and the children. That way, you will arrive there in more fitting condition, rather than . . .''

"Looking like something the tide tossed up?" Dominique answered coolly.

"I didn't mean . . .''

"Don't equivocate. I know perfectly well how we look. Do you imagine I've liked it for one moment? Don't you think I wanted better for Nicole and David? They are so young and full of life. When I think what might have happened to them—"

It was too much. All the fear and anguish of the past months—indeed, years—abruptly caught up with her there in the supping room of Mrs. Mullworth's inn. To her horror, great, hot tears began pouring down her cheeks. She choked on a sob and tried to rise. But before she could do so, strong arms were around her. She was lowered once again onto the bench, only this time she was not alone. Paul cradled her to him, holding her head, with its tumult of ebony curls, to his broad chest.

Huskily, he murmured, "It's all right, sweetheart. There's no shame in crying. I've done it myself a time or two."

"Y-you . . . ?" she asked shakily as she looked up at him. He appeared so indomitable in the warm glow from the fire, like a statue cast of bronze, the masterwork of a genius sculptor seeking to personify all that was good and true in man.

"Oh, yes," he said. "I've wept over lost patients, lives thrown away, my own stupidity, and the futility of trying to change large chunks of the world. What I've discovered is that it's possible to make only a small difference, and that only through dint of great effort, but in the end, what counts is simply having tried."

"I wanted to try," she said, the tears still flowing, soaking the broadcloth of his jacket, working their way beneath the crisp linen of his shirt to touch his warm skin.

"I thought I could help simply by staying where I was, by refusing to accept what was happening. I thought I could make things be the way they ought to be. But it isn't possible."

"Nay, love, if wishes were beggars, and all that . . ."

Love. The word touched her softly, penetrating the fog of her grief like a faint ray of light beckoning her onward.

Love? She looked up at him, acutely aware in that instant of all he had been to her and was—friend, enemy, rescuer.

He was the person she had idolized when, as a child, she had known little of the world. Then she had made him something more than human in her mind, and in the process, denied what he truly was—a man.

But her heart had always known the truth. He was the other half of herself, once lost, now found—the completion and fulfillment of all her most dearly nurtured hopes and dreams. He was before her—strong, whole, alive, breathtakingly real, and so completely male that the woman in her could not help but respond.

Slowly, she raised her head. Slowly, her lips parted. A soft sound escaped her. He was scant inches away. She could see the day's growth of beard darkening his lean cheeks, hear the rapid rise and fall of his breath, smell the tang of wool and linen, leather and salt air, mingling with the wine he had drunk.

Taste . . .

She moved slightly, enough. Her mouth touched his. Shyness was beyond her. She was enveloped in the need for him, caught up in emotions too primal to be denied, borne on a wave of joy and carried upward, higher and higher, without restraint. He tasted of sunlight and grapes, of summer rain and autumn harvest, of the earth and her infinity of promise. Her lips parted as she pressed closer. Her hands tangled in the thick golden pelt of his hair and drew his head down.

Shadows born of fire danced on the rough-hewn walls. The image of a man and a woman entwined, drawn to each other by forces that were old when the world was spun, flickered around them as they clung together. Nothing mattered except each other.

Suddenly a shutter banged and abruptly, remembrance flooded back.

Paul raised his head. Through hooded eyes heavy with passion he gazed down at the small, vibrant woman in his arms. She was perfect in every sense—beautiful, sensual, responsive, a dream brought to enthralling life. Yet she was also caught in the midst of emotional turmoil. It would be so easy for her to act on impulse, only to bitterly regret the action later.

He could not bear that. The new accord that had existed between them since she had admitted the necessity of escape was infinitely precious to him.

Not for anything could he bear to return to the enmity that had been present before—not even to assuage the rampant hunger of his body, which threatened to devour all reason and honor.

Before that could happen, his hands closed with gentle firmness on her shoulders. Putting her from him was an act so difficult that its accomplishment astounded him. For a long moment, he stared at her. Finally, he said shakily, "Go to bed, Dominique."

A soft sound of protest broke from her. Instinctively, she tried to press closer to him, but he pushed her away even more firmly and stood up. With his back to her, he said desperately, "You're behaving like a child. Go to bed before I do something we'll both regret."

In her heightened emotional state, his words stung like the lash of a whip. She moaned faintly and jumped up. Mortification burned her cheeks as she clutched her skirts and ran from the room.

Paul waited until her footsteps had faded completely away before he turned back. His gaze fastened on the table and the remains of the feast they had shared. Like it, he felt spent and torn apart.

An angry curse rose to his lips. He quenched it with a long, hard draught of the wine but found no sweetness there—only the bitter remains of what might have been.

Chapter
12

In the night, the tide turned. It came lapping at the wooden staves along the row of piers, frothing beneath the docks, whispering against the shingle beaches. Drawn by the pale December moon, it rode high, silver-etched, glittering.

While the tide rose, Dover slumbered. Watchmen making their rounds called off the hours, their voices falsely loud in the darkness, as though they needed to reassure themselves of their own valor. Here and there a rat skittered between barrels, but otherwise, the streets were empty. The last drunken navvy had found his bed, the last hard-working doxy had done the same. Save for the watchmen, no one with any but the devil's own business was about.

Wrapped in night, a figure moved. The shape was indistinct, blurred by the black cloak in which it was clothed, but the walk was that of a man, cautious but sure-footed, purposeful in his direction.

He paused beside a warehouse wall and raised his head,

sniffing at the air even as the rats did. His face was long and narrow, the eyes hard like flint and his mouth so narrow as to seem almost lipless. Like the rat, he had a sharp, agile nose that flared as he caught the scent of a nearby garbage heap. Hinges creaked as a sign blew in the wind. Bathed in cool moonlight, the sign of a wayfarer caught the man's eye. His smile bared small, yellow teeth. Moving swiftly, he crossed the cobblestone road and hid himself within the shadows of the door. There he remained motionless, hardly breathing, listening until he was certain that no one remained awake within.

Pale, white hands emerged from beneath the cloak. A sharp, black pick gleamed. It was the work of moments to open the lock and slip inside.

The entry hall of the Wayfarers' Inn was deserted. Mrs. Mullworth and her able husband had long since retired. The scullery maids were asleep in their narrow box beds behind the kitchen. The stable hand slumbered outside in the barn. Even the cat who occupied the premises was not on hand, having gone visiting earlier in the evening.

The dark, elusive shape moved up the steps so lightly that no tread creaked. He paused at the top of the stairs and glanced around. A corridor ran the length of the inn. Two rooms gave off to the right, three to the left. He checked those on the right first, only to find both empty. A fine sheen of sweat gleamed on his pale skin as he moved to the other side of the hallway. His hand on the third door shook slightly. He eased it open and peered inside. Immediately, his confidence returned.

He had been afraid for a moment that his information might have been incorrect, that the dock rat who had provided it might have lied, and returning to France without accomplishing his mission was unthinkable. He would suffer any fate rather than have to face Robespierre with news of failure.

But he would not fail. He was certain of that now. The curtains in the room had been left slightly apart. Through them light fell on the figure on the bed.

The man lay on his side, facing the door. There was no mistaking the gleaming helmet of golden hair or the aristocratic features that had been so well described.

The assassin reached once more beneath his cloak. The knife handle was cool, familiar, stimulating. He had used it many times before, always successfully. Now he was about to do so again.

Long ago he had learned the art of moving soundlessly. Balanced on the balls of his feet, he inched forward. The man on the bed did not move. His breathing remained deep and regular. The assassin's gaze fell on an empty wine bottle lying on the floor. He smiled again. Robespierre's instructions had been precise: kill them all. He had screamed the words, fists pounding on his desk, eyes wide and glittering with rage.

Kill them all. No one dared to escape his justice and make a fool of him to boot. His power rested on the illusion of invincibility. Let it once be shattered and the harm could be incalculable. He had said nothing about how it was to be done, but the assassin knew it would have to be fast. Too bad. He would have enjoyed toying with them, especially the woman.

Still, he would be well paid, and perhaps not only in money. If he pleased Robespierre well enough, he might be given access to some of the hapless souls who still lingered in the Paris prisons, awaiting whatever fate the masters of the state chose to give them.

A blood-red flush suffused his pale skin. He grasped the knife more tightly and moved closer to the bed. His intent was to slit Paul's throat, both to prevent him from crying out and to assure that he would die in a properly bloody and memorable fashion.

In the morning, when the four bodies were found, word would spread through Dover like fire cast on bone-dry tinder. In its wake would come terror. Men who might have been predisposed to help refugees would instead look over their shoulders with no thought but for their own safety.

The news would have the same effect in London. Robespierre's name would be whispered with hatred, certainly, but also with awe born of fear.

All that was needed was a single slash, downward across the carotid artery, through the cartilage surrounding the larynx and windpipe, and up the other side—the work of a moment. The assassin licked his lips. He bent forward, tensed and ready, his arm raised.

Never to fall. Without sound or warning, Paul came at him. The killer slammed backward, a scream trapped in his throat, flailing wildly. The lion had sprung, silent, merciless. Pain smashed into him, driving him into a well of darkness.

Paul straightened slowly. He stared down at the unconscious man with the regard generally reserved for a piece of offal encountered on the street.

Robespierre. Not for a moment did he doubt whose will guided this ferretlike being or the razor-sharp knife that lay glittering on the floor, inches away from his hand. Or what his fate would have been had not he awakened in time.

He stooped to pick the knife up and a groan escaped

him. Only then did he realize that in his brief but frantic attempts to break free, the assailant had wounded him.

The cut across his upper left arm was nasty, but not serious. Absently, he noted that had the blow been even slightly more accurate, a vein would have been cut. With his teeth, he ripped off a length of shirt and was in the process of tying it around the wound when Dominique ran into the room.

Her green-gold eyes were huge against her white face. She had let her hair down in a single braid that flowed over one shoulder. Loose tendrils curled around her forehead.

She wore the nightgown Madame Renée had insisted she take with her. It was many times too large, with the result that she looked almost like a child.

Almost, but not quite. Beneath the thin cotton, the outline of her breasts was clearly visible. He could see the dark crests of her nipples pressing against the fragile cloth. His body tautened as his gaze swept lower, over the slender curve of her waist and hips to the shadowed place between her thighs.

"Paul!" She gasped as her eyes flew to the man lying at his feet. "Who? My God, what has happened?"

"Nothing," he said quickly as he went to her. In one swift motion he seized his cloak off the wall peg and draped it over her. Dominique barely noticed. She looked from the man to the wound on his arm and drew her own conclusions.

"He attacked you."

"And got his head bashed in for his trouble. Now, go back to your room and stay there. I'll take care of this."

She ignored him as thoroughly as if he had never spoken. "Stay here. I'm going downstairs to find the Mullworths."

"There's no need for that," he began, reaching out to stop her. But already she was gone, running lightly on bare feet.

He would have followed, but a wave of dizziness swept over him, making him realize that his wound was more serious than he had wanted to admit. He sat down abruptly, fighting to remain conscious. By the time Dominique returned scant minutes later, Paul was reasonably sure that he was back in control of himself. He had finished tying the bandage and was gratified to see that the flow of blood was already lessening.

"I've never 'eard o' such a thing," Mrs. Mullworth said as she bustled into the room. She was wrapped in a thick robe, her nightcap askew. She looked thoroughly put out at having been awakened at such an hour, until she saw the man lying on the floor. Than she looked horrified.

"This is a respectable place," she squeaked, taking a quick step back. Her hapless husband had the luck to be in her way. She pushed him forward angrily as she glared at Paul.

Forgetting herself, she demanded, "What's that rat's arse doing in my inn?"

"Now, now, dear," her husband murmured as he surveyed the unconscious man tremulously. Mr. Mullworth was a small man, slightly built and clearly overshadowed by his far more assertive wife. But he was not without courage, as he promptly demonstrated.

"No point upsetting yourself, sweetling," he went on. "I'm sure there's a simple enough explanation for this."

"Of course there is," his wife hissed. "It's what comes of taking Frenchies in."

At Paul's quick scowl, she added more diplomatically, "It's not ye I mean, Doctor. We all know yer as Irish as yer anything else, an' besides, we've always been beholden to ye for treating Mac here when he had the ague. But the others . . .'' Her gaze spanned Dominique, then drew all their attention to the door, where two small forms huddled.

"Nicole, David," Dominique exclaimed, "what are you doing here?" Hastily, she put herself between them and the unconscious man, hoping they had not already seen too much.

Her hope was in vain. They craned their necks to see around her, appearing stunned but thrilled, as only children can.

"We heard noises," Nicole explained, "and came to see what was wrong. Did he break in? Oh, Monsieur Delamare, you're hurt!"

"It's nothing," Paul assured her gently, "merely a misunderstanding. Mr. Mullworth, if you would be so good as to assist me, we can get this fellow downstairs and turn him over to the watch."

"Glad to," the innkeeper said gallantly, "but don't trouble yourself. I'll get the stable boy to give me a hand. Your arm needs tending to."

"I asked for hot water," Dominique said.

"And ye'll get it," Mrs. Mullworth shot back. She sensed events slipping beyond her control and bristled at the notion. "But that's all ye'll get. I'm sorry, Doctor, but I want the lot of you out of here by morning. This is a respectable place. We can't afford this sort of thing. Why, what would people say if—"

"That's enough, dear," her husband said so firmly that she stared at him in astonishment. Before she could recover herself, he took her arm and led her swiftly from the room. Over his shoulder, he said, "Pay no mind to my wife.

Not herself, that's all. I'll be back in a jiff with the boy. The water won't be much longer.''

Paul had a bemused look on his face as he sat down again on the edge of the bed. "That's a surprise."

"What is?" David asked.

"The sudden emergence of Mr. Mullworth." At the boy's puzzled look, he said, "Never mind. Now that you've seen there's nothing to be worried about, the two of you should be back in bed."

"That's right," Dominique said firmly. "Off with you both. We've a long day tomorrow and you both need your sleep."

"Aren't you coming?" Nicole asked.

"After I've seen to Paul's injury. He can't do it all himself, you know, even though he's a doctor." She shooed them toward the door.

The children stubbornly hung back. "Will you be very long?" David asked.

"No, I . . ." Seeing what was in her brother's mind, she touched his cheek gently. "I'll tell you what, why don't you and Nicole lie down in our room? You can keep each other company till I get back."

That cheered them both up and they went without further argument. Barely had they disappeared down the hallway than Mr. Mullworth was back on the scene.

With him came the stable boy, a husky lad with broad shoulders and a bemused stare. Under Mr. Mullworth's supervision, the lad half hoisted, half dragged the assailant out of the room.

"I've sent for the watch," Mr. Mullworth said self-importantly. "They'll take this fellow off our hands, though undoubtedly they'll want a word or two with you tomorrow."

Paul assured him that he would be available. His shoulder was beginning to throb. He was relieved when a serving girl arrived with the hot water as Mr. Mullworth took his leave. The girl followed quickly, though not without a wide, admiring smile for Paul.

"This will sting," Dominique said with a hint of asperity. She undid the improvised bandage and placed a clean, hot cloth against the wound. Paul flinched but made no sound.

The circumstances of her life had required her to become adept at treating all manner of injuries, but she was nonetheless grateful for his instructions. When the wound had been thoroughly washed, he guided her to the small stockpile of medical supplies he had brought with him. Dominique's fingers trembled slightly as she applied a soothing salve, then covered it with a linen bandage.

By the time she finished, her knees felt weak. She sat down suddenly and clasped her hands together to keep them from trembling.

All the while she had been doing what needed to be done, she had managed to hold her fear at bay. But now it surged back, relentless and demanding, battering at the walls of her frail defenses and swiftly overcoming them. With them crumbled caution, reason, and even the memory of Paul's earlier rejection that had sent her weeping into a dream-tossed sleep. It might never have happened, for all the significance it seemed to have now. Nothing mattered except that Paul was still alive, despite having brushed so perilously close to death.

Rage rose in her—raw, primitive fury at the fates that had already robbed her of so much and would attempt to take yet more. Instinctively, she sought to defeat them in the most absolute way possible.

Paul was startled when she stood up again. He had been searching within himself, trying to find the strength to tell her once more to return to her room. That sort of fortitude seemed suddenly in dangerously short supply.

She stood and the cloak fell, leaving her standing clad only in moonlight and the thin nightgown. She was ebony and alabaster, emerald eyes and lips like wine.

He had drunk heavily to find sleep, and felt as though his senses were still befuddled, yet his body was achingly, perilously alert.

"Go," he rasped.

Holding his eyes with hers, she shook her head. Slowly, deliberately, she began to unweave the long, silken braid, strand by strand, until her hair lay loose and free around her shoulders.

The scent of it filled his breath. He closed his eyes and saw again the lilac-strewn fields of Montfort, the girl child racing through them, felt his own swift joy and the tender strength of all-encompassing love.

"*Dominique*—"

She laid a cool, gentle finger against his lips. "Hush, Paul. You've done everything you could; no one can blame you for anything."

It was absolution, sweet as the balm with which she had soothed his wound. It came to him at that instant that she knew him almost too well. Without having to be told, she understood that he was a man who felt his responsibilities keenly.

To him, honor and decency were all. He could not lightly put the burden of them down. Only she could lift their weight from his shoulders, as she had just done.

"I won't leave," she murmured as her hand went to the neck of her gown. Her mouth—soft and ripe as summer fruit—lifted at the corners. "Unless you want another scene, you will simply have to admit defeat."

"At what cost?" he murmured, lost in the miracle of her eyes, as in a sun-dappled forest virgin to any man.

"Your illusions? The ones that tell you I'm a child to be protected. The same ones that insist you mustn't give in to yourself, that you must always be strong, noble, exemplary."

A bubble of amusement rose within him. "You make me sound like an unbearable prude."

"Oh, no," she said. "At least, I don't think you are. Shall we see?"

"It seems inevitable," Paul murmured. Her hand moved and the gown slipped away, baring first the smooth perfection of her shoulders, then the full lushness of her breasts, and the tiny indentation of her waist. For a moment, it rested on the curve of her hips, before she pushed it away and stepped out unhesitantly to stand before him proudly naked, unashamed, magnificent.

"Like Aphrodite," he murmured, "rising from the waves."

She smiled sweetly, surely—a smile as old as time. "No goddess—only a woman."

His hands settled lightly on her hips, the callused touch almost reverent against her velvet smoothness. "Not quite," he murmured, drawing her closer. His lips brushed her belly and he felt her tremble. "But soon . . . very soon."

"Now," whispered Dominique. Only his arms held her upright as her head fell back, the silken hair brushing her rounded buttocks. A tremor ran through her, as though the earth itself quivered.

She cried out softly as he rose, slowly, tantalizingly,

his mouth trailing fire along her abdomen, up to the curve of her breasts, to the crests that throbbed and ached for his touch.

Her fingers tangled in his amber hair. The rough wool of the breeches he had slept in—instinctively resisting the urge to relax too completely—rubbed tantalizingly against her silken skin. She was engulfed in the heady male scent of him. A wild thrumming surged through her veins. On the brink of the unknown, she felt not fear but exultation.

Despite his raging desire, Paul went very slowly. His only other alternative was to lower her at once onto the soft bed and thrust between her silken thighs until he found his release. That was unthinkable; he would not treat any woman in such a way, much less a virgin whom he loved.

The sweet, shy girl child of that long-ago summer afternoon was transformed into a tantalizing nymph trembling in his arms, on the brink of full awakening. He was a man who had seen enough of life and death to know how infinitely precious such a moment could be. It was meant to be savored, then safely stored away against the world's vicissitudes.

Groaning, he lifted her, holding her high for a moment against his chest. Her head was languorously bent, the midnight sheen of her hair obscuring her features, but he could feel the rapid-fire beat of her heart and was reassured that her desire was as intense as his own, or nearly so. He was confident that before very long, any discrepancy would be more than rectified.

Gently, he laid her on the bed, drinking in the sight of her lying like ebony velvet and purest alabaster. Beneath the thick shading of her lashes, emerald eyes gleamed with a light as old as time. Her lips were parted slightly. He could see the tip of her tongue as she caught it between her teeth.

"Don't," he murmured almost harshly as he came down beside her. When she looked at him uncomprehendingly, he said, "I don't want you to feel the slightest hurt—not this night, not with me."

Her gaze widened. Hesitantly, she murmured, "Is that possible?"

His smile was utterly male, yet masterfully reassuring. "Oh, yes, I should think so. But," he added as his fingers stroked lightly up her arm, "shall we find out?"

At his touch, Dominique started. A ripple of almost unbearable pleasure ran through her. She gasped softly at the same instant that Paul's mouth claimed hers.

He kissed her with devastating thoroughness, seemingly making no concessions to her innocence. His tongue plunged deeply, evoking another and far more intimate possession about to come.

Far from being shocked, Dominique's response was of unbridled sensuality. She met him teasing stroke for stroke, her fingers digging into his shoulders lest he have any thought of pulling away.

When he at last raised his head and gazed down at her, his breathing was labored and the gentleness she had seen in his eyes earlier was gone.

"Dominique," he rasped, "you undermine my greatest resolve."

The corners of her mouth lifted in unconscious provocation. "Perhaps this isn't the place for nobility, Paul."

He stared at her for a long moment before laughter abruptly broke from him. He felt suddenly much younger than his years, a love-struck boy with all of life before him and no heavy sense of responsibility or duty to hold him back. The difference in their experiences—the women he had known, the cynicism he occasionally felt—all faded away. Within the shelter of her arms, held close against her high, firm breasts, he knew the beginnings of rebirth.

Slowly, he stepped away. Without taking his eyes from her, he undid the buttons of his breeches and stepped from them. Naked he returned to her, reassured that what he saw in her gaze was admiration rather than fear.

"Oh, Paul," she whispered as she gathered him back to her, "you are so very beautiful."

In the tender fierceness of her look, the unabashed touch of her hands, the movement of her body beneath his, he felt as well as heard her thoughts. With a sense of barriers cracking wide, he realized that she meant exactly what she said. He was beautiful to her as a magnificent force of nature is beautiful, as beauty is to be welcomed, treasured, delighted in.

His thighs, corded with muscle, slipped between her own. Slowly, drawing out each moment, he touched her with his hands, his eyes, his mouth, in ways that wrung soft cries of pleasure that fell like balm upon his soul.

Not until he had brought her once, twice, three times to the edge of ecstasy and beyond did he at last lift himself above her. Her hair was a tangled glory spread out over the pillow. Her cheeks were flushed, her lips swollen. Deep within her eyes danced the pale moon. He turned for an instant and glimpsed the milk-white face of Earth's first mother hovering beyond the window. Then Dominique drew him back and there was nothing save the two of them lost in a dream of rapture.

Chapter
13

London, January 1793

Lady Amelia Haverston, duchess of Clarendon, tapped the marble-inlaid top of her dressing table idly. Before her was the same glazed and gilded mirror that had been reflecting her image for more than fifty years, recording the transition from young bride to aged matriarch. Hovering immediately to one side was Danvers, the maid who had served her for almost as long.

Dithering old fool, Danvers, Lady Amelia thought. *She should have been put out to pasture years ago*. Instead, her softhearted mistress had kept her on, even employing a younger maid to help her, and what did she get in return? Aggravation.

"I am not trying to be difficult, madame," Danvers said stiffly. "I merely feel it my duty to point out that the young lady is very unhappy."

"You exaggerate," Lady Amelia said. "She is simply

experiencing a perfectly natural and inevitable period of adjustment.''

"This morning she looked as though she had been crying.''

"A slight chill, nothing more. Enough to make the eyes and nose red. Undoubtedly, she will be fully recovered in a day or two.''

Lady Amelia lifted a gnarled, blue-veined hand to forestall any other comment. "This is quite enough chattering. I will wear my peach velvet today with the lace tucker and the smaller pearls. That should be adequate.''

Despite her age—Lady Amelia had turned seventy-three on her last birthday—she saw no reason to change the tastes that had directed her throughout a long and relatively contented life. Besides, the peach velvet flattered her complexion.

"Get on with it,'' she said smartly as she rose, supporting herself on a gold-handled cane. "I've no more time for twaddle.''

Danvers sniffed audibly but made no further argument. She trundled over to the clothespress and began removing the required garments. When the young undermaid—a mere chit of forty—tried to assist her, she brushed her off peremptorily.

Forty-five minutes later, Lady Amelia was dressed and powdered, and ready to face the day. In particular, she was ready for her granddaughter.

Very much the grande dame, she descended the curving marble staircase of the Haverston town house and marched smartly across the domed center hall.

Footmen bowed in her wake. A young housemaid dropped a curtsy. Lady Amelia ignored them all. She moved on, regal and oblivious, not unlike a great sailing ship refusing to take note of lesser craft.

An underbutler sprang to open a door for her. Once inside, she paused and glanced around. The small drawing room—so it was called in deference to the larger and more formal reception room on the other side of the hall—was Lady Amelia's personal favorite. She had decorated it herself shortly after becoming duchess of Clarendon, and though over the years the furnishings had been updated, they had not been substantially changed.

She had chosen yellow damask for the walls and a bright chintz pattern for the upholstered pieces. The colors blended well with the marquetry-worked tables and chairs scattered about.

Despite the season, crystal vases were filled with a profusion of blossoms brought directly from the Clarendon estate outside of London. The greenhouses there had always been a source of pride to her, not to mention a good investment, given the cost of fresh flowers in London in January.

Prudence, Lady Amelia thought. *Prudence and practicality.* They might as well be the watchwords of the Haverstons, who had survived longer and more ably as a family than almost any other noble lineage in Europe. That was no accident. They had backbone, as the young woman before her was proving yet again.

Shorn of any sign of tears, Dominique sat at a small, exquisitely made harpsichord, a creation of the late Florentine, Bartolomeo Cristofori, widely recognized as a master builder of stringed instruments. This particular harpsichord was one of the last he constructed. It had been purchased for Lady Amelia more than thirty years before.

Dominique's touch on the keys was light, almost reverent. Despite that, a discordant note sounded. She broke off and smiled apologetically. "I haven't played in so many years, I scarcely know how to begin again."

"It will come back to you," her grandmother said. She seated herself on a settee across from Dominique and continued to regard her steadily.

At least it could be fairly said that the pale, thin creature who had arrived at her door less than a month before now appeared considerably improved. Good food, warmth, and security had done much to banish—or at least mask—the haunted look.

Lady Amelia did not care to dwell on her own shock and sadness when she beheld the eldest child of her only daughter. Nor would she reveal to anyone the tears she had shed while berating herself for not having been more insistent about removing the young de Montforts from that cesspool of madness and brutality that France had become. It was enough that the girl was showing improvement.

"That's very pretty," Lady Amelia said, gesturing at the gown Dominique wore. It was fashioned of watered silk in a soft shade of mauve that complemented the gray-green hue of Dominique's eyes.

Her ebony hair gleamed from a crown of curls held in place by emerald and diamond clips. More jewels—appropriate to a young unmarried woman but nonetheless impressive—shone at her throat and wrists.

Silently, Lady Amelia made a note to compliment Dominique's maid, who had sole charge of dressing her, since Dominique herself took absolutely no interest in such matters.

"Thank you," she said absently, as though she wasn't quite sure what her grandmother was referring to. That did not, however, mean that she had forgotten her manners. Rising, she went to stand before the older woman and kissed her gently on the cheek. "You have been so very kind, *grandmere*."

"Nonsense," Lady Amelia said huskily. "I have merely done what is right. You are, after all, an heiress."

Dominique smiled ruefully. "I still can't get used to that."

"And I can't understand why your late father never explained it to you, but I suppose he thought you were too young and presumed there would always be time later."

Lady Amelia stared off into space for a moment as she added, "I've known so many people who did that, and invariably they died before they could complete half of what they intended. For myself, I prefer to leave as little as possible to chance."

"I would say you have managed that very effectively," Dominique murmured. At her grandmother's insistence, she had spent an illuminating if tedious day the week before with the family barrister.

To her astonishment, she had learned that her mother, an only child, had been the beneficiary of a substantial trust left to her by a devoted aunt. Upon her marriage to the marquis de Montfort, control of it had passed to him, but upon his demise it reverted to Lady Amelia to await Dominique's coming of age as her direct heir.

This had now occurred, with the result that the money was hers, at least until such time as she married and her husband took charge. While she remained unattached, she was in that rarest of positions for a female of her time— in possession of her own independent funds.

The Montfort estates might be irretrievably lost, but

Dominique would not suffer for it. Neither, for that matter, would Nicole or David.

"Where are the children?" Lady Amelia inquired. She saw the two younger de Montforts several times a day, merely to assure that everything was being done for them properly.

That she could have simply presumed that was the case, or sent a servant to check, didn't trouble her. They were lively children, exuberant and good-natured, despite everything they had been through. If anyone asked, she would say that it amused her to be with them.

Dominique was not fooled. She had been at first surprised, then intensely grateful for the love their grandmother showed them. She might be a crusty old lady with a tart tongue, but she had a bountiful heart.

"They are upstairs," she said, "with Mrs. Remington, having their lessons."

"Ah, yes," Lady Amelia said. Her mouth twitched. "I remember those. Dreadful things. I was always looking out the window, wondering when they would be done."

"Mrs. Remington seems to have a way of making them interesting. At least, the children appear to like her very much."

"Then you made a good choice," Lady Amelia said. It had been her inspiration almost immediately upon her grandchildren's arrival to involve Dominique in the selection of a governess for them. As she had hoped, the task had helped to take Dominique out of herself and concentrate her attention on the future.

"So long as she wasn't for me," the young woman said with a soft laugh. "I admit that my education has been catch as catch can, but I have no urge to return to the schoolroom."

"Actually, my only regret concerning your upbringing is that you have been exposed to things no young girl should encounter."

Lady Amelia paused. Her least desire was to do or say anything that would distress Dominique, but she also believed very firmly that it was best to bring matters out into the open rather than attempt to suppress them. Quietly, she asked, "What news from Paris today?"

Dominique's smile fled. For a moment, the haunted look was back in her eyes. Quietly, she said, "The trial continues but is expected to end soon."

Lady Amelia murmured something under her breath best not repeated. She went on, "I am at a loss to understand how it has come to this. That the rabble should dare to put a sovereign monarch on trial, to judge him like a common criminal, is simply inconceivable."

"I suppose that's because it couldn't happen here," Dominique said.

"There are a few harebrained hysterics who would disagree with you, but you are quite correct. Our system of government is far too advanced to allow for any such goings-on."

Which was not to say that nothing of the kind had ever happened in England. Lady Amelia was hardly ignorant of the fate of Charles I, who in the previous century had lost his head at the pleasure of Cromwell's rabble. She would not, however, mention that—especially not since she was certain that Dominique already knew all about it.

"Ah, well," the duchess said, "let us all be grateful that we are in England. The day is quite pleasant. What do you say to an outing?"

"If you wouldn't mind, I would really prefer to remain here."

"Nonsense. You can't stay cooped up all day; it isn't healthy. Now that your cough is gone, you must get out more."

Dominique sighed. Her grandmother spoke in a tone that brooked no further disagreement. She couldn't really claim to be surprised.

Lady Amelia was naturally impatient with her desire to remain within the sheltering walls of the Haverston town house. She wanted her out and about, meeting new people and beginning to lay the foundation of a new life for herself.

She had no way of knowing, or at least so Dominique presumed, that what kept her at home day after day was not any true disinclination to go out in society. Rather, she remained there in the stubborn but increasingly forlorn hope that Paul might decide to call.

She had not seen him in a fortnight, since shortly after their arrival in England. He had delivered her forthwith to her grandmother, remained on hand long enough to ascertain that all was well, and then taken his leave. Lady Amelia had graciously offered to put him up, but Paul had refused. He had friends at the Royal College of Physicians whom he was anxious to see.

And with whom he had presumably been ever since.

"Come along then," Lady Amelia said as she rose. "We shall go for a ride in the park and talk about Lady Saltonstall's soiree tonight."

Dominique winced. She had managed to completely forget about that event. Her grandmother had promised that it would be a small affair, but she somehow doubted that would be the case. Nothing she had seen in London so far appeared to be small.

Nonetheless, she had said that she would go and she

would stay with that with as much good grace as she could possibly muster.

"By all means," she said as she offered Lady Amelia her arm, "let us discuss it. You must tell me who will be there so that I will know what to say and not appear too thick."

As though she could, Lady Amelia thought. Her granddaughter had no idea of the sensation she would cause when she walked into Diana Saltonstall's drawing room that evening.

If she had lived longer at Versailles, she would have known. But the last three years of her life had been spent shut away from the world in an increasingly grim and treacherous environment.

Not that others would perceive it that way. They would see only the young woman who had been lady-in-waiting to Queen Marie Antoinette, an intimate of the French royal family, and now an exile who had escaped under the most romantic and difficult circumstances.

Those credentials alone would be sufficient to assure Dominique's social cachet. But when her beauty and wealth were added to them, they made a combination that was—as the French would say—*formidable*.

Paul Delamare had understood that. Lady Amelia smiled inwardly as she remembered her conversation with him the day after her grandchildren's arrival. He had been very formal, very correct, and very direct—up to a point.

To begin with, he had stated boldly that if there were any difficulty in Dominique and her brother and sister finding a home with the duchess, it would be no imposition for him to find shelter for them elsewhere.

Lady Amelia had assured him such was not the case. All the de Montforts were more than welcome. Indeed, should Paul entertain any notion of attempting to remove them, he would not enjoy the consequences.

He was grimly amused by that, but had swiftly moved on to other things.

If there was any shortage of funds, he would not hesitate to provide them, his only stipulation being that their source not be revealed.

Stiffly, Lady Amelia told him that this, too, was not required. Far from being in any need, Dominique was about to find herself an extremely wealthy young woman. Indeed, there were few wealthier ones in England.

That at least gave him pause. The hard, bronzed face revealed a hint of regret that told Lady Amelia volumes. It was quickly masked, but not before she guessed a great deal about the extent of his feelings for Dominique.

Were he to follow his heart, he would seek to tie her to him in every possible way, but he was sensible and honorable enough not to attempt it.

Or was he? There was something between those two that gave Lady Amelia pause. She had seen them together only very briefly, but she was still convinced that all was not as it should be.

She sensed an aura of yearning combined with guilt that disturbed her deeply. It all too easily recalled memories of her own youth and a certain Guy Fawkes Day when, amid the traditional bonfires and straw men, she had strayed rather far from the limits of propriety.

Fortunately, the good doctor seemed genuinely to care for Dominique and to want what was best for her. Which clearly meant marrying a man of her own class and outlook, and settling down in England to raise Lady Amelia's great-grandchildren.

No, Paul Delamare would not interfere in her plans for

Dominique. At least, Lady Amelia equivocated, she didn't think he would. Such uncertainty was not like her.

She stiffened her back, spoke sharply to the butler who held her cloak, and sailed regally down the front steps of the town house with Dominique in tow.

They rode through Hyde Park, past the high stone walls that surrounded it—a remnant of its prior incarnation as a private preserve—and along the wide, elegant road perversely called Rotten Row.

Or perhaps not so perversely. To it came all manner of ladies and gentlemen, and those wishing to be mistaken for such, to see and be seen, gossip and slander; in short, to indulge in one of the finest pastimes of civilization, promenading.

Dominique tried not to gawk. She really must remember that she was the daughter of a marquis, granddaughter of a duchess, and hardly a country miss to be easily impressed. Compared to the distantly remembered glory of Versailles, London was little more than a bagatelle. But the memory was fading and she was left with very little to buttress her assumed air of sophistication.

Lady Amelia chatted on happily, pointing out various individuals or not, depending on whether they were in good odor. The more gaily dressed women—the ones with two or three patches on their ivory faces and eyes rimmed with kohl—were pointedly ignored.

Several gentlemen favored with a signal of recognition drew up beside the duchess's barouche and attempted to engage Dominique in conversation. She was not precisely mute, but she was certain they went off with the impression of a young lady with little to say for herself.

Lady Amelia, however, was not displeased. She thought

Dominique struck precisely the right note of mystery and rectitude. The duchess sat back against the tufted leather upholstery and smiled to herself. The evening promised to be extremely interesting, indeed.

The entire family met at luncheon. David and Nicole regaled their grandmother and sister with tales of their morning. Mrs. Remington—a young woman in her mid-twenties with a plain but pleasant face and a sensible manner—laughed along with the rest of them.

Dominique had suggested her inclusion at informal family meals—an unexpected courtesy that had caused the young governess to take a thoughtful look at her charges' elder sister.

Rumors had been flying about her ever since her arrival. Tonight a few would be put to rest, but undoubtedly others would immediately sprout in their place. Though she sometimes regretted her own relatively uneventful life, Mrs. Remington decided she would not wish to change places with Dominique—not when it meant bearing the concentrated scrutiny of a society that seemed required to feed regularly on shredded reputations.

At her grandmother's urgings, Dominique spent a quiet afternoon. She endeavored to find solace in a book, but found her thoughts wandering directly back to Paul. A warm flush suffused her cheeks as she remembered what had passed between them.

Surely no woman had ever had a more tender or passionate awakening. She could still feel the touch of his hands and mouth all along the length of her body. Despite his own raging need, he had restrained himself to bring her to a peak of exquisite desire before at last piercing the final barrier between them.

All the girlish whispers she had heard about the pain of

that were proved naught, at least in her case. A moment's slight discomfort and she was his, or he was hers. The distinction did not seem to matter.

How glorious it had been! So beyond any part of ordinary life, so magnificently right that it seemed as though the world itself must be changed by what they did.

Sadly, that was not the case. Morning brought reality, and regrets—at least on Paul's part. She could not find it in herself—even weeks later—to regret an instant of it, but he clearly had. He had been rigidly proper, aloof, and restrained throughout the remainder of their journey to London.

Only once had he unbent slightly to tell her where he would be staying should she have any need of him. It had taken her a moment to understand precisely why she might require his presence.

He could not have made himself clearer—should the night they had shared bear fruit, he would not attempt to shirk his responsibility. Otherwise, he thought it best for them both to get on with their own separate lives.

So be it. If pride alone had not been enough to keep her from pleading with him, generations of imbued female instinct would have assured that she did not. He could go his own way all he wished; she would never seek to constrain him.

Shortly after tea, she adjourned to her room, where she suffered herself to be bathed and dressed by the redoubtable Margaret, lady's maid *extraordinaire*.

"Just so, miss," Margaret murmured as she assisted Dominique to rise from the dressing table, where she had applied the final touches to her coiffure.

Because Lady Saltonstall's soiree was regarded as an informal get-together, Dominique's hair had been left unpowdered. The ebony tresses were brushed to silken perfection, then swept up in a cascade of curls that fell halfway down her back.

The style, with its Grecian overtones, perfectly suited the new mode of dress introduced since the Revolution. Much though the noble ladies of England despised the politics of the rebels, they adored the fashion that had resulted from them.

Gone were the heavy, hooped skirts and absurdly elaborate headdresses of only a few years ago. In their place were light and airy gowns made of gauzelike fabrics. The more propriety conscious wore sufficient layers of the tissue-thin silk and wool to cover their charms. The more daring wore only the absolute minimum, consisting of little other than a tantalizing veil through which the female form could be admired in all its glory.

Dominique's gown, naturally enough, was hardly among the most daring. Nonetheless, Margaret was well satisfied with it. Her young charge would be without a doubt among the most dazzlingly beautiful women present that evening. Moreover, everything about her spoke of her position and heritage.

No gentleman could mistake her for anything other than she was—a young woman deserving of nothing less than the best.

Margaret was slightly misty-eyed as she saw Dominique down the stairs and into the care of her grandmother. Lady Amelia had enlisted an old friend as their escort, Baron Richard Fitzstephen-Smythe. Sixty, silver-haired, a veteran of the unpleasantness in the Americas, he was both gracious and good-humored.

As he bent over Dominique's hand, he said, ''My dear,

I count it a great privilege to witness your debut. London society will never be quite the same.''

''Now, now, Dicky,'' Lady Amelia interjected, ''don't make the lass any more nervous than she already is. After all, this is just a little soiree.''

Dicky exchanged a speaking glance with the duchess before shrugging tolerantly. ''If you say so, my dear. Shall we be off?''

As she was assisted into the carriage, Dominique searched within herself for any sign of the nervousness her grandmother had mentioned. She could find none, which she knew was not a good sign.

By all rights she should be excited and apprehensive about the evening, exactly as Lady Amelia presumed her to be. Instead, she felt only pleasantly numb, as though nothing mattered very much.

She might only be nineteen years old and freshly out in the world, but she had all the sense needed to realize what a very dangerous illusion that could be. A great deal mattered, not in the least what she was going to do with the rest of her life.

Which was far too much to think of in her present state. Doing her best to think of nothing at all, she glided into Lady Saltonstall's drawing room.

Chapter
14

Exactly as Lady Amelia had predicted, there was a most satisfying hush at the moment of Dominique's entrance. It was followed almost at once by a tide of murmured comment which could, to the untutored ear, pass for normal conversation. Certainly, Dominique gave no indication that she understood herself to be the object of so much attention. She responded politely to Diana Saltonstall's greeting while either ignoring or failing to notice her hostess's razor-eyed scrutiny.

Lady Saltonstall—formerly one Mary Murphy of Limerick, small-time actress and sometime light skirt—had not climbed so improbably high in life without a remarkable talent for assessing potential. She took one look at Dominique—albeit a long one—and smiled.

"My dear," she said, "at last. We have all been so eager to meet Amelia's granddaughter, and of course so concerned about you. Do come in."

Dominique knew her words were insincere, although

the woman tried to appear otherwise. She did, after all, understand the power of influence. Dominique was young, beautiful, exotic, and wealthy. Whoever happened to introduce her to her future husband would be most kindly remembered by that gentleman.

Aware as she had been for the last week that Dominique would be in attendance that evening, her ladyship had taken care to invite several of London's most eminently eligible bachelors. None of them, however, could hold a candle to her supreme catch, William Charles Douglas, duke of Devonshire. Lady Saltonstall had not been absolutely certain that he would come, despite the lures she had tossed out in his direction. Not until he appeared on her doorstep approximately half an hour before Lady Amelia's arrival had she known for certain that the evening was going to be a singular success.

"Your Grace," she said smoothly, "may I have the pleasure of introducing Mademoiselle Dominique de Montfort? She has but lately arrived in England, and this evening is her first opportunity to broaden her acquaintances among us."

Indeed, Lady Saltonstall could have saved her breath for all but the bare minimum of courtesies. Certainly the duke heard nothing more, nor did Dominique. They merely stood in the center of Lady Saltonstall's chinoiserie drawing room, surrounded by the *glitterati* of London society, and gazed at each other.

Dominique saw a pleasant young man, a shade under six feet in height, well built, with broad shoulders and attractive features. He had deep-set gray eyes alive with intelligence and a mouth that smiled instinctively.

Without thought, she smiled back.

William blinked once, then again. He beheld a young

woman of surpassing loveliness, made all the more beautiful by unstudied charm. But he also saw, or felt, something more——a certain vulnerability, a fragileness, and the echo of pain that called to all his protective instincts.

His smile turned rueful, which caused Dominique to draw back slightly. "Is something wrong?" she asked.

"Oh, no," he assured her quickly. "I was only reminded of an incident when I was eight years old and shimmied up an oak tree to rescue an imprudent kitten. She clawed my arm deeply enough to still give me an occasional twinge."

"What happened to the kitten?"

"Oh, I kept her, of course. Wasn't her fault that she was scared. Turned out to be quite a good cat, in the long run. Liked to sit behind the books in the library and peer out at people. Gave them an awful jolt when they caught her at it."

Dominique laughed. She had no idea why they were talking this way, as though they were old friends picking up a conversation only recently left off. But she did know that she felt utterly at ease with William Charles Douglas, duke of Devonshire, and she was grateful for it.

"We had cats at Montfort," she said as he led her over to a settee, away from Lady Saltonstall and, for that matter, everyone else. "A vast clan of them that I imagine had been there for centuries. They were forever breaking into the dairy to steal cream."

At her wistful look, William said quietly, "It must be very hard to lose one's home. I haven't suffered it myself, but I can imagine how adrift one must feel."

Dominique's throat tightened. His simple, matter-of-fact sympathy undermined her defenses as nothing else could. Softly, she murmured, "It has been . . . very difficult."

"I'm sorry," William said, seeing her distress. "I shouldn't have said anything."

"No, I'm glad you did. Everyone else has evaded the issue, even *grandmere*."

"Lady Amelia? It's hard to imagine her being evasive about anything."

"I don't suppose she can be blamed. It's all so . . . awful."

In that single word was wrapped a multitude of meaning, none of which escaped William. Instinctively, he placed his hand over hers. He had no ulterior purpose other than to offer whatever comfort he could, but at the first touch of skin against skin, a jolt went through him.

His eyes widened slightly. At twenty-six, he was unusually sophisticated, which is not to say he was debauched. His intelligence and innate self-control made that an unappealing avenue in life.

Still, he understood full well the forces that could undo the most resolved men and women, and he realized that he was well and truly in the grip of them. The thought both dismayed and enthralled him.

Dominique gave no indication that she knew what he was feeling. She accepted his touch as she would that of a brother or a friend. Her innocence was as artless as her charm, and it enabled her all unknowingly to spin a web no other London miss had managed, the best of them having tried.

All in a moment's work, sitting on the settee in Lady Saltonstall's drawing room, His Grace, William Charles Douglas, duke of Devonshire and heir to sundry other titles and courtesies, not to mention a fortune rivaled only by the holdings of the throne itself, rescuer of kittens and despair of fond mamas, was smitten.

* * *

"I quite enjoyed it," Lady Amelia said the following morning. Already the household routine had been disrupted by Her Grace's unheard-of decision to breakfast downstairs.

Nothing less than the chance to indulge in supreme understatement could have drawn her from her boudoir at such an hour. Unfortunately, her audience was ill-equipped to appreciate the extent of her verbal restraint. Nicole and David had no idea of their sister's inordinate success.

Neither, for that matter, did Dominique, who merely believed she had passed an unexpectedly pleasant evening, due almost entirely to William's congenial company. He had not strayed from her side for so much as an instant, despite the efforts of various gentlemen to insinuate themselves in his place. As a declaration, it was as good as a printed announcement in the *Times*. Certainly, everyone else present took it as such. And today, in all the drawing rooms of Mayfair and St. James, the rest of society would do the same.

"Lovely morning," Lady Amelia murmured, staring absently out the window. Mrs. Remington suppressed a smile. It was, in fact, a perfectly murky and unappealing January day.

The leaden sky hung low over streets that appeared stripped of all life and color. A snowstorm threatened but had yet to materialize. London lay wrapped in gray, murmured over by an icy wind, and stripped of any pretense of gentility. It was the sort of day when people grew nostalgic for their country homes. It was therefore surprising when the butler interrupted breakfast with news of early morning visitors.

William and Paul had met on the doorstep. Paul was

raising his hand to the brass knocker when William stepped out of his carriage. Both men were enveloped in heavy winter cloaks, both were bareheaded. Both looked grim-faced and intent.

They eyed each other warily.

"Sir," Paul said, inclining his head an eighth of an inch.

"Your servant," William said, doing the same.

"Gentlemen," the butler murmured as he opened the door and stood aside to admit them.

"What a pleasant surprise," Lady Amelia claimed as she came out of the breakfast room to greet them. She was happy enough to see William, but Paul was another matter entirely. How very unfortunate it would be if Monsieur Delamare chose this moment to try to gum things up.

In fact, Paul had a very different purpose in mind.

"Good morning, Your Grace," he said to the duchess. "I trust you will forgive me for coming so early, but it is necessary that I speak with Dominique."

William frowned. He handed his cane to the butler and turned to regard Paul again, even more closely. What he saw gave him pause. Beneath the inherent strength and resolve, he sensed deep conflict mingled with sorrow.

Quietly, William said, "Is it possible that we are here for the same reason?"

Lady Amelia looked from one to the other of them. "What do you mean?"

William hesitated a moment before he said gently, "I received word early this morning from contacts of mine in France. I am afraid I have very bad news. Dominique must inevitably learn of it, but I thought it would be best for her to be told in the gentlest way possible."

The duchess laid a hand to her throat as dread filled her. "And you, Monsieur le Docteur, is His Grace correct that you have come for the same reason?"

Somberly, Paul nodded. "Apparently so, although I also have something more to tell. I am leaving England shortly and wished to say good-bye to the de Montforts."

He did not add that in particular, he wanted to ascertain Dominique's condition for himself. He could not depart without being absolutely sure that he was doing what was right for her, no matter how painful that decision was to him.

"Leaving . . . ?" Lady Amelia began. "But, for where?" A terrible suspicion dawned in her. "Surely you aren't thinking of—"

"I am returning to France," Paul said quietly. "It is essential that resistance to Robespierre and the Jacobins be increased. There is no other way for them to be overcome."

"You will be walking into a hellhole," William said quietly. Although he did not know Paul, indeed had encountered him for the first time only moments before, he marveled at the audacity and courage that enabled any man to think of voluntarily returning to France. The doctor did not seem either stupid or insane—far from it. Yet what he was contemplating could turn out to be little more than suicide.

Lady Amelia was of the same opinion. Brusquely, she motioned both men into the drawing room. It was her intention to try to persuade Paul to leave without seeing Dominique.

But before she could suggest any such thing, Dominique herself appeared from the breakfast room, drawn by the sound of their voices. Sensing he brought bad news, she stood for a moment, pale and regal, staring at Paul. Her green-gold eyes appeared enormous, yet seemed to see nothing but him.

"Why are you here?" she said at length. Her voice was little more than a whisper. She swayed slightly and reached out a slender hand to support herself.

Paul did not dare to touch her. Were he to do so for even an instant, he knew that he would be lost. All his noble resolve would vanish and he would think of nothing except claiming her as his own.

William felt no such restriction. He reached Dominique's side and put an arm gently around her narrow waist. "Come and sit down," he said quietly.

Lady Amelia bestowed an approving glance that went unnoticed as William guided Dominique into the drawing room. Paul and the duchess followed. The young under-butler who had been observing the scene with great interest reluctantly closed the door behind them.

Dominique sank onto the couch with scant awareness that she did so. All her attention was needed to refrain from staring at Paul like a lovesick ninny, or worse yet, throwing herself at him. Inwardly she trembled at the mere sight of him, but on the outside, she managed to appear calm.

Only a hint of sarcasm betrayed her distress as she murmured, "What a surprise to see you, Monsieur le Docteur. I had no idea you intended calling again."

"Monsieur Delamare escorted Dominique and the children to England," Lady Amelia explained. "Naturally, we are always pleased to see him." With a warning glance, she sought to remind Dominique that to appear otherwise would arouse unwanted suspicions.

It was an admonition Dominique chose to ignore. She

was not in the best of moods, having realized only that morning that her night with Paul was not going to bear fruit. Torn between relief and regret, her nerves were badly frayed. It would take very little to snap them.

"My dear," Lady Amelia said, "I am afraid that Monsieur Delamare has some unfortunate news for us all." So long as he was still on hand, Lady Amelia decided to let him be the one to tell it——whatever it was——since the aura of ill tidings tended to cling to the messenger who brought them.

Paul hesitated. What he had to say was difficult enough without doing so in front of an audience. Abruptly, he made up his mind. "If you please, Dominique, come into the garden with me."

"The garden?" Lady Amelia protested. "Why, it is far too cold. Besides, what reason could there be for not speaking before us all?"

Paul did not answer. He merely looked at Dominique, willing her compliance. After the barest delay, she rose. "I will need a cloak."

He had not parted with his at the door but merely opened the frog closing at the neck. Now he removed the sumptuous length of fine wool in a single motion and draped it over her shoulders.

Tall French doors led from the drawing room to the walled garden beyond. Watched by Lady Amelia and William, who were both too startled to protest further, Paul opened one of the doors and guided Dominique out. Behind them, her ladyship murmured, "Well, I never . . ."

They walked a little distance down a gravel path framed on either side by snow-shrouded flower beds. Skeletal trees rustled against the leaden sky. It was very quiet. Only the faint, muted sound of horseshoes on the cobblestones beyond punctured the stillness.

Dominique stopped at a small fountain, empty now and shorn of life. She took a deep breath and lifted her head. "Tell me."

Wrapped in his cloak, she looked little more than a child. He hated himself for what he was about to do. But how else was she to hear? From the town crier, who within hours would be shouting the news from every corner in London? From the society drones who would relish every gory detail as only the terminally bored can? Or perhaps from that quiet, self-possessed young man Lady Amelia called His Grace? The same young man who watched Dominique with such tender intensity.

Paul's throat tightened. With unintentioned harshness, he said, "The trial is over. Louis was found guilty. Two days ago he went to the guillotine."

He had prepared himself for tears, screams, perhaps even fainting, but Dominique did none of those things. She simply stared at him silently for what seemed like a very long time before she said at last, "Poor, poor man. He deserved far better."

"Dominique . . ."

She held up a slim white hand in entreaty. "No, please, don't say anything more. I understand how hard this was and I appreciate your coming to tell me, but right now what I need most is to be alone."

He was loath to leave her, especially looking as helpless and vulnerable as she did, but Dominique insisted. "Only for a few minutes," she assured him with a wan smile. "Then I will join you inside. Besides," she added when he would have protested further, "it's far too cold for you out here without your cloak. You don't want to take a chill.''

The look she gave him was of such consummate sadness that Paul could not bear it. His throat was tightly clenched as he turned on his heel and strode back toward the house.

In his absence, William had informed Lady Amelia of the king's death. She sat straight-backed, her hands resting on the silver pommel of her cane. Her mouth trembled. ''My God,'' she murmured, ''that I have lived to see such horror.''

William had the good sense to know that nothing he could say would offer any comfort. He remained silent and watchful, standing by the mantel. As Paul entered, he stiffened. ''Where is Dominique?''

He went over to the fire and thrust his hands toward it before answering. ''She wanted a few moments by herself.''

Lady Amelia nodded mutely. She stood with great effort, as though the last few minutes had aged her decades, and rang for the butler. When he appeared, she ordered tea, then informed him of what had happened.

''Kindly tell the staff. Naturally, we shall put on mourning. Indeed,'' she added, ''the entire court will don black, although for some of them that will be no more than an excuse to order new clothes.''

She spoke with such bitterness that both young men glanced at each other. Catching their surprise, Lady Amelia said, ''Do you wonder that I am angry? England could have prevented this. We could have gone to Louis's assistance when it first began and put a stop to it right then. But men who should have known better imagined that a shattered France would be to England's advantage. We shall pay a heavy price for that bit of shortsightedness, mark my words."

Before either of the men could reply, the door to the garden opened and Dominique stepped in. She removed Paul's cloak and handed it to him, then she went to warm her hands in front of the fire.

With her back to the rest of the room, she said quietly, "I will speak with Nicole and David in a few minutes. I hope you all understand that I prefer for them to hear this from me."

"Of course, dear," Lady Amelia murmured. Privately, she was astounded by her granddaughter's composure. Indeed, it struck her as almost frightening that Dominique was so much in possession of herself. A nineteen-year-old girl of gentle breeding would never have been able to exercise such self-control. Only one who had lived too closely with the darker side of life could do so.

She turned and looked directly at Paul, her back straight and her features utterly composed. "I would like to know your plans, if you care to tell me."

For an instant, he was surprised, but that faded before the realization that she knew him well enough to strongly suspect. Intimacy that went so far beyond the physical was a new experience for him. He savored it even as regret filled him for how quickly he must part from her.

"I leave tomorrow for France," he said.

"Which is madness," Lady Amelia broke in. She had recovered herself sufficiently to speak her mind. Violent, premature death was a hideous offense against nature, no less to the old than to the young. That even one more life should be offered up to the bloody maw of revolutionary France enraged her.

"I cannot conceive of any reason for you to return," she said sharply. "There is more than ample work for you here. I, myself—and I am sure William, as well—will see that you make the right connections, reach the right people. We will . . ."

Paul held up a hand wearily. He had argued it all out with himself and was not inclined to do so again for anyone's benefit. Thank God Dominique needed no such explaining.

"Whatever I could accomplish here," he said quietly, "I can be far more effective in France itself. You see, I know Robespierre very well. I can anticipate his actions and see where he is weakest."

"If that weren't true," Dominique interjected softly, "we would all still be in the Temple Prison. It was only because he understood Robespierre so well that Paul was able to trick him and get us out."

The words cost her dearly; she was, in essence, agreeing with his decision to go. Yet she could not conceal a note of pride. He was more than worthy of her love, however futile it might be.

"I see," William said thoughtfully. He looked at Paul in a new light, remembering the conversation he'd had at the Foreign Office only that morning. There was a growing awareness, however belated, of the need to cooperate with moderate elements in France. Paul could be a direct line to them.

William hesitated, still vividly aware that the man could be going to his death and wanting no hand in persuading him. Under any circumstances, that would have been unacceptable. But given what he suspected about their mutual feelings for Dominique. . . .

"Is there any possibility whatsoever," he asked bluntly, "of your being convinced to remain here?"

"None," Paul said with equal firmness. Out of the corner of his eye, he saw Dominique flinch and cursed himself for an insensitive idiot. But what was he supposed to do, reveal his feelings for her and damn them both?

She deserved so much more than he could offer—safety, position, wealth. Moreover, he was convinced that if he were to selfishly take what he knew could be his, she would end up hating him for it when she discovered all that might have been hers.

Confronted by the complex, conflicting demands of love and honor, Paul did what generations of men before him had done—he found escape in the call to war.

"In that case," William was saying, "before you depart, there are some people I would like you to meet. It may be that we could assist each other."

Paul frowned. "Let me be clear, Your Grace: I am a Frenchman first and last. I will do nothing to betray my country."

"Of course not," William said. He did not question that for a moment. Monsieur Delamare was a man of integrity, heaven help him. It was at once his greatest strength and his most dangerous weakness.

Dominique looked from one to the other of them. In the pale winter light filling the drawing room, Paul looked remorselessly big and hard. His presence dominated the gathering, yet William was not without his own impact.

More slightly built than Paul and lacking his golden radiance, the duke was nonetheless impressive. The day before he had offered her what—in the blindness of her love for Paul—she took to be simple friendship. Now she was doubly glad that she had accepted it, because William's presence, his legitimate business with Paul, and his gentle understanding, combined to give her the protection she desperately needed at that moment.

Above all, she must not be alone with Paul again. Were that to happen, she knew beyond question that she would forget all her brave resolve and beg him not to go. To do so would only embarrass him and shame her.

Only lately had she experienced for herself the courage that could come from love. She had spoken the truth when she said that the queen had been as a mother to her. Certainly, Marie Antoinette had loved her far more than the gay, careless young marquise de Montfort ever did. Yet Antoinette had sent her away without tears or pleading, with no final encounter to instill a burden of future guilt and remorse.

At the very least, she could do the same.

"If you would excuse me," she murmured softly, "I would like to write a brief letter. Provided," she added, looking at Paul, "that you would not mind carrying it with you?"

"Of course not," he said. "I won't be able to give it to Her Majesty directly, but I believe I can arrange for her to receive it."

Dominique nodded. She, too, was unsurprised by the lack of explanation required between them. He knew her better than anyone else.

She left the room swiftly, before her resolve could weaken. Ahead lay painful and difficult tasks of which writing the letter of sympathy to the queen was only the first. She must then tell Nicole and David what had happened and somehow find the strength to comfort them, despite the fact that all her strength would be needed to say good-bye to Paul.

She paused on the stair landing and took a steadying breath. Deep within her she felt pain stir. Soon enough she would be locked in its grip, but for a short time yet she could hold it off. She would get through this terrible day with courage and dignity, as she would endeavor to get through all the empty, frightening days ahead. She had survived, and she would continue to do so. But the brief, enthralling glimpse of joy she had found in the little inn in Dover seemed gone forever. Only duty and honor remained.

Silently, she promised herself that they would be enough, but the words were hollow. She blinked back tears and ran up the rest of the stairs, a pale, slender figure in flight from what could never be escaped.

Below, in the entry hall, Paul watched her go. He stood motionless, straining for the last glimpse of ebony hair, the last rustle of silk, the last tantalizing hint of perfume.

A pulse beat in his hollowed jaw. His crystalline eyes gleamed with yearning so intense as to be all but unbearable. With a low curse, he smashed his fist against the marble banister. The pain was intense, but he hardly felt it. Indeed, he felt nothing but blessed numbness as he turned and walked back into the drawing room.

Lady Amelia shot him a quick, all-encompassing glance and silently took her leave. William said nothing, but went over to the sideboard and poured them both a drink. Handing a healthy measure of brandy to Paul, he said, "I have to admit, Delamare, I envy you."

Paul barely heard him. He was thinking only of Dominique. The brandy tasted sour. He set it aside and shook his head wearily. "Why?"

William hesitated. He seemed about to say something, then changed his mind. With a faint smile, he murmured, "Oh, being in the center of the action, that sort of thing."

Paul thought that a singularly odd thing to envy, but did not say so. Instead, he said, "You are rather well-positioned yourself—enough so that I would ask a favor of you."

"Of course," William replied.

"I am . . . concerned about Dominique." He hesitated, choosing his words carefully. This man cared for her. It would not do to give him any reason to be suspicious of her, and he did want her to be content.

"We have known each other for many years," Paul went on, "and as you know, we came to England together. I am concerned that she may worry about me overmuch." Surely, he thought, he had struck the right note of merely wanting to spare a friend anxiousness.

"I would like to get news to her from time to time that I am all right. Would you be willing to pass such messages along?"

William was silent for a moment, staring down into his brandy. He seemed to be wrestling with himself. At length he looked up, met Paul's eyes, and said, "Of course."

Chapter
15

London, Spring 1798

The boy who bounded up the steps of the Haverston town house was tall for his age, with long legs and arms and the gangliness of a puppy. His brown hair was disheveled, his frock coat unbuttoned, and his cravat askew. An excited flush darkened his high-boned cheeks and his hazel eyes glowed.

He hammered energetically on the bronze knocker, then danced impatiently from one foot to the other until the door was opened.

With a quick grin for the imperturbable underbutler, he raced past. "Her Grace is in the drawing room, sir," the butler called just as the boy was about to mount the stairs.

He changed course without pause and dashed in that direction, but drew up short before entering. In a quick bow to propriety, he smoothed his hair, then darted into the room.

"Mornin', *grandmere*," he said. Going over to her chair, he gave Lady Amelia a quick kiss on the cheek.

She looked up at him chidingly. "Where have you been at this hour? And whatever was Wilburs thinking of to let you go out in that condition? I declare, boy, that's the worst tied cravat I've ever seen. Come over here and let me straighten it for you."

David Francis Phillipe, marquis de Montfort, complied. His recently acquired height—he had turned fourteen the previous month—necessitated that he kneel before his grandmother so that she might make the necessary repairs. Her gnarled hands trembled slightly but her touch was gentle and filled with love.

"Wasn't Wilburs's fault," he said as she clucked over him. Matter-of-factly, he added, "Does his best but says I'm too much for him."

"I daresay Wilburs has some justification for that," the duchess murmured. She adored her grandson but was hardly blind to his faults.

David was an intense, intelligent boy who seemed driven to accept every challenge life offered. His masters at Eton—he was home from there for the Easter holidays—believed that he had a brilliant future, provided that he could learn to rule his boundless energy rather than be ruled by it.

Gazing at the boy fondly, Lady Amelia said, "Sit down now and tell me what you've been about." A dawning suspicion made her frown. "Not the coffeehouses again, I hope?"

David shrugged lightly and dropped into the chair across from her. He had no desire to upset his grandmother, but already he was very much his own man. Gently, he said,

"There's no harm in them if a fellow keeps an eye out, which I do. Besides, there's no better place for ferreting the news."

"The news," Lady Amelia grumbled. That seemed to be all she ever heard from the boy.

In all his letters from school he beseeched everyone to send him the latest word from the Continent. Whenever he was in London, he frequented not only the coffeehouses, where at least members of Parliament and other respectable men could be found amid the riffraff, but also the docks, where he rubbed elbows with all manner of lowlife.

Lady Amelia's best efforts to dissuade him from such behavior had failed utterly. He was, in his way, as obstinate as his eldest sister.

"Don't scowl so, *grandmere*," he said mischievously, "it will give you wrinkles."

She swatted at him but could not forbear smiling. He could be quite charming when he chose, this grandson of hers who already showed the bearing and manner of his illustrious ancestors. If the French ever got their mess sorted out, he would make an excellent suzerain of Montfort.

"Besides," David went on, reaching for a scone from the silver tea tray set nearby, "today it happens that there really is news. Boney's truly done it this time."

His grandmother sniffed. She was more interested than she cared to admit. "Such a vulgar term, but appropriate to the man."

"Perhaps," David said noncommittally, "but whatever one thinks of his politics, no one can deny he is a great soldier. If he weren't, he wouldn't have set off to invade Egypt with the biggest fleet anyone has ever assembled.

Can you imagine? Egypt's absolutely vital to us because it commands the Mediterranean and the route to India. If Boney should succeed . . .''

Lady Amelia's eyes widened. She caught herself, but not before an exclamation of astonishment escaped her. ''Well,'' she murmured after a moment, ''I never . . .''

''Neither did a good many others, Your Grace,'' William said as he strolled into the room with Dominique on his arm. He bowed to the elderly lady and gave David a grin. ''Bit of a surprise, I'd say.''

Dominique smiled as she slipped off her gloves and sat down gracefully on the settee. On this lovely spring day, she wore a long tunic dress of striped silk cut in the Grecian style so well suited to her tall, slender figure. Her ebony hair was coiled in braids at the back of her head with a few curly tendrils brushing her forehead.

A walk in the park with William had heightened the glow of her cheeks and eyes. She looked elegant, self-possessed, and inexpressibly beautiful—particularly to the duke of Devonshire, who watched her with the cautious restraint that marked all their encounters. More than four years after their first meeting, William remained as fascinated by Dominique as ever, if not more so.

Each year, on the anniversary of that meeting, he asked her to marry him. Each year, she turned him down gently and regretfully. He did not press her, sensing that were he to do so, she would end their friendship rather than encourage him to believe that there was hope where none existed.

She was ruthlessly honest, he thought wryly, this beautiful young woman who had taken London by storm and who remained its darling despite her own natural reticence and disinclination for society. Her very aloofness added to her charm and made her attendance at any event all the more desirable.

Ambitious hostesses courted her, admiring men desired her, the world as a whole offered her its very best. Yet Dominique remained curiously disengaged, as though her mind and heart were somewhere else.

William suspected where that might be, though he was loath to admit it—especially now.

"What's a surprise?" Dominique asked lightly. She had been out late the previous evening, at a ball given in honor of the crown prince, and was feeling a bit tired. Moreover, a vague feeling of unease had been growing in her recently, which she could not completely ignore. She had the sense that a relatively peaceful interlude in her life was coming to an end, but did not know why.

"Boney is going to invade Egypt," David said eagerly. "Admiral Nelson has been dispatched with the fleet to intercept him but it's touch and go whether he will succeed."

Dominique darted a quick glance at William, who stood near the mantel. "You knew about this?"

"I heard something to the effect late yesterday. You may recall that His Majesty left the festivities early?"

So he had, though it had been given out that he was merely feeling indisposed. Hardly surprising when one considered the vast quantities of food and wine customarily ingested by the profligate Prince of Wales—the man who, given the erratic health and occasional insanity of his royal father, might rule England before too long.

"You might have mentioned it," she said, not critically, for she never reproached William on any matter, but as a simple statement of fact.

"It seemed too pleasant a morning to spoil with such

talk," he responded mildly. Unspoken between them was the knowledge that if he possibly could, William avoided speaking to her of events concerning France. They were simply too painful.

He had broken with that rule only a handful of times in the past several years. In the hot, fiery autumn of 1794, when Dominique was still struggling to adjust to her separation from Paul and her life in a new land, it was William who gently and compassionately told her of Marie Antoinette's death. The doomed queen had followed her husband to the guillotine, preserving her pride and dignity to the end, despite the howls of the mob who demanded her death.

Her son did not survive her by long. He succumbed to inherited ailments aggravated by the grim circumstances of his captivity. Alone of the little family, Maria Theresa still lived, having been allowed to find sanctuary with her mother's people in Austria. Undoubtedly, they would continue to protect her despite Boney's recent victory.

Death had reached out its grasping hand far beyond the royal family itself. In a matter of months, more than a thousand aristocrats—men, women, and children—had perished on the guillotine, all sent to their deaths by Robespierre and those like him.

Madmen, they sought to birth a new society in blood, and instead achieved only their own destruction. Eventually the tide had turned and Robespierre had suffered the same fate reserved for his victims; his decapitated body lay unmourned in an anonymous grave.

"Pleasant," Dominique said absently. Aware suddenly that she had been silent too long and that the others were looking at her with concern, she managed a faint smile.

"Perhaps it will be. Surely with this new threat on the horizon, England will think of making peace?"

"I wouldn't count on that," William said quietly. In fact, he knew there was great resistance to anything of the sort. "The gentlemen at Whitehall seem to feel that Boney is at least as formidable a villain as any of those who actually claim to rule France."

"But he is subject to the Directory and the constitution," Dominique said, color flooding her cheeks. Despite all that had happened, she still regarded France as her home and was reluctant to hear any outsider, even one as dear as William, criticize it.

"Perhaps," the duke said noncommittally. "But whether the government in Paris has the same goals as our Corsican friend remains to be seen."

"It is rather ironic, don't you think?" David interjected. "A few years ago, no one had even heard of Napoleon Bonaparte, and now we seem to speak of little else."

"That's because he's given us so much to talk about," William said dryly. "Three years ago he was an obscure officer who happened to be at the right place at the right time to put down a royalist uprising. His reward was an army, which appears to have been all he was waiting for. In the scant time since, he has used it to conquer Italy, acquire Belgium, and defeat Austria—all in the name of France, of course, although one wonders how long General Bonaparte will remember that."

"As I recall," Lady Amelia said, "I predicted that we would rue the cost of our failure to put down the revolution at its very beginning, and I am more certain of that now than ever. The day will come when we have to face the Corsican on the battlefield."

"Not if a peace treaty could be worked out now," Dominique insisted. "Surely it is in England's own best interest to recognize the reality of France and strike an accord with her before there is any more bloodshed?"

"So others are undoubtedly preparing to claim," William said. He hesitated a moment, looking at her inscrutably. At length, he said, "We have been advised to expect an emissary from the French government. Nothing official, of course—that wouldn't be appropriate under the circumstances. But still, an attempt will be made to see if we can't sort the matter out once and for all."

"How wonderful," Dominique exclaimed. This was the first genuinely solid indication she had received that peace might actually be possible. Without stopping to think, she said, "If only Paul were here. William, surely by this time you must have had some news of him?"

William's face went blank. From behind a carefully guarded mask, he murmured, "I'm afraid not, my dear."

It was the same answer he always gave her when she asked about Paul. Lately, she had begun to wonder if he might not know more than he admitted. William was extremely well-connected; he heard and saw a great deal. Yet on the single subject of Paul Delamare, he claimed ignorance. It was almost as though he did not want to admit that Paul existed.

Nonetheless, Dominique was delighted by the news of a French emissary coming to London. Peace between the two nations was among her most cherished hopes. Only one far more private yearning surpassed that. Despite her best resolve and efforts, she ached with longing for Paul. Waking or sleeping, she thought of him. Sometimes she believed that if she were never to see him again, she would not be able to live. Then she would rebuke herself for being weak and melodramatic, two traits she could not abide.

Caught between need for him and dismay at herself, she felt deeply confused. The passage of time, generally thought to be so beneficial in such cases, only worsened her situation. Desperately, she grappled for some distraction on which to focus. William and the political situation provided it, if only up to a point.

"It all sounds very clandestine," she said with a smile. "Will we be able to meet this emissary?"

"I rather suspect so," William murmured. A hint of bleakness shone in his eyes before being quickly concealed. "In fact, I imagine he'll be certain to arrange it."

A thousand dancing lights illuminated the windows of Carlton House, the residence of the Prince of Wales and on this night the scene of a royal ball to which all of London society had aspired to be invited. For the lucky four hundred so honored, it appeared as a fairy tale palace rising above the cobblestone streets of Pall Mall.

A steady stream of carriages disgorged passengers before the stately columned entrance. Up a flight of stone steps, through gilded doors, the gloriously arrayed guests streamed. Beneath a dozen crystal chandeliers, they twittered and chirped like so many overexcited cockatoos until the satin-garbed majordomo intoned each one's name and sent them fluttering down into the majestic ballroom.

"Sweet heaven," William murmured as he looked around dazedly, "I can never set foot in this place without being stunned."

"Well, you should be," Dominique said dryly, "considering what it cost. I hate to be mundane, but a good chunk of London could have been rebuilt for the cost of the gilt alone.''

''Something I'm sure you would never be so tactless as to mention to our beloved prince.''

''Actually, I have mentioned it. He merely squeezed my hand all the more tightly and peered down my dress.''

William laughed, not entirely without a hint of malice. ''No one has ever claimed that royal birth endows one with even the rudiments of common sense.''

They left it at that and allowed themselves to be caught up in the whirl of color and sound, which for all its brittleness couldn't help but be a bit beguiling. Both had numerous acquaintances among the crowd and easily fell to talking.

Dominique found herself confronted by an elderly dowager, the marchioness of Bath, who peered at her through her lorgnette and demanded, ''Where is your grandmother, girl? Not feeling the thing tonight?''

''Lady Amelia preferred to remain at home,'' Dominique said courteously. Since an illness two years before, her grandmother had lacked the strength to go out in society very often. Only her most intimate friends knew this, however. The marchioness was not among them.

''Ought to have more sense,'' she declared, ''letting you run about harum-scarum, unmarried gal and all. In my day it would never have done, let me tell you. Devonshire's a fine lad, none better, but a man for all that. Ought to mind what people are thinking.''

''I can't say that I've ever worried much about that,'' Dominique said coolly. She knew her own behavior to be perfectly proper and saw no reason to explain it to anyone else. Nonetheless, she listened to the elderly woman for several more minutes until she could politely remove herself.

William had become caught up by the crowd. He was talking with a stout man Dominique recognized as being with the Foreign Office. They were both frowning and shaking their heads. It didn't look as though they ought to be interrupted.

She moved on, accepting a glass of wine proffered by a passing waiter carrying a silver tray, and found herself a relatively quiet corner. William would rejoin her eventually, and in the meantime, she was hardly bored—not when there were so many interesting people to watch.

The Prince of Wales had entered the room. The bobbing sea of heads indicated his presence. Dominique made her own curtsy automatically. As she straightened, she dimly noted that His Majesty appeared even more jovial than usual. His round face beamed as he spoke to the tall, elegantly dressed man at his side. A man who . . .

For an instant, she stood utterly immobile, unable to breathe or think or feel. Sensation returned in a near-painful rush. Her starved lungs dragged in air as her heart hammered against her ribs.

Paul.

No, not Paul—or at least, not the memory of him that she cherished. This man was older, even more powerfully built than she remembered, and far more formidable.

He was also the perfect image of an aristocrat.

His golden hair was worn slightly long, as fashion dictated, and secured in the back in a neat queue. The style emphasized the leonine strength of his features, a quality in no way diminished by the meticulous elegance of his dress.

His gleaming black satin frock coat bore all the marks

of superb tailoring, as did the embroidered waistcoat worn beneath it. Narrowly fitted white silk breeches revealed strongly muscled legs that appeared well suited to the glittering ebony boots with which they were paired.

Beside the fluttering popinjays of the court in their pastel costumes, nipped-in waists, and absurdly exaggerated collars, he was an unrelieved study in masculinity. Not surprisingly, all eyes were on him as he strode with the Prince of Wales across the width of the ballroom, until they stood scant yards away from Dominique, separated only by a wall of courtiers pressing in on them eagerly.

The turbulent sea of emotions that had engulfed her the moment she set eyes on Paul left her dizzy and confused. She took a deep breath, struggling to regain her composure. When she looked in their direction again, it was to find the Prince of Wales eyeing her benignly.

"Ah, my dear Miss Montfort," he said as he started forward. Automatically, the crowd parted before him. Equally instinctively, Dominique curtsied. As she straightened, the prince smiled broadly.

"Here is someone you must meet—a compatriot, as it were. Mademoiselle de Montfort, this is the marquis de Rochford, but lately arrived on our shores. Undoubtedly, the two of you have many mutual acquaintances."

Belatedly, it dawned on the prince that if that indeed had ever been true, it was no longer likely to be the case, the ranks of the French aristocracy having been sorely thinned in recent years. Mentioning absent members was perhaps insensitive.

He cleared his throat and tried again. "That is, common interests . . . a bit of home . . . not that this isn't your home now, of course," he rattled on, apparently addressing Dominique. "Still always nice to talk over old times, don't you think?"

He shot Dominique a frantic glance that left her more bewildered than ever. Why on earth was the prince doing this?

He rarely took on the task of introducing any two individuals, but when he did so, he certainly didn't make a hash of it as he was doing now. Why did it seem so important for him to publicly present them to each other?

Slowly, an explanation suggested itself. She was known, through no particular effort of her own, to have the prince's esteem. Though he had never approached her directly, he had made no secret that he found her both desirable and charming.

By introducing her to his guest, he was in essence announcing that the gentleman held his favor. With a single gesture, he established Paul's identity and credibility with London society.

Very clever, Dominique thought—the perfect way to assure that Paul would be able to come and go as he pleased amid the highest precincts of power. It was a privilege that most certainly would have been denied to someone suspected of being an emissary of a government with whom England was still very much at war.

Resentment filled her. In all her fantasies, she had never imagined that her reunion with Paul would occur in so cold-blooded and calculating a fashion. That it would happen at all she had hardly dared to hope. But now here he was, standing directly before her, his turquoise eyes watchful and challenging.

Coolly, she smiled. The hand she offered to him was perfectly steady. "How nice, Monsieur le Marquis. The

French community in London is always delighted to welcome a new arrival.''

''Indeed, yes,'' the prince interjected. He was gazing at them both with blatant approval, his small eyes fairly dancing with relief. ''Always eager for news from the other side. Some of them still think about going back, you know. 'Course, with the place still hopping like a kennel in heat . . . ah, beg your pardon, my dear. Carry on, you two, carry on.''

Puffing himself up majestically, the prince drifted off, taking the current of attention with him.

Dominique and Paul were left alone. He retained possession of her hand. When she attempted to withdraw it, his fingers tightened.

Slowly, deliberately, he raised her hand to his lips. ''Mademoiselle de Montfort,'' he murmured tauntingly, ''the toast of London, beloved of the duke of Devonshire, dear friend of His Majesty.''

His lips narrowed in what no one would be so foolish as to consider a smile. ''How you have blossomed in your new home, Dominique.''

From the depths of her forest-green eyes, daggers leapt. A lesser man would have quailed. Paul merely laughed.

His mouth against her skin was warm and slightly moist. She stood perfectly still, willing herself to be unaffected —willing the stars to drop from the sky. One had as much likelihood as the other.

Damn him!

A lifetime of love, a single night of passion, years of sweetly cherished memory, and now this? This mocking, accusing, threatening man.

With a single glance, he ripped away the fragilely woven threads of her security. In an instant, he banished the intervening years and made her once again the passionate, yearning girl she had been in Dover.

A thousand times damn him.

She should have torn him from her heart, married William, gotten on with her life. Instead she had waited, secretly nurturing a foolish hope, like a lovesick calf.

In an instant, she made the decision: he must not know. Pride alone demanded that she deny him the knowledge of her own stupidity.

He believed her worldly, experienced, shopworn? Then let him believe whatever he damn well pleased. He deserved nothing else.

"So nice to see you again, Paul," she murmured serenely. "I did wonder from time to time how things were going for you—whether you were still alive, you know, or if all that nastiness over there had proven too much."

She stopped, well aware that she was overdoing it. Paul was looking at her with outright perplexity, as though a small house pet had suddenly addressed him.

Beneath unruly locks of golden hair, his broad forehead creased. "I thought William kept you informed. That was part of our arrangement."

That was news to her, but then, it was always so stimulating to discover hitherto unsuspected facts.

"Indeed?" she murmured. "I do seem to recall him mentioning you occasionally, but I can't say I attended very closely." She waved a hand vaguely. "You do understand, the hustle and bustle of a new life and all that."

"Indeed," he said, mimicking her disingenuous tone. His expression was anything but. The look he gave her was nothing short of fierce. Inwardly, she trembled. Outwardly, she remained perfectly self-possessed.

He had made his choice three years before, as had certainly been his right. She had understood and even supported him in it. But the years since had nonetheless been empty and arid—the nights spent wondering, yearning . . . and now this.

No, he could not now blame her if he didn't like the results. And she could never let him see how deeply his disapproval wounded her, piercing past the layers of numbness and false calm to find the girl she had once been. Slowly, painfully, Dominique woke again to sensation in all its rudely glorious reality.

Off to the side, silent and watchful, William, duke of Devonshire, observed them. His handsome, aquiline features were tautly drawn. Anyone in turn observing him would have wondered what could possibly have happened to make the normally imperturbable duke appear caught between anguish and rage.

Chapter
16

Lying between silk sheets of the finest weave, protected from the night coolness by a blanket of incomparable softness, his head cradled on a pillow of down, Paul chafed.

It was several hours past midnight. By all rights, he should have been asleep, storing up strength for the day to come. Instead he was vividly, vexatiously awake.

Moreover, it was his own fault. If ever a man had been offered the means to assure his relaxation, it was he. Not far from his elbow, on an inlaid satinwood table, sat a crystal decanter of brandy. If that were not sufficient, there was a fine selection of cigars, several interesting books, and a tray of biscuits all laid out for his enjoyment.

The butler who had come with his rented town house had seen to it all. Say what you would about London, they still knew how to do things there.

Should he prefer more vigorous entertainment, there were any number of ladies who had made it clear they would be pleased to share his bed. The gay, indiscreet city abounded with them. Only pure stubbornness and an odd disinclination accounted for his solitary state.

He stretched slowly, willing the tension from his body. The Prince of Wales's ball had ended scant hours before. It had to be accounted a success. Ruefully, Paul reflected on how very well the prince had done his part—far too well.

Damn her.

He stared up unseeingly at the ceiling fresco of prancing gods and goddesses. A cherub leered at him, unnoticed.

Damn her.

His body was all fire and deep, roiling wind, viciously alive with need, torn by memory, denied rest.

How many times—how many brutal, god-awful times —had he lain in fear and near-despair dreaming of her? Seeing again the hair dark as night, eyes like the forest under soft rain, lips that beckoned and promised, and the body that . . .

And all for what? His noble sacrifice, walking away so that she might achieve the life that by rights should be hers, had apparently been for naught. She had not married William—he felt fierce joy at that, but also shock. She had not married anyone. Dominique remained as she had always been—gloriously, impudently independent.

Abruptly, he sat up and ran a hand through his already disheveled hair. Brandy, that was the thing. He'd drink himself into oblivion and count the headache that followed a fair price.

Except that the brandy—undoubtedly of excellent vintage and perfectly decanted—tasted bitter. Only the remembered sweetness of her skin tempted him. He needed it as a man in the desert needs water. His survival depended on it.

With a muttered curse, he got out of the bed and strode naked to the windows. Staring out at the empty avenue of St. James and the park across the way, he thought back over the previous evening.

Set a fox among the hens. So Talleyrand had said, but the foreign minister was comfortably ensconced back in Paris while Paul was on the front line in London. Where, he had already noted, there appeared to be a significant shortage of chickens waiting to be plucked.

Not that anyone had said it would be easy. Peace never was. Still, he hadn't needed the added complication Dominique represented.

A cool breeze wafted across his broad, bared chest. He sighed softly. If only he could think of her that way—as a complication. Nothing terribly important—just a small annoyance that could be safely ignored.

He smiled ruefully. Whatever else Dominique was, to ignore her was to court disaster. Besides, it was flatly impossible.

He'd seized on every bit of information about her that came his way, even when it maddened and worried him. Now that he was at last once more within touching distance of her, almost, he could hardly be expected to walk away.

Besides, she could be useful.

William, the prince, who else? He had no right to be angry; freely, he admitted having forfeited that privilege. But what he felt went beyond mere rage into the netherworld of cold, clawing jealousy.

He was a stranger there, having never before experienced the emotion. In a maze of conflict and uncertainty, he could see no way out, except to make use of her.

He arched his neck, willing the muscles to unclench. A few moments longer he lingered beside the window, drinking in the cool, inviting air. Weariness at last forced him to return to the bed.

He lay down reluctantly and closed his eyes, willing his mind to remain blank. Just this once, let him not dream of Joseph and the others. Let him rest undisturbed by the ghostly, disembodied heads that murmured to him of guilt and failure, time wasted and hopes lost, and the still desperate, driving need to redeem himself.

Dominique woke early. She lay wrapped in the quiet of her bed, not certain what had disturbed her sleep. She felt heavy and muzzy, yet perversely alert, as though she hadn't really slept at all.

Perhaps the dreams were the cause. Strange, half-recalled images flitted through her mind. She stirred restlessly and pushed the covers back.

On bare feet, her white lace nightgown wafting about her, she went over to the screen set in a corner of the room and stepped behind it. A small mahogany table held a pitcher of water and a basin. The water, having been there all night, was cold. She had only to ring and a maid would bring her some fresh, hot water from the stove, but she didn't bother. Cold was what she wanted—the colder, the better.

Vigorously, she splashed water on her face, then toweled herself dry. She felt marginally improved as she went back to the bedroom proper and plopped down on the side of the bed. Staring at her toes, she tried to decide what to do. Perhaps she should get dressed, have breakfast, write a few notes, visit the lending library, change her life?

She knew where Paul was staying. He had happened to mention the town house the previous evening. The butler could summon her a carriage if she didn't want to borrow her grandmother's. He would raise his eyebrows, but no attempt would be made to detain her. Everyone knew that Miss Dominique went her own way.

She laughed, a sound perilously close to a sob. Everyone was a fool, but she was the worst of all even to consider going to him. She would not, absolutely not, throw away the last shreds of honor and pride to pursue a man who had looked at her with contempt.

With a mutinous gleam in her eyes, she rose and went over to her clothespress. Half an hour later, when she came to draw back the curtains, Margaret found her rummaging through a heap of silk and satin, muttering to herself.

Rushing to the rescue—of the garments, not Dominique—the maid exclaimed, "Really, miss, I'd no idea you were awake already. Here, let me have that." Snatching a lace manteau away from her young mistress, she said sternly, "I'll lay out your clothes for you, miss. I always do. There's no reason for you to trouble yourself."

"I don't care what I wear, Maggie," Dominique said disconsolately, "just so long as I can get out of here quickly. I need some fresh air."

"Just as you say, miss," the maid murmured. She tried very hard to maintain her firm demeanor, but without great success. Four years of serving Dominique had gradually eroded the young Cornish girl's innate caution. She liked Dominique, though she genuinely despaired of her ever developing any fashion sense.

Maggie shuddered at the thought of what combination of clothing Dominique would have put together on her own. Briskly, she ushered her over to the dressing table and began loosening her braids to give her hair a nice, long brushing.

"Where are you off to in such a rush, milady?" she murmured, her sharp look betraying the casualness of the question. Independent though Dominique was, and living with an indulgent grandmother to boot, there were still certain things a young lady didn't do—not if she was to retain any claim on the eventual grand marriage for which Maggie yearned. Nothing could be better than to be lady's maid to a duchess, and one as adored and indulged as Dominique would be if she ever had the sense to accept William.

"I don't know," Dominique admitted. "I just thought I'd take a walk, clear my head."

"The shops aren't open yet, milady. But when they are, we could go together, perhaps look for that white faille you need, or a nice new bonnet. You could use some new gloves, too, while we're about it, not to mention an additional reticule for day wear. While we're about it, it isn't too early to be talking with Madame Delphine about this fall's fashions."

Dominique shot her a look of purest alarm. If she permitted it, Maggie would soon have her entire day arranged for her, all of it spent in the maid's dearest pursuit, shopping.

"I'll tell you what," Dominique said with a smile. "Suppose you do it all for me? And while you're at it, get yourself a new dress—something Patrick would like."

Her ploy worked. Maggie turned bright red and ducked her head. Gone was the supremely confident professional. In her place was a shy and disconcerted girl.

"Oh, miss, I couldn't possibly do that." Her eyes met Dominique's in the mirror. "Could I?"

"I don't see why not. After all, you'd be doing me a favor, as well as acting on my instructions. Besides, we both know that if I were to go along, I'd just end up buying whatever you told me to anyway."

Perhaps there were advantages to having a fashion dunce for a mistress, Maggie thought absently. Certainly she knew of no one else who would make so generous an offer.

"Well, if you insist . . . ?"

"I do," Dominique said firmly, "but first, let's get me dressed."

Maggie complied, swiftly and efficiently, so that in a very short time, Dominique was on her way down the front steps. On the last of them, she paused and lifted her head.

It was a spectacular morning. A fresh breeze blew out of the south, carrying with it the scent of the sea. Only a few white tufted clouds dotted an otherwise clear sky.

All around her was the rustling, stirring, murmuring promise of spring. Odd that she had spent two other springs in London and never taken much notice of them. Suddenly she was acutely, vividly aware of every nuance.

Her step was light as she started down the street in the general direction of Green Park, near where Mayfair met the neighborhood of St. James. She chose that destination rather than the nearer Hyde Park because it was smaller, more relaxing, and less likely at that hour to contain anyone she knew.

The scent of the gardens laid out in the previous century greeted her as she walked toward the entrance. She was almost there, within sight of the high stone pillars, when a sudden sound drew her up short.

Around the corner came a milk wagon bearing a load of fat tin jugs that rattled with each step the plodding horse took. There was nothing unusual about the sight, this being the hour when such deliveries were made to the great households in the area. Nor was there anything unusual about the two ragged boys who lurked in the wagon's wake, waiting for the moment to strike.

It would take two of them, Dominique thought, to roll off one of the large jugs and escape with it. And even then they would be lucky, she realized, judging by the size of the man driving the wagon, who would undoubtedly defend his property.

Doubt moved her. The poverty of London was unspeakable. She knew that full well because she spent a good deal of her yearly income doing whatever she could to help alleviate it. Wealthy though she was, for every person she touched, a thousand more went unaided—like the two boys eyeing the milk truck.

Yet the driver, too, was deserving of compassion. She had little difficulty imagining his life—rising well before dawn each day, making his rounds, returning with the few coins that meant the difference between survival and disaster. For him, as well, a case had to be made.

The wagon had stopped before a large, well-appointed house. As Dominique watched, the boys faded into the shadows of an adjacent building. The man got down and went around to the back of the wagon. He unfastened one of the jugs and hoisted it onto his shoulder. With it in place, he strode off toward the side entrance of the house.

The boys made their move. They darted forward swiftly, one clambering into the wagon to free another of the jugs. Dominique took a step forward, still not sure of what she was going to do, but certain that she had to do something. She was across the street, almost to the wagon, when two things happened at once: the boys got the jug loose, and the man became aware of them.

He dropped the jug from his shoulder with a roar and

sprinted back to the wagon. One of the boys got away, but the other was not so fortunate. He was yanked from the wagon by his scruffy neck and sent flying to the ground, where the man proceeded to hold and beat him.

"Stop." Without pausing to think, Dominique threw herself at the pair. She got hold of the man's shirt and succeeded in distracting him enough to earn a grunt and a quick swat that sent her reeling back like a brushed-off fly.

She landed hard on her bottom and for a moment sat stunned, until a surge of outrage propelled her back onto her feet and into the melee.

"'Cor, lemme me go, yer bastid!'' the boy was screaming as he twisted and turned in the man's grip. He had his arms up over his head to protect himself and was lashing out with his feet.

"Bastid, is it?" the man demanded. "Devil's spawn, ye be! Robbin' from an honest workin' man. I'll teach you. What . . . ?"

He broke off, startled by the sudden thud of a warm, inexplicably soft body against his. Even more surprising was the cultured, female voice assaulting him. "Unhand him, sir! How dare you mistreat a child like that? I'll have you before the watch. I'll . . . *Umph.*"

This time, when the great hairy paw knocked her off her feet, Dominique stayed down. More than simply the wind was knocked out of her. Her head made contact with the cobblestone street. She felt a sharp, blinding pain down the side of her face, followed by a rush of all-encompassing blackness.

"Oh, sweet lord," the man moaned when he saw what he had done. Bad enough he'd hit a woman, but a lady to boot. "Now see wha' ye've made me do, ye little cur," he said, giving the boy a further shake. The lad took advantage of his shock to slip agilely from his grip. With a swift, bemused glance at Dominique, he went racing down the street.

The man hesitated only a moment before leaping onto his cart and lashing the horse to a gallop. He was a decent family man who would have preferred to stay and at least make sure that Dominique was all right, but he knew full well what could happen to a man of his class responsible for injuring a lady. If he landed in Newgate Prison—a real possibility—his wife and three daughters would face starvation. Thinking of them, he sped around the corner and was soon lost to sight.

Dominique regained consciousness slowly. She was dazed and confused. Slowly, as she grasped the fact that she was hurt, she also became afraid.

With great difficulty, she managed to lift herself from the cobblestones. The effort wrung a groan from her. She was winded and badly bruised. Worse yet, she remained disoriented. Clearly, she needed help, but at that moment, she had no precise idea of where to find it.

Hesitantly, going step by step, she managed to make her way down the street. Her sense of direction was uncertain. She knew only that she was drawn forward until at least a glimmer of recognition dawned.

Paul's house—the place she had heard he had gone to stay after arriving in London. With a heartfelt sigh of relief, she stumbled up the steps and all but collapsed in front of the door, but not before she managed to grasp the brass knocker.

The butler who opened the door did no more than raise his eyebrows fractionally. Perhaps he was already accustomed to injured people arriving unexpectedly.

"May I be of assistance, miss?" he inquired.

Since it was patently obvious that someone had to be, Dominique did not try to reply. With the last of her breath, she murmured, "*S'il vous plaît—Monsieur le Docteur . . .*" In her confusion, she instinctively spoke in French. The butler frowned. Like most Britishers, he wasn't too fond of the French just then. That business with their king had been bad enough, but lopping people's heads off in public was going too far. Every decent person knew that the proper place for such activities was behind discreet prison walls. Not that there weren't exceptions—the doctor, for example. He was a gentleman through and through, unfailingly reserved and considerate, not at all like this impertinent miss who seemed to think that . . .

"*What in bloody hell . . .*"

The butler turned, eyes widening, as Paul strode toward the door. Perhaps he ought to consider revising his opinion of his employer. The man before him looked almost savage with rage. Valiantly, in the finest tradition of his calling, the butler held his position—but only barely.

"Sir, this young lady . . ."

Paul shot him a look that silenced the man as effectively as a bullet. Kneeling beside Dominique, he could see only her crumpled form and ashen face, with the livid bruise already forming. There was scant comfort in the fact that her pulse was steady and her breathing normal.

Swiftly, he lifted her and started for the stairs. Behind him, the butler had recovered sufficiently to remember his duties.

"May I be of some assistance, sir?" he inquired cautiously.

Paul wasted no words. "Hot water, Samuels, upstairs."

"Very good, sir," the butler murmured as he carefully shut the door behind him.

Paul gave him no further thought as he climbed the steps. Dominique stirred slightly and moaned. He looked down at her and blanched. A thin trickle of blood shone at the corner of her mouth.

At the top of the steps, he stopped for an instant. The master bedroom, which he occupied, lay directly ahead. At the opposite end of the house were two smaller guest rooms, both empty. Propriety—what little of it was left —dictated that he take Dominique to one of them.

His face was set and his turquoise eyes glinted dangerously as he shrugged off the notion. She would rest exactly where she belonged, in his own bed.

And if she had any doubts about the propriety of that later on, he would be more than happy to convince her of it.

Chapter
17

Was it a coincidence? Dominique wondered, but sitting in the enormous, high-posted bed, garbed in an incongruously ruffled white linen nightshirt that was yards too big for her, and feeling dazed for reasons that had nothing to do with the blow to her head, Dominique could not be sure. Fate appeared to have suddenly taken a very firm hand in her affairs. How else could she explain Paul's sudden appearance? Moreover, this was the Paul of old, as she remembered him, not the cold, glittering stranger she had encountered at the ball.

"How are you feeling?" he asked gruffly as he wrung out a cloth in a basin of cold water and applied it gently to her cheek.

"Fine," she murmured. Her voice was soft and breathless, as though she had run a great distance. "It's nothing, really."

His scowl informed her that he did not believe her. "What happened to you?" he demanded abruptly.

Dominique told him how she had intervened in the robbery, then stumbled to his doorstep.

"You could have been even more seriously hurt."

"What was I supposed to do?" she shot back, her green-gold eyes glinting. He might as well have taken the basin of water and upended it over her for the effect his words had.

She'd been wrong, as always, when she was fool enough to nurture tender thoughts of him. He was as uncompromising and annoying as ever. And how dare he criticize her behavior, when his own had been no better.

"At least I'm not sailing under false colors," she said acidly. "I know what I believe in and I'm willing to act on it. But you, Monsieur le Docteur, seem to feel the need for a great deal of pretense."

He stared at her blankly for a moment before uttering a particularly nasty invective. While she was still blanching from it, he rose from the bed, leaving her to catch the cloth and lower it, forgotten, onto the towel beside her.

Paul stared out unseeingly at what was really a very pretty garden at the rear of the house. Ordinarily, he would have enjoyed the sight, but at the moment, he was thoroughly preoccupied by the war of emotions going on within him. It was a singularly uncomfortable experience for a man who had only survived the past few years by hardening himself against any feeling at all.

He had known the moment he saw her the previous evening that Dominique was the sole individual who could breach his defenses. He had merely to look at her for the fire storm of passion, rage, and jealousy to threaten to overcome him. And now? Slowly, he turned and made a valiant attempt to see her dispassionately. It failed miserably. Her beauty was so piercing as to make his chest tighten painfully.

In the struggle with the man, her hair had come down. It lay in seemingly wanton disarray over her slender shoulders. Aside from the livid bruise on the left side of her face, her features were perfection. Her eyes were wide and luminous, watching him questioningly. Her lips were full, soft, ripe. He breathed in convulsively as he remembered how they had felt beneath his own.

Four years—four long, hellish, seemingly endless years.

The ridiculously large nightshirt had slipped off one of her shoulders, revealing alabaster skin gleaming in the sharp morning light. For almost any other woman, that light would have been ruinous, revealing as it did the slightest imperfection. For Dominique, it was merely a golden benediction confirming her loveliness.

His hands trembled. He put them behind his back and regarded her levelly. "What makes you think I'm pretending? I am the marquis de Rochford by right. Besides, I could hardly be blamed for finally tiring of France and deciding to seek sanctuary here."

Dominique made a sharp, dismissive sound. "Don't be absurd. No one who knows you could ever believe that."

"Why not?" he asked, genuinely curious. Sheltered though she had been during most of the years of terror—thank God for that!—he still suspected that she knew only too much about what they had been like.

Why then should she find it unbelievable that he would at last sicken of the experience and leave?

"Because," she said quietly, "if you are anything at all, Paul Delamare, marquis de Rochford, it is loyal. You are utterly, blindingly, infuriatingly committed to the ideal of liberty. I cannot see you giving it up for any reason whatsoever.''

His feet carried him back to stand beside the bed. He seemed to have very little control over the matter. Indeed, he hardly noticed what he was doing as he sank wearily into a nearby chair.

''That ideal,'' he said softly, ''has proven a harsh mistress. I have had very little joy from her over the years.''

A murmur of surprise escaped Dominique. She had not expected him to be so honest, or for that honesty to affect her so profoundly. She looked away hastily, lest he see the sudden sheen of tears in her eyes. ''Some men at least have to cling to belief,'' she murmured huskily. ''Otherwise, what would happen to the world?''

He laughed, a sound of bitter self-mockery. ''What, indeed? I daresay it would somehow manage to muddle through, perhaps with a good deal less anguish.''

Her eyes met his. Disillusionment was so foreign to his nature that she had difficulty recognizing it. Yet it was there, along with something else. Despair?

''Paul . . .'' She sat up in the bed and reached out a hand to him. There was no thought in her mind except the overwhelming need to give comfort. It eclipsed even passion.

Her skin was smooth and warm against his. At the first touch of her hand, he thought very clearly that he must resist. He must get up and walk away, out of the room, out of the house. It had been madness to bring her here —sweet, irresistible madness.

She was sitting on her knees on the edge of the bed. The nightshirt had slipped down slightly. Through the ruffled edges, he could see the gentle swell of her breasts. His mouth was suddenly very dry.

"Don't berate yourself," she said gently. "I'm sure you've done everything you could—far more than anyone could have expected. If there is any single person who can hold his head up after all that's happened, it's you. And now, thanks to your presence here, there may actually be a chance for peace."

He started slightly, his hand tightening on hers. "How do you know that?"

"William told me. That is, he said there was an emissary coming from the Directory to begin peace negotiations. When I saw you with the prince, I realized that it must be you."

Despite himself, Paul smiled ruefully. All their careful preparations, all the effort made to provide him with the perfect cover story, and she had seen through it in an instant.

"That was . . . indiscreet of William."

"Also uncharacteristic," she said tartly. "He's normally far too close-mouthed."

"So I gathered. We did, as I mentioned yesterday, have an arrangement."

"That he would keep me informed and that in return you would provide him with whatever information was consistent with your loyalty to France?"

"Exactly. It doesn't seem as though he kept his side of the bargain."

"I'm not so sure," Dominique said slowly. "I have always known that you were alive and in reasonably good health. That meant a great deal to me. But beyond it, I'm not sure you would have wanted me to know the particulars of what you were doing."

Paul had a quick flash of memory—the nights spent on the run after his return to France, hiding in damp, rat-infested cellars, knowing that at any moment he could be betrayed. He remembered the long, savage hours of helplessness and frustration as plans failed to mesh or luck went against them; the horror and anguish of knowing that each day meant the loss of more lives. Finally, there had been success. The destruction of the Jacobins and the first real chance for sanity had ultimately prevailed. But this newly found peace was nearly destroyed on the rocky shoals of war.

No, he could say nothing of that to her. Besides, he suspected that she already—somehow—knew.

She was close enough for him to smell the perfume of her skin. It wafted toward him on the spring breeze—lilac and jasmine, roses and pure woman. It was heady, intoxicating, achingly reminiscent of the single night they had shared when he had found that scent all over her body, along silken limbs and in hidden, secret places.

"Dominique," he murmured through lips that were suddenly taut, "am I a fool?"

She shook her head slowly, ebony hair gleaming in the light, dancing with shards of silver before his dazzled eyes.

"Oh, no," she whispered. "If you were, I wouldn't be here. I'd have married William, settled down, forgotten you. But I couldn't, you see, no matter how hard I tried."

Her voice caught. She took a deep, shaky breath, struggling for some remnant of self-control. "What," she murmured, "are we going to do?"

He looked at her solemnly for a moment, and then he smiled—a broad, warm, heart-shattering smile of utter confidence and masculinity. It curled through her like the gentlest and most potent of caresses.

"That depends," he said, "on whether we want to be noble or human."

"Human," she said promptly, "please."

He frowned slightly, suddenly all seriousness. "Are you sure? I must be honest with you, Dominique. When my mission here is over, however it ends, I must return to France. If peace is not achieved, the situation there will continue to be dangerous and chaotic. This man, Bonaparte . . ."

"Forget him," Dominique said, placing a finger against his lips. "Forget all of them. There is only us . . . only now. Let's not waste it."

Once before, in the inn in Dover, he had allowed himself to be persuaded by her beauty and his own need, but this time he hesitated.

Only the conviction that she was older now and vastly more sophisticated reassured him. Dominique was a child no longer. Her wishes could not have been clearer, and they agreed perfectly with his own.

Besides, he was frankly sick of always doing the right thing, always putting aside his own desires and needs for the greater good. Paul Delamare—healer, idealist, fighter for freedom and almost martyr—might be an admirable enough chap from a distance, but living inside him all the time could get a bit tedious.

He was also, quite simply, a man, with all the strengths and weaknesses that implied. Before him was the woman of his dreams, the one woman he had always desired above all others. She was the only woman with whom he was perfectly, utterly happy.

Dominique—silk and fire, skin like honey-warmed cream, and passion so wholehearted and unfeigned as to leave him dazzled.

His mouth hardened. Beneath hooded lids, his eyes were piercing. Men who had felt the full force of his will would have recognized the look. He had made up his mind and he would not be stopped.

He reached for her. She gasped faintly, not having anticipated the move, but went unresistingly. Her body was infinitely soft against the rock-hard strength of his own. Without thinking, he grasped her close and took her mouth with his.

It was a kiss of desperation, utterly lacking in tenderness. His lips parted hers instantly, his tongue plunging in to taste her sweetness. At the same time, he bent her backward so that she felt disoriented, unbalanced, and completely helpless. She gasped again, her nails digging into his broad shoulders.

The situation had suddenly slipped beyond her. The first time they had made love she had frankly been the instigator, knowing that there was simply no other way it would happen. This was different. This time she was in the grip of a man whose self-restraint had suddenly snapped. That realization should have been terrifying, and indeed, she was a little afraid.

But she reminded herself that it was Paul who held her so demandingly, Paul whose hard, callused hands were slipping the nightdress from her body, Paul who pressed her back down onto the bed, his long, heavily muscled form covering hers.

His clothes were the only impediment between them. He left her long enough to make short work of them. She lay unmoving, watching him through heavy, slumberous lids.

His body was magnificent, perfectly honed, utterly male. There wasn't an ounce of softness about him. Only the ragged white scar across his abdomen marred what was otherwise perfection.

Scar? Granted, she had only seen him nude once before, in Dover, and then she had been so overcome by passion that it was possible certain details had escaped her attention—but not a scar of that size.

She sat up slowly and stretched out a finger, stroking it along the length of the raised white ridge.

A tremor raced through Paul. He clasped her hand at the wrist and pulled it away. "Be merciful, Dominique," he said with a faint grin. "I want this to last, and it's been a long time for me."

Her eyebrows rose. She wasn't quite sure she understood him, but he seemed to be saying that he hadn't . . .

"You mean," she ventured as he rejoined her on the bed, "there haven't been . . . other women?"

He smiled down at her ironically. "Does that surprise you so much?"

"Yes," she answered frankly. He was a supremely attractive man; it was inconceivable to her that women would not be readily available to him, even under the most difficult and trying circumstances.

Indeed, the closer such a man came to death—and Paul had been surrounded by it in recent years—the more he would instinctively reach out to the life force that women represented.

She recognized that without having to like it. What took her aback was the idea that he had not availed himself.

Paul sighed suddenly and turned over on his back, away from her. Instantly, she felt bereft. Her body was cold, her nakedness embarrassing. She reached for the sheet to cover herself.

"No," he said, his hand coming out to stop her. "Come here instead."

She did as he said, puzzled by the change in him but

glad nonetheless that he wanted her near. His embrace was reassuring. With her head cradled on his broad shoulder, she listened as he spoke, almost to himself.

"Sometimes it's damned inconvenient to be a man."

She lifted herself slightly to look at him. He was staring up at the ceiling, his eyes impenetrable. What struck her most were the lines of weariness carved into his face. At that moment, he looked older than his years and far too vulnerable.

"I wouldn't have thought that," she said slowly. "It's always seemed to me to be very much a man's world."

"Yes, I suppose it does, but still, there are certain expectations . . ." He sighed deeply and turned on his side, facing her. "There have been women in the last few years, Dominique, and opportunity enough. That's one thing that never stops, no matter what sort of madness is going on. But I couldn't . . ." He broke off, unable to go any further.

It was unnecessary. She understood. Without needing any great explanation or experience, she realized what he was saying. And though she colored slightly, she dealt with it quite calmly.

"That . . . uh . . . doesn't seem to be the case any longer."

He stared at her for a moment before suddenly laughing out loud. "No," he admitted, "it doesn't."

Whatever combination of love for Dominique and deep, debilitating sorrow had prevented him in the past was gone now. He was unmistakably, implacably restored, to such an extent that he was suddenly afraid he might hurt her.

There was so much she wanted to ask him—about the years they had been apart, the future—but this was not the time. With a soft, barely audible murmur, she twined her fingers in his golden hair and drew him to her.

It was enough. Whatever hesitation Paul had felt vanished in an instant. He gasped her name inarticulately and came over her with almost bruising force—almost, but not quite. Never did he forget that she was Dominique, the woman he loved more than life itself. But in the back of his mind, he was fiercely, sardonically grateful that she was no longer the innocent young girl she had once been.

His mouth traced a line of fire from her lips down the vulnerable line of her throat to the scented hollow between her breasts. They were taut and swollen, the nipples erect, begging for his touch. But he passed on for the moment, tasting the silken skin of her flat abdomen, delving his hands between her slender thighs, urging her open to him.

She cried out softly when his breath touched the tangle of dark curls between her legs. He raised his head, his expression wolfish. Her features were tightly drawn, almost as though she was in pain. The bruise stood out lividly.

A wave of remorse washed over him. For a few minutes, he had actually forgotten what had happened to her. Lifting himself off her, he touched the side of her face gently. "Is it hurting?"

She looked at him blankly for a moment before the words made sense. "No, not that, but . . ." She broke off. It was impossible to tell him.

The bruise did not matter at all—she'd lost all awareness of it—but every other part of her body was vividly, tormentingly alive.

She felt as though she was being drawn as taut as a bowstring. The sensation was almost unbearable. "Paul, please . . ."

His gaze flicked over her, taking in the ivory skin gleaming with a sheen of moisture; the magnificently formed body, slender yet voluptuous; the look on her face—the look of a woman passionately, totally in love. Not merely in the throes of desire but truly loving, with all the fierce, all-encompassing gentleness that entailed. Only once in his life had he seen that look directed at himself—the night in Dover—and even then he had not truly appreciated it for what it was.

Always he had loved her, for as long as he could remember. But now, for the first time, he suspected that she loved him, or at least believed that she did.

He could work out the difference later, if there was one. For the moment—

His mouth was hot and wet on her nipples. Dominique moaned convulsively as he suckled her. It was too much; she would die from this. But when she tried desperately to draw him to her, he stopped her. His big hands held hers as slowly, deliberately, he settled himself between her thighs.

"Don't deny me, Dominique—not this or anything else."

It was half plea, half command. She was helpless to reject either. Her eyes opened wide as his mouth found her, driving her to an apex of pleasure so acute that existence itself seemed to cease. She hovered on the edge of a shimmering, golden plane that reached beyond infinity.

It was there that he entered her, plunging hot and full with his demand. Belatedly, he realized how very tight she was—almost as tight as the first time—and tried to draw back, but she was beyond letting him go. Fiercely, she held him to her until he relented and sank once more into her.

"Dominique," he whispered thickly against her hair, "I thought . . ."

"I know—William, perhaps more. But there's been no one, Paul—no one except you."

He believed her. How could he otherwise, when her body itself gave him the proof? He could feel her struggling to accept him and held himself in rigid check until the accommodation was made. Even then he had only to move to the slightest degree to make her cry out with pleasure.

It was too much. So long denied, his need so fierce, he could not hold back. His big hands cupped her buttocks, raising her to him.

A harsh groan escaped him as he plunged once, and again, driving them both over the brink into ecstasy.

Chapter
18

Dominique stirred languidly. Her body felt so utterly content and replete that she was loath to move. Only the lengthening shadows in the bedroom compelled her to do so.

She sat up reluctantly, lifting the heavy curtain of her hair away from her face, and smiled down at Paul. He was deeply asleep.

His breathing was slow and regular. His features, which a short time before had looked so harsh, were now completely relaxed.

Profound satisfaction filled her, not merely at the passion they had shared but at the fact that she had been able, at least for the moment, to banish the ghosts that haunted him.

Silently, she slid from the bed and padded across the room. Her clothes were behind the screen. She dressed with some awkwardness, not being accustomed to performing the task alone, but quickly enough she was ready.

When she emerged, Paul was still asleep. She gazed at him for a long moment before going over to the small desk near the window.

There she found paper and ink to pen him a note. Leaving it where it was sure to be found—on the pillow where her head had lately rested—she tiptoed out.

The butler was crossing the entry hall as she came down the stairs. He looked at her expressionlessly and bowed. "May I call you a hack, madame?"

For all his surprise, slightly disheveled young women might have been coming and going from the house daily.

With a slight smile, she shook her head. "No, thank you, I prefer to walk."

He held the door for her, murmuring something appropriate as she passed. Dominique scarcely heard him. She felt reborn, as though the arid sorrow of the past few years had never happened. It was an illusion, of course, but one she was pleased to cherish, if only for the moment.

Absently, she noted that she received more than the usual number of stares as she walked the distance to the Haverston residence.

Unaccompanied women, particularly those of quality, were sufficiently rare on London's streets to make her reception unsurprising. It wasn't until she reached her grandmother's door, and was greeted by the underbutler, that she remembered the bruise.

"Good afternoon, milady," the young man began, only to break off abruptly at the sight of her. "Great heavens, what happened to you?" Belatedly, he remembered himself. "That is, I beg your pardon, milady, but . . ."

"It's quite all right, Rogers," she said with a grimace. "I had a slight accident, that's all."

He clearly did not believe her, but he was far too well

trained to say anything more. He merely accepted her hat and gloves. "Her Grace is in the small drawing room, milady," he murmured. As a rather broad hint, he added, "I believe she has been somewhat concerned about you."

Dominique nodded. She had been well aware of the worry her absence would cause. Nothing less would have drawn her from Paul's bed.

Forcing herself to smile, she opened the drawing room door and stepped inside. Lady Amelia was seated at a small inlaid table. She appeared to be reading a book, but the printed page scarcely held her attention. The instant she looked up and saw Dominique, her expression was of intense relief.

"There you are. I've been . . . *Oh, my dear, what has happened*?"

"I'm sorry, *grandmere*," Dominique said hastily as she went to her side. "I would have warned you if I could. I had a silly accident while I was out walking, but I assure you, it looks far worse than it feels."

Actually, her face had begun to throb painfully. She marveled that she hadn't felt it sooner, even though she fully understood the reason why.

"An accident?" Lady Amelia repeated. She touched Dominique's cheek with gentleness that belied her stern expression. "Tell me."

Dominique smothered a sigh. She hated the very idea of lying to her grandmother, but she knew there was no possibility of telling her what had happened with Paul. To do so would be to burden the elderly woman with knowledge she neither wanted nor needed. Instead, Dominique sought some middle ground that would include enough of the truth to salve her own conscience without telling too much.

"I had trouble sleeping and decided to go for an early morning walk," she began. "Near Green Park, I witnessed an altercation between a dairyman and a beggar boy who was trying to rob him. The man was understandably angry, but I still didn't think he had any right to beat the boy. When I tried to intervene, I got hit by mistake."

"I see," Lady Amelia said slowly. Her shrewd old eyes looked her granddaughter over closely. "That was this morning, you say? Where have you been between then and now?"

"I . . ." Dominique swallowed hard. No wonder she had always shied away from falsehood. It was damnably hard!

"The man was very upset. He . . . insisted I come home with him so that his wife might tend to me."

It was what could have happened had she not been near Paul's house, but it was still a lie. As such, it left her feeling decidedly uncomfortable—all the more so because she suspected Lady Amelia did not believe her.

"Indeed," her grandmother said at length. "Well, in future, you really must be more careful. Now, run along upstairs and let Margaret see to you."

As an afterthought, she added, "I shall send a note around to Lord and Lady Sanders's explaining why you shan't be able to attend this evening."

Belatedly, Dominique realized that she could hardly go out in public looking as she did. That would give rise to all sorts of unfortunate speculation. But beyond that, the bruise provided her with an excuse for not seeing William immediately.

He had been scheduled to escort her to the Sanders's supper party. Though she felt guilty about letting him down, she knew that she couldn't possibly have faced him just then.

Although she did not love William, she did care for him, and wanted, if at all possible, to avoid hurting his feelings. He had been a good and steadfast friend to her all these years. He deserved far better than a woman who was given heart and soul to another man.

She was thinking of Paul as she sank into the hot bath that Maggie speedily prepared for her. And she continued to think of him through the remainder of the day. It passed quietly enough.

She spent some time with David and Nicole, both of whom were quite impressed with her injury. After sending a note to William explaining her incapacity, she curled up in a window seat in her room and tried steadfastly to read. Afterward, she could not have said what book she held, let alone what it was about.

Maggie came and went, straightening her mistress's clothes. If she noted the dreamy, enraptured expression on Dominique's face, she was careful not to mention it.

Lady Amelia spent the day brooding. This was unlike her, but under the circumstances, it couldn't be avoided. She was quite well aware that Dominique had not told her the truth—at least, not all of it—but she was uncertain as to what the girl was concealing. For some time now, she had been worried about her granddaughter. On the surface, Dominique had everything necessary to assure a happy life, yet she was clearly far from content.

Not that Lady Amelia had ever caught the slightest hint of self-pity from her—Dominique was made of sterner stuff than that. But there was a sense about her of something not yet complete, something waiting to happen, which made the older woman uneasy.

With a sigh, she reached for the carefully folded copy of the *London Gazette* on the tray beside her. As always, she turned first to the court calendar.

She had been following the comings and goings of her fellow aristocrats for more than sixty years, and continued to find them amusing, even if these days there were few of her own generation still mentioned.

She scanned the column with casual interest until a name leaped out at her. A soft gasp escaped Lady Amelia. She brought the paper closer, thinking that perhaps her eyes were failing her.

No, there it was. *"At Carlton House, evening last. The marquis de Rochford, lately arrived from France. Residence: St. James Sq."*

Yesterday evening, Dominique had also been in attendance at Carlton House. Her name was, in fact, mentioned farther down in the column. It was possible that she had not encountered Paul, but not likely.

And today she had gone walking near Green Park, only a short distance from St. James Square.

Had they met at the ball and arranged a further rendezvous? Or had the morning encounter been accidental?

That Dominique had seen Paul again, Lady Amelia did not doubt for a moment. She was less certain of what, if anything, he had to do with the bruise Dominique sported. Granted, she had met the marquis de Rochford only briefly, but she could not imagine him striking a woman. Still, if they had argued. . . .

She was still mulling that over when the butler appeared to announce that His Grace, the duke of Devonshire, was calling.

"I received a note from Dominique," William said with scant preamble, "saying that she was unwell and couldn't attend at the Sanders's. Naturally, I was concerned, so I thought I would just drop by and see for myself how she is doing.''

Lady Amelia was not fooled. William had also been at the prince's ball. Even if Dominique had not been aware of Paul's presence, it was likely that William had known he was there. After four years of extraordinary devotion and patience, His Grace could be pardoned for being concerned.

''Please sit down,'' Lady Amelia said quietly. ''I believe we have something to discuss.''

Briefly, she told him what had happened—or at least the version of it she thought he should hear.

In her account, Dominique went for a morning stroll accompanied by her maid. She returned hours later, bruised and disheveled, and said she had been in an altercation with a dairyman who was beating a young boy. The maid supported her story.

As William listened to her, his normally pale features darkened. Lady Amelia had not mentioned Paul's name. Only by a pointed glance at the copy of the *Gazette* lying open before her to the court calendar did she make it clear that she knew.

The sight of the newspaper brought back all the memories William had been struggling to suppress since the previous evening.

Four years before, he had suspected that Dominique's feelings for the handsome Dr. Delamare went far beyond mere gratitude and affection. Paul, too, he guessed, felt far more than was proper for a woman who, by all rights, should never be his. Now he was certain. Watching them standing in the midst of the glittering array, utterly unaware of anything except each other, he realized that he was looking at love so pure and radiant as to transcend all else.

That love filled him with despair and rage.

With an immense effort he controlled himself, but only just. His eyes were narrowed to razor-thin slits. His mouth trembled slightly and his knuckles shone whitely.

"Bruised, you say?"

Lady Amelia nodded slowly. She had been watching him with interest, observing the play of emotions across his face. What she saw disturbed her, but also gave her hope.

"Apparently, the boy was trying to rob the dairyman. Dominique attempted to intervene and was accidentally struck. It's the sort of thing she would do. Still, I admit to some concern—"

Not even to suit his greatest convenience could William convince himself that Paul had hit Dominique. But in the final analysis, it didn't matter. He had merely to pretend to believe it, and everything else would follow automatically.

He cast a shrewd glance at Lady Amelia, wondering for a moment how much she had guessed. Not that it mattered. She was as determined as he was to prevent Dominique's involvement in any unsuitable entanglement.

"Dear William," Lady Amelia said. She leaned closer and laid her gnarled hand on his. "Is there nothing that can be done?"

On the surface, the question made no sense. But they were far beyond the surface now, dealing in the nether realm of innuendo and implication. There they understood each other perfectly.

"I shall see, Your Grace," William said softly. He

raised her hand to his lips, kissed it lightly, and rose. "Under the circumstances, I don't believe it will be necessary to mention this visit to Dominique, do you?"

"What visit was that, William?"

He smiled, bowed, and took his leave.

Paul's hand, thrust deep in the pocket of his morning coat, curled around the paper hidden there—Dominique's note. Why he had brought it with him, he couldn't say, except that it gave him some obscure comfort.

"My love," the note read, "I must go lest my grandmother be concerned. Only send me word that we may be together again. Dominique."

My love.

He suppressed a smile and strove to attend to what the man before him was saying.

"All very well and good for His Highness, but peace isn't going to come dropping out of a tree at us. Pitt needs this war. He's got to keep the military engine going, or the whole bloody business will fall apart."

"No one doubts the prime minister's brilliance," Paul said, "or his implacable opposition to revolution. But surely even Pitt must see that the war is doing nothing good for England?"

Charles Fox shrugged. Of all the men in the British government, only he was regarded as Pitt's equal. Together they were twin colossi who utterly dominated the lesser men around them. They were also devoted adversaries who saw nothing alike.

"It's true that the financial strain has been immense," Fox allowed. His broad face crinkled in an ironic smile. "Frankly, I suspect that's behind H.R.H.'s desire for peace. He'd rather have the money to spend elsewhere."

Paul returned the smile. He was well aware of the Prince of Wales's reputation for extravagance. But even if he had not been, the visit to Carlton House would have told him enough. He also knew that Fox was being too modest. Unlike the Tory, Pitt, whom the Prince of Wales despised, Fox wielded enormous influence over the future king. Indeed, it was thought that he provided most of his opinions.

"It must be frustrating," Paul said quietly, "to have a protégé seize upon an idea and take it further than had been intended."

Fox stared at him for a moment. His face reddened and his small, bright eyes gleamed dangerously. "You surprise me, Monsieur de Rochford," he said at length. "Frankly, I've not been overly impressed by the caliber of men in the French government these days. Robespierre and the others may have been mad, but at least they knew what they wanted. The same can't be said of this new bunch, can it? Still, you seem to have your sights clear."

Paul shrugged. "I am a temporary diplomat, milord, and perhaps not a good one, but my goal is simple. I seek peace for my country. Prolonged war will lead to dictatorship, the mere thought of which I abhor."

Fox settled back in his leather wing chair and regarded Paul steadily. "Dictator," he repeated, as though savoring the word. "It has a fine Latin sound to it. The Romans knew what they were about when they feared giving too much power into the hands of any one man. In the end, they couldn't manage to avoid it. I'm not sure you'll be able to either."

"Maybe not," Paul said noncommittally, "but we must try."

Fox rubbed the bridge of his impressive nose. He stared off into space for several moments before he said, "Contrary to your implication, monsieur, I don't feel His Highness has gone too far in receiving you. However, that's not to say I think you have any chance of success. Should Mr. Pitt get wind of what you are about—"

"I don't think that's likely. The only other person who knows why I'm here is the duke of Devonshire, and he's a Whig, like yourself."

"Aye, William's a good man. It's only a pity that—" He broke off abruptly. "Never mind. What counts is this: I support you in theory, but I'm not about to put my head on the political chopping block until I've got a good indication that you can succeed. Understand?"

Paul nodded curtly. He was certain that Fox had not chosen his words carelessly. On the contrary, he had deliberately recalled to Paul's mind images that he must know needed desperately to be forgotten. Heads on chopping blocks were not a popular subject among French aristocrats these days. Paul could hardly miss the point.

"You've made yourself quite clear," he said, rising.

Sensing that he had gone too far, Fox was magnanimous. Walking with Paul to the door, he said, "I hope at least you'll enjoy yourself while you're here. All work and no play . . ."

Paul smiled coldly. He had every intention of taking Fox's advice, but he wasn't about to say so. While there was much to do, he didn't plan to work twenty-four hours a day. What time he had free would be spent with Dominique—provided, of course, that he could get her away from her grandmother, who was bound to be extremely protective.

After he took leave of Fox, he strolled along the riverfront, past the Palace of Westminster and the adjacent medieval abbey, where generations of English kings had been crowned. On impulse, he went inside and found himself a quiet spot in a corner not far from the main altar. When he emerged half an hour later, he felt calmer and more determined than ever about what he was going to do.

Fox was right—the chances of peace between England and France were extremely slim, and not only because of Pitt's opposition. There was a strong desire on both sides to keep the war going.

It might be that there wouldn't be much he could do about that. But he could do his damnedest to put his personal life in order. He would start immediately.

Not far from the abbey was a line of flower stalls. He stopped at one and delighted the elderly woman who ran it by purchasing an armload of daffodils, tulips, and irises. She was further pleased to provide a young nephew to deliver the flowers. He gave the boy Dominique's address and flipped him a shilling—extravagant pay for such a task.

But then, he was in an extravagant mood. Whistling, he set off toward his lodgings. His hands were stuck jauntily in his pockets; his golden head was bare. He looked like an exceptionally attractive man out for an afternoon's stroll, with nothing on his mind except the woman he loved.

It wasn't true, but it might have been, and for the moment, that was enough.

Chapter
19

"Tell me what happened," Dominique said softly. It was the following day. They were lying together in Paul's bed after making love.

Her ebony hair coiled over the white pillows and across his bare chest. The silken strands lifted slightly in the soft breeze coming from the open window.

Beneath her cheek, she felt the hard, solid curve of his shoulder. Beneath her hand was the raised ridge of the scar running across his abdomen.

"A narrow escape," he said quietly. With her in his arms, the memory seemed very distant and far less painful than usual.

Still, his turquoise eyes were shadowed as he said, "Robespierre was still in power; I was on the run. I'd hidden in a house outside of Paris, waiting to make my way into the city, but the location had been betrayed. I had to fight my way out."

She flinched, her imagination easily filling in what he

wasn't saying. Against his skin, she murmured, "It's a miracle that you're still alive."

He twined his fingers in her hair, bending her head to look at her. "A few days ago I would have said that I didn't believe in miracles, but now I've changed my mind."

She laughed softly and dropped a feather-light kiss on his mouth. But a moment later her smile faded and she was suddenly somber.

"Paul," she said quietly, "this can't go on. I love my grandmother and I can't bear deceiving her. Besides," she added, "I'm not at all sure that I've succeeded. She's definitely suspicious."

He could well believe that. His reception when he had arrived that morning to collect Dominique had been less than cordial. Lady Amelia had made no secret of the fact that she was displeased to find him back in London and even more so to find him on her doorstep.

Yet she could hardly refuse to allow Dominique to go with him for what was supposed to be an innocent ride in the park. Her suggestion that a young lady shouldn't be seen in public while still so bruised was waved aside with the promise that Dominique would wear a veil. It lay now in the tumult of their clothes, not far from Paul's bed.

"You can hardly tell Lady Amelia how you spent this afternoon," he reminded her gently.

"No, of course not, but I can be honest about my feelings for you, if only to prepare her for when—"

She broke off, suddenly acutely aware of the fact that she might have been presuming too much. After all, Paul had said nothing of the future.

"Never mind," she said hurriedly. "I'll take care of it myself. But now I must get back."

She made to rise from the bed, only to be stopped by a steely arm around her waist. Firmly ignoring her protests, Paul drew her close against him. Her buttocks nestled against his lower body, making her acutely aware of his resurgent desire.

"Have you noticed," he asked, sounding amused, "that we always seem to be rushing away from each other? It's a habit we really must break."

"Paul, I have to get back. And you have people to see." She paused, then added faintly, "That's always been the problem—the world intruding."

He wrapped his arms more securely around her and nuzzled the back of her neck, sending shivers of pleasure down her spine. Against her warm, scented skin, he murmured, "We've never had more than stolen moments, Dominique. I'm not content with that anymore."

Her eyes widened, reflecting the gilded expanse of the ceiling above. "W-what are you saying?"

Ah, well, there came a time when a man simply had to take the plunge. Heaven knew he'd been in tougher spots before. But this . . .

He took a deep breath, steeling himself. "I'm saying that I would like you to be my wife."

Her immediate response was not what he had imagined. She went rigid and glanced at him warily over her shoulder. "Are you serious?"

"I'd hardly be inclined to joke about something of this magnitude."

A moment longer she stared at him before her face was lit by a smile so radiant, so filled with happiness, that he could only stare in awe.

Joy filled her—exquisite, enthralling, all-encompassing joy. So much so that she thought she could not bear it.

For a moment, it seemed as though the world had skidded to a stop—as though ordinary, everyday existence had simply ceased.

It started up again quickly enough.

"Wait a moment," Paul said hastily. "You must listen to me, Dominique."

This was made all the more difficult by her squirming against him. He tried to stop her, but she succeeded in turning over.

Her breasts rubbed lingeringly against his chest, their limbs were intimately entwined, and when she pressed her mouth to his in a passion-drugged kiss, he felt like a man on the verge of tumbling into paradise.

"I love you so," she whispered against his lips. "I didn't want to tell you, isn't that silly? You were so horrid at the ball . . ."

"I'm sorry," he said humbly, the picture of contrition while below, beneath the sheet, his legs gently urged hers apart. There'd be time to talk later. At the moment, other considerations had suddenly become more urgent.

"It's all right, I don't mind now. But Paul . . . oh . . ."

Whatever she would have said was lost in the surge of passion as he entered her. Their earlier lovemaking had left her gloriously replete, but still moist and fully ready to receive him again. Nonetheless, he moved slowly, carefully, until he saw her head tilt back, her eyes half closing as desire seized her.

Some time later, Paul raised his head from the pillows and said faintly, "As I was saying, you must listen to me."

She nestled against him and smiled serenely. "By all means."

"Hmmm, don't pretend to be so compliant, my love—

it doesn't suit you. But never mind that now. I love you and I want you for my wife. However, I must be sure that you understand the situation. If the peace negotiations fail, France will remain in turmoil. Anything could conceivably happen—even a return to the desperate conditions of the past few years. Under those circumstances, I could not in all good conscience take you there. It would be far safer and wiser for you to remain in England.''

"Never mind about that," she said blithely. "We'll work it out as we go along. All that matters is that we be together.''

He frowned, knowing that it could not possibly be that simple, but reluctant to disillusion her. Life had a habit of doing that anyway, without his helping out.

Gently, he gathered her to him, stroking the long, slender line of her back. Her breath rose and fell with his; her mouth was sweet on his skin. Silently, he shut his eyes and willed time to stop.

It didn't, of course. Inexorably, the moments fled one upon the other, until it became essential for Dominique to leave.

Paul escorted her back, continuing the charade of the afternoon ride. He did not see Lady Amelia again, but he felt her lingering disapproval in the cold stare of the butler and the unnecessarily sharp crack of the door behind him, all of which served only to renew his purpose. He had already arranged meetings with several members of Parliament on the Whig side who might be sympathetic to the notion of peace.

Like Fox, they were hesitant, but at least willing to listen to what he had to say. Yet by the time he left them several hours later, his resolve had been replaced by a lingering sense of pessimism.

As one of the men had put it, "Our two countries have been at war for six years now, Monsieur de Rochford, and before that we were none too fond of each other. It's hard to think of there ever being peace between us."

Another had chimed in, "Especially so long as you've got that Boney fellow running around trying to conquer everything in the name of France."

And there he had the crux of the problem. France simply was not trusted. Despite all his pleas that the Directory truly wanted peace, he could see that he was not believed.

Unless and until the Corsican general was reined in, that would not change. Yet how could he be? It was no exaggeration to say that Bonaparte was rapidly emerging as a law unto himself. That filled Paul with cold, remorseless dread. It was all very well for Fox to talk lightly of dictators; he was an Englishman. It was France that had suffered for generations under the hand of tyranny.

Since the destruction of the Jacobins and the institution of the Directory, there had been a brief period of respite. But he was desperately afraid that it was too fragile to last.

He was in a gloomy frame of mind when he returned to his lodgings to dress for the evening ahead. Thanks to the patronage of the Prince of Wales, he had received several last-minute invitations to various social events. Riffling through the embossed cards as he dressed, he tried to find a glimmer of enthusiasm for any of them.

At length, he made his selection and set out. The evening was fine, clear, and pleasantly warm. He decided to forgo a hack and walk instead. The streets around St. James were filled with people hurrying to and fro on the evening social round.

He had walked five blocks and was nearing his destination when a large, somberly dressed man suddenly approached him. In the fading twilight, the man's face was ruddy, pockmarked, the nose set at an odd angle, as though it had been broken at some time in the past. He had the look of an old prize fighter, too often wounded in the brutal, bare-knuckle matches that passed for entertainment.

"Yer pardon, guv'nor," the man murmured. "Could ye be tellin' me the way to number fifty-seven?"

As he spoke, the man appeared to stumble. He reached out a hand to steady himself. At the same moment, Paul felt something slipped into his jacket pocket.

"Down that way," he said, gesturing with his hand in the direction of the address the man claimed to be seeking. He touched a finger to his hat, murmured his thanks, and moved hastily away.

Paul waited until he had put some distance between them before cautiously slipping a hand into his pocket. When he withdrew it again, he found himself staring at a small piece of paper folded down the middle and secured with a blank dab of sealing wax.

Swiftly, he opened the note and read it.

Your identity is known to P. Arrangements for your arrest are being made. We have not met. F.

Paul exhaled sharply. There was little doubt as to who P was. F must be Fox, writing to warn him that Pitt had discovered his true purpose in being in England, to secretly negotiate a peace. Pitt and his followers had sworn they would never lay down arms against France until every revolutionary was crushed. He would do anything he had to in order to stop Paul.

All this, of course, presumed that the note was genuine. There seemed little reason, however, for his enemies to fake any such warning. Why give him the chance to escape when they could gain far more by confining him and exposing his mission?

Swiftly, he turned on his heel and returned to his house. He was there, in the study, when William arrived. He smiled apologetically as the butler showed him in, then waited until the man had withdrawn before stepping forward to offer Paul his hand.

"I'm sorry we didn't have a chance to meet the other night. The crowd was a bit much."

"Of course," Paul said, gesturing for him to sit down. He was surprised to see the duke, as well as a bit wary.

Dominique had made it clear that she could have married William, had her feelings been different. She wasn't the sort of woman to be mistaken about something like that, or to lie about it.

William accepted the offer of brandy. He swallowed a good part of it down without appearing to taste it.

Paul had taken the seat opposite him. From where he sat, he could see the small clock on the mantelpiece. It reminded him of the passage of time and the pressing issue he must deal with.

Still, he did his best to hide his impatience, and a moment later was glad that he had done so.

"Fox doesn't know I'm here," William said. He smiled again, self-consciously. "He wouldn't approve, but I thought . . . well, that is, the situation's a bit rough, don't you think? Bad luck Pitt finding out, but one has to salvage whatever one can. The thing now is to get you out without anyone being the wiser."

"I see," Paul said slowly. It made a certain sense. William and Fox were on the same side—both Whigs, both opposed to Pitt and his policies. Moreover, Fox would be inclined to confide in the younger man, who by virtue of his birth and demeanor, seemed utterly trustworthy.

Paul was less certain of that, but he didn't see much alternative to listening to whatever William had to say.

"It's good of you to want to help," he told his guest.

The younger man shrugged lightly. "Don't think it's entirely altruistic."

At Paul's quizzical look, he went on, "If Pitt gets his hands on you, any chance of peace will be over and done with. He'll create a scandal so vicious that no one will be able to take the risk of speaking out for an end to the war. Everyone, including Fox and the Prince of Wales, will have to repudiate you. Personally, I'd rather not see that happen."

"What's the alternative?" Paul asked quietly.

"If you get safely away to France, Pitt won't be able to prove what you were doing here. There won't be any scandal. You'll have gotten your message across and you'll have outsmarted him. Quite a few people will enjoy that. It will put them in the mood to think very seriously about what you've had to say."

William made a persuasive case. He didn't minimize the problems or exaggerate the chance for success, but he did spell out a realistic scenario.

At any rate, Paul didn't have much choice. Arrest would mean the exposure of his mission, and that would mean disaster.

"It isn't only Englishmen who would have to deny me," Paul said quietly. "The French government would have to do the same or risk bringing Bonaparte's wrath down on them."

William took another long swallow of his brandy, finishing it. "All the more reason to go now."

Still, Paul hesitated. Slowly, he said, "There is a . . . personal complication."

The duke raised his head and looked at him directly. "Dominique?"

Paul suppressed a smile. Would he be as blunt in battle, this heir to generations of Norman and Saxon warriors? Probably.

"I must see her before I go."

William frowned. "That really isn't advisable. Your acquaintance with her is known. In all likelihood, the house will be watched."

"Nonetheless, it is essential."

"If you must communicate, I suggest it be by letter, which I will be glad to carry for you."

"Thank you," Paul said coolly, "but no."

Unspoken between them was the knowledge that William was not, after all, completely trusted. And why.

The duke's mouth thinned. He stared off into the distance. Paul waited, patient, unmoving, until he came to a resolution within himself.

"Very well. I will try to arrange it. But in the meantime, you must leave here. Every moment counts."

Paul was willing enough to believe that. Pitt wouldn't wait around forever to arrest him. He had taken a chance as it was, simply returning to the house.

"I'll be in touch," he said quietly as he rose and held out his hand again. "Thank you for your assistance."

William hadn't been expecting so direct a dismissal. Caught off guard, he said, "But you must tell me where you will be."

Paul walked toward the door, giving him no choice but to follow. "As I said, I'll be in touch." He smiled again, leaving no room for argument.

Clearly displeased but uncertain as to what else he could do, William departed. Barely had the door closed behind him than Paul moved.

He took the stairs to the second floor two at a time. In his bedroom, he yanked open the closet door and shoved aside the various silk and velvet garments hanging within—garments suitable to his stature as the marquis de Rochford, but not at all to his taste, and not at all suitable for where he was going.

Half an hour later, a tall, powerfully built man in the rough dress of a laborer slipped out the back door of the town house. He made his way through the garden, scaled the wall, and dropped to the other side. With a quick glance around, he set off down the street.

To satisfy his own curiosity, and confirm whether or not he was doing the right thing, he deliberately backtracked through alleys and side lanes until he stood near his residence.

Standing in the shadows, he observed the two men watching the front entrance. They were speaking between themselves while glancing up and down the street, as though expecting someone else to arrive.

They didn't have long to wait. As Paul watched, a carriage drew up in front. Half a dozen men emerged. They spoke briefly with the other two, then moved in a close-order drill toward the house.

One banged heavily on the door. The butler answered, appearing surprised and then distressed. He stood aside as the men pushed their way in.

Paul had seen enough. The warning had been correct; he had only just evaded arrest—hardly for the first time, and possibly not for the last.

Grimly, he set off down the street.

Chapter
20

"It is simply too much," Lady Amelia said angrily. "To not be able to walk about without being importuned. *Be off with ye.*"

She took a swat with her cane at the beggar who had dared to come too close. He ambled away, but his place was quickly taken by another.

Dominique was walking with her grandmother along New Bond Street. On either side of them were the fashionable shops patronized by the ton. Emblazoned carriages rolled up and down the thoroughfare, gloriously dressed ladies and gentlemen strolled by, windows overflowed with luxurious offerings of all sorts.

And the beggars abounded.

It was impossible to take a step without encountering them. They spilled over the pathways, loitered in the store entrances unless they were driven off, and generally made a nuisance of themselves. Some were children; others were fully adult. Both sexes were represented in about equal numbers. All were dressed in filthy, flea-infested rags that gave off an unmistakable stench.

"Fie," Lady Amelia said. "The authorities are much too soft. Put a few of them in jail and the rest would disappear quickly enough."

Dominique suppressed the retort that sprang to her lips—that the beggars only existed because of London's grinding poverty—and took her grandmother's arm more securely. Lady Amelia was an old woman, long since set in her ways. There was absolutely no point in arguing with her.

"Don't upset yourself," she murmured gently. "This is supposed to be fun."

"Don't cosset me, girl," Lady Amelia snapped back. Her spleen sufficiently vented, she softened somewhat. "But you're right. Let's try that new place—Danvers, what's the name of it?"

"Philips's, madame," Lady Amelia's elderly maid replied. If possible, age had made Danvers even more crotchety than her mistress. She had grumbled at going out, complained of their destination, and continually muttered under her breath until Maggie, who was accompanying Dominique, was ready to throttle her.

The younger maid tried to inject a note of enthusiasm into the excursion. "Would that be the new auction house, miss?"

Dominique nodded. "I understand they have some very good pictures. Shall we take a look, *grandmere*?"

Lady Amelia agreed and they continued on down the street until they came to number seven. The management of the auction house kept sturdy young men posted out in front to keep the beggars off. Lady Amelia and her party were not disturbed as they stepped inside.

Once there, Dominique relaxed slightly. Her grandmother, who was as acquisitive at seventy-seven as she had been half a century before, was quickly absorbed in the pictures. Danvers trailed after her, still muttering, as she moved about, peering at them through her lorgnette.

A respectful young man from the auction house had attached himself to them. He could answer whatever questions Lady Amelia might have.

Meanwhile, Dominique had other plans.

"My grandmother will be here for a while," she murmured to Maggie. "I'm going to get some fresh air."

The maid raised her eyebrows in surprise, but didn't quibble.

"If Lady Amelia asks for me," Dominique instructed, "tell her I'll be back directly."

"As you wish, miss," Maggie murmured. Her expression belied the propriety of her words. Plainly, she thought Dominique was mad.

Fresh air on New Bond Street? The effluvia of horse-drawn carriages, scattered wastes, and general rubbish made even the thought of any such thing absurd. But if that what was Miss Dominique wanted, she would not argue.

Outside once again, Dominique walked swiftly down the street until she came to the nearest corner. There she turned in the direction of Grosvenor Square. Barely had she done so than a large, especially filthy beggar accosted her.

"Spare a pence, miss?" he cajoled, falling into step with her.

Dominique was about to pay him off, simply to get rid of him, when she happened to glance at the grime-encrusted face in which turquoise eyes gleamed brilliantly.

"*Paul!*"

"Sshh," he said quickly, raising a finger to his lips. "Come on, this way."

Baffled, she followed him through a crack between two buildings and down a narrow alleyway.

"Watch where you go," Paul murmured. "This isn't the cleanest . . ."

With a stifled groan, she saw what he meant and hastily picked up her skirts. "Slow down. I can't keep up with you."

"This is far enough," he said, stopping before a high wooden fence that closed off one end of the alley. Turning, he smiled gently.

"Forgive me for not greeting you properly, my love, but I don't think you'd want the evidence of it smeared all over your fine clothes."

"Just out of curiosity," Dominique asked, studying him, "however did you manage to get so thoroughly foul?"

"Coal dust," he said succinctly. "It's a trick I've used before."

She didn't ask for details; there wasn't time, and besides, she had the distinct impression that she really didn't want to know.

Stilling the fear and worry she had been feeling for him ever since learning of Pitt's actions, she said, "Your note told me very little." Pointedly, she added, "William was more forthcoming."

Paul grinned wolfishly. "Is he still waiting for me to get in touch with him so that he might arrange our meeting?"

"I believe so. Really, it's too bad of you to play with William like this."

"Play? I'd hardly call it that. He was too damn close to having his life in my hands. I preferred to put some distance between us."

"You can't really believe he'd betray you," Dominique said, genuinely startled. "He's been a very good friend to me, and besides, he's a duke."

There were times when her naïveté shocked Paul. He didn't know how she had managed to preserve such innocence despite all that she'd been through.

Never mind, it wasn't important now. What counted was making her understand him.

"He's also a man," Paul said curtly, "and as such, is better left out of this. It concerns only the two of us."

He took a breath, readying himself to launch into the speech he had prepared, but Dominique forestalled him.

"I'm coming with you," she said.

"What?" He might have looked comical standing there in his beggar's disguise, except that the expression on his face was far too dangerous for humor.

Dominique did her best to ignore it. Sticking her chin in the air, she said, "You heard me. I understand that you must leave England at once. However, there is no reason for me not to go with you. *Grandmere* will be upset at first, but she's a realist, and will reconcile herself to it. Nicole and David will miss me, as I will them, but they're both growing up now, and besides, they'll be extremely well cared for. So, as you can see, nothing stands in our way."

She had been speaking very fast, wanting to get the words out before he could interrupt. When she stopped, the silence between them seemed very loud.

Finally, Paul said, "I realize this is very hard . . ." What in God's name was he to do? Surely she understood how mad such a scheme was, yet she seemed so set on it.

"Not hard at all," Dominique said. "I'm happy to go. England has definitely begun to pall. Besides, conditions are so much better in France now."

"Are they?" he demanded, suddenly fierce. "Because they're no longer lopping off heads in the Place de la Revolution?"

His hands came down hard on her shoulders. "By God, I thought I'd made myself clear. It could all start again tomorrow. Don't you understand that? I lost far too many friends, people I cared about, to take the risk of your being caught up in it. You'll stay here in England, where you're at least safe, or I'll damn well know the reason why."

Dismay surged through her. Surely he didn't really mean to leave her behind? Spurred by the fear that he meant exactly that, she lashed out impulsively.

"You aren't my master. Whatever you may think, I make my own decisions. I can return to France with or without your approval."

"To what end?" he demanded scathingly. Foolishly, without thought, he used the weapon that came most readily to hand. "Disobey me in this, Dominique, and I swear our relationship will be at an end. You'll achieve nothing by following me."

That did it. Her eyes shot fire as she said, "Following you? Why, you loutish swine! I'm not some lovesick sheep to trail after you. If I go to France, it will be for my own benefit, not yours. And that's what it would have been, *Monsieur le grand Marquis*, if I'd been fool enough to plight my troth with you. When I think . . ."

"*Quiet*," he roared, somewhat defeating his own purpose. No matter. He'd heard enough and more. Independent women were all very well and good until they got out of hand, which this one most definitely had.

Such circumstances of extreme distress will make a fool of the most sensible man, and never more so than when he thinks himself in possession of a brilliant idea. Forgetting himself, forgetting her, Paul tried a different tack—one that was singularly ill-advised.

"Dominique, sweetheart, be sensible. We can be married here before I leave. That way we'll still be together, in a sense, but you'll be safe."

And William would be nicely shut out, he thought. That was an altogether ideal solution. He was quite proud of himself for thinking of it.

"Married?" Dominique repeated frostily. "So that I can sit here anguishing over you while you chase your dreams of a perfect France? No thank you, Monsieur Delamare. I have better ways to spend my days."

And with that, she turned neatly on her heel and made to depart. The effect was only slightly spoiled when her toe snagged the hem of her gown and she almost fell forward, but she recovered herself before Paul could come to her aid. Shooting him one last glacial glare, she stomped out of the alley, heedless of whatever lay in her path.

"*Sacred heaven*," Paul muttered under his breath. He'd made a mess of that, for sure. To make it even worse, there was nothing he could do at the moment to rectify the situation. He had to avoid arrest and return to France to report what had happened.

But he could come back. That was it. In a few weeks, a couple of months at the worst, he'd slip back into the country, and then, nothing would keep him from Dominique.

There was something familiar about that. It had the

irksome ring of a mistake he'd heard somebody else make. No, not so much a mistake . . . a delusion.

He shook his head wearily. Time was running out; he had to go. But at least Dominique would still be safe.

He wondered if that was another delusion. Yet he had no choice but to believe it. He struggled to do so all the way out of London, to Dover and the ship that carried him home to France.

"Please try to understand, grandmother," Dominique said softly. "I love you dearly and I appreciate everything you have done, but the time has come for me to leave."

"It's all because of that man," Lady Amelia said. She banged her cane on the parquet floor, heedless of whatever damage it might do.

"I rue the day I ever let him into my house. And you —whatever can you be thinking of? What about your life here, Nicole and David, William?"

"William is only . . ." Dominique broke off. She didn't know quite what to say. Certainly, her grandmother knew of her reluctance to marry the duke, and must have discerned the reason.

"I'm sorry," she murmured at length. "I simply don't love William, and if I were to marry him under such circumstances, I would be doing him a terrible disservice."

"Such nobility," Lady Amelia said. "The ultimate indulgence of youth. You'll learn, my girl, to your sorrow, that you must make the best of what life hands you. William is a good man, whereas Delamare . . ."

"I'm not going to France because of Paul," Dominique said firmly. "It's all over between us."

"What is over?" Lady Amelia demanded shrewdly.

When her granddaughter failed to reply, she went on, "Exactly how far has this gone?"

Belatedly aware that she had revealed too much, Dominique flushed. Tears shone in her green-gold eyes. "Please, Grandmother," she murmured brokenly, "I don't think I can bear . . ."

"Oh, sweet lord. You foolish chit. Don't tell me you've . . ."

Without further ado, Lady Amelia gathered her granddaughter to her. She held Dominique tenderly as the young girl sobbed, rocking her back and forth and crooning to her gently until at last, the paroxysm of grief spent itself.

Dominique raised her head to find herself staring into eyes filled with wisdom and compassion. "So," her grandmother said brusquely, "you'll go after a man who couldn't bring himself to do the honorable thing."

"On the contrary," Dominique said wearily, "he was all set to drag me off to the altar before his departure."

Despite herself, Lady Amelia smiled. "And you resisted?"

"I refused outright. How dare he imagine I would agree to such a thing—to be stamped and sealed, then left behind like an unwanted parcel. When I think . . ."

"All right, dear, I believe I'm fully in the picture now. So you don't want to marry Monsieur de Rochford, but you still think you should return to France?"

Slowly, Dominique nodded. Even as she sensed that she was not being completely honest, she said, "This is my best possible chance to reclaim our estates. I can't let it go by without at least making the attempt."

Lady Amelia herself understood the lure of land and honor far too well to argue. Still, she did not relish her granddaughter going into so uncertain a situation. Rather, she would have preferred her to remain sheltered and protected, at least a little while longer.

But then, Dominique had never truly been that, not since the first days of the Revolution, when all semblance of security had been ripped away from her.

Slowly, Dominique reached for a slender gold chain around her neck. She lifted it to reveal an inlaid locket still warm from lying against her heart.

The locket clicked as she opened it. Inside was a miniature portrait of the French royal family. Marie Antoinette smiled out of the tiny canvas. Seated next to her husband, surrounded by her children, she looked utterly content— a woman untouched by any shadow of the future.

"They were only human beings," Dominique said softly, gazing at the portrait, "who happened to be born to tremendous responsibilities. They made mistakes; there were things they should have done and didn't. *But they didn't deserve to die.*"

"Child," Lady Amelia said shakily, "life is so very often unfair."

"I know that, but don't you see? I loved them, yet there was nothing I could do to help. The queen . . ."

She bent her head again, struggling for composure. "She was all alone, with no one to comfort her in those final hours. She had to face it all by herself. She must have been terrified for her children and filled with despair, but she gave no sign of it. She behaved with dignity right to the end."

"To her eternal credit, but what has that to do with you?"

"I can't do less than she did. I have to face my fears —all the terrors of the past that you and Paul are trying to protect me from. For my own sake, and for the sake of the future, I must go back.''

Lady Amelia closed her eyes. Behind the worn, wrinkled lids, a universe of darting lights danced and played. She was tempted for an instant to let everything go and sink into them.

Abruptly, she opened her eyes. ''All right, you must go back. But not, you say, to resume your relationship with Monsieur Delamare. Then what, precisely, do you expect to achieve? Surely, I have the right to know that much?''

Dominique closed the locket. She tucked it back into place beside her heart and stood up. The smile she gave her grandmother was filled with purpose.

''I am going to reclaim Montfort,'' she said calmly. ''It is our family's heritage and David's birthright. It will be ours again.''

Her smile deepened, bright with confidence and anticipation. For too long she had allowed herself to be buffeted this way and that, without taking any direct hand in her own destiny. Now that was going to change.

''And then,'' she said softly, ''we shall see.''

Chapter
21

Leaning against the wall in Dominique's gilded drawing room, Paul surveyed the passing scene. The wall was covered in white embossed brocade. By contrast, he was dressed in black, as unrepentantly masculine as his usual attire and compellingly attractive despite its absolute rejection of fashion. His thick golden hair was brushed back from his high forehead and his turquoise eyes glinted with a wolfen gleam as he watched the peacock-garbed men and women flitting about beneath the crystal chandeliers.

Trust Dominique. Little more than a year after returning to Paris, she possessed it completely—or at least the portion of Parisian society that mattered to an ambitious young woman.

Her salon was the most fashionable, eclipsing even that of the legendary Madame de Stael. Her parties were the most glittering, her clothes the most discussed, her every action and word repeated, analyzed, and delighted over to a degree that was nothing less than fawning.

Beautiful, fickle, enraptured Paris had found in Dominique exactly what it was looking for—a young woman of surpassing beauty, wealth, and heritage who by her mere presence signaled that the days of violence were over. Now all that mattered was gossip, romance, intrigue—the truly important things in life.

She was looking particularly lovely this evening, Paul thought sardonically. Her high-waisted tunic dress of cloth-of-gold over ivory silk was the height of fashion, perhaps even a little beyond. No matter, whatever Dominique wore, the *modistes* of the rue St. Honore would be frantically copying within a day or two. Her ebony hair was drawn up to the crown of her head, then allowed to fall in a cascade of silver-black curls. Watching her from across the room, he could see the green-gold sparkle of her eyes, the slight flush of her cheeks, the full, rose softness of her mouth.

Infuriating woman. He took another sip of his drink— champagne, of course; Dominique served nothing else— and scowled. Beside him, a tall, narrow-faced man laughed.

"She's in superb form tonight, isn't she?"

Paul didn't bother to glance at the other man. His eyes remained on Dominique as he said, "When isn't she?"

Charles Maurice de Talleyrand laughed. Foreign minister of France, diplomat, statesman, and intriguer *par excellence*, he was a man of keen sensibilities who was thoroughly enjoying himself, not in the least because of Paul's discomfort. To see the brilliant, respected, and even feared marquis de Rochford thrown by a young woman was a sight so rare as to deserve relishing.

"There now," he said soothingly, "surely it isn't so bad? At least we were invited. The alternative, my friend, would be a fate worse than death, or so I am informed by the social arbiters who rank an invitation from the lovely Mademoiselle de Montfort among the necessities of life."

Paul muttered an expletive under his breath and continued watching Dominique. She was enjoying herself thoroughly, as always. The party was a brilliant success, the food and wine perfection, the house magnificent, the guests suitably enchanted. Ah, yes, Dominique had every right to be pleased. She appeared to have exactly what she wanted.

"Of course," Talleyrand murmured as he, too, watched her, "all that money does help."

Paul shot him a chiding look. "I thought we were all supposed to believe that the Directory was simply happy to assist a loyal daughter of France by returning her family's property."

Talleyrand snorted into his champagne. He didn't bother to dignify with a reply what both men knew to be patently untrue. Since her return to France, Dominique had cut a swath through the highest reaches of the government. Talleyrand was by no means alone in succumbing to her charm. Charm, as he said, glazed by judicious applications of money, not to mention influence.

"It's really a shame," the foreign minister said, still eyeing Dominique, "that she wasn't born a man."

Paul choked. He couldn't think of any more outlandish or unlikely violation of nature. "Why on earth do you say that?"

"Because she's brilliant, politically speaking. She knows exactly what to do and say to achieve her ends. And she does it all with a minimum of fuss. In fact, anyone watching her would swear she was having a marvelous time.''

Reluctantly, Paul had to agree. It was that, more than anything else, that rankled. Dominique went blithely on her way while he suffered a slew of emotions, none of them pleasant.

When he had first discovered her presence in Paris the previous summer, he had been shocked and concerned, with good cause. Yet another coup had been underway as members of the Directory were deposed and others put in their place. For a time it had been unclear which way the country would go—rightist, leftist, anarchist. In that atmosphere, Paul had felt compelled to go to her and offer his help—which had been promptly refused.

Moreover, she had wasted no time making it clear that, far from hoping to resume their relationship, she considered it at an end. She had, in effect, called his bluff—something he was still, all these months later, having difficulty dealing with.

How dare she upset his plans, make a mockery of his honorable self-sacrifice, and gaily go her own way, as though he didn't even exist? Moreover, how dare she be so incandescently beautiful and so stunningly successful to boot?

Not that he was still angry at her; of course not. That would be absurd. He had far more important matters with which to concern himself. Watching Dominique make fools of other men was merely an amusement—one that was, unfortunately, ultimately less than satisfying. He took another sip of his champagne and discovered that the glass was empty. A passing waiter recovered it and supplied him with a fresh one.

Talleyrand lingered, chatting. Paul listened to him with

half an ear. He wasn't in the mood to talk about Bonaparte, who rumor had it would be arriving in Paris at any moment, fresh from his so-called victories in Egypt.

He was being proclaimed the conqueror of that land, but Paul privately had his doubts. Too many of the reports from the battlefields suggested that the great general might have met his match. Bonaparte might simply have decided that the wisest strategy was to declare victory and get out.

"I understand Mademoiselle de Montfort has become great friends with the lovely Josephine," Talleyrand said. "But then, it's hardly surprising. Despite the difference in their ages, they come from similar backgrounds."

"I suppose," Paul murmured, still hardly listening. Dominique was talking with a tall, well-built young man he recognized as the son of one of the government Directors. The fellow was staring at her in delighted bemusement as though she was an angel only lightly touched down to earth.

He turned away in disgust, only to find Talleyrand staring at him oddly. A tiny smile quirked the foreign minister's mouth. "Would you like me to start over?"

"I'm sorry," Paul said. "I seem to be rather preoccupied this evening."

"I can't imagine why," Talleyrand murmured dryly. "But at any rate, what I was saying was that it is perhaps inevitable that your Mademoiselle de Montfort and Madame Bonaparte have become friends. After all, before she wed Napoleon, Josephine was married to a viscount of the old regime. He died in the Terror, as you may know. At any rate, they both lost a great deal in the Revolution, although I must say they have both recovered very nicely."

"So Dominique—not my Dominique, by the way; she

has made that quite clear—so she and Bonaparte's wife are friends. Why should that interest me?''

Talleyrand shrugged. ''It is one more reason for you to be wary of her, my young friend, if you aren't already sufficiently so.''

Paul took another swallow of his champagne and said blandly, ''I have no argument with Bonaparte.''

The foreign minister shot him a hard, swift look. ''Indeed? I had thought otherwise.''

''Why?'' Paul countered smoothly. ''Surely we can all agree that France's legitimate military objectives have been achieved. Peace must now be regarded as inevitable. Bonaparte has done all that could be asked of any man and more. He must welcome the successful conclusion of his efforts.''

''Ah,'' Talleyrand said softly, ''is that how you see it?''

Paul turned a hard eye on him. There was no further pretense between them as he said, ''General Bonaparte would do well to remember that we did not fight a revolution in order to exchange one form of tyranny for another.''

Talleyrand leaned forward slightly. He glanced around to make sure that no one else could hear them. Paul wasn't sure whether his concern was genuine or for effect, but it didn't matter. The foreign minister had his attention as he murmured, ''All I am asking is that you not condemn him out of hand.''

''I'm not in the habit of doing that with anyone,'' Paul responded, a shade stiffly.

Talleyrand raised an eyebrow. Pointedly, he glanced in Dominique's direction. ''Oh, really?''

Half an hour later, still lounging against the wall, still

drinking champagne, Paul admitted to himself that the foreign minister had a point. Talleyrand had gone off to put a word or two in other ears. Several ladies, all lovely, had attempted to engage Paul in conversation, without success. He was in no mood to relinquish his self-imposed solitude. He was fully involved thinking about Dominique.

"*Monsieur*?" The sotto-voce interruption of the waiter at Paul's elbow jolted him back to awareness momentarily. Absently, he exchanged his empty glass for another that was full and emptied it in turn, hardly aware that he was doing so.

Across the room, Dominique laughed. She was standing at the center of an admiring crowd of gentlemen, one of whom must have said something amusing. Her head tilted back, the cascade of curls brushing the small of her back. The sound of her laughter, like water rippling over mossy earth, unheard yet remembered, washed through him. He felt his body harden and cursed under his breath.

His eyes narrowed to glinting shards of turquoise ice. Abruptly, he straightened and crossed the room toward her.

Dominique saw him coming, although she gave no immediate sign of that. Not counting the first meeting, when she had made it clear that she intended to maintain her independence, they had seen each other only a handful of times, always in public and very briefly. There was no reason to think this wouldn't be the same, which did not at all explain the sudden flutter in her stomach as he approached.

"Paul," she murmured when she could no longer pretend not to see him, "how nice. I had no idea you were here."

Instantly, the adoring crowd around her seemed to disintegrate and drift away. It was as though a silent signal had been given. The men looked at Paul—leonine, predatory, relentless—and saw danger. The women saw obliviousness; he literally did not know they were there. They quickly decided there was no point in lingering.

All around them the party continued, bustling, loud, filled with the deliberate gaiety of people determined to demonstrate that they belong.

But to all intents and purposes, Paul and Dominique might as well have been alone.

He lifted his glass to her in mock salute, drained it, and set it down on a nearby table, all without taking his eyes from her.

"May I say, Mademoiselle de Montfort, that you look lovely?"

She stared at him for a moment, her eyes widening. His cheeks were unnaturally flushed and there was a glint in his eyes she didn't quite recognize—at least, not at first. Slowly, understanding dawned.

Incredulously, she said, "You're tiddled." Her amazement was genuine; she had never seen Paul in such a state. Indeed, she wouldn't have even thought it possible.

He was offended and showed it. Drawing himself up on his dignity, he said, "Don't be ridiculous. I am never tiddled, as you put it." Deftly, he helped himself to another glass from the tray of a passing waiter and drained it, too.

Dominique was having second thoughts. Maybe her first impression was wrong. Certainly, he seemed to be a man perfectly in control of himself.

Perhaps too perfectly. She sensed a certain iron will in play that worried her.

Cautiously, she said, "I wasn't sure you would be here tonight."

Despite herself, she couldn't keep a faint note of yearning out of her voice. For the past several months, she had been away from the capital, staying at Montfort. At first, she had gone merely to ascertain the estate's condition and determine what needed to be done. But she had quickly come to take a personal interest in the reconstruction and decided to stay on for a while to observe it. And she had lived constantly with the apprehension—or was it the hope—that she would encounter Paul on the neighboring estate which had, after all, been his father's.

It wasn't until several months had passed that she learned he had sold the land and was using at least part of the money to finance the construction of a private hospital in Paris, where he had also resumed the practice of medicine, a practice that apparently kept him far too busy for society dillydallying, at least so far as her invitations were concerned.

Meticulously, in keeping with his recognized position in society, she invited him to all her large parties. To do otherwise would have raised questions she did not care to answer. It was bad enough for Paul to decline her hospitality. At least people could excuse that on the grounds that Monsieur le Marquis was simply very busy and didn't seem to care much for such pursuits anyway. Only Dominique knew that the affront was personal and gnashed her teeth over it, even as she contrived to appear completely unaffected.

Once she glimpsed him at the opera during the interval, but they were quickly separated by the crowd before she could even think of speaking to him. Another time she caught sight of him while strolling near the Louvre. He was going into one of the government buildings that lined the nearby streets and didn't notice her.

None of these encounters helped her temper any. For

all that he might prefer to claim otherwise, he certainly knew where she was should he choose to call upon her. But the months passed without his putting in an appearance at the renovated and restored town house not far from the fashionable rue St. Honore. There were days when it seemed that all the rest of Paris dropped by to visit. Paul, however, was never among them.

Until now.

Trust him to come on this particular evening, when the tension in the air was all but palpable. No one seemed interested in talking about anything other than Bonaparte's imminent arrival. Speculation was rife as to what he would do, what demands he would make, whether the Directory would be able to withstand them.

Dominique was no more immune from the tension than anyone else. Hardly aware that she did so, she signaled for a waiter, took a glass of champagne, and drank it in a single gulp. Paul watched her with amusement. He was cynically glad to see her so discomfited. He believed it served her right after what she'd put him through.

"Aren't you cold?" he murmured.

She eyed him warily. "No, why?"

"That slip of a gown you've sort of got on. I'd have thought you'd be freezing. In fact," he added with an unholy smile of satisfaction, "aren't those goose bumps?" Deliberately, he gazed at the generous expanse of alabaster skin exposed by her neckline, where indeed the skin had puckered, though not from the cold. Dominique flushed, knowing full well that what she was feeling was the effect of his presence solely. If anything, the drawing room was too warm, and growing warmer by the moment.

"Well, it was certainly nice of you to drop by . . ." she ventured.

He smiled, sending a tremor through her. He really was the most dangerous man. She had been a fool to ever nurture tender feelings for him. He saw the world strictly on his own terms and was relentless in his approach to it. Hadn't he been willing to leave her behind in England while he trotted back to Paris and had all the fun? Hadn't he virtually ignored her ever since? Never mind that she had done everything possible to encourage his disinterest.

"You know," she said, "I've been having the most wonderful time."

"Somehow, I'm not surprised."

"I mean, everyone has been most kind. Did you know I've had Montfort returned?"

"I heard the Directory practically tripped over itself doing so."

She frowned at his sarcasm. "Well, why shouldn't they? After all, it does belong to my family. Besides, other people are getting their property back."

"Buying it back, you mean. And the only reason they're allowed to do so is that the government has needed money to prosecute this damnable war. I'm sure your contribution came in handy."

Dominique glared at him. "I don't like the war any more than anyone else. If you remember from when you were in England, *if* you can cast your mind back that far to so obviously inconsequential a time in your life, I was all for peace."

Perversely, her words pleased him. He liked her angry, on the offensive, ready to challenge and contest him. That was the Dominique he knew and loved.

No, dammit. He wasn't falling into that again. She was too independent, too impulsive, too strong-willed—everything he might admire from a distance in a woman but be dismayed to find in a wife.

But she was also Dominique—beautiful, sensual, responsive. He swallowed hard, aware suddenly that he was having trouble breathing.

"How much longer . . ." he muttered.

"What?" she asked, staring up at him, seeing only him.

With an effort, he said, "Will this party go on?"

She looked surprised, as though she'd forgotten there was a party, other people, anything standing between them. Abruptly, she recalled herself. "Hours yet." Reluctantly, she added, "Naturally, as hostess, I have to circulate."

"Naturally," he muttered.

They stood moments longer gazing at each other until the ebb and flow of the crowd seized them again and gradually, inexorably, drew them apart.

It was hours later, well after midnight. Paul sat slumped in a chair in what appeared to be a library. At least, the room was lined with books which he kept thinking about looking at, but somehow didn't manage. Instead, he remained where he was, staring into the fire.

A butler came and went occasionally. The last time he removed the empty bottle of champagne at Paul's feet and replaced it with a fresh one in a nicely chilled silver bucket of ice.

Paul hadn't touched it. He'd had enough to drink, probably more than enough. But he didn't feel drunk, much as he rather thought he'd like to. Instead he felt coldly, unrelentingly sober. More's the luck.

He sighed deeply. His stock was undone and the catch

of his shirt was open. He had his feet propped up on an embroidered ottoman. Firelight reflected off the tips of his highly polished boots.

He might have been asleep. That was certainly Dominique's first thought when she entered the room. Her guests had gone home, the last of them departing in jovial good humor out into the snow-strewn street not fifteen minutes before. She had sent the servants to bed. The house lay wrapped in stillness, punctuated only by the crackle of the fire and the soft murmur of the wind beyond the high, curtained windows.

She took a step closer, watching the man stretched out long and lean before her. On second thought, she didn't think he was asleep. There was too much coiled energy about him for that. But neither did he look as though he wanted to be disturbed.

With a sudden, surely misplaced sense of tenderness, she said, "Shall I fetch you a blanket?"

Her voice was soft but the words seemed to ring loudly in the little room. Paul didn't straighten, but he did open his eyes and look at her.

"That presumes I'm staying."

She lowered herself gracefully onto the settee across from him and smiled. Perhaps she was merely too tired to be angry anymore, but she was suddenly feeling absurdly calm. Lightly, she said, "It's after two o'clock and snowing."

He raised an eyebrow. "Heavily?"

"Heavily enough." She sighed and leaned back against the tufted velvet cushions. The tension she had been feeling all evening, since realizing that he was there, seemed to have evaporated. She closed her eyes for a moment, grateful for the surcease. When she opened them again, Paul was looking at her.

"After two o'clock" he said quietly. "That means it's my birthday."

Her eyes widened. Only then did she remember what had been buried so deep within her consciousness as to almost be forgotten. "Why, so it is." A moment passed, another. On impulse, she held out her hand to him. "Happy birthday, Paul."

He took the slim, cool fingers between his own. They were scented with her perfume—lilac, jasmine, woman. The nails were perfectly shaped and buffed. On one finger, she wore a ruby surrounded by diamonds.

"Pretty," he murmured. "Who gave it to you?"

"What makes you think I didn't buy it for myself?" she countered.

He shrugged. "Beautiful women never have to buy their own jewels."

"Not have to, but perhaps want to. I like being independent."

"So I have noticed," he said dryly. He glanced at the ring again, trying hard to believe that she really had bought it for herself. "There's no panting admirer in the wings?"

"Dozens. Is that what you want to hear?"

He sat up further, still holding her hand, the lion awakening.

"Oh, no, sweet Dominique," he murmured, "that's not at all what I want."

A shiver ran through her. She tried to reclaim her hand, only to find herself pulled suddenly off balance. With a soft exclamation, she fell against him.

"Let go."

He shook his head, laughing at her. "I don't think so."

"I mean it, Paul, let go."

"You have a short memory, sweetheart."

She looked at him apprehensively. "W-what do you mean?"

"That last night in London, I told you we kept running away from each other and that it had to stop."

"And then you promptly did it again," she said tartly. "Short memory, indeed."

"All right, I made a mistake," he conceded. "But it was for the best of motives. I really did think Paris would be too treacherous for you."

He laughed again, dangerously soft, infinitely male. "I should have known you'd be able to hold your own and more."

"I've managed."

"Brilliantly, as always."

"No," she murmured, bracing her free hand against his chest, only to instantly regret it. Beneath her skin, she could feel the measured beat of his heart. It reminded her of when she had last felt that, lying side by side with him, naked, entwined. . . .

"Paul, it's late."

"An astute observance."

"I have things to do tomorrow—today, that is. I must get some sleep."

"Busy on my birthday?"

"I'm going to church," she insisted. "It's permissible again, and besides, I want to. Afterward, Josephine de Beauharnais is giving a party. I promised that I would go."

"Josephine Bonaparte," Paul corrected grimly. "Poor

old Beauharnais was her first husband. He died, remember?''

Dominique swallowed hard. She hated reminders of that time, as did most everyone she knew. Quickly, to change the subject, she said, "Poor Josephine. I think she wants to forget sometimes that she married the Corsican."

"Why did she?" Paul asked idly. He really didn't care. Dominique's hair had caught his eye. It was coming undone. He wound a silken curl around one finger and tugged lightly.

"Ouch," she protested, "stop that. She thought he had money."

"Did he?"

"Of course not. He was just a newly minted general and church mouse poor. He thought *she* was rich."

"Poor Josephine, indeed," Paul said with a grin. "And poor Boney."

"Don't call him that; he hates it."

"All the more reason."

She sighed and sat up slightly, looking at him. "You're going to be difficult, aren't you?"

He frowned slightly. "Is that how you see me—a troublemaker?"

Softly, she smiled. "No, not that, worse. An idealist."

"Perish the thought."

Her gaze fell to his mouth, watching him shape the words, remembering . . .

"Paul, please . . ."

"Please what?"

"Please be sensible, be prudent. For once in your life, do what's best for you."

He shrugged dismissively. "I always have."

"You never . . ."

He stopped her with a look. "I'm serious, Dominique. I have lived a singularly selfish life, in the sense that I have always done precisely as I wished. Or almost always. The only times I've wavered from that have been when you were involved."

"You wished to leave me in England," she reminded him.

"No, not entirely, not even mainly. It was . . . complicated."

Her breath touched his cheek—warm, sweet, remembered. "Why?"

He raised her hand, carrying it to his lips. Holding her gaze with his, he murmured, "Because, sweet Dominique, you make me feel as though the world has turned upside down and I am floating off into space, never to touch land again."

She breathed in sharply, partly because of what he said, partly because he was drawing her fingers one by one into his mouth, sucking on each one gently and biting the soft nub of each just hard enough to hurt.

Desperate now, she whispered, "I don't believe you. You never lose control of yourself."

He raised his head slightly and smiled. "As I said, a short memory."

She flushed, realizing what he meant—the heated, golden hours in London when all restraint had vanished; the passion and the power she had felt pouring from him, engulfing her, making her his.

Oh, lord, she was still so terrifyingly vulnerable to him. Why had she been mad enough to come in here? Better she should have gone straight to bed.

She was unaware that she'd spoken out loud until she realized that Paul was gazing at her sardonically.

"Is that an invitation?" he inquired.

"*Of course not*. Don't be absurd."

"What's absurd about it? I've shared your bed before."

"You hardly need to remind me of that," she shot back, and immediately resumed the struggle to free herself, to no avail. A steely arm wrapped around her waist held her snugly in place. All her efforts succeeded in doing was making her abruptly aware of his arousal.

"Oh, I didn't mean . . ." To his delight—or his chagrin, he wasn't sure which—she flushed red.

"Why so surprised?" he countered. "Surely you must know by now that when an extremely beautiful and desirable woman does certain things to man, whether she intends it or not, certain results occur."

Dominique considered that thoughtfully. She was no longer merely beautiful but *extremely* so. Not to mention desirable. But then, there was also that passing reference to the level of her experience.

"You're not going to start that again, are you? Thinking that I've been with other men?"

"No," Paul said promptly. She was surprised and said so. "It's simple," he explained. "If I let myself think of you with anyone else, I'll go mad, and I'd rather avoid that."

"Oh . . . all right, then. It's just as well, since there's still only been you."

"I admit to being relieved to hear that," he said, giving her a crooked grin.

"I'm not sure I am. Mind you, there have been plenty of opportunities."

"I don't doubt it for a moment," he said solemnly.

"Too many by far. Sometimes I think it's all anyone in Paris thinks about."

"Possibly." Hastily, he added, "With the exception of the two of us, of course."

"Of course," she murmured. What was he doing now—that hand moving down her back. "Paul . . . ?"

"There's something to be said for the practice of medicine," Paul murmured, "not to mention the associated discipline of surgery. It teaches a man to be dexterous."

A warm puff of air touched Dominique's bare skin. She flinched, only to utter a soft exclamation of dismay when her gown fell forward from her shoulders. Dexterous by far. Paul had undone the buttons in the back with greater skill than any lady's maid could have managed, and in the process, left her nearly nude.

"You," she muttered, "are incredibly presumptuous."

"Oh, no, sweet Dominique," he murmured as he stood suddenly with her in his arms and crossed the narrow space to the fireplace. Before it lay a thick Persian carpet and on that he laid Dominique.

"Not presumptuous," he said, lowering himself beside her. "Only desperate . . . and resigned."

She gazed up at him, watching the play of firelight across the sculpted planes of his face. So beautiful a man, though he would undoubtedly scoff at the word. So unyielding in his faith and his determination. So far above the ordinary tawdriness of everyday life.

A man not for the moment but forever.

Heaven help her.

"Is this surrender I hear?" she asked with the softest and gentlest of smiles. Generous in victory, always magnanimous.

"I very much fear it is," he said as he slid the cloth-of-gold and ivory silk dress from her. Beneath it she wore only the thinnest of chemises and fragile silk stockings held up by garters embroidered with rosebuds.

"Total surrender," he murmured thickly as he gazed at her. "Absolute and complete."

She smiled again and raised her arms, drawing him to her. Drawing him home.

Chapter
22

Of course, it wasn't that simple.

By morning, they were arguing again. It happened easily enough. They had made love once in the library, again upstairs in Dominique's wide bed. In between, they had held each other and talked. Neither had felt any urge to sleep. All very well and good, but by morning they were both tired, and paradoxically, given the pleasure they had shared, out of sorts.

Perhaps they were both simply afraid.

"I promised her I would go," Dominique said stubbornly as she sat wrapped in a froth of silk and lace at her dressing table. "A promise is a promise."

"She won't even know you aren't there," Paul insisted. He lay in bed, hands folded behind his head, the sheet no higher than his hips. Dominique tried very hard not to stare at his powerfully muscled, bare torso as she said, "That isn't fair. Josephine is always aware of such things."

"All the more reason not to go. She sounds shallow."

"She's my friend," Dominique protested.

"She's convenient. The great Bonaparte's wife—one more conduit for you to the people you imagine are important."

"Oohh." Dominique slammed her hairbrush down hard on the inlaid table and turned on him. Her green-gold eyes flashed daggers.

"You," she said succinctly, "are a bigot. You think anyone who happens to be in a position of influence is automatically suspect, someone to be avoided. It doesn't occur to you that she might actually be a nice person who cares for others and wants to help."

"More pity her," he shot back, angry at himself, angry at her. She was right, of course. He had nothing against Josephine de Beauharnais Bonaparte, except perhaps her taste in husbands. And even that, according to Dominique, had been inadvertent.

What he disliked was having to share Dominique with anyone so soon after their reunion. He wanted to keep her all to himself, far from the interference of the world, which wasn't even remotely fair.

"All right," he said finally, relenting. "We'll both go."

Dominique wasn't yet willing to forgive him. Stiffly, she said, "You weren't invited."

"Sneak me in."

"Perhaps . . ." She turned back to the mirror and began brushing her long, luxurious hair.

He grinned at her in the glass.

Whatever financial problems had caused the Bonapartes to marry three years before had seemingly been overcome. The house to which Paul accompanied Dominique later that day was situated in one of Paris's most exclusive neighborhoods, not far from the opera. The three-story marble residence was elegant, spacious, a throwback to the days before the Revolution. It was also magnificently furnished and amply staffed.

"All gifts from his admirers," Dominique explained in a whisper as they were admitted by a butler outfitted in satin and lace, no less glorious than those she remembered from Versailles.

In fact, she wasn't absolutely sure, but it was possible that the uniform was the same. No, surely not? Not even Bonaparte, staunch anti-royalist that he claimed to be, would go that far. Or would he?

"How thoughtful," Paul murmured. He held Dominique's arm lightly as they proceeded through the crowded entry hall. It seemed as though all of Paris had only one objective on this day—to pay their respects to the man of the hour, Napoleon Bonaparte.

He had arrived in the city secretly, coming by way of Cairo and his extraordinary succession of disputed victories. Word of his coming had been greeted with intense anticipation.

"No one is quite sure what he will do next," Dominique acknowledged. "But surely he must be tired of fighting."

Paul cast her a skeptical look. "More to the point, the people of France are tired of it."

"Do be sure to tell him that," a voice behind them said dryly. They turned to find Talleyrand, looking tired but alert, an old war-horse relishing the scent of battle, political or otherwise.

"Do you think he would listen?" Paul asked with a smile.

"Perhaps. He seems willing to listen to anyone about almost anything. That's one of his great strengths."

Paul shrugged, unimpressed. "It costs nothing to listen. And it keeps people guessing about what he actually intends."

"An idealist who is also a cynic," Talleyrand said with a sigh. "What are we to do with him, mademoiselle?"

"I could make one or two suggestions," Dominique said lightly, "but I fear that Monsieur le Marquis would not approve."

The foreign minister looked at her admiringly. "A woman of restraint—such a rarity."

Paul swallowed a laugh, encouraged in doing so by a quelling glance from Dominique. "Never mind," he said. "Whatever I think of Bonaparte, I am anxious to meet him."

"Then, by all means . . ." Talleyrand said with a wave of his hand that seemed miraculously to part the crowd before them and open up a pathway directly to the inner sanctum, where the general was holding court.

"It's like a royal levee," Dominique murmured under her breath as they entered the glittering, overheated room.

"Don't be silly," Talleyrand countered, a teasing gleam in his eye. "How could it be anything of the sort when everyone and the world knows of the general's devotion to republican values?"

Paul muttered something that suggested everyone and the world had been fooled before. Whatever he said was lost as Talleyrand exclaimed, "Ah, there he is. General Bonaparte, what a delight! At last, after so long an absence . . ."

Heedless of anyone else, the foreign minister plowed a furrow across the room to stand directly before the great man, thereby completely obscuring him from everyone else's view. Paul had to crane his neck to confirm his first suspicion: the conqueror of Italy and France, scourge of the British, terror of Europe, looked like the runt of a not particularly good-sized litter.

Not that he was unattractive. His features were strong and well-formed, his eyes compelling. He was well-built, with a broad chest and shoulders, and the erect posture of a soldier. He looked amused but wary.

"Monsieur Talleyrand, so glad you could stop by. And this is . . . ?"

Bonaparte was looking not at Paul but at Dominique, with a warm, approving look that left no doubt that he found her attractive. Marriage to Josephine had not restricted his interest in other women, which was rumored to be immense.

"Mademoiselle de Montfort," the foreign minister murmured. With a hand at Dominique's back, he pushed her forward.

The general's expression changed. The approval was still there, but so was cautious respect. "I have heard your name, mademoiselle, though admittedly it was some time ago and in an entirely different context."

She inclined her head slightly, not taking her eyes from his. "I left Paris rather suddenly almost seven years ago. Before then, I had the honor to serve the late queen as lady-in-waiting."

Had there been any doubt as to whether or not people were eavesdropping, it was promptly answered. All conversation around them ceased. Dominique was aware of a collective inhalation of breath, as though everyone in the room was deeply and profoundly shocked.

"I have made no secret of my background, Monsieur le General," she said pointedly. "On the contrary, as you indicated, it is well known."

"Indeed, Mademoiselle de Montfort," Bonaparte said with a slight smile, "as is your courage."

Paul relaxed marginally. He had been poised to intervene between Dominique and the general to protect her from the consequences of her bold words. Now it appeared he would not have to.

Point to Bonaparte. Willingly or not, Paul couldn't help but be impressed. If the man had nothing else, he knew the value of restraint.

"And you, Monsieur le Marquis," the general said, turning his attention to Paul. "I understand you have opened your own hospital and that some of my soldiers have been treated there."

"We care for a wide range of cases, General," Paul said noncommittally. He was tired of ambitious, greedy men who pretended an interest in humanitarian work merely to appear noble at no cost to themselves.

All hint of amusement vanished from Bonaparte. He looked suddenly fierce and determined. "They deserve the very best after the great sacrifice they have made for France. It is only a shame that public money is not always forthcoming to provide for them."

"Not that the Directory isn't willing," Talleyrand intervened hastily. "However, we do all recognize that there are certain financial difficulties . . ."

"Which makes your contribution all the more valuable, Monsieur Delamare," Napoleon continued. "I would like to speak with you about it, and about what else could be done, when I have more time. Please call on me."

"Marvelous," Talleyrand murmured when they were safely away. "Absolutely marvelous. I knew the two of you would hit it off."

"I wouldn't say that precisely," Paul replied. He was glad that the encounter had gone as well as it had, though far more for Dominique's sake than his own. For his part, he remained extremely wary of the general.

"He needs men like you," Talleyrand insisted. "And he knows how to reward ability. Join him and I daresay there would be almost nothing you couldn't accomplish."

"Join him?" Paul repeated with a faint smile. "Are you suggesting that I enlist in the army?"

"Of course not," the foreign minister said with a hint of asperity. "You know perfectly well that isn't what I mean. The general has many civilian advisers, and there will be more now that . . ."

"That he is making his objectives clear?"

Talleyrand's response was a Gallic shrug. Paul wished he could be as philosophical. But uppermost in his mind was the memory of the day not so many years before when Robespierre had made him a similar offer, trying to enlist his support. Robespierre had been mad; there was no evidence to suggest that Bonaparte was the same. So far.

"You're very quiet," Dominique said as they drifted around the outer drawing room. Word of their encounter with the general had apparently spread. They were greeted with courteous nods and cautious smiles.

"I'm sorry," Paul murmured. With a sudden smile, he added, "You should have better company."

"Oh, I don't know about that." The glance she gave him from her magnificent green-gold eyes was redolent of the passion they had shared scant hours before. At the sight of it, a tremor raced through Paul. It was all he could do to keep from seizing hold of her right there and then, in the midst of the Bonapartes' glorious drawing room.

He was still wrestling with the problem when a soft, honey-drenched chuckle interrupted him.

"Why, my dear," a tall, darkly beautiful woman said, "you never told me he was this handsome."

The color drained from Dominique's face, only to rush back in a flood. For a moment, she might have been listening to Marie Antoinette teasing her about Paul all those years ago. But the queen was only memory, bittersweet, and still drenched in the pain of loss.

"Josephine," Dominique said when she had regained control of herself, "if truth be told, I don't remember telling you much about Monsieur le Marquis at all."

The general's wife laughed. She was a slender, almost willowy woman with short, elaborately curled brown hair, enormous gray eyes, and delicate features. In her mid-thirties, she retained the vivacity and sensuality of a young girl. Undoubtedly, that accounted for Napoleon's willingness to marry her, even when he discovered that rumors of her financial well-being had been grossly exaggerated.

"Truth is such a rare commodity," Madame Bonaparte said as she extended her hand to Paul. "Sometimes it's almost impossible to recognize."

"Very wise, madame," he murmured as their eyes met. "Naturally, I prefer to believe that Dominique has spoken of me often and at length."

Josephine laughed again, delightedly. "Marvelous. I adore romance, but there is so little of it. All most people want to talk about is war and politics."

"Most people" were clearly her illustrious husband and his associates, about whom she seemed to think the less said the better.

"Come with me," she said in a conspiratorial whisper

as she linked one arm through Dominique's and gave the other to Paul. "I've got something special to show you, but it's private."

Chattering brightly, Josephine drew them down a long corridor to a back staircase and up to the second floor, where she and the general occupied adjoining suites. Her own rooms were done all in white and gold, a fitting foil for the dark loveliness of the woman who lived in them.

Paul hesitated before crossing the threshold. Even in Dominique's presence, it seemed less than wise to enter the bedroom of the general's wife. But when he ventured that it might be indiscreet, Josephine shrugged that off.

"You're a doctor, aren't you? Doctors are always going into ladies' boudoirs. Besides, it would never occur to Bonaparte to be annoyed. His vanity is such that he can't imagine me ever being attracted to another man."

She spoke so matter-of-factly that both Paul and Dominique were taken aback. If that were indeed true, it seemed that the general was not as perceptive as he liked to believe.

Despite Josephine's urgings, Paul continued to feel ill at ease in the intensely feminine surroundings. He stood by the window, staring out at the swirling snow as behind him the women talked.

"Now, where is it?" Josephine murmured as she pulled open an exquisite little writing desk and began rummaging through the various pigeonholes. "Ah, here. Oh, I do hope you like it. I was so excited when I realized what it was."

With an eager smile, Dominique took the small package. She knew that Josephine delighted in giving her friends impromptu presents. She had in fact received several in the past—all pretty little trinkets that she cherished for the affection they represented. But even as her fingers undid the wrappings, she sensed that this one was somehow different. Inside was a velvet box that opened to reveal two exquisite diamond-and-emerald earrings. It was a lovely gift, generous, even extravagant, and clearly chosen specifically for her.

It was also hauntingly familiar.

"The dealer assured me that they really had belonged to the queen," Josephine said eagerly. "In fact, he absolutely swore it. Of course, there's no way to know for sure, but I thought if anyone could be certain, it would be you. And then I thought perhaps you would like to have them, so I . . ."

She broke off, aware that Dominique was trembling. Her finger shook as she lightly, tentatively, touched first one of the earrings and then the other.

"The dealer was right," she said, her voice hardly more than a whisper. "I remember these."

"They are lovely," Josephine acknowledged. "Marie Antoinette had superb taste."

Dominique nodded slowly. "Yes, she did. But these were particularly special. The king gave them to her after the birth of the dauphin."

"Why, I had no idea of that," Josephine exclaimed. She was all the more delighted to know that her gift had such special significance.

"They were part of a set," Dominique said, her eyes still focused on the jewels, "along with a necklace and two bracelets. There was an official gift as well, naturally, but this was private, just between the two of them."

"I wonder if I might be able to find the rest," Josephine said thoughtfully. "Various things are beginning to turn up now—furniture, clothing, books. Not many jewels, though. I suspect most of them have already been broken up."

"Most likely," Paul said. He had stepped away from the window and was standing beside Dominique's chair, his hand on her shoulder. Beneath his fingers, he could feel how shaken she was.

"Perhaps we should get back," he suggested softly.

"Of course," Josephine said quickly. "I didn't mean to keep you away." She turned, her hand on the doorknob. Her gaze was filled with concern as she looked at Dominique. "But . . . you do like them, don't you?"

"Very much," Dominique said. She stood with some effort and managed a warm smile. "Truly, Josephine, this was very kind of you. I have so little to remember her by . . ."

Relieved that she had not made a faux pas, Josephine gave her a quick hug. Her enormous eyes were moist as she said, "Believe me, my dear, I understand. It's as though our entire world vanished in some sort of horrible cataclysm. There are just bits and pieces of jetsam washed up on the shore. We must cling to them as best we can."

That so perfectly reflected how Dominique felt that she could say nothing more. With the velvet box and its precious contents hidden deep in the pocket of her skirt, she accompanied Josephine and Paul back to the drawing room. The general's wife was shortly called away, and not long after that Dominique and Paul decided to leave.

Neither mentioned the earrings again until they were in the carriage returning to Dominique's town house. Then Paul put his hand over hers and said gently, "She meant well."

Dominique nodded. "I know that. She has a kind and loving heart. And it isn't as though I don't appreciate the gift; I do. It's just that it brings back so many memories . . ."

He could have said that this was one of the reasons why he had not wanted her to return to France, because he had known that on every side she would find reminders of what had been.

It was bad enough for him—he had held out to the very last, fighting every step of the way against the insanity of the Jacobins, and ultimately, helping to bring them down. But for Dominique, who had been safe in England, the guilt of the survivor must be unbearable at times. It was misplaced guilt, of course, but potent all the same.

And beyond his ability to erase—at least, not all at once. However much he longed to, he could not wipe away Dominique's sorrow. He could only hope to replace it with something far better.

Chapter
23

"Come for a carriage ride, *mignon*," Paul said. He had just come in from outside, arriving in a flurry of crisp autumn air and swirling leaves, his cloak billowing around him, his golden hair gleaming. His cheeks were slightly flushed from the brisk wind and his eyes held glistening shards of splintered sky. When he held out a hand commandingly, Dominique was loath to refuse him.

Still, she tried, "You've only just arrived, and you must be tired after a day at the hospital. Why not have a drink first, something to eat?"

"Later. Right now, I want to ride with you." Laughing at her surprise, he said, "All those years you lived in Paris and I'll hazard a guess you have never seen *l'heure bleu*? How can you call yourself a Parisian?"

"I don't believe in it," Dominique said stubbornly, even as she allowed the butler to fetch her cloak. "It's only a legend."

"We shall see," Paul said with a grin. He waved the

servant away and stood before her, his fingers lightly brushing her cheeks as he raised the hood of her cloak over her head. Her face was framed in ermine, her eyes sparkled, and despite her disclaimer, she looked excited. All in all it was an improvement from the pale, quiet young woman he had left that morning.

He was doing the right thing, he was certain of that. Indeed, the only thing. They had not come so far, through so much, to turn back now.

"Come," he said peremptorily as he guided her toward the door.

She smiled chidingly but went with him readily enough. Autumn twilight was settling over the city. The air was crisp, slightly moist, altogether pleasant. The streets were almost deserted, which was a shame, as Dominique quickly saw. For the air was indeed a ghostly, ethereal, glimmering blue, unlike anything she had ever seen before.

"Does this happen very often?" she asked wonderingly when their carriage paused on the Pont Neuf, the oldest bridge in Paris and still without doubt the noblest. "And if it does, how could I have never noticed before?"

"First," Paul said as he put an arm around her shoulders, drawing her closer, "it isn't all that common, requiring as it does a particular combination of temperature and other weather conditions." With a smile, he added, "That's the scientific explanation. Others say that it happens all the time but can only be seen by those in love."

"Oh . . ." She paused, gazing up at him. He looked indomitable, as always, yet also preoccupied, as though some part of himself was not fully with her. She supposed she should be used to that, since the responsibilities he carried were so heavy. Whereas she . . .

Since the return of Montfort, she seemed to have been

drifting. No immediate challenge occupied her, no goal fueled her days. She had actually thought on occasion of returning to England, if only briefly, to see her grandmother, Nicole, and David.

Despite the war's continuance, it was still a relatively simple matter to go back and forth. Certainly, letters were no problem. She heard frequently from Lady Amelia, as well as her brother and sister. Her grandmother in particular did not stint with her opinions. She thought what Dominique had accomplished was admirable, but the time had come to return. Unspoken between them was the knowledge that Lady Amelia still clung to the hope that Dominique would marry William. It was a misplaced hope, if ever there had been one.

"What are you thinking about?" Paul asked suddenly. Despite all he had on his mind, he couldn't help but notice that Dominique had seemed suddenly very far from him. Naturally enough, he wanted to know why.

"William," Dominique said without thinking. It was true enough but it was also misleading.

However, before she could explain, Paul said coldly, "How touching. Here you are with one man and your thoughts are occupied by another. If I am boring you, sweet Dominique, we can easily enough return to your home and I can take my leave. Certainly there are more than enough other pursuits for me to . . ."

"Oh, stop being so touchy," Dominique said with asperity. "It's not like you at all, and I don't understand why you're always doing it with me."

At his startled look, she added, "Most of the time you're the soul of rationality, but for some reason, that doesn't seem to apply when we're together. Really, Paul, it isn't very nice of you to think that I'm not worth the same consideration as you'd give most anyone else.''

"Consideration?'' he echoed, as though the word was meaningless to him. "When on earth did anything between us ever come down to a matter of consideration?''

"There happens to be nothing wrong with that,'' Dominique insisted, even though she sensed that she had already lost this particular battle. They'd never had time for anything so weak and proper.

"Besides,'' he went on relentlessly, "we were discussing the duke of Devonshire, who so occupies your thoughts.''

"Only because it was his betrayal of your identity to Pitt that forced you to flee England.''

For the first and only time that she could remember, Dominique had the intense satisfaction of seeing her beloved looking totally befuddled. With delighted venom, she said, "It did cross your mind that he was responsible, didn't it?''

"Of course,'' Paul murmured, still staring at her. "But I had no idea you knew, much less that you would admit it.''

"And why not? William was a good friend to me—still is, for that matter. But he's also human, and perfectly capable of making a totally abominable mistake. Incidentally,'' she added for good measure, "he's still ashamed of what he did.''

"How do you know that?''

"He told me in the letter he sent a few months ago. Apparently, he felt the need to confess.''

"I'm not surprised,'' Paul said thoughtfully. "He is at heart an honorable man.''

"Who is nonetheless capable of treachery."

He shrugged, undisturbed by the apparent contradiction. "Most people are a combination of conflicting feelings and traits. It's what makes life interesting."

Dominique sighed. She leaned her head back against the tufted upholstery and gazed out the window at the incredible light. "So blasé, Monsieur le Marquis. How do you reconcile that with all your ideals?"

"Simple—I accept people for what they are, but I still want the best for them. That's understandable, isn't it?"

"I suppose," she acknowledged slowly. "But for it to be true, you would have to be very tolerant."

"Which I am of everything except cruelty and tyranny."

"And me."

He was silent for a moment, his mouth quirking. At length, he said, "You stab me to the quick, sweet Dominique. Indeed, you have discovered my secret weakness —the same great failing that caused poor William to act so uncharacteristically."

"Don't you dare tell me it's me," she insisted. "I refuse to take responsibility for either of you."

"Really?" he inquired softly, turning so that he was suddenly much closer to her. Much too close, or else the carriage was far too small. And warm . . . She felt suddenly uncomfortably hot, despite the cool air drifting through the carriage windows.

"Is that the truth?" he asked, his breath brushing her cheek, his mouth almost but not quite touching her. "Do you really wish to disavow me?"

"I only meant . . . that is . . . I don't control you."

He laughed, infinitely male, insufferably proud. "Of course not." Clearly, the very idea was comical. Yet in the next instant, he added gravely, "Any more than I control you. I used to think that I'd like to, but recently I've been having second thoughts.''

"Oh . . . ?'' And just what did that mean? Was he sorry they had become involved again? Was he washing his hands of her? No, she mustn't be silly. No man brought a woman to so romantic a spot merely to break off with her.

"I love you, Dominique,'' Paul said abruptly. He looked like a man stating an implacable fact, not necessarily something he welcomed.

"Oh, well, I thought perhaps you did.''

"You're not supposed to say that,'' he chided gently. "You're supposed to act surprised, flustered, all that sort of thing.''

"Is that what you want? For me to act rather than be myself?''

"Oh, no,'' he said, suddenly serious. "You, my sweet girl, are an original, and my fondest hope is that you will stay that way.''

Slowly, tentatively, she smiled. "I could almost believe you.''

"Please do,'' he murmured, gathering her to him, his hard chest teasing her breasts through the velvet of her cloak. "Because a very kind gentleman is expecting us to come by in a few minutes so that he can marry us, and I think that would go much better if we were in as much agreement as possible.''

"Marry?'' It came out as a squeak. Dominique dragged in air and tried again. "Marry?'' Better, though not much.

"It can hardly be such a shock to you,'' he said matter-of-factly. "After all, this is the third time I've asked.''

"Correction, you have never asked.''

"What?''

"You heard me. You have never said, 'Dominique, would you please marry me?' You have always simply informed me of your wishes."

"I see."

"It's all right," she broke in, laughing, because how could she not when the world was suddenly, gloriously perfect? "For all your republican ideals, you still have a touch of the autocrat at heart. It must come from all those generations of marquises."

"Not so many," he reminded her. "Truth be told, the Delamares are still scraping the bog off our shoes."

"And what were you in Ireland then? Clan leaders, chieftains?"

"Troublemakers, I suspect. But let's not get off the subject again. My apologies for my lack of tact. Please, my beautiful and beloved Dominique, will you marry me?"

He almost managed to sound humble. Not quite, of course, but then, she wouldn't have wanted that. Which shouldn't be taken to mean that she was through teasing him.

"Perhaps . . ."

"You have five minutes," he informed her.

Her eyes widened. "And then what happens?"

"I drag you into Notre Dame and shock the poor priest silly."

"You'd enjoy that, wouldn't you?"

"Probably, but I'd enjoy it even more if you would come willingly."

"We'd need witnesses," she pointed out, always practical.

"I've taken care of that."

"Flowers?"

"All arranged, as well as a champagne supper for the two of us and a week in the countryside."

"You *have* been busy."

"I had help," he admitted, "as you shall see."

What Bonaparte would make of it, he didn't know, presuming of course that the general ever found out. Josephine didn't impress him as the sort of woman who felt compelled to tell her husband everything. She was, all the same, an inveterate romantic. When Paul had gone to see her that morning and confided his hopes, she had thrown herself into the preparations for the wedding.

"My own was a little hole-in-the-corner affair," she said as she briskly set about the business of turning Paris on its ear in pursuit of everything that was needed. "The second one, I mean. Not that I minded, under the circumstances, but Dominique should have something better, don't you agree?"

Paul had, wholeheartedly, and had left it all in her more than capable hands. He had no cause to regret that. Barely had they stepped into the hallowed sanctuary of Notre Dame than they were greeted by a flustered, respectful priest.

"Ah, monsieur, mademoiselle, please come this way. All is in readiness."

"The license?" Dominique whispered as Paul propelled her gently but firmly up the aisle toward the chapel. "The dispensation for not calling the banns? Are you sure you haven't forgotten something?"

"Of course he hasn't," Josephine said. She looked radiant in a gown of silver-gray silk trimmed with sable. Beside her stood a young, wide-eyed maid who stared at the couple with unconcealed fascination.

"Oh, I might have known," Dominique murmured. "Who else would he turn to?"

"No one, I hope," Josephine said. "If there is absolutely anything I know, it is how to arrange a wedding." She repeated her hole-in-the-corner comment, laughed gaily, and took the priest off to one side to give him last-minute instructions. He was a middle-aged man, worldly despite his calling, and well aware of the identity of the lady. He was therefore totally, utterly attentive to her every wish.

"I suppose," Dominique said, "that it would be horribly boorish of me to try to back out now?"

"Futile, too," Paul replied with a look that firmly canceled any lingering doubts she might have had.

With a sigh of pleasurable defeat, Dominique removed her cloak. Beneath it she wore a gown of emerald silk and gauze that perfectly complemented her eyes. Because she had not been planning to go out for the evening, her hair was loosely arranged in curls around her shoulders. On an impulse earlier that day, she had put on the earrings Josephine had given her, determined to find in them the pleasure their giver had intended.

At the sight of them, the general's lady smiled tremulously. "You know," she whispered, "I almost feel as though the queen is here today watching all of this." With a glance at Paul, she added, "I'm quite certain she would approve."

"Yes," Dominique said softly, "I believe she would."

An odd sense of peace was settling over her as she stood bathed in the light of the magnificent rose window above the altar. The great cathedral was almost empty except for the wedding party. Within its hushed immensity, a silent, unknowable presence seemed to dwell. It entered Dominique with each breath she drew and filled her with serenity.

"Mademoiselle," the priest murmured, "Monsieur . . ."

Following his instructions, they knelt at the prie-dieu before the altar, side by side but without touching. Josephine and her maid took up their positions behind.

In the instant before Dominique knelt, Josephine pressed a bouquet of white lilies into her hands. Their intoxicating scent, so rare in Paris in the autumn, joined with all the other soaring, enthralling elements of the moment to complete her transfiguration.

She had entered the cathedral a surprised and uncertain young woman. Kneeling at the altar, within the sight of the Almighty, she was a supplicant boundless in her gratitude for the love that had come to her despite all the vicissitudes of the unruly world.

Paul felt much the same. If pressed, he would have said that he didn't think of himself as a religious man. Certainly there had been a great deal in his life to turn him away from the simple faith of his childhood. Yet it lingered, strong as ever, the ultimate teacher and guide.

The priest had begun to speak. The words, ancient and beautiful, flowed over them. Dominique's head was bent, her gaze on the delicate white blossoms she held, until from the corner of her eye, she saw Paul slip a hand out for hers.

Gladly, she gave it, heedless of whatever breach of protocol they were committing. The priest apparently did not notice, or was far too diplomatic to show it. Moments later, he gestured for them to rise.

"My children," he said solemnly, "you are now united in the holiest state decreed for mankind. May your marriage be as a beacon unto the world, shining the light of love and faith on all."

Dominique's throat was tight; she was too moved to speak. Thankfully, she was not required to. Nothing was required except that she accept Paul's kiss, gentle and reassuring, filled with a multitude of promise.

Behind them, Josephine sniffed delicately. The sound was lost as the great carillon of Notre Dame chimed out the hour, ringing joyfully over the heart of Paris, over the reborn city, over a world from which the moment all darkness seemed banished.

Chapter
24

"Paul . . . ?" Waking uneasily in the wide, soft bed, Dominique stared at the dark silhouette of her husband, standing alone and brooding by the window.

Despite the downy quilt covering her, she felt suddenly cold. Ever since their marriage three weeks before, she had sensed that an enormous struggle was going on within Paul. She knew that it had to do with the rumors convulsing Paris that there was soon to be a change of government, but beyond that she did not want to think.

"Paul . . ." she said again, more loudly this time, to penetrate his thoughts.

He turned, startled, and gazed at her. "Dominique . . . I thought you were asleep."

"I was," she said with a gentle smile, "until I felt your absence." Pale in the fragile light streaming through the curtains, she raised her slender arms to him. "Please come back."

He hesitated for a moment before cold—of the spirit, not the body—drove him to comply.

As he slipped into bed beside her, Dominique nestled close against him. Both were naked. They had made love long and lingeringly during the earlier part of the night. Ordinarily, the exquisite ecstasy she had experienced would have led Dominique to sleep heavily until morning, but a deeply buried part of her mind had felt Paul's unease and been stirred by it.

"Talk to me," she murmured against his skin. "Tell me what you are thinking. Perhaps I can help."

He smiled and stroked a tender, loving hand down her back. "Sweetheart, you already have, simply by being here."

Desperately, she wanted to believe him, but doubts lingered. He was used to being alone, to making his decisions strictly according to what he believed was right. Now, suddenly, he had a wife to consider at a time when he might have preferred to be unhindered.

"Do you regret . . ." The words were out before she could prevent them. They seemed to echo harshly in the silence of the room.

Paul turned sharply. He gazed down at her with eyes that were at once tender and chiding. "You can't honestly think that."

"No . . . perhaps . . . I don't know. It just seems to me that you might be easier in your mind if you didn't have to be concerned about me."

"Undoubtedly."

At the quick rush of color to her cheeks, he laughed softly. "Ah, Dominique, don't you see? Three weeks ago I faced up to the fact that you and I belong together, no matter how infuriatingly independent you may be. Nothing will ever make me regret that.''

He was speaking the truth while also teasing her. Moreover, she sensed he was trying to arrange a distraction, changing the subject from his concerns to her independence.

For once, she wasn't going to let that happen. Pushing aside the heavy weight of her unbound hair, she said, "Why are you so convinced that General Bonaparte is a danger to France?"

Paul shrugged. "Instinct, experience, call it what you will. All I am certain of is that to place civil power in the hands of a military man is foolish at best and possibly disastrous.''

"Most people would disagree. The crowds adore Bonaparte."

"Oh, yes," Paul said bitterly. "I've seen that kind of blind willingness to be led before. So have you.''

"The general is no Robespierre," Dominique protested.

"No," Paul agreed, "but I'm not sure that he doesn't have just as much potential to harm innocent people, possibly even more.''

Dominique sighed. The last thing she wanted was to get involved in a political discussion while lying naked in bed beside her husband. Yet she could understand Paul's concern. The search for freedom was the ruling passion of his life. To his way of thinking, Napoleon threatened all he had fought for through so many years and at such dire cost.

"What are you going to do?" she asked softly.

"I don't know," he admitted. "It depends on how far Bonaparte tries to go.''

"If you could reach some accommodation with him . . . ?"

"Is that what you think I should do?"

"Perhaps . . . why not? After all, haven't you done enough? You've been through so much. What's wrong with stepping back a little and doing something for yourself?"

She was afraid her words might anger him, but instead, he merely looked at her gently. "Always so pragmatic, Dominique."

He made that sound like the most endearing of traits, yet she still felt compelled to defend herself.

"I've had to be. There were always people depending on me for the simple necessities of life. That doesn't leave a great deal of room for ideals."

"No," he acknowledged quietly, "it doesn't. In many ways, you had a far more difficult time than I did."

"That isn't true. I was safe in England when you were . . ."

He stilled her mouth with his lips—hard, insistent, persuasive. "Let's not talk about that now. The important thing is that there are no regrets, correct?"

"None," she said honestly, "not between us. I have loved you for so many years. Being your wife is the fulfillment of every dream I ever had."

That simple, heartfelt statement struck him to the quick. He buried his head in the smooth, scented skin of her breasts and proceeded to love her with a degree of desperation, almost of ferocity, that left her stunned. She clung to him frantically in the maelstrom of their passion, wanting to understand, wanting to help, yet terrified that something was going terribly wrong.

* * *

"I see," Talleyrand said slowly. He lowered the crystal paperweight at which he had been idly gazing and smiled at Paul. "Well, I think you are making the right decision. Certainly, the general is very eager to have your support."

"I haven't said that I will give it," Paul said coldly. He had slept not at all the previous night, lying awake with Dominique in his arms long after exhaustion claimed her. Staring up at the ceiling, all he had been able to think of was the responsibility he had to her. She had every right to expect him to act prudently, not merely out of noble ideals, which had already caused them both to suffer far too much.

But could he do it? That was the key question that preoccupied him as he stood in Talleyrand's sumptuous office in the Luxembourg Palace, where the Directory was headquartered. As foreign minister, he merited a superb suite of rooms overlooking the magnificent gardens. But on this particular day, Talleyrand seemed oblivious to his surroundings. All his attention was concentrated on the proud, self-possessed man before him.

"Do you ever wonder," Talleyrand asked suddenly, "why Bonaparte wants your support badly enough to ask for it? He doesn't ordinarily bother, you know."

"I had suspected that," Paul said dryly. "Suppose you tell me."

The foreign minister sat back in his capacious chair and eyed the younger man benignly. "You possess something extremely rare. Not merely power or money, which if anything, are all too common. Your particular attribute is integrity. People trust you. What you say and do is believed to be right, simply by virtue of your reputation."

Paul shrugged. He was faintly embarrassed, although not unduly so. At heart, he thought Talleyrand was merely trying to flatter him.

"I don't see . . ." he began.

"Ah," the foreign minister interrupted, "but I do and so does Bonaparte. He knows that he will need men like you after the first flush of enthusiasm has worn off and the serious business of governing takes over."

Paul's eyes narrowed. No other change of expression revealed the impact of what he had just heard. Had Talleyrand inadvertently revealed the general's true intentions, or was the revelation deliberate?

"Correct me if I am wrong," Paul said quietly, "but to the best of my knowledge, Bonaparte is not a member of the government."

"Not at present," Talleyrand conceded, "but many of us feel that is an omission which should be speedily rectified."

"And which of the current directors do you intend to have step aside in order to make room for the general?" Paul asked sardonically. He knew perfectly well that none of the five men who together made up France's ruling council would deliberately allow his power to be set aside.

Talleyrand knew it, too. He gave Paul a sardonic smile. "Ah, well, it is true there is still some persuasion to be accomplished."

"Peaceful persuasion?"

"Of course, what else? As you yourself have pointed out, France has had quite enough of war."

Paul frowned. He was not at all convinced that Talleyrand was being completely straightforward with him. But his keenly felt responsibility to Dominique made him want to believe. At any rate, it would cost him nothing to meet with Napoleon—or, at least, it should not.

"Come to tea," Josephine had said, "and bring that delightful husband of yours. We will have a marvelous tête-à-tête without a lot of silly interruptions."

And just how was she going to arrange that, Dominique wondered as she stepped from the carriage that had brought her and Paul to the Bonapartes' residence. As usual, a crowd was gathered out in front, staring avidly at anyone who went in or out of the house and cheering whenever a familiar face was seen.

Barely had Paul emerged from the carriage than a roar of approval went up. It took both him and Dominique by surprise. A path cleared for them, leading toward the front door. Paul took Dominique's elbow and they began to make their way, met at every step by smiling men and women.

"Good day to you, Doctor," someone murmured respectfully. Others echoed it.

"God bless you, sir," a woman said.

Paul stopped and looked at her. Gently, he asked, "Why do you say that?"

The woman looked taken aback to suddenly be at the center of attention, but she recovered quickly. Raising her voice to be sure she would be heard by all around her, she said, "Why, because you saved my son's life, that's why. He was sent home from Egypt terribly wounded and they could do nothing for him at the military hospital. Said it was just too bad."

Outraged mutterings fueled her recital.

"But your hospital took him in. The doctors there cared

for him and now he's back home recovering. We all know you paid from your own purse to build the place and that it's your standards that make it what it is.''

"That's right,'' a nearby man said. "Everybody's heard of Doctor Delamare and all he's done.'' Proudly, he added, "My boy was with the resistance during the Terror. He's told us stories about how you kept everyone going during the worst of times.''

Bemused, Paul shook his head. "I did very little . . .''

"Of course you think that, Doctor,'' another woman said. "You're that sort of man. But we all know the truth, and don't think we don't appreciate it, because we do.''

Paul meant to protest further but a quick squeeze of Dominique's hand on his arm stopped him. She was looking at him through eyes filled with love and perilously close to tears.

"I'm so proud of you,'' she murmured for his ears alone.

He sighed, realizing that this was not the time or place to insist that he had only done what any rational, compassionate man would do. If anything, such a statement would only set off another round of adulation—something he could manage very well without.

With a courteous nod to the crowd, he led Dominique inside.

"What nonsense,'' he said when they were alone in the entry hall, except for the blank-faced butler who was taking their cloaks.

"Certainly not,'' Josephine interjected as she swept out of the drawing room to greet them. She looked lovely as always, her cheeks glowing and her eyes dark with excitement. "I was looking out the window,'' she explained as she gave Dominique a quick hug and kissed her cheeks. "Did you truly not realize how people think of you?''

Paul shrugged self-consciously. "I suppose I haven't had much time to notice."

"And even less interest?" another voice suggested. They all turned to behold Bonaparte himself coming forward to join them. As always, he wore the uniform of a general in the National Army, but without the multitude of medals and ribbons other men in his position affected. By contrast, he looked unpretentious and innately confident. A smile played across his well-shaped mouth as he inclined his head slightly in recognition of their surprise.

"I hope you won't mind too much, Monsieur le Docteur, but we have gotten you here under somewhat false pretenses. That is, Madame Delamare is more than welcome to take tea with my wife. However, I would prefer for you to join me in a private conversation."

Paul suppressed a surge of irritation. He could hardly blame the general, who had previously indicated his desire to speak with him. Moreover, Talleyrand had certainly dropped a broad enough hint that such a meeting would take place. With a curt nod of his head, he signaled his acquiescence.

Bonaparte stood aside to show Paul into his private study. The two women exchanged a hopeful look as the door closed behind them.

An hour later, in the carriage returning them home, Dominique turned eagerly to Paul. "What did he say?"

"A great deal, mostly having to do with France's place in the world and our destiny."

"Oh." Dominique frowned. She heard the hard, cynical note in Paul's voice and was worried by it. Not that she could blame him for being suspicious of such grandiose topics—especially not when so much that was hard and down-to-earth remained to be settled.

"Was that all?" she ventured.

"Not quite." Paul shut his eyes wearily for a moment. When he opened them again, he found Dominique gazing at them, her lovely features suffused with concern.

Instantly, he regretted worrying her. "I'm sorry, sweetheart. Really, there's no need to be so apprehensive. Bonaparte and I had a perfectly amicable talk."

"Really?" She couldn't hide her disbelief. Indeed, it was so overt that Paul laughed.

"Really." More seriously, he added, "He is brilliant, I give him that. And he understands people, though whether or not he understands himself is another matter entirely."

"What does that mean?"

"That he seemed to me to be almost two men. On the one hand, there is the genuinely great leader with a noble vision of what his country can become. On the other is the man who seeks power merely to assuage his own vanity. That worries me."

It was on the tip of Dominique's tongue to say that he was surely mistaken, there was nothing to be concerned about, but she stopped herself. Truth be told, she didn't know Bonaparte better than anyone else. Indeed, Paul, with his calm perceptiveness and understanding, probably knew him at least as well as those who claimed to be his intimates. And if he were worried . . .

"What did he ask you for?"

"At first for my support. When he saw that I was still hesitant to give that, he asked that I simply not speak out against him. Apparently, he remains of the opinion that my words would carry some weight."

"As he should be. You saw what the crowd was like, but even more important, there are many in the government who would listen to you. Talleyrand wouldn't be courting you so intently if that weren't true."

Paul smiled faintly. "You have the advantage over me in this matter, sweetheart. When it comes to political maneuverings, I'm a novice."

"Ah, well," she said, snuggling against him, "it's only fair that for once I be more experienced than you." Teasingly, she added, "Why don't you just settle back, relax, and let me show you how it's done."

The light gleaming in his eyes told her that he was enjoying the game but that she shouldn't expect to keep the initiative too long. A shiver of anticipation ran through her. She was almost unbearably eager to be home with him again, alone in her quiet, high-ceilinged bedroom, where they could shut the world out.

As his proud head bent, his lips claiming hers, she closed her eyes and made a silent vow that nothing would take him from her.

Chapter
25

"He didn't say that he would oppose him," Dominique insisted quietly. "What he said was that so long as the general respected the integrity of the constitution and acted peacefully, he would not speak out against him."

Josephine made a sharp, exasperated sound under her breath. She and Dominique had met by chance at the shop of the fashionable *modistes* on the rue St. Honore. The two women had not seen each other since Paul's discussion with Bonaparte the previous week. Dominique wasn't absolutely sure that Josephine was avoiding her, but she suspected it.

"Doesn't he understand," Josephine demanded, "that one simply cannot impose conditions on Napoleon? He is too consumed by his own visions to be hemmed in like that."

"But it's hardly as though Paul was asking a great deal," Dominique protested. She kept her voice down to avoid attracting the attention of anyone else in the shop, but she could not completely hide her dismay. Her hand trembled as she laid aside a length of fine white lace she had been examining.

"All any of us wants is peace," she said tightly. "Surely that is not so much to ask?"

"Peace . . ." Josephine murmured as though she were not certain what the word meant. "I am truly not sure that any such thing exists."

Dominique was still pondering that when she returned home. She entered the house anxious to speak with Paul, only to be told that he had not yet returned from the hospital. That really wasn't so unexpected; it was still early. Yet she remained apprehensive and was glad of the stack of letters that had arrived to distract her.

David wrote as usual of his fervent desire to return to France. He was convinced that the war was almost over, peace would shortly be declared, and his two beloved countries would become friends at last. Dominique only wished that she shared his optimism. She put the letter aside with the intention of writing him a gentle but firm refusal. David was just beginning his final year at Eton. He could wait until that was completed before claiming his heritage in France.

Meanwhile, Nicole appeared not at all to share her brother's discontent. She wrote a gay, chattering letter filled with cheerful gossip and brimming over with the enthusiasm of youth. Dominique laughed out loud several times as she read her sister's perceptive comments about mutual acquaintances. It astounded her to realize that Nicole had only three more years in the schoolroom before she would make her entrance into society. She shook her head wryly as she wondered whether London would ever be ready for that.

There was also a note from Maggie, which Dominique opened with special anticipation. Though she well understood her maid's reluctance to leave England for France during a time of war, she missed her terribly. Her replacement, a long-suffering Frenchwoman who nurtured the best of intentions, knew her business well enough, but no one would ever replace Maggie.

It was therefore with delight that Dominique learned the young woman was seriously considering the move. She and her Patrick had married and were eager to make a fresh start. With peace appearing more likely each day, they wondered if Dominique would have places for them.

Most assuredly, she thought as she sat down at her escritoire to pen a hasty response. Mademoiselle Helene would have no difficulty finding another position. Indeed, she would most likely be far happier with a mistress who understood and cared about fashion, instead of being totally oblivious to it. And Maggie would adore Paris—the promenades, the shops, the great *modistes*. Oh, yes, Maggie would be very much in her element.

By the time she had finished the last of the return letters, it was after dark. A butler had come in silently to light the lamps, then gone out again. Preparations for dinner were underway. Dominique could smell the odors of food wafting up from the kitchens.

She sniffed appreciatively, realizing for the first time that day that she was absolutely ravenous. But a moment later, her appetite vanished as a wave of queasiness washed over her.

Gasping, she clung to the edge of the desk until the

world righted itself once more and she felt safe to take a breath.

Slowly, a thoughtful expression crossed her face. This was the third time—no, the fourth—that she had experienced such a sensation in the last few days. Was it possible that . . . .

A smile of purest happiness lit her eyes as she placed a hand reverently on her abdomen. Beneath her narrow silk dress, her body felt unchanged, yet Dominique knew better. She felt herself quickening with life, stirring to the great, eternal mystery that lay at the heart of existence.

The knowledge was at once exalting and humbling. She sat very still and thought about how delighted Paul would be. Surely, no man would love a child more or be a better father. She could hardly wait to tell him.

With a sudden frown, she glanced at the clock. It was later than she had realized. Paul should have been home by now. Swiftly, she stood and went out into the entry hall.

"Francois," she said when she encountered the butler on duty, "has there been any message from Monsieur le Marquis?"

The young man shook his head. "None, madame, but if you like, I can send someone to the hospital to determine if he is still there, or I can go myself."

Surprised by the suggestion, Dominique said, "Oh, I don't really think that's necessary, Francois. He was probably just delayed with a patient."

The young man gave her a puzzled frown. "I thought you had heard, madame, but then, you have been at home most of the afternoon, haven't you? General Bonaparte has taken command of the army in Paris. The Directors have been arrested. There is talk of a coup."

All the color vanished from Dominique's face. She swayed on her feet, and would have fallen if the young man had not caught her. He shouted for help from the other servants, even as he carefully lowered her onto a nearby chair.

In the tumult that followed, the maid, Helene, wasted no time taking charge. A stern-faced, no-nonsense woman of forty who had been a lady's maid before the Revolution, she knew very well how to give orders.

"Send someone for Monsieur le Docteur at once, then madame must go upstairs and get off her feet. You, Jules, and you, Henri, lift her in the chair. Careful, you dolts! That's it . . . slowly . . ."

Dominique was hustled up to her boudoir with a minimum of comfort and a maximum of fuss. But once there, she recovered sufficiently from her shock to take command.

"I am perfectly all right, Helene," she informed the maid, "although I thank you for your concern. Henri and Jules will go together to find Monsieur Delamare." They were both strapping young men who had always seemed to have all their wits about them. Nonetheless, she felt compelled to add, "However, they are not to linger on the streets. If they cannot find his lordship quickly, they must return. It may be dangerous out there."

Thankful for her consideration, the men bobbed their heads and quickly took their leave. When they were gone, Dominique forced herself to sit very quietly in the chair next to the window. She accepted her maid's suggestion of a cup of tea, simply to gain some time by herself.

Somehow, she had to find the strength to face what she was sure was coming. Yet by the time Helene returned with the steaming cup of chamomile, Dominique was no closer to that goal than before. She continued to stare, white-faced and tense, at the empty street, praying that Paul would miraculously appear.

Jules and Henri returned a short while later with word that Paul had been called away from the hospital in the early hours of the afternoon and had not been seen since. Dominique accepted that news with outward calm, but inside, she was consumed by fear.

The hours passed with aching slowness. Paris seemed wrapped in stillness, as though the entire city was holding its breath. The streets remained ominously empty as the citizens remained within their own walls, finding whatever comfort there that they could.

For Dominique, there was none. Throughout the long hours of the night she remained in the chair by the window, waiting for what she slowly realized was not going to happen. By morning, she had accepted the truth.

She dressed with great care, for once astounding Helene by her attention to detail. Once she was satisfied with her appearance, she instructed Henri to bring her carriage around. It was still early when she left the house and set off for the Bonapartes' residence.

More than anything else, the absence of the usual crowd told her all she needed to know. If nothing untoward had happened, the general's supporters would be in their accustomed place, ready to cheer his every appearance. Instead, even they were lying low, waiting to see what would happen.

Josephine, however, was not. She was already up and dressed, seated in her drawing room with a silver pot of tea before her and a plate of brioches.

"Sit down," she said gently when she caught sight of

her guest's pale, strained figure. "It will do no one any good for you to collapse."

"I know that," Dominique murmured as she took the chair that was offered. Now that she was actually here, her courage threatened to desert her. Her slender hands twisted in her lap as she stared at her friend.

"Oh, Josephine, what am I to do?"

The older woman sighed. With brisk kindness, she held out a cup of tea. "First, drink this, then have something to eat. The way you look right now, those have to be the priorities. Afterward, we will talk."

"You know about Paul . . . ?"

"I didn't think you were here for any other reason. But, really, Dominique, what else could you think would happen?"

"I didn't know. I hoped . . ."

Josephine smiled wryly and set a plate with a perfect, golden brioche on it in front of her. "That he would be sensible and do what was safe? Perhaps even more, that he would seize this opportunity to advance himself with Bonaparte?"

"No, I knew he would never do that. He doesn't trust the general."

"A sensible man," Josephine said with resigned amusement. "But he could have chosen safety."

Dominique's hands clenched all the tighter. She closed her eyes for a moment, fearful that she was going to cry.

"Oh, my dear," Josephine exclaimed, instantly contrite, "it was too cruel of me not to tell you at once. He is perfectly all right. All that has happened is that he has been . . . removed from circulation."

"Arrested?" Burgeoning hope so great as to be painful

almost choked her. Now that she knew the worst had not happened, she believed she could deal with anything.

Josephine nodded. She had the grace to look embarrassed as she said, "There was a list, you see. Apparently, after last week, Paul's name was on it."

"So it wasn't enough that he promised not to interfere so long as Bonaparte respected the government and kept the peace?"

"Of course not. The general has never had any intention of doing either."

Dominique took a long, shaky breath and let it out slowly. "What does he intend?"

"To rule France, absolutely and utterly, whatever he says to the contrary. But don't feel bad that you didn't realize. There are still many people who haven't, including plenty who ought to know better."

"Talleyrand?" Dominique ventured, struggling to fill in the blanks and understand what had happened.

Josephine laughed. "Heavens, no. That wily old fox has always known exactly what was going to happen. He and Napoleon understand each other perfectly. However," she added, "you mustn't blame him for trying to enlist Paul on their side. He has the highest respect for your husband."

"How nice," Dominique muttered tautly. "He respects him enough to acquiesce in his arrest."

"It was that or his execution. Which would you have preferred?"

Dominique stared at her hostess with wide, dark eyes. "You are . . . very blunt."

Josephine shrugged her slim shoulders unapologetically. "Life has taught me that there is little point in being anything else.'' Deliberately, she added, ''I would have thought that you had learned the same.''

Dominique set down her teacup. Slowly, she nodded. For a moment, she glanced around at the elegant, gracious room. Beyond, through the tall, open windows, she could hear the street sounds of Paris, at least so far as they occurred in this most exclusive of neighborhoods.

All of it was achingly familiar and dear to her. This was her home, the only place where she had ever truly felt she belonged. Despite everything that had happened, this was still where she most wanted to be.

With a sole exception.

Quietly, she said, ''I believe I understand what needs to be done.''

The entrance to the Luxembourg Palace was guarded not by the usual ceremonial troops, but by a cavalcade of battle-hardened veterans who stood grim-faced and silent, observing everyone who came and went. Those compelled to pass them looked at best cautious and at worst frightened.

Dominique contrived to appear neither. She approached the first guard she saw, her head high and her gaze direct. With the merest touch of hauteur, she said, ''I have a note for His Excellency, General Bonaparte, from Madame Bonaparte. I must see him at once.''

The guard scowled and looked at her suspiciously. He held out a large, hairy hand. ''Give it here.''

Dominique shook her head firmly. ''Absolutely not. It is for the general only.''

''The first consul,'' a younger, amused voice corrected. Dominique turned to find herself confronting a handsome, perfectly uniformed officer in his midtwenties, who surveyed her appreciatively.

"You are . . .?" he inquired as his gaze wandered over her.

"Madame la Marquise de Rochford," she said coldly. "I have a personal note for the general . . . the first consul . . . from Madame Bonaparte."

"May I see it?" the young man asked.

Reluctantly, Dominique held it out. He took the heavy embossed envelope and turned it over. Silently, he studied the wax-imprinted seal holding it closed.

"I see," he said slowly as he returned the note. "Very well. Please come with me, madame."

The unnatural silence hovering over Paris was absent within the precincts of the government palace. There, it seemed as though chaos reigned. Barely had Dominique entered on the young officer's heels than she was assailed by a barrage of sights and sounds.

Men—most in uniform, a few civilians—were running along the gilded corridors, shouting instructions or questions to one another, bustling in and out of antechambers, and generally looking extremely preoccupied. Yet despite the seeming disorganization, there was no hint of panic. On the contrary, the mood was one of relentless purpose that frankly chilled Dominique.

Softly, she asked, "What was it that you called the general?"

Over his shoulder, the officer said, "First consul." Proudly, as though he himself had brought it about, he said, "The Directory is abolished. France is now governed by a consulate headed by Bonaparte."

To rule France, Josephine had said. It seemed as though

he had already achieved that ambition. And yet Dominique wondered if there wasn't more to come.

"Are there other consuls?" she asked.

The young man nodded. "The general will share power with two others."

She was tempted fo ask how long anyone imagined that would last, but held her tongue. They were approaching an immense set of double doors at the end of the corridor. The doors stood open, revealing an office so large that several hundred people would fit inside it. At least that many seemed to be hovering about.

The officer shoved a path through for them and whispered a few words in the ear of the guard stationed before an inner door. A moment later it opened and Dominique was ushered inside.

Bonaparte was alone. He stood with his back to the room, staring out the single window. By contrast with the magnificent antechamber beyond, this room was bare to the point of austerity. It might have been the command tent of an officer in the field.

Uncertain of what to say or do, Dominique stood without moving until Bonaparte abruptly turned. He had removed his uniform jacket and was dressed only in a plain white shirt, black breeches, and boots. No insignia indicated his rank, but then she supposed none was needed. He radiated strength and energy in almost superhuman amounts.

He smiled as he held out a hand toward a nearby chair. "Sit down, Madame la Marquise. I have been expecting you."

Pride demanded that she give no indication of her surprise—or her fear. Calmly, she held out the letter. "Madame Bonaparte sent a note."

"Ah," he said, an amused look in his eyes. "Well, let's see what she has to say."

He took the note and opened it, scanning the few lines in seconds. His smile faded. With a sigh, he tossed the paper into the fire and shrugged. "My wife sees fit to reprimand me."

Dominique froze in surprise. That she had most certainly not expected. When Josephine offered to provide her with the means to gain entrance into the palace, Dominique had presumed that she would write something innocuous. Certainly, the most she hoped for was that her friend might make a gentle plea on her behalf. Now it seemed that Josephine had gone much further.

"I will never understand women," Bonaparte said. He sat down matter-of-factly in a canvas chair and propped his feet up on a nearby chest. His eyes were dark, inscrutable, penetrating, as he added, "I surround her with every luxury, endow her with power and honors beyond any she has ever known, and this is only the beginning. Nonetheless, she berates me for being cruel to young lovers."

With a grimace, he said, "Sometimes I understand why Beauharnais went off to fight in America. After all, a man must have some peace in his life."

The inherent contradiction of that apparently did not disturb the first consul. With a resigned shrug, he said, "Undoubtedly, I shall find some way to placate her." Abruptly, he pulled open a drawer in his desk and dumped out several canvas pouches. Dominique gasped as a glittering shower of precious gems spilled across the battered surface.

"Beautiful, aren't they?" Napolean said, though with no more emotion than a busy man might award a good meal or a pleasing bottle of wine. "Do you think Josephine would like them?"

"Undoubtedly," Dominique said dryly. "Where did they come from?"

"Who knows? I was given them this morning by a gentleman who was anxious to purchase my favor. He went off quite content, imagining that he had succeeded."

And undoubtedly, Dominique thought, he was not alone. The men whom the Revolution had made wealthy and powerful would be fawning around Bonaparte, anxious to prove their support to the audacious man who had seized authority from beneath their very noses. He was one of them—brash, determined, remorseless—yet also more, in that he acted alone, driven solely by his own vision. And that, more than anything else, would terrify those who always needed the mob at their backs, propelling them along.

"So you will become rich beyond your dreams," she said quietly, wondering what that must mean to a man born into a respectable but hardly affluent family in the backwater province of Corsica.

Napoleon shrugged. "The money is unimportant. What counts is the power."

Dominique did not doubt him. She heard the hard, relentless purpose behind his words and winced.

He smiled chidingly. "Why so fastidious, madame? It is the way of the world."

"Your world, monsieur, not mine . . . or my husband's."

Bonaparte's smile deepened. "Ah, yes, the indomitable Doctor Delamare. Whatever are we to do with him?"

Dominique forced herself to remain silent. She found

the first consul's amused, teasing tone to be utterly outrageous, and would gladly have told him so but for the
repercussions that might well follow.

Abruptly, Bonaparte turned serious. "I will tell you
truly, madame, if there were more men in the world like
your husband, there would be no chance for fellows like
me."

The compliment—for that was indeed what it sounded
like—was so unexpected that Dominique could do little
except stare at him. After a moment, Napoleon went on,
"However, as it happens, Doctor Delamare is very much
in the minority—a man of honor and integrity who can be
neither bought nor coerced. Such men are extremely dangerous."

"Only to those who would harm others, monsieur,"
Dominique said softly.

"But what does harm mean?" Napoleon demanded. His
eyes gleamed as he threw out his arms in a sweeping
gesture. "I shall raise France to magnificence unlike any
she has ever seen. I shall make her the most powerful and
the most feared nation on the face of the earth. And in the
process, I shall make a great many Frenchmen rich. Where,
I ask you, is the harm in that?"

"There would be none," Dominique acknowledged quietly, "if one could overlook the fact that *in the process*,
a great many Frenchmen and others will die."

"Gloriously, madame. Their names will live forever."

Sadly, Dominique shook her head. "No, Monsieur le
General, *your* name will live forever, which I suspect is
exactly what you intend. But very few, if any, of those
who die in your battles will ever be remembered. *That* is
the way of the world."

Napoleon sat back in his chair with a resigned sigh. He gazed at her benignly. "You have been listening to your husband, madame."

Regretfully, Dominique shook her head. "Not enough, I think. Paul has always maintained that no compromise is possible with tyranny. It must be opposed utterly. Until this moment, as I listened to you speak so casually of the deaths you will cause, I didn't fully appreciate what he meant. You have no respect for the lives of individual human beings. He holds them precious."

Abruptly, Napoleon swung his feet onto the floor and sat up. From the edge of his camp chair, he stared at her intently.

"Do you love him?"

For all the unexpectedness of the question, Dominique did not hesitate. Firmly, she said, "With all my heart."

Napoleon gazed at her a moment longer before he appeared to come to some decision. "I will tell you something, madame, and if you ever repeat it outside of this room, people will think you are mad. Always, since I was a small boy, I have known my destiny. Always the path to glory has unfolded clearly before me. I know that I will triumph, but I also know that in the end, it will count for nothing."

"I don't understand you," Dominique murmured.

"Because in the end it is the vision of men like your husband, the vision of freedom, that will determine the fate of the world. Right now, his vision is hard for many people to grasp. They fear it. But the day will come when they have finally had enough of men like me. Then they will seize the vision and make it their own."

"It could be yours now," Dominique exclaimed. "You have the power to choose freedom over tyranny."

Regretfully, Napoleon shook his head. "No, I do not. It is my preordained role to be one of those who teaches the world this harshest of lessons. In that regard, at least, I will help prepare the way for what is to come."

"And Paul?"

"He does have a choice. To remain here in France and attempt—futilely—to fight me, or to accept exile. I care enough about my place in history not to wish to be held responsible for such a man's death. But I will do it nonetheless if he presses me."

Dominique swallowed hard, fighting against the wave of sickness that threatened to overwhelm her. She was desperately, horribly afraid that Paul would not see the danger he was in, or would not care. Hadn't he left her in England to go back and fight Robespierre? Hadn't he lived underground, always on the run, his life constantly at risk? It was perfectly possible that he would believe that he could do so again.

As though he had read her thoughts, Napoleon said, "I am not Robespierre, madame. Stress that to your husband. I nurture no insane infatuation with death, and I do not see him as the angel of my destruction. Rather, I will destroy him before I permit him to disrupt my destiny."

"You wish me to persuade him to go," she said slowly as the full impact of what that would mean settled over her.

"I wish you to plead with him, to beg, cajole, threaten—to do whatever it is a woman must do."

"To be your weapon against him."

Napoleon looked at her narrowly—a long, hard look, as though he was discovering an adversary he had seriously underrated. Finally, he said, "I had hoped you would not see it that way, madame."

"But that is what it amounts to, isn't it? You want me to use his love for me and his sense of responsibility to convince him to give up everything he has fought for these many years."

Bonaparte sat down once more behind the desk. He reached for a sheaf of papers and began to read. Without looking at her again, he said, "The decision is yours, madame, but I don't blame you for hesitating. You would make a charming widow."

Chapter
26

Each step farther into the bowels of the Conciergerie carried Dominique nearer to her most deeply held fears.

The grim stone fortress that had been the final stopping place for so many victims of the Terror—the place that Dominique herself had so narrowly escaped—seemed alive with whispers and sighs. Old friends and acquaintances, not to mention people she had loved, appeared to waft pale and ethereal just beyond the limit of sight.

How long did it take unhappy spirits to finally fade away? Only a few short years had passed since the tumbrils had made their regular trips back and forth from the Conciergerie to the guillotine. Was it foolish to believe that some remnants of those hapless victims still endured within these walls, crying out for vengeance?

Shivering, Dominique clutched her cloak more tightly around her as she followed the guard. By the time they stopped finally in front of a low, iron-studded door, it seemed as though they were so deeply interred within the earth that they would never find their way out again.

That impression was heightened when the door swung open and she found herself staring into a dank, dark hole lit by a single candle. Within the hole, a large, powerful figure loomed.

"P-Paul . . . ?" All her promises to herself that she would be brave and stalwart went by the board. Tears coursed down her cheeks as she threw herself into the darkness, into his arms.

"My God," he murmured, clutching her. His embrace was heaven—strong and warm and so lovingly real. She clung to him with all her strength, until at last, the first shock wore off and she was able to regain some semblance of control.

Shakily, she straightened up and managed a wan smile. "I'm sorry. I really had no intention of doing this."

He shook his head bemusedly. "It doesn't matter. I can't believe you're here. What happened?" Abruptly, he stared down at her with fear. "You haven't been arrested, too, have you?"

"No," she assured him hastily, "nothing of the sort."

Grimly, Paul said, "Nonetheless, you shouldn't be here. There's no point. They're letting me out in a few hours."

"Letting . . ." In the faint light of the candle, he could not see how all the color drained from her face. But he could feel the sudden trembling of her body in his arms.

"Dominique, what is wrong?"

"Oh, God," she murmured tautly, "it is even worse than I thought. He realized that he can't keep you here; the people would be outraged and you'd become a rallying point. But if he lets you go . . ."

"He will regret it," Paul said implacably, "but I still see no reason to tell him that. If he is foolish enough to release me . . ."

"He isn't. You will never leave here alive, or at least you won't get very far. You'll be just one more body floating in the Seine." Abruptly a flood of memory returned. Her father had been one of those bodies, though his death had been a purely personal tragedy with no larger overtones.

Nonetheless, it had affected her more deeply than she had ever wanted to admit, even to herself. From that moment, she had fully assumed the responsibility of raising her brother and sister. She had never looked back from that, but there were still times when the burden of her love for them seemed almost too heavy to be borne.

Was that how it would seem to Paul?

For long moments, neither spoke. In the small, low-ceilinged chamber the silence rang like iron striking stone. Finally, Dominique said, "There is an alternative."

She felt him stiffen, even as she carefully avoided looking at him. "Bonaparte has offered you exile instead. If you will agree to leave France, he will allow you to go unhindered."

Paul inhaled sharply. "That is unexpected. Why would he do such a thing?"

"Because he says he doesn't want history to hold him responsible for the death of a man like you."

Before Paul could comment on that, no doubt sardonically, she said, "I understand what is important to you and I love you far too much to ever stand in your way. I will tell him you have agreed, that we are leaving France together. He will believe me, and that will give you the chance to escape."

"To go into hiding as I did before, to strike at him where he will least expect it?"

Numbly, she nodded.

"And you?"

"I . . . I really will leave. I couldn't remain here, knowing that you were in constant danger. Besides, I would always be watched, on the chance that I might lead them to you."

She was perfectly correct about that, Paul thought. In fact, she was correct about everything. The perfectly correct wife making the perfectly correct decision. Putting aside her own needs and desires to do what was noble.

If he took her offer, he would be free to follow his dream wherever it led. All the concerns of ordinary men —wife, home, possibly children—would be left behind. He would once again be the solitary, visionary warrior concerned only with the highest ideals. Moreover, she was inviting him to do it without guilt, surely the rarest of all gifts.

Borne only of love.

The temptation to accept was there, he had to admit it. But so was the yearning to remain with her, to choose love over war and find a different path.

She watched the battle within him through eyes lit by understanding and compassion. He was a proud man in an untenable situation. Desperately, she struggled to find a way to help him.

And there in that dark, dank chamber, in the place where the light of freedom was never seen, a sudden, illuminating hope came to her.

"Paul," she said slowly, "there must be someplace in the world where a man can live in freedom, and work to make others free, yet still stay alive."

"There is," he said readily enough, proof to her that he had already been thinking of it. "The same place Lafayette was drawn to and poor old Beauharnais, not to mention so many others. But I'd hardly expect you to ever agree to . . ."

Angry now that he should be so obtuse, she grabbed hold of his broad, hard shoulders and glared at him. "I would go with you to the ends of the earth if it meant keeping you alive, you stubborn, infuriating man. Do you think anything else matters to me? If I spent my life in palaces surrounded by every luxury, so long as you weren't there, I would have nothing."

His mouth crooked in a smile as he looked down at her. She was so radiantly beautiful, so compellingly alive, that her mere presence seemed enough to overcome the greatest despair. Always it had been that way, even in his most desperate days. Always she was a light unto the darkness, leading him to the best in himself and in the world.

Nonetheless, when he spoke again it was with caution. "Dominique, the place I am speaking of is . . . America."

She looked at him blankly for a moment. "Oh, you mean the Colonies."

He laughed, his eyes alight with loving amusement. Generations of aristocratic ancestors would have been pleased. Gently, he corrected her. "They aren't colonies anymore. Those people fought to free themselves and succeeded. Now they are fighting to build a country. Life isn't easy there; it never is at the beginning of something. But I believe what they accomplish will ultimately reach far beyond their own borders."

"America . . ." she repeated slowly, trying to accustom herself to the word. Not England. Not the country that was her second home, the land she knew, but a wild and untamed place beset by all sorts of strange notions about what people could be.

"America . . ." The candle flared. Shadows danced on the stone walls. A murmur of air moved through the cell. On it she thought she caught the scent of flowers where there had never been any, of budding trees and wide expanses of fertile land, glittering beneath a golden sun. A place of new beginnings for anyone who dared to seize them.

She raised herself on tiptoe and twined her arms around his broad neck. Their bodies pressed close together— warm, alive, filled with the promise of life.

"To the ends of the earth," she said.

Paul laughed again and bent his head to hers. Against her mouth, he murmured, "Not quite. Only as far as . . ."

"America."

Three days later, a plain black carriage drew up alongside the Quai d'Orsay. Masts of sailing vessels split the sky. Hard autumn sunlight bathed the bustling scene, including the dock beside which rode the *Marie Clare*, shortly to be outward bound for Boston.

A man leaned forward slightly to look through the carriage window. His face was inscrutable, only the dark, gleaming eyes appearing to be alive. They lit upon the man and woman making their way through the crowd to the gangplank.

Paul had a protective arm around Dominique. His big, powerful body effectively shielded her from all others. She had been ill upon waking that morning but had tried to convince him it was only because of the excitement of the last few days. He hadn't believed her, of course, but he had yet to tell her of his joy that they were to have a child. That could wait until France was safely behind them.

The man in the carriage turned to his companion.

Quietly, he said, "I could still stop them."

"But you won't, my dear Bonaparte," Talleyrand said.

The first consul's mouth quirked. "Why not?"

"Because by letting Paul Delamare live, you are putting your stamp on the future in a way neither he nor anyone else will ever realize."

Napoleon was silent for a moment, then slowly he shook his head. "No, there is another reason."

Talleyrand shot him an inquiring look. "What is that?"

Abruptly, Napoleon rapped on the roof of the carriage. As the driver moved on, he glanced once more out the window, then looked determinedly away.

"Because to stop him, to kill him, would be to admit how much I envy him. Indeed, how much I envy them both."

His eyes alight with painful awareness, he said, "You and I, my friend, we will have all the power and glory of this world. But those two have love—and freedom, both of which come from a far higher source. Which of us do you suppose is therefore the victor?"